FLEMISH LIFE.

IN

FOUR STORIES

BY

HENDRIK CONSCIENCE

Fredonia Books
Amsterdam, The Netherlands

Flemish Life in Four Stories

by
Hendrik Conscience

ISBN: 1-4101-0441-9

Fredonia Books
Amsterdam, The Netherlands
http://www.fredoniabooks.com

In order to make original editions of historical works
available to scholars at an economical price, this
facsimile of the original edition is reproduced from
the best available copy and has been digitally
enhanced to improve legibility, but the text remains
unaltered to retain historical authenticity.

CONTENTS.

	PAGE
AUTHOR'S ADDRESS TO HIS FRIENDS, . .	3
THE RECRUIT, ...	7
MINE HOST GANSENDONCK, ...	101
BLIND ROSA, ...	215
THE POOR NOBLEMAN, ...	247

THE AUTHOR TO HIS FRIENDS.

ANTWERP, *Nov.* 15, 1849.

RESPECTED READERS,—To you, my good friends, who have remained true to the story-teller, however much his name and office have been abused, I bring good news to-day.

I have been ill. My spirit was weary, my soul disenchanted, my body sick. I, endowed by God—if with nothing else, at least with energy, life, and universal love—sank into the deepest dejection, and became alarmed as I felt a deadly poison—it might have been misanthropy—taking possession of my soul.

Have I not seen, for the first time in my life, in these incomprehensible times, every selfish passion rage—naked! shameless? Gross injustice and crime legalized by the struggle for existence, as murder is legalized by war? And the holiest thing of all—the elevation of Flanders—the aspiration of my youth, the endeavour of my manlier years—but let us not speak of that; I have a wound in my heart which might begin to bleed afresh. Let us talk of sweeter memories.

Three months I lived upon the heath—you know it well—that beautiful spot where the soul returns into itself and is at rest; where everything sings of peace and calm; where the spirit, face to face with the primeval creation of God, throws off the wearisome veil of conventionality, forgets mankind, and with renewed youth frees itself from all restraint; where every thought forms itself to a prayer; where everything disappears from the heart which is not in unison with fresh, free nature.

Oh! yonder, yonder is peace for the weary spirit—yonder the strength of youth is still in store for the toilworn man.

And so passed the days of my illness—days of inexpressible joy for my soul. To go to meet the sun with a smile, when in full majesty it pours its first rays over the horizon; to wait upon nature at her awaking, when the first tones of her great song of praise ascend to heaven; to wander over heath and through bush, questioning my own soul, and reflecting—looking into the life of plants and animals, and wondering; inhaling the pure air in full draughts; now standing, now moving on, retracing my steps and speaking aloud in my solitude; dreaming of things inconceivably beautiful—of God, of the future, of Flanders, of peace, and of love.

And in the evening, to sit in the old inn, under the broad projection of the fireplace, my feet in the ashes, and my eyes towards the star which blinks down upon me from above through the opening of the chimney, as if it had a message for me; or, with wandering thoughts, to look into the fire, and watch how the flames take shape, rise, pant, crackle, and blow, and press against one another as if in rivalry to lick the kettle with their fiery tongues; and to think, *that* is human life,—to be born, to labour, to love, to hate, to grow to maturity, and to perish. The smoke flies upward out of the chimney, and nothing more comes of all this panting and crackling.

And then again, to awake out of my dream, and listen to

the villagers' talk. To see in motion around me a little narrow world, with its unconcealed weaknesses and passions; to read into the heart of man, and follow out his instincts laid bare in their workings; and to revel in this simple country life which uncorrupted nature painted with so fresh a colouring.

Meanwhile, to remember to collect a store of things which everybody there knew how to relate, that on my return home I might be able to offer my friends some presents from the Kempenland.

Here am I now, p   nts and all,—modest wreaths, dreamily woven by my own hand, of heath and corn-flower.

Some among you, honoured readers, may not be pleased with these quiet, peaceful Tales. Simple as the soil from which they grew, they are diametrically opposed to the reigning fashion; they are no medley of blood, thieves' slang, dishonour, connubial infidelity, barefaced debauchery, mocking unbelief, or destructive and morbid despondency: they do not make the reader anxious about his own virtue, or the future of humanity. No, no; the demon of Despair and Hate finds here no place. Nature in her unspotted freshness has woven these tales out of humble material, here and there lighted up by a pure pearl of a human heart. To enjoy them, one must still have some poetry in one's soul; for they are addressed only to the finest chords of the heart, the tender sources of life-enjoyment—love to God and our fellow-man, which alas! too soon grow weak, and wear out by contact with grasping selfishness.

Accordingly, readers, if I here promise to tell you stories which I have heard narrated in the old inn, or picked up in my wanderings over the heath, expect nothing but a faithful description of the peaceful manners of the dwellers there; and be indulgent with me when I attempt to write a whole book for your amusement out of such slender material.

To you, my Flemish friends, do I dedicate, in this tale of THE RECRUIT, the first blossom of the wreath. May your friendly reception of it be my reward, and encourage me to fulfil my whole promise in the course of time!

THE RECRUIT

CHAPTER I.

THE earliest sun of spring beamed with full splendour in the blue heavens, as if it were the exalted countenance of the Deity looking down beneficently, and calling out to creation, "Up! up! the winter is past, live and rejoice before me!" The young light diffused itself over heath and field, and the moist earth smoked with its genial warmth.

A few plants had already heard the call of the world-friend; the little snow-drops shook their silver starlets on the borders, the hazel-bushes unfolded their catkins, the wood-anemone put forth its first leaves among the underwood; while the birds hopped joyously in the warm light, and sang in clear notes of the approaching time of love.

Not far from Zoerselbosch stood two mud cottages, solitary and forgotten. In the first dwelt a poor widow with her daughter; all she possessed was a cow. The other was also inhabited by a widow, with her aged father and two sons, one of whom had just attained the years of manhood. They were wealthier than their neighbours, for they possessed an ox as well as a cow, and rented far more land.

Spite of this, the inhabitants of both huts—for their dwellings were little better—had for many years formed only one family, loving and helping one another. John and his ox worked on the poor widow's field, while Trien fetched fodder for the ox, herded for her neighbours, and helped them at harvest-time; and neither ever thought of reckoning which had done most for the other.

Simple-minded, and knowing nothing of all that befel in the stirring masses of human life beyond their native parish, they lived contented with the bit of black bread which the Almighty had granted them. Their world was very limited; on one side of the hamlet a humble little church, on the other, the immeasurable heath, and the unbounded sky.

And yet dwelt laughter and song around this lonely habitation; joy and merriment were there in full measure, and not one of these poor people would have exchanged their lot for one apparently far better.

It was love which, with its magic power, had breathed life into solitude. John and Trien, though they knew it not, loved each other with that unexpressed and shy feeling which makes the heart beat quick on the slightest occasion, and the brow redden at the most trifling word; which changes life into a long dream—a blue heaven sparkling with stars of happiness—an immeasurable deep, as if the human heart must ever remain that which the first sigh of love—the pure and holy incense of the soul—has made it.

Poor people! they thought not of the vast masses swarming in the distant cities; and, as they desired nothing from them, they imagined that they likewise would be forgotten, and, full of confidence, lived on in their sweet and beautiful poverty.

But suddenly came one and demanded blood-tax from these poor mud-huts. The only young man who dwelt there—the only one who had the strength to make the ungrateful soil fruitful by the sweat of his brow—was to draw lots and become a soldier, if his trembling hand should draw an unlucky number; bid a long it might be an eternal farewell to his mother, his friends, and his native heath; and pine, perchance die, of the wounds which the wild and dissolute soldier-life would inflict on his yet pure and peaceful soul.

The sad March day in '33, which Trien had marked with a black cross, arrived. The young man had gone out of the village to Brechts, with about ten companions, to draw lots.

Within the huts, both mothers and the little boy were kneeling in prayer. The old grandfather tottered silently up and down for a time, and at last remained standing before the door leaning on a vine-stem, with his head bent down, as if he were looking into a grave. The maiden stood in the stable, gazing long and wistfully into the eyes of John's cow, and gently stroking its head, as if consoling it under the approaching misfortune.

A gloomy silence brooded over both houses, unbroken save by the occasional lowing of the ox. Trien soon approached the grandfather, silently, but with a beseeching and inquiring look. The old man awoke out of his painful reverie, and seizing his heavy staff, said—

"Do not lose courage, Trien; God will aid us in this dreadful extremity. Come, the time is up, let us go and meet the poor recruits."

Trien followed the grandfather over a footpath which ran past the house and led to the village. Though driven on by a burning impatience, her steps were slow and heavy. The old man turned round, and, when he saw her sunken head and pallid countenance, he took her hand sympathizingly, and said—

"Poor child! how dearly you must love our John. He is not your brother, and yet you are more alarmed than we. Keep up your spirits, Trien, dear; you do not yet know what God has determined."

"I am so terrified!" she sighed, visibly trembling, and looking through the wood in the direction of the town.

"Terrified!" repeated the old man, while he exerted his eyes to discover the cause of her terror.

"Yes, yes," said Trien, covering her eyes with her apron, "it is all over, and we are unfortunate—the lot has fallen on him!"

"But how can you know that? You make me tremble too," said the old man anxiously.

Trien pointed with her finger beyond the trees, and replied, "There, behind the wood—listen!"

"I hear nothing. Come, let us make haste; it must be the recruits—so much the better."

"O God!" cried the maiden, "I hear a sound—so sad and pitiful, it sounds in my ears like a deep and heavy sigh."

Perplexed and anxious, the old man looked at the girl for a time, while she seemed to listen to a distant sound. He also listened attentively in order to catch the noise as it came over the quiet heath. A friendly smile lighted up his countenance as he said—

"Foolish little thing! it is the wind sweeping through the fir-wood."

"No, no!" she replied; "further, further, behind the wood. Do you not hear a wailing sound?"

After some moments' attention, the old man rejoined—

"Now I understand what you mean; it is Farmer Claes's dog which is howling over some one dead. The farmer's wife, who had consumption, must have died last night. May God receive her soul!"

The girl, whose mental tension and excitement had made her regard the howling as foreboding some calamity, acknowledged her error, and, quickening her pace, hastened after the old man, in silence and in tears. At last he said—

"If *you* are so inconsolable, Trien, what shall his mother and I, his grandfather, say? With hard toil have we brought him up, and loved him as the apple of our eyes. Now we are old and feeble, and he in his turn should work for us. And ah! if God has not sent his good angel to direct his hand, then must he be a soldier, and leave us in our necessity."

These words made Trien's tears break out afresh, and with an attempt at consolation she replied—

"That matters little, father—I have strong arms; and as you are no longer able, I myself will go behind the oxen, and do all the heavy work. But he—but John, poor fellow! To hear nothing but cursing and swearing, to be beaten and imprisoned, and pine away from sheer vexation of mind, like the unfortunate Pauw Stuyck, who was tortured to death in four months; and never to see one of all those who loved him on earth, neither you nor his mother, nor his little brother, nor—any one, save wicked and dissolute soldiers!"

"Oh! do not speak so, Trien," said the old man with a choking voice, "your words make me sad. Why lament so bitterly? You grieve and tremble as if there were no doubt of his being unfortunate, while I, on the contrary, have a feeling that he will draw a lucky number; I have confidence in the goodness of God."

Insensibly the maiden smiled through her tears, but so full was her mind of sad forebodings, that she could not speak. Both walked on in silence till they reached the village. Here, on the road which led to Brechts, were assembled a great number of people, clustered in little knots all full of impatience to learn the result of the lot-drawing. It was easy to distinguish those whose son, brother, or lover had gone to Brechts. Here and there one might see a mother with her apron to her eyes; a father, who endeavoured in vain to conceal the anxiety too visibly imprinted on his countenance; a maiden, with pale face and bashful look, going from one knot to another, as if haunted by some secret fear.

Many others had collected there out of mere curiosity, and spoke and jested with a loud voice. The old smith, who in former times had been one of Napoleon's dragoons, was loud in his praise of a soldier's life, and was seconded by the miller's drunken son, who, after serving eleven months, had returned to waste his paternal property in riot and debauchery. The smith did it with a good intention, for he wished by his fine description to console his anxious friends, and kept always repeating—

"Every day soup and meat, plenty of money, good beer, pretty girls, dancing, leaping, and fighting. There's a life for you! you have no notion what a jolly life it is."

But his words had quite a contrary effect, for they made the tears of the mothers flow faster, and gave fresh cause of grief to many hearts.

Trien could restrain herself no longer; in this jesting speech there was one word especially which had wounded her deeply. With an angry and threatening mien she went up to the jester, and said—

"Shame on you, abandoned man! Is it necessary that they should all be drunkards like you, forsooth, or dissolute fellows like that loose vagabond there, who has learned nothing else among soldiers but to lead a bad life, and bring his parents with sorrow to the grave?"

The miller's son went passionately up to the bold girl, and

would have attacked her rudely, had not some one just at that moment exclaimed—

"There they are! there they are!"

In the distance, the recruits might be seen emerging out of a wood upon the highway, shouting and singing as they approached. Some were joyfully throwing their hats and caps high into the air, and all together had the appearance of a troop of drunkards returning from a feast. But it was impossible to see which of them were merry and sang, and which were sad and silent.

As soon as the recruits had gained the highway, their relations and friends hastened from all sides to meet them. The old grandfather could not go so quickly as the others, though Trien now led him by the hand, and dragged him on. At last the maiden could restrain her impatience no longer when she saw mothers and young women embracing some young peasants with loud rejoicing, and, letting go the old man's hand, she ran forward as fast as she could. Suddenly she halted in the middle of the road, as if deprived of motion by some unknown power; then tottering to the roadside, she leant her head on a tree and wept bitterly.

The old man overtook her and asked, "Is John not among them, that you remain standing there, Trien?"

"O God, it will be my death!" she cried. "See yonder, father, he comes behind the others, with sunken head and pale face. He is half dead already, poor, poor fellow!"

"Perhaps it is from excess of joy, Trien?"

"How fortunate you are," she cried, "in not seeing more clearly!"

Meanwhile John approached the place where his grandfather stood, and went slowly up to him.

Trien did not go to meet him, but buried her face in her hands, and sobbed audibly.

The youth seized the old man's hand, and showing him a number, said with a choking voice—

"Father, the lot has fallen upon me."

Then turning to the maiden, he sighed, and a flood of tears gushed from his eyes.

"Trien! Trien!" was all he could utter.

The old man was too much overpowered to be able either to speak or think; the tears rolled slowly down the furrows of his face, while he stood silent and stupified, with his eyes fixed on the ground.

For a time the deepest silence reigned, till John exclaimed with a despairing voice—

"Oh, my poor mother! my poor mother!"

Scarcely were these words uttered than a wonderful change seemed to take place in the maiden. She was a noble and courageous girl. While there was uncertainty, she had given free vent to her tears; but with the certainty of misfortune, her heart found the needful energy, and now, when an elevating sense of duty awoke her out of her grief, a strength which was peculiar to her beautiful character returned to her soul. She raised her head, and drying her tears, spoke calmly and collectedly.

"John, my friend, God has so willed it, and who can strive against Him? You have still a year with us; perhaps some way may cast up. Let me go, _I_ will tell your mother; if another should tell her the dreadful news, it might be her death."

With these words, she hastened into the fir-wood and disappeared. The old man and the unfortunate youth kept the usual path to the village. They heard songs, and shouts, and hurrahs, but were too deeply sunk in grief to heed them.

As they approached their poor dwelling, Tried, accompanied

by both the women and the little brother, came out to meet them weeping.

The young man gave Trien a look of the deepest gratitude, for he could well perceive from the countenance of his mother that the noble girl had roused in the heart of the sorrowing widow a feeling of hope. He was encouraged when he saw this, and, repressing his grief, he hastened towards her with open arms.

At first there was violent emotion, deep sorrow, and many tears; but despair yielded to calmer feelings, and by degrees peace returned into the widows' huts.

CHAPTER II.

THE hour of departure is come. Yonder, before the hats, stands a fine young man—his staff on his shoulder, and a bundle on his back. His eyes, once so quick and lively, now move slowly and heavily, his face is calm, and everything seems to indicate in him a tranquil and collected mind; but his heart beats quick, and his breast heaves with repressed emotion.

His mother holds one of his hands in hers, and overwhelms him with the tenderest expressions of love; the poor woman sheds no tear, and her lips tremble under the restraint which she puts on herself to conceal her grief. She smiles on her son to console him; but this forced and melancholy smile is sadder than the bitterest lamentation.

The other widow is endeavouring to console the little boy, and make him believe that John will soon come back again; but the melancholy feelings with which, during the past year, his parents had looked forward to this day, had taught him to regard the departure as a dreadful calamity—and nothing could comfort him.

The grandfather and Trien are within doors, making the last preparations for the journey; they have cut a great hole in a loaf of bread and filled it with butter; carrying this with them, they go out and stand beside the young man.

The stable is open, the ox turns its head and looks with a

sad expression towards its master, uttering at intervals a low and melancholy sound. One might have supposed that the beast knew what was going on.

All is ready, and he is about to depart. Already he has firmly pressed his mother's hand, and advanced a step; but he pauses a moment longer to cast a last look of affection around him—on the humble cot where his cradle stood—the heath, and the wood where he had wandered when a child—and on the barren fields, which, as a young man, he had so often made fruitful by his labour. Then by turns his glance falls on all the objects which he loved, even on the ox, his trusty friend during many a hard day's toil; he covers his face with his hand, to conceal the tears which roll over his cheeks, and sighs inaudibly, " Farewell!"

Now he raises his head, shakes back the long hair from his brow, and walks forth with a determined air.

All follow him; for they will not leave him yet. A little farther on, there hangs under the linden-tree, at the cross roads, an image of the Virgin. Trien had hung it up there on a beautiful May evening, and John had made a bench for the knees at the foot of the tree. At this sacred spot, where they daily kneeled and prayed, their trembling lips were to pronounce an anxious adieu.

The linden-tree may now be seen in the distance—the spot which is to witness their fatal separation. The young man slackens his pace, while his mother, in the midst of tender caresses, thus addresses him—

" John, my son, do not forget what I have told you; at all times have God before your eyes, and never omit to say your prayers before lying down at night. So long as you do this, your heart will remain pure; but should it happen that you forget it on any occasion, then think next day on me—on your mother, and again may you return to the right path, and be

3   B

good; for he who thinks on his mother and his God is strong against all evil, my dear child."

"I will always, always think on you, mother," replied the young man in a low tone; "and if I am sad, and lose heart, then shall the thought of you support and console me—for I feel too well that I shall be unhappy; I love you all too much."

"And, then, do not swear, my son, and lead a profligate life. You will go to church regularly, will you not? And as often as possible, you will let us know how you are? And ever keep in mind, that the most trifling news from her child, makes a mother's heart glad. Oh! every day will I pray to your guardian angel, that he may not forsake you."

The sweet tone of his mother's voice moved the young man deeply; he did not venture to look at her, so overpowering an emotion did her beaming maternal glance raise in him at this solemn hour; he listened to her with sunken head. His only reply was now and then a firmer pressure of the hand, or a deeper sigh, while, "Mother, dear mother!" were the only words he could utter.

Silently they approach the cross road. The old man going on the other side of the youth, said to him, with an earnest voice—

"John, my son, you will do your duty, will you not, without murmuring, and with pleasure? You will obey your superiors; and if injustice is done you, bear it in silence? Be courteous and obliging to all; show good-will towards every one, and what is given you to do, do thoroughly. Then will God aid you, and your superiors and comrades love you."

Trien, her mother, and the boy, are already kneeling on the grass under the linden-tree, beside the bench, and are engaged in prayer. John has no time to reply to his grandfather's exhortations; his mother leads him to the bench—all kneel down and pray with uplifted hands.

The wind sounds gently among the firs; the spring sun beams mildly on the sandy highway—the birds overhead sing a joyful song—all is calm and solemn, and the pious whisperings of the praying family ascend audibly through the linden branches.

It is over; all stand up, and every eye is filled with tears. The mother embraces her son with bitter lamentation, and though the others stand ready to say the melancholy farewell, she will not let her dear firstborn go: again and again she kisses away the tears from his cheeks, and utters unintelligible words of love and sorrow.

At last she sits down on the little bench exhausted and fainting, but still weeping.

John hastily embraces his grandfather and Trien's mother; with kindly force separates himself from his little brother, who clung crying to his legs; once more presses his mother to his breast, kisses her brow, and with a final adieu, hastens towards the village without venturing to look round, till he has turned the corner of the wood, and is out of sight of his relations.

It was with difficulty that Trien, carrying the bread under her arm, was able to follow and overtake him.

For a long time both young people stood beside one another without speaking; their hearts beat quickly; a dark blush of modesty suffused their brow and cheeks—they did not venture to look at each other. Great hour! in which two human souls tremble in each other's presence, with the consciousness that a long-cherished and holy secret is about to be revealed.

John took Trien's hand shyly and timidly, as if to touch it were a crime, and let it fall again as if it burnt him.

After a pause, during which perfect silence reigned, he

took her hand again, and, in a tone unlike his ordinary, sighed—

"Trien, will you not forget me?"

A flood of tears was the maiden's only reply.

"Will you wait till John comes back from soldiering?" said the young man again. "May he take with him that one consolation at least, that he may not die of grief?"

The maiden raised her large blue eyes, and gazed on him with a long sad look, penetrating his soul like a ray of fire, and filling his heart with a blessedness hitherto unknown to him.

He continues to stand there unconsciously: how it happens he knows not, but his burning lips have touched the young girl's brow. As if terrified, he draws back and leans upon an oak. There before him beams the maiden's countenance with the fire of modesty and of happiness; he lays his hand upon his heart, for he feels as if it would break in pieces, so violent is its beating. Yet an indescribable smile plays upon his face, his eyes sparkle with a manly glow, proudly and confidently he raises his head; a single glance from his beloved seems to have infused into him a giant's strength and courage.

Behind the wood a well-known voice is heard; some one approaches singing a merry song. It is Charles, who is also to be a soldier, and is now on his way to the village.

Trien makes great efforts to hide her confusion. The surprise awakes her out of her dreams; she casts a hasty look on her friend, and urges him to go, that Charles may not overtake him, and that no strange eye may perceive what has taken place between them.

But Charles advances rapidly to join his fellow-traveller. Trien perceives it, and says hastily—

"John, when you are gone I will care for your mother,

grandfather, and little brother; I will go behind the plough, as it is proper I should do, and care for the ox that it come to no harm. I am strong and healthy, and will manage so that on your return you will find everything as you left it."

"Everything?" repeated the young man, looking deeply into her eyes, "everything?"

"Yes, everything; and I will not go to any merry-makings so long as you are away, for without you I can have no pleasure in them. But—you, too, must not drink, nor take up with pretty girls, as that profligate smith talks about, for were I to learn that, I would soon lie in the churchyard"—

Just at this moment Charles slaps John's shoulder with his heavy hand, while he sings, with a tone of mock sadness—

> "Alas, my love, I now from thee must part,
> Must to the wars—ah, how it tears my heart!
> Farewell!—forget me not!"

The young girl blushed deeply. John, perceiving her perplexity, replied to his comrade's jest in a careless tone, and seizing him by the arm, proceeded with him to the village, while Trien walked silently behind.

At last they reach the village. Before the "Crown" stand three young fellows with knapsacks on their backs, waiting for John and Charles.

Every one is kissing parents and friends. Trien alone kisses nobody; but in the secret glance which she exchanged with John as she gave him the bread, lies an affecting utterance of the soul.

The recruits set out towards the city.

Trien leaves the village without shedding a tear; but, behind the fir-wood, her heart is too full. With her apron to her eyes she returns to the hut, where all would be empty but for memory, which fills up the gap caused by the departure of the son and the lover.

CHAPTER III.

On a clear day in August, Trien left the village on her way home, in high spirits; she seemed in great haste, and happiness was painted on her smiling countenance; light were her footsteps in the dusty sand of the highway, and now and then some unintelligible sounds escaped from her panting breast as she talked with herself.

In one hand, she held two great sheets of writing-paper, and in the other, a prepared quill, and a little bottle of ink, which the parish-clerk had made her a present of.

On the way, pretty Kate, the wooden-shoemaker's daughter, came singing out of a side-path, with a bundle of clover on her head, and compelled her friend to stop, by calling out—

"Ho there, Trien! where are you running with the paper? Why such haste? Is there a fire anywhere? Tell me, how goes it with your John?"

"With our John?" replied Trien, "*that* the Lord God alone knows, Katie dear. Since he went away, we have heard from him only thrice, that he is in good health. It is now half a year since a comrade from Turnheutz left a message from him to us at the 'Crown.' But it must be a difficult thing to send word, for he is somewhere beyond Maestricht, and it isn't every day that an acquaintance comes from so great a distance to our quarter."

"Can he not write, then, Trien?"

"He used to be able to do so; for when we were little, and went together to school in the parish-clerk's house, he once carried off the prize for his writing. But I daresay he has forgotten it all, like me."

"What are you doing with the paper, then?"

"Why, Kate, two months ago I sought out my old writing-book, and have been learning it all over anew; and I wish to see now whether I can write a letter. Whether it will succeed or not, I cannot tell; have you ever written a letter in your life, Kate?"

"No; but I have heard many letters read; for my brother, Dries, who dwells in the city, writes almost every month to us."

"What kind of a thing is a letter? What is in it? Is it just the same as if you were speaking to some one?"

"Save ye, Trien! that would be a fine thing, indeed! It is always full of compliments and big words, which *you* could scarcely understand."

"Ah! Kate, how shall I ever manage it rightly? But if I were to write like this, for example—'John, we are anxious, because we do not know how you are. If you do not send us news quickly, your mother will fall ill,' and so forth; he will understand that, won't he?"

"Yes, you simple little heart; but that is no letter; every body speaks that way—those who have been taught, as well as those who have not. Wait a moment—ay, this is the way it always begins—'Much-honoured parents,—Trembling, I take the pen into my hand to—to'—now, I can't find out what comes next."

"To—write!"

"Oh, you know more about it than I! You think me very stupid. That is bad of you, Trien."

"But, Kate, what can you be thinking about? If he takes

the pen into his hand, he doesn't do it to spread a piece of bread and butter. I can't help laughing at you. I do not understand why your brother Dries always trembles when he begins a letter. Writing must surely be very difficult to him. It is a bad thing, too ; for when one trembles, one never writes well."

" No, that is not it; but Dries follows his own ways in the city, and is always wanting money, and father is so angry with him, and that's why he trembles. But tell me, Trien, how is your cow ?"

" Pretty well, now. She has suffered much, poor thing ; but she has come through it safely, and is almost herself again. We have sold the calf to a peasant from Wechel-ter-zande. It was a mottled calf—a dear little thing !"

Meanwhile the girls had moved a few paces, each in her own direction.

" Well, a kind greeting to your family, Trien," cried Kate, as she walked away ; "see that you manage your letter properly ; and send John our compliments."

" Adieu till Sunday, after church ; then I shall tell you how I have got on with it. Kind remembrances to your sister."

Kate's voice already sounded in the fir-wood ; merrily and clearly she sang the burden of a well-known May song—

> " See ! with wreaths and flowers adorn'd,
> The village May-pole, planted high,
> And the boys and peasant girls
> Dancing round it merrily.
>
> Up, maidens ! seize the hour,
> Up ! and join the gleeful throng ;
> Youth comes but once, and when it goes,
> Go with it dance and song."

Trien stood dreaming till the beautiful voice of her friend died away behind the wood. Then she bounded along the road, half skipping, half walking, and soon reached her dwelling.

Here sat both widows at the table, and waited impatiently for Trien's return. The old grandfather, who had taken cold, lay in bed, and pushed his head through the curtains, that with eye and ear at least, he might be present at the great work in which they were engaged.

So soon as the girl made her appearance, the women hastily cleared off everything that lay on the table, and wiped it clean with the corner of their aprons.

"Come here, Trien, seat yourself on grandfather's chair, it is more convenient."

The girl seated herself silently at the table, spread out the paper, and then stuck the end of the pen thoughtfully in her mouth.

Meanwhile the women and the grandfather looked at her with the liveliest curiosity. The little brother had spread out both arms on the table, and fixed his gaze on her mouth and eyes, watching what she would do with the pen. But Trien rose from her seat as silent as they, took a little coffee-cup from the shelf, poured the ink out of the bottle into it, and set it on the table, where she kept turning the paper this way and that nine or ten times.

At last she dipped the pen in the ink, and disposed herself to write. After a few moments, she raised her head, and asked—

"Now, tell me, what am I to write?"

Both widows looked inquiringly at one another, and then to the sick grandfather, who had pushed out his head far beyond the curtain, and kept his eyes fixed on Trien's hand.

"Why, write that we are all well," said the old man, coughing; " a letter always begins so."

The maiden smiled, and said—

"Ah, that were fine, to be sure! That we are all well, and you have been lying ill in bed this fortnight!"

"But you can say that at the end of the letter, Trien, all the same."

"No, child, do you know what you must do?" said John's mother. "You must first ask how *he* is, and after you have written that, we shall add all the other things."

"No, child," said the other widow; "write down first that you take the pen in your hand to inquire after his health. That is the way the letter of Peter-John's Tist began, which I heard read at the miller's last night."

"Yes, that is what Kate the wooden-shoemaker's daughter said too. But I'll not do it for all that—it is far too childish," replied the maiden, impatiently. "John knows, without being told, that I can't write with my feet."

"In the first place," said the grandfather, "set down his name at the top of the paper."

"What name? Braems?"

"No, no—John!"

"You are right, grandfather," replied the girl. "Go away, Pawken, take your arms off the table. And you, mother, pray sit back a bit, else you will jog me."

She put the pen to the paper, and, while seeking for the place at which she should begin to write, she spelt, in a low tone, the name of her absent friend.

Suddenly John's mother rose, and, seizing the girl's hand, said—

"Wait a little, Trien. You do not mean to say, surely, that John is not good? That is so short a way of beginning; would it not be better to set down, *Beloved son*, or, *Dear child?*"

Trien scarcely heard her; for she was busy licking the paper, and half angrily exclaimed—

"Look there! that comes of it all. A great blot on the paper; and no licking will do any good—it will not go out. I must take the other sheet."

"Now, Trien, what do you say to it? *Beloved son*—that sounds much better, don't you think?"

"No, I will not put down that," grumbled Trien, in a slightly irritated tone. "Can I write to John as if I were his mother?"

"Well, what will you write, then?"

The maiden blushed all over, while she replied—

"Let us write, *Dear friend*. Does that not sound well?"

"No, no, I'll not have that," said the mother. "I would rather have *John*, short as it is."

"*Beloved John*—will that do?"

"Ay, ay, that's right!" replied the others all at once, as if overjoyed at the solution of the heavy problem.

"Now, keep off from the table all of you," cried Trien; "and keep Pawk away, that he may not shake me."

She now began the work. Immediately after, pure drops of perspiration stood upon her brow; she held her breath, and her countenance glowed. Soon after, she heaved a deep sigh as if she felt a great burden lifted from her, and said joyfully—

"Ah, it is the most difficult of letters that *B*. But there it stands now, with its thick head."

Both women stood up and looked with great admiration at the letter, which was as big as a finger-joint at least.

"Well, that is clever!" exclaimed John's mother; "the thing looks like a wallet, and it stands for *Beloved John!* Well, well, writing is a fine thing; one would almost think it was witchcraft."

"Come, let me get on," said Trien courageously. "I shall manage it famously now; if only the pen would not spirt so."

Trien now laboured on, perspiring and groaning. The grandfather panted and coughed; the women were silent, and did not venture to stir; the little brother busied himself dipping his fingers in the ink, and bepainting his little arms with black spots.

After a time, the first line was full of great letters, and the girl paused a moment.

"Well, Trien, how far are you now?" asked John's mother. "You must read us what you have got on the paper, there."

"Do not be so very impatient," said Trien; "nothing more stands there yet than, *Beloved John.* All goes on well. Just look how the sweat breaks out on me! I'd rather muck the stable; you seem to think, surely, that writing is no labour.—Pawken, let alone the ink, you rascal, else you will upset the cup."

"Come now, go on, girl," said the grandfather, "otherwise the letter will not be written till next week."

"Yes, that's true enough," replied Trien; "but tell me what I shall put down next."

"In the first place, and before anything else, inquire after his health."

She wrote on again for a time, wiped out two or three incorrect letters with her finger, annoyed herself very much with efforts to get hold of the hair which had found its way into the slit of the pen, scolded the parish-clerk because the ink was so thick, and then read, with a loud voice, "*Beloved John, how is it with your health?*"

"That is as it should be," said the mother. "Now, write that we are all well—both ourselves and the cattle—and that we wish him good-day."

Trien reflected for a moment, and then went on with her writing. As soon as she was ready, she read—

"*God be praised, we are all in good health, and the ox and the cow likewise, except grandfather, who is ill; and we all together wish you good-day.*"

"Heavens!" cried her mother, "Trien, child, where have you learned all that? The parish-clerk himself"—

"Do not confuse me," interrupted Trien, "and make me forget something. I feel now that all will go capitally."

For half an hour the deepest silence reigned. The work seemed to go on more easily, for Trien smiled at times while writing. Pawken alone annoyed her, for he was now dipping his whole hand in the ink, and his arm was black all over. She had pushed the cup to the other side of the table several times; but the little fellow was so bent upon playing with the ink, that nothing could take him away from it.

Spite of that, the two first pages were now full to the edge. At the request of the women, Trien now read what she had set down, with a certain self-satisfaction, and it was as follows:—

"'BELOVED JOHN,—How is it with your health? God be praised, we are all in good health, and the ox and the cow likewise, except grandfather, who is ill; and we all together wish you good-day. It is now six months since we heard from you. Send us word, then, whether you are still in life. It is not right of you so to forget us—us, who are so fond of you that your mother speaks of you all day long, and that I dream of you every night—dreaming that you are unhappy, and that I hear sounding in my ears without ceasing "Trien! Trien!" so that I start up in my sleep and leap out of bed. And the ox, poor thing! is always looking out of its stall and heaving sighs, which it would almost make you shed tears to hear. And that none of us know anything at all about you is a great cause of grief to us, and you ought to have pity on us, John, for it will make your poor mother quite ill. Poor woman! if she only hears your name, a spasm seizes her throat, and she begins to weep, so that it almost breaks my heart to see her'"—

While she was reading these lines, the eyes of the listeners gradually filled with tears; at the sad tones of the last words, they could no longer restrain their emotion, and the maiden was interrupted by loud sobs and groans. The grandfather had laid his head on the bedstead to conceal his tears; John's mother, too deeply affected to be able to repress her feelings, sprang up and fell speechless on the young girl's neck, who beheld with surprise the effect of her writing.

"Trien, Trien! where did you find these words?" cried the other widow. "They go like a knife through my heart; and yet they are very beautiful!"

"Ah! it is the simple truth," sighed John's mother; "it is better that he should know what I have suffered in my heart. Read on farther, Trien dear; it quite astonishes me that you can write so well—there never was the like of it. Your hands are much too good, child, to milk cows or till the land; but God lets many strange things happen in the world."

Pleased with the praise she received, Trien said with a self-satisfied smile—

"I will cope with any one in writing. Now, at last, have I discovered the proper way of writing a letter. But listen still, for there is more yet:—

"'Ah, John, if you but knew all, you would not neglect to send us news The clover has failed on account of the severe frost, and because the seed was bad; but the sainfcin smiles at you when you look at it, as mellow as butter. And the grain has suffered a little from the drought; nevertheless, our dear heavenly Father has blessed us with beautiful buckwheat, and a large crop of early potatoes. And the joiner is married to a girl from Pulderbosch who squints, but she has brought a little dowry with her. John Sus, the butcher, fell from the brewer's roof on our old smith's back, and the smith lies at the point of death, poor fellow.' "——Trien paused, and looked up at her audience.

"Is that all?" asked the mother, disappointed. "Will you not tell him that the cow has calved?"

"O yes, I forgot that.——See, there it is already—'Our cow has calved; all went well, and the calf is sold.'"

"Will you say nothing about our rabbits, then, Trien?" asked the grandfather.

After it was written, the maiden read—

"'Grandfather has made a rabbit-warren in the stable; they are as fat as badgers; but the biggest buck shall not be killed till you come back, John, and then we shall have a glorious feast.'"

All burst into a hearty laugh; the little fellow, who saw everybody happy, and was himself somewhat moved by the word *feast*, clapped his hands. Unfortunately, however, he struck the coffee-cup so violently that it rolled over the table, and the ink was poured over the beautiful letter like a black flood. Laughter disappeared from every countenance; they looked at one another astounded and silent, and held up their hands in despair, while Pawken, who was afraid of a beating, was howling and screaming by anticipation. A considerable time was spent in overwhelming the child with reproofs, and in bitter lamentations over the mishap, till at last it occurred to some one to say—

"O Heaven! what is to be done now?"

"Come, come," said Trien in a decided tone, "the mishap is not so bad, after all. I had some inclination to write the letter over again at any rate, for at first it did not go so well as I wished—the letters were too big, and the writing crooked. Now I shall do it much better—I feel in spirits to attempt it. Just let me run as fast as I can into the village for paper and ink, and to get my pen made again, for it has become far too soft."

"Then go quickly, child," was the reply. "You have the five-franc piece you got for the calf; get the parish-clerk to change it, for we must send at least eighteen-pence to our poor John.—Pawken! get out of the house, and don't show face till evening, if possible."

Trien hastened out of the door on her way to the village, with a pleased expression on her face. The victory she had gained, the conviction that she could henceforth write to John, and above all, a kind of pride she felt in her accomplishments, filled her heart with a secret pleasure.

At the linden-tree, by the cross-roads, she saw the letter-carrier at a distance approaching. This made her stand still, and her heart beat quick with expectation; for as this road led nowhere but to the mud-huts, and the uninhabited heath and wood beyond, she had no doubt that the postman brought some news from John. And in fact, as he approached, he took a letter out of his pocket, and said smiling—

"Trieny, I have got something here for you, which comes all the way from Venloo; but there is thirty-five cents to pay."

"Thirty-five cents!" murmured Trien, as she took the letter with a trembling hand, and dreamily gazed at the super-scription.

"Yes, yes," said the letter-carrier, "it is written there on the outside. Am I likely to cheat you for such a trifle?"

"Can you change this?" asked Trien, giving him the five-franc piece.

The letter-carrier changed the piece of money for her, deducting the postage, then greeted the maiden in a friendly way, and returned to the village.

Trien ran joyfully home. But unable to resist her impatience, she tore open the letter, and was not a little surprised to see another fall out of the envelope. She lifted it up. A modest blush overspread her brow and face, while a smile played round her lips, and her eyes sparkled with pleasure. On this letter there was written, in large letters, "*For Trien alone.*" For Trien! here, in this bit of paper, John's soul was shut up; his voice spoke out of it to her—to her alone! It was a secret between John and her!

At once moved and perplexed, she stood for a moment looking to the ground : a flood of thoughts flowed through her head, till the distant lowing of the ox recalled her to herself, and she remembered that it was not right to stay away so long. She hid the second letter in her bosom, and hastened to the hut, where she surprised the two widows, who were waiting for her return, with the joyful exclamation, " A letter from John! a letter from John!"

Both came to meet her with joyful surprise, and the good old women almost skipped with delight. The grandfather bent himself so far forward to see the letter, that he almost fell out of bed.

In a few hasty words, Trien told them how she had met the letter-carrier by the way, and how he had asked thirty-five cents; but she was interrupted by the others, who kept calling out: " Oh, Trien, read it! read it, Trien!"

Trien seated herself at the table, and began to spell out the letter with a loud voice; and as the writing was not very distinct, she had to do so with every word, and had to repeat many of them before she could bring out any sense. She read as follows :—

"MY VERY DEAR PARENTS,—I take the pen into my hand in order to inquire into the state of your precious health, and I hope to hear from you soon also. I have got sore eyes, and am at present in the hospital; and I am very anxious, dear parents, and somewhat afraid, because so many comrades have become blind from the same disease."

Trien could read no more: she let her head sink on the ill-starred paper, while the women and the grandfather shed bitter tears, and bewailed their misfortune with loud sobs.

"O God! O God!—my poor child! my poor child! my poor child!" cried the mother, raising her hands to heaven, and walking about the room in despair. "Blind! blind!"

The maiden raised her head again, and said through her tears—"For Heaven's sake do not make it worse than it is —it is bad enough already. Let me go on; perhaps it is not so bad as we suppose. Be still, and listen.

"But tell mother not to be anxious, for I am already a little better, and I hope to recover, if it please God. The worst thing of all is want of food, for we are on half rations in the hospital. We could take in one mouthful the allowance of bread and meat for a whole day; and in addition to that we have a dish of *Ratatul*,* without salt and pepper, and that is all. When the heart is sound, one may live on that. But, dear parents, if it is in your power, send me a little money. We are wretched enough here, sitting all day in the dark, and mourning, for we can't bear the light. Many compliments to grandfather, and Trien, and her mother, and Pawken, and I wish you all health and long life.

"Kobe, the son of Tistje the crofter, has been made a corporal. The rats in the barracks have bitten a great hole in my knapsack, and they have set down a new knapsack to my account, and it costs seven francs and seventeen centimes. Were it not for this, I should have no debt. All my superiors like me; and the sergeant, who is a Walloon from Liege, is pleased with me also.

---

* *Ratatul*, or *Ratatoull*, a Walloon word, is a kind of soup, or ragout, made of scrape of meat.

" Charles, the farmer's son, has written this letter for me, and he is in the hospital too, with sore eyes; but you must not let his father know it, for he is almost well again. The other friends from our village are still in good health. We send you, beloved parents, our respectful greetings. Your dutiful son."

After she had read it, Trien held the corner of her apron to her eyes, and mourned in silence; the grandfather had sunk behind the bed-curtains; the two widows sat weeping.

For a long time a painful silence reigned, only interrupted now and then by sighs and sobs, till Trien rose, and taking a sickle from the wall, went to the door and said—

" Our grief would soon have made me forget our poor cow. I go to fetch sainfoin. Try, in the meantime, to pick up a little courage, and think on what we should do."

No one answered. The maiden took a wheelbarrow from before the door, and wheeled it past the house. Behind an oak-tree, and concealed by the brushwood, she stopped and sat down on the barrow. With trembling hands, she put aside her neckerchief, and took out the letter. When she had opened it, she spelt out aloud what follows, while tears more than once bedimmed her eyes, and she had almost fainted.

" This letter, too, is written by Charles, but I have told him word for word what he should set down.

" TRIEN,—I have not ventured to write it to my mother, because the news is too terrible. Trien, I am blind—blind for my whole life. Both eyes are gone. It does not grieve me so much that I have lost my sight, as that I can see you no more on earth, nor mother, nor grandfather, nor any of those who love me ; and that this will be my death, I feel too well.

" Trien, since I grew blind I always see you before my eyes, and it is that alone which keeps me alive; but now I may no longer think of that, nor you either. Ah, my dear friend, you may go to merry-makings now as you used to do; do not stay away from them on my account, but enjoy yourself while you are young. For were you to suffer for my sake, then should I die an earlier death.

"Trien, I have written this to you alone, that you may acquaint my poor mother with it by degrees. For Heaven's sake, do it gently, Trien!—Your unhappy John, till death."

Scarcely had the girl read, with the greatest effort, the closing words of the letter, when her face became as pale as death, her arms sank powerless by her side, her eyes closed, and her head fell slowly back on the wheelbarrow. There she lay unconscious, in a deathlike swoon.

The sultry breeze from the heath lazily stirred the oak twigs overhead, and the quivering leaves threw their shadow on the maiden's pale brow; the honey-bee buzzed and hummed round her head; high up towards the heavens, the skylark soared with its song; far away into the solitude was heard the ceaseless chirping of the crickets—and yet all was still and silent. Nothing awoke the maiden out of her death-like slumber.

The sun advanced gradually in its path, till a warm beam penetrated the foliage, and fell on her face. The unhappy girl slowly opened her eyes, and the blood began to flow again through her veins. She raised her head and looked round with a confused expression, unable to understand where she was. The letter, which still lay open at her feet, recalled the fearful calamity to her mind. She picked it up, and, folding it carefully, put it into her bosom, and bent her head in deep reflection.

After some time she rose, and wheeling the barrow hastily to a little field, half tore and half cut the sainfoin. In less than a minute the barrow was fully laden. With as much rapidity she returned home, threw down the fodder before the cow, and then entering the house, said abruptly—

"To-morrow, at daybreak, I go to John."

"Oh, child!" cried her mother, "it is at the other end of the country. What are you thinking of? You will not reach it in a year!"

"I go to John, I tell you," replied the girl decidedly, "and I shall find him out were it three hundred miles from here. Our parish-clerk will tell me the way."

John's mother went up to her with folded hands and with supplicating mien, and sighed—

"Ah, Trien, dear angel! will you really do that for my child? I will bless you till my dying day!"

"Do it!" cried Trien, "do it! The king himself will not prevent me. I will see John, and console him, or perish in the attempt."

"Oh! a thousand thousand thanks, Trien!" exclaimed the mother, and clasped the maiden to her breast.

CHAPTER IV.

IT is just seven o'clock in the morning; but the heat is
great notwithstanding, for the sun glows brightly in the deep
blue sky.

See, yonder on the highway, not far from the beautiful river
Meuse, a peasant girl is walking forward vigorously. Her
dress shows that she is a stranger here: for such plaited caps
ornamented with lace, and such straw hats, are not worn by
the women of Limburg. She walks barefoot, carrying her shoes
in her hand. The perspiration drops from her brow; and
though weary even to fainting, she directs her look with inexpressible joy upon a distant church-tower; for there lies the
city Venloo, the termination of her long journey.

Poor Trien! for four days now she has walked steadily on,
asking her way, and suffering pain and fatigue. She has allowed herself short repose and little food; but God and her
strong nature have aided her. She has found it—the place
where her unhappy friend lies suffering and languishing far
from his friends and home. All her grief is forgotten; her
heart leaps with joy and beats with impatience. Had she
wings, she would fly like lightning to those turrets, from whose
roofs the sun is reflected as from a mirror. Increasing her
speed, the young peasant girl pushed on, till she came close
upon the entrenchments of the city of Venloo. She then

quickly put on her shoes, brushed off the dust a little, arranged her dress, and entered the open gate with a stout
heart.

After she had advanced a few steps between the outer ram-
parts, she observed a soldier with a musket in his hand walking up and down before a little house. While still at some
distance, she smiled in a friendly way to the sentinel; but he
looked at her with perfect indifference. Spite of this, however, she approached boldly, and asked, with an agreeable
smile—

"Friend, can you tell me where I can find John Braems?
He is here among the soldiers somewhere."

The sentinel was a Walloon, from about Liege.

"Can't understand," he grumbled, and wheeled round to
call the corporal.

The latter walked out of the guard-house, and came kindly
up to the maiden, who courtesied politely, and inquired—

"Mr. Corporal, can you tell me, if you will be so good,
where John Braems is to be found?"

The corporal looked amazed, like one who is disappointed
in his expectations, and, turning to the guard-house, he called
out in the Hainault dialect—

"Ho, Fleming! come here. Here's a chance of earning a
pot of beer."

A young soldier sprang down from the wooden board on
which he was sitting and came out, still rubbing a heavy
sleep from his eyes, and looking rather cross; but as soon as
he saw the girl, his expression became more friendly.

"Now, then, Mieken," he asked, "what do you want?"

"I have come here to see John Braems. Can you tell me
where he is to be found?"

"John Braems! I have never heard the name."

"But he is a soldier among the Belgians, like yourself."

"Yes, that may be; but does he serve in the cavalry or the infantry?"

"What do you mean, friend?"

"Is he in the horse or foot?"

"I don't know that; but he is a soldier in the Rifles. Are they not in the city?"

"There!—no wonder I didn't know him; we are of the ninth."

During this conversation, the corporal, and three or four soldiers beside the sentinel, had approached the girl. Trien could not understand why they peered into her face in so strange a way, laughing and jesting in the Walloon dialect. She began, however, to feel ashamed, and said to the Fleming, imploringly—

"Ah, friend! be so good as to show me the way; I am in such great haste."

The obliging soldier answered quickly—

"Go through the gate, strike into the first street on the right, then to the left—then once more to the left, and after that to the right again, till you come to a chapel; you leave this on your left, and turn to the right, behind the big house, where you will see a shop; when you have gone a considerable way further, then take to your left again, and this will bring you to the market-place; ask there for the barracks of the second Rifles, and any child will show you where it is to be found."

Trien was almost out of her senses; her head whirled with all the lefts and rights which she had endeavoured to fix in her mind. She could make nothing of it, however, and was about to beg a clearer explanation, when, suddenly, the sentinel shouted as loud as he could—

"*Aux armes!*"

Every one ran hither and thither, and hastened to the guard-house to get their arms; while the soldier said hastily to the terrified girl—

" Off with you! off with you!—run, or we shall be put into the lock-up. The town-governor is coming."

The maiden did not wait to be told twice; for at the city gate she saw an officer on horseback, who looked to her like a king, and had a great moustache. Angry, because he had surprised the guard while speaking with a young woman, he looked at the poor peasant girl as if he would eat her, but rode past without saying anything; but she heard with trembling how he scolded the soldiers, without being able to understand what had caused such violent anger.

She hastened into the city, and at last found the market-place. Here and there she saw soldiers in various costumes; but the occurrence with the guard had made her prudent. She now addressed herself to a citizen's wife—

" Do you know Flemish, friend?"

" Dutch? Yes."

" Will you be so good as tell me where the Rifles lie?"

" Certainly. You must turn round the corner there, and go straight on to the end of the street; there you will find the riflemen's barracks."

" A thousand thanks!" said Trien, setting off in the direction pointed out. She easily enough recognised the barrack when she reached it, both on account of the many soldiers going out and in, and the noise of the drums inside.

Smiling with joy, she went straight up to the gate with the intention of entering, but the sentinel called out in a gruff tone—

" Halt! back!—there is no admission here."

And when the girl still ventured to advance a step or two, he pushed her back with his hand.

" Ah, friend! I wish very, very much to speak with an acquaintance who is a soldier here; what must I do?"

" In what battalion, and in what company is he ?" asked the sentinel.

"Ah ! I can't tell that," she replied in a disheartened tone.

" Wait for half an hour," rejoined the sentinel ; " the signal for soup is just about to be given, and immediately after is the call to parade. Then you will see every man in the barrack march out, and if you have good eyes, may single out your friend. Go, meanwhile, and drink a glass of beer in the 'Falcon,' hard by, and leave me, for I see the adjutant looking at us."

The sentinel now let the perplexed girl stand there unheeded, struck his right hand forcibly on the butt-end of his musket, threw back his head, and marched up and down like a proud soldier without casting another glance at poor Trien.

She remained for a moment sunk in deep thought, and tortured herself to find out how it could be a misdeed to show a stranger the way. Her grief and vexation began to overpower her. Impatient as she was, however, half an hour seemed to her not too long to wait, and she accordingly determined to stand near the barrack-gate when the Rifles were marching out, and take such great care that not one should escape her eye. She would see and recognise John ! But with this charming thought, her countenance was suddenly overcast ; for it all at once occurred to her that it was impossible that a blind man could march with the rest of the soldiers. Still, what could she know about it ?   Everything here was so singular and extraordinary to her.   In her despair, she followed the sentinel's advice, and slowly went towards the " Falcon."   Arrived in the tavern, she called for a glass of beer, and sat down, weary and ashamed, at a table in the corner.

In the tavern room there were eight or ten soldiers standing beside the bar, and gossiping in a rough and loud way of things connected with the " service."

When the maiden entered, they had all turned towards her, and exchanged their remarks, at the same time exchanging a smile. As they all spoke French or Walloon, however, Trien did not understand what they said about her, and although the impudent glances of the soldiers annoyed her, she smiled notwithstanding, and said—" Good-day to you all, friends."

These soldiers seemed to her to be fine, gallant fellows, with the exception of one, who was older than the others, and assumed a certain superiority over them. He wore coarse gloves of chamois leather; the buttons of his waistcoat shone like gold; the military cap hung over his left ear, while his magnificent moustache was made to stand up with black wax. He stood with the upper part of his body bent back, and his hand planted on his side, like a perpetual challenge. This haughty warrior must be provost of the regiment, or fencing-master at least, thought Trien.

It was not his exterior and his bearing which made the girl form a bad opinion of him; but it was the shameless way in which he compelled her to hold down her eyes before his impudent gaze, and his appearing to make jests on her in a loud coarse tone, which annoyed her. Nor did she hide what she felt, for the proud rifleman could easily see from her face that she had no friendly feelings towards him.

While both parties were thus looking at each other, the hostess brought a glass of beer to the maiden. A young soldier, with a mild expression and friendly eyes, approached her, put forward his glass, and said in the dialect of the Kempenland—

" Mieken, let us touch glasses. You are certainly from the Antwerp country."

"No, comrade, I am from the St. Antonis district, from Schilde or Magerhalle, whichever you please."

"And I am a young man from Wechel-ter-zande, so we are neighbours."

Joy lighted up the maiden's countenance, and she gave the young soldier as affectionate a look as if she had found a brother in him.

Meanwhile, the other riflemen also had advanced to the table, some sitting down upon it. The soldier with the brushed-up moustache sat down so close to Trien, that he almost touched her.

Trien could not bear his mocking and confident air, and trembled as if afraid. She then seized the hand of her countryman, and begged in the friendliest way—

"Oh, my good friend, you must sit by me, if you will be so good, for I am afraid of the Walloons. What does *he* suppose that I am?"

"Bah, bah!" replied the other, "he is an empty braggart. Let him only dare to touch you, and I will bring my fist down on his moustache, were he a hundred times fencing-master."

Encouraged by these words, Trien turned to the mocking fellow, and said confidently—

"Mr. Soldier, I would beg you to sit along a bit. What do you imagine? what do you take me for?"

The fencing-master burst into a loud laugh, shoving his stool back a little at the same time however, while he made various jesting remarks, which the maiden fortunately did not understand.

"Tell me, friend," said Trien to her protector, "what is your name, if I may be so bold as to ask?"

"Sus Caers."

"Sus Caers! Ah, well, how wonderful! A fortnight ago

we sold your father a calf—a pretty mottled calf. I have still some of the money in my pocket."

"Ay! and what is my father about? Is he well?"

"Quite well—a man like a tree. I remember now he told us that you also were in the army. Do you know our John?"

"What is his second name?"

"Braems."

"O Heavens! as if I didn't know John Braems! We were in the same company, and we were great cronies till he took weak eyes."

Deeply affected, the maiden now seized him with both hands, and said, with a deep breath—

"Ah, friend! how grateful am I to my heavenly Father that He brought me into this tavern. You will show me where I can find John, will you not? The young men from our quarter are all good-hearted fellows."

"Certainly. I shall take you to the hospital. You know, I suppose, that he is blind?"

"Alas, yes," sighed Trien; "but it is the hand of God, and cannot be helped now. Many are the tears we have shed over the thought of his calamity."

The soldiers had seen with a kind of envy the sudden intimacy and mutual confidence which had sprung up between the Kempener and the young maid. The fencing-master, above all, slid backwards and forwards on his stool, and made all kinds of demonstrations. In the meantime, he had gradually come quite close to the girl again, and even chucked her under the chin in a familiar way, as if she cared in the least for him.

The Fleming started up and threatened him; but Trien, whose countenance burned with indignation, stood up, and with the flat of her hand struck the fencing-master in the face with such right good-will, that he did not know whether his head was off or on.*

As soon as he had recovered from his confusion, the tavern became a fearful scene of battle. He seized a jug, and would have broken the girl's head with it, had not the young Kempener, who was a stronger man, seized him by the throat and wrenched it out of his hand. The other comrades sprang forward to separate the combatants, calling out that the sabre alone, and not the fist, could decide a soldier's quarrel. Trien, in the greatest anxiety and trembling with fear, is compelled to listen to a multitude of coarse and violent words, while the soldiers struggling with one another tumble about the room and the hostess is screaming out that she will fetch the watch. Suddenly, however, a sound of drums is heard proceeding from the barracks :—

"Soup! soup!" cried those who took no part in the contest, and leaving the others, hastened out of the tavern.

The fencing-master still poured forth threats, but at last went out, saying to the Kempener as he passed—

"*A ching heures sol terrain! edj vindrai vos quérie.*"†

"Be it so, braggart!" replied the challenged youth, with a laugh of mockery.

"Ah, Sus, what anxiety have I suffered!" sighed Trien. "Is it all settled now?"

"Settled! I must this evening fight a duel with that sword-eater."

"O Heavens! and all on my account!" cried the maiden, pale and trembling.

"Do not annoy yourself about that, child; it is only a matter for laughter. It will end in our going to drink together. That is the way the Walloon takes of getting a little gin

---

* This rather rough mode of self-defence is pretty customary among the peasant girls of the Kempenland, and is regarded among them as a point of honour.

† Walloon: "At five o'clock on the fighting-ground. I will seek you there.

if he can get it into the bargain. Such things happen twice a week with that fellow, and it is known by everybody. Come quickly, and I shall take you to the hospital where John Braems is."

Trien paid her beer and left the tavern with the soldier. He took her through several streets, talking all the way, and then left her saying, while he pointed with his finger—

"Do you see the soldier yonder, sitting on a bench before the door of that large building? That building is the Infirmary. You must speak to the soldier and he will let you in, if it is possible to gain admission. A safe return home to you, and many greetings to my father, if you chance to see him."

"A thousand thousand thanks, my friend," replied Trien, as she left him and proceeded on her way to the hospital.

So soon as the maiden found herself alone, a feeling of despondency took possession of her, and she could scarcely muster courage to speak to the soldier on the bench. As she came nearer, however, a joyful smile lighted up her face, for she thought she recognised him. And, in fact, when yet some paces from him, she called him by his name, for it was Crofter Tistje's son, Kobe, who had been made a corporal, as John had written, and who now sat here on the bench in that capacity.

So soon as he saw Trien, he sprang joyfully up, and hastened to her with pleasure and surprise.

"What! Trien dear, is this you? Heavens! how glad I am to see you here! How goes everything in our village? Has my mother recovered? How is Verbaet's daughter Loken? Do they know yonder that I am a corporal now? And what did Loken say when she heard it?"

"All is well," replied Trien. "Your mother was at church last Sunday; she has got rid of the fever, and one can scarcely see that she has been ill. I myself told Loken, in passing, that you had been promoted."

"Well, and did she not smile with pleasure?"

"No, she blushed up to her very hair; but she was so delighted that she could not say a word: I could see that in her eyes."

Kobe the corporal slowly hung his head, and looked to the ground—the expression of his features was suddenly altered: he, too, felt his face redden, and his heart beat fast. His native village, with its heath and fields; the modest glance of his beloved; his mother's affectionate smile; the Sabbath enjoyment, after a long week of toil; the songs under the linden trees; the prattle of the tame magpies; the barking of the house-dog; the rustling of the fir-wood;—all came before his eyes fresh and living, all sounded in his ears with irresistible sweetness, and he was lost in the enchanting contemplation of the life for which he longed.

"What have I said then, Kobe, that vexes you?" asked Trien gently.

"Ah, Trieny dear, I do not know. There came before my eyes all at once our village, and so clearly, that I saw the very sun shining on the church-tower. My father was busy raking the stubble out of the field; my mother stood beside him, and I heard them speaking about me. I had quite forgotten myself—but now it is over."

"Come, Kobe," said Trien, "lead me to John as quickly as you can—he will be so glad to see me."

"You know, then, his misfortune?"

"Alas! yes; I come to talk with him, and comfort him, poor fellow! Do not let me stand here any longer, but lead me to him at once."

"Trien dear, how sorry I am for you!" sighed Kobe, truly grieved.

"And why?" cried Trien. "Ah, Kobe, you make me anxious. Has anything happened?"

" Unfortunate Trien !" he replied. " No one is admitted to the blind and diseased; it is forbidden under a severe penalty."

The poor girl uttered a painful shriek, and covering her eyes with her apron, she wept and bewailed her bad fortune.

" Alas ! alas ! four days have I walked and suffered, and after all cannot see him. From this place I do not go alive; of that you may be certain."

" Trien, you must not make such a noise in the street," said Kobe; " otherwise people will collect round you to gape and stare. Be quiet, if you can."

The maiden dried her tears, with a mingled expression of courage and despair, and exclaimed—

" If I have to break into this house as a thief, and were a sabre to pierce my heart, I *will* see him, and speak with him —let them prevent me if they can."

" Listen, Trien dear," said the corporal gently; "I may perhaps lose my place by it, but I will help you, for all that. Keep quiet, and act as if you knew nothing. The sergeant is just going with the report to the governor; the doctor has been there already; and the director is unwell, and will not come into the sick-ward. When the sergeant is gone, I will bring you quietly into the blind-room. But, Trien, if I am put in the lock-up, and lose my rank, then remember to tell Loken and mother that it was owing to friendship and pity, and not from any misconduct."

" Be sure of that, Kobe," replied the girl, with moist eyes; " I will be grateful to you all my life long; let me only do what I wish now, and Loken shall write you a letter when I get home again."

" Ah, she can't write, Trien," sighed the corporal.

" But *I* can," she rejoined; " and I will do it for her; and I will set down such delightful things that you wil actually leap with joy."

' Do you see, Trien, I do not stand here as sentinel; **I am**
Planton, and am forbidden to speak with any one. Come,
sit down on that bench, and take no notice of anything, till
the sergeant has passed out. I shall say that you are my
sister, otherwise he will thwart our plans. Let us talk a bit,
meanwhile, of our friends at home. Is Ned, the brewer's son,
married yet to farmer Dierikx's dairy-maid? Is the filly,
which we sold to the landlord at the ' Crown,' grown a fine
horse ?"

They sat down on the bench, purposely at some distance
from each other, and began to chat about the absent.

———

Within the hospital, there was a room set apart for those
with diseased eyes, its windows securely covered with shut-
ters of green paper, so that not a ray of light could enter. To
those who could see, it was a horrible place; for a shade of
light, gloomier than the deepest black, threw a painful colouring over everything, oppressing the heart of the spectator
with mingled sadness and fear. It could be called neither
light nor darkness; and it was necessary to accustom one's-
self to the green and deathlike day, before any object could
be distinguished. In addition, there reigned throughout
this abode of affliction the stillness of death, only broken
from time to time by a cry of pain, when the eyes of some
poor patient were being burnt with caustic. Along the
walls on wooden benches sat the blind and diseased, like
a row of spectres, motionless and silent in the darkness.
Each had on a large green shade, which so entirely covered
the brow and face, that the features could not be distinguished.

In the furthest corner sat John Braems with sunken head,
sadly dreaming of things which he loved, and should never
see again. Under the green shade, a quiet smile played round

his mouth, while his lips moved, as if he were conversing with some invisible beings. He had just conjured up the image of his darling friend, and made her whisper in his ear once more the modest confession of her love, when an almost inaudible noise was suddenly heard upon the stairs. He seemed to hear his name mentioned. All trembling, he sprang from his seat, as if moved by some invisible hand, and sighed involuntarily, " Trien ! Trien !"

The door was opened from without, and the maiden, accompanied by the corporal, stood on the threshold. Trien shuddered as she looked into the dark chamber, and saw rows of spectre-like shadows all masked with green shades. She drew back with a cry of alarm ; but John Braems had recognised her voice, and advanced with outstretched hands, groping his way towards her. She perceived her unfortunate friend, and hastening up to him, fell weeping on his neck. For a time nothing was heard but " Trien !" " John !" uttered in tones of love, sympathy, and sorrow. The maiden lay weeping on the young man's breast, and seemed at last to have fainted with her emotion ; for her head lay on one side, and her hands hung powerless from her lover's shoulders.

Meanwhile the rest of the blind had collected in a circle round the girl, and were feeling her, as if they too might perchance recognise some friend. Their touches awoke her out of her forgetfulness, and drawing back, half afraid, she said with alarm—

" Heavens ! John dear, what is all this ? Tell them to let me alone, otherwise I can't stay here."

' Don't be afraid, Trien," replied John ; " it is nothing. The blind see with their fingers. They are feeling your clothes ; and find out in that way from what quarter you come. They mean no harm."

" Ah, poor fellows !" sighed Trien, " since that is the reason, I forgive them with all my heart; but I don't like it much. Let us go into that dark corner and sit down on the bench, John; I have so much to say to you."

With these words, she led her friend to the bench, and sat down beside him, holding his hands in hers.

The conversation which now began must have been very moving, though almost inaudible; for joy, sorrow, smiles, and tears, often succeeded each other on Trien's face; and from time to time, one might see her press John's hands with deep feeling. She was, without doubt, endeavouring to infuse the balsam of consolation into the unfortunate man's heart, for the few sounds of her voice which one could catch were as tender and impressively sweet as the sweetest tones of some love-song. John had pushed the shade higher up on his brow, and on his countenance there was visible a peculiar expression of dreamy attention, and at the same time of sadness and despair, like one listening out of the abyss of suffering to words which cannot make him forget his sorrow, though they may delude him for a moment with imaginary happiness.

The blind stood round them in silence, and listened attentively to catch what they were saying, and pick up some of those consolatory sounds. The corporal remained outside the door, marching up and down, and every now and then putting his head into the room to see if Trien was ready to leave. Suddenly he grew pale, and intense fear was depicted on his face,—he saw the sergeant ascending the stairs. Without making any remark, he opened the door and admitted him into the blind-room, following him with sunken head, and a look of conscious guilt, like a malefactor who awaits his sentence. Scarcely had the sergeant perceived the girl, when he broke out into a storm of angry words, and at last turning to the corporal, said—

"Ha! and so you have admitted a stranger—and a woman too! I'll not be long of relieving you of your duties, my good fellow, and getting fourteen days from the Governor for you. It will not be my fault, I can tell you, if you retain your corporal's dress."

Trien rose and said imploringly to the enraged sergeant—

"Oh, sir, be pitiful! I alone am to blame, for having prevailed upon him with my tears to admit me. Do him no harm for having been so kind-hearted"—

The sergeant shook his head impatiently, and prevented her from adding more.

"What has all that to do with the matter?" he interrupted. "I know my duty, and what I have to do; and you, Mieken, out at once, and that quickly too!"

The maiden was grieved and surprised when she heard this order; he seemed to be in earnest, however, and she went all trembling up to him, and entreated—

"Ah! grant me, I beseech you, only one half hour! I will often pray to God for you, and kiss your hand with joy."

"Come, come, make an end of this stupid game," snarled the sergeant; "not one minute longer!"

"But oh, sir," cried the distracted Trien, "I have come on foot all the way from the other end of the land to bring comfort to our unfortunate John, poor fellow, and you will not, surely, drive me out. I have scarcely spoken with him yet."

"Are you going, or are you not?" said the sergeant, adding a few coarse threats, which made her tremble.

The tears gushed out of the maiden's eyes; she raised her folded hands to the sergeant, and sobbed out—

"For God's sake, friend, only one quarter of an hour! Do not kill me! Have compassion on a poor blind man; it may happen to you too. Would it not tear your heart *then,* if your mother or your sister were to be hunted away like a dog? Ah, sir! take pity on us; all my life long I will love you for it."

John and the other blind men, who were all angry at the sergeant's severity, urged the maiden's petition, and the whole room was in confusion, as if the blind were rebelling against their inexorable overseer. This only enraged him the more; he threatened to put all on bread and water, and suddenly seizing Trien by the arm, was about to drag her forcibly out of the room. She, however, perceived his intention, and tearing herself loose, ran weeping to John, whom she embraced, with loud lamentations. As deeply grieved as she, but yet convinced that nothing could prevent their separation, the young man tried to console her, and hastily said to her a multitude of things which had been forgotten during their quiet conversation. The sergeant, however, was not slow in following her, and had again laid hold of her arm. He attempted to tear her from John, but the sorrowing girl kept her arms locked round her blind friend like an iron band, and resisted the sergeant's violence with determination; whereupon he called out to Kobe, who was standing in perplexity at the door—

"Corporal, what are you doing standing there? Come here; I command you to turn that peasant woman out of the door, or you will pay dearly for it. Do you hesitate?"

Kobe approached the girl, and, taking her arm, said—

"Trien dear, I am very sorry; but it can't be helped. Go out peaceably, otherwise they will throw you down stairs. Such is the order; the sergeant must do what his duty commands."

Trien separated herself from her friend, and holding up her head with quiet dignity, she advanced to the sergeant, and said—

"Mr. Overseer, I will go; but, friend, forgive me and Kobe also; it will be well done, and God will certainly reward you. You have a heart in you as well as others; and all men in this world are brothers. You will be so good as to forget, Mr. Sergeant, will you not? I will remember you in my prayers."

The wrath of the sergeant was appeased when he saw his commands humbly obeyed; the sweet voice and expressive blue eyes of the maiden also had touched his heart, and he replied, in a more kindly tone—

"Now, then, only go out without further delay; and if the fault is concealed, I shall say nothing about it, and forgive it out of compassion for you."

"Ah, you kind man!" cried Trien; "I knew it; you speak Flemish, like ourselves. I go in a moment—only one farewell!"

She once more embraced the unhappy blind man, who speechlessly received her farewell kiss—murmured in his ear a few consoling words, and then walked to the door weeping and sobbing. There she turned her head, and uttering a piercing cry, endeavoured to return, struggling with the sergeant, who, however, now held her fast. The truth was, she had seen that her unfortunate friend had fallen to the ground, and lay as if lifeless, with his head upon the bench, and the sight of this excited her to such a degree that she trembled with anxiety and grief, and struggled wildly with the sergeant to free herself. He dragged her out, however, and shut the door behind him.

Exhausted, powerless, and almost dying with despair—obedient as a martyr, and almost unconscious—she walked down stairs and into the open court, between the sergeant and the corporal. Here, she let herself be pushed and dragged along; for her feet refused the motion which was to distance her from John. She did not speak a word; the quiet tears which streamed over her cheeks was the only sign of her sorrow.

At the threshold of one of the doors which opened into the front court, stood a richly-dressed lady, with noble features. She beheld the weeping girl from a distance, and seemed desirous to know what had happened. The nearer they approached her on their way to the gate, the more strongly did her countenance express a deep concern and sympathy.

Trien observed it, and a ray of hope entered her breast. It did not escape Kobe, for he whispered to her—

"That is the wife of the governor of the hospital; and oh, so good and kind! She is from Antwerp."

The girl now made haste, as if she were eager to reach the gate; but as she approached the richly-clad lady, she turned round and threw herself on her knees before her with outstretched arms, crying out—

"Ah, lady, help!—pity, for a poor blind man!"

The lady seemed surprised and perplexed by this unexpected appeal. For a short time, she looked at the young peasant girl, who held her beautiful blue eyes fixed upon her as if in earnest supplication, at the same time smiling hopefully through her tears, as if already thanking her for a benefit received. She took Trien by both hands, raised her up, and said, with a friendly voice—

"Poor girl! Come in, my dear child! what is it that troubles you?"

With these words, and without looking at the sergeant, who put his hand politely to his forehead, she led Trien into the house, and pushed forward a chair for her to sit upon.

In the room, she found an officer of the Rifles, who stood before a desk writing. He raised his eyes from his work, and looked at the weeping maid curiously and sympathizingly, but waited, without making any observation, to get an explanation of the matter.

The lady—she was the officer's wife—again took Trien's hand, and said—

"Come, come, my girl, be comforted; no harm shall happen to you. Tell me what terrifies you so much; if it be possible, I will help you."

"Ah, lady!" sighed Trien, while she kissed warmly her protector's hand. "God will bless you for your kindness. I am a poor peasant girl from between St. Antonis and Magerhalle in the Kempenland. The lot fell upon our John, and he had to be a soldier. Four days ago he wrote to his mother, saying that he had sore eyes; but to me privately he wrote that he was blind for his whole life. I lay for two hours as if dead, under an oak-tree. I did not venture to tell his mother the truth, for fear she should die of grief. On the next day, early in the morning, I set out barefoot, without knowing the road, to walk from our village to Venloo. I asked my way; often wandered from it, and made long roundabouts; suffered shame and pain enough; walked night and day, with scarcely any food or drink, till the blood dropt from my feet. After I had suffered three days, like a stray sheep, I arrived here. A young man from our village, who is corporal, let me into the hospital out of compassion. I saw our John with his eyes all gone, and was just comforting him, when the sergeant came and drove me out. Now I shall not see John again; I must leave him, poor fellow, without consolation; and oh lady! I cannot, cannot do that. Pray think, if you will be so good, what I have endured to come here; and have compassion with the innocent lamb who wastes and pines away with grief yonder in the dark room."

"I be your brother?" asked the officer behind the deek.

The maiden hung her head to conceal the blush which suffused her countenance at this question.

After a short silence, she raised her eyes and said—

" Sir, I am not his sister; but from childhood we have
dwelt under the same roof; his parents are mine; he loves
my mother; his grandfather has carried me before I could
walk; labour, gains, joy, and sorrow, all,—we have had in
common."

After a pause, she again looked down, and said in a lower
tone—

" Since he has met with this misfortune, I too feel that I
am not his sister!"

Moved by the girl's words, the officer had left the desk, and
gradually approached Trien.

" Poor child!" sighed the lady; "you must drive the
thought out of your mind, and try to console yourself. You
cannot continue to love a blind man?"

Trien trembled, for this wounded her deeply.

" Forsake him!" she cried; "forget him because he is to
be for life blind and miserable! Oh, lady! be so good as
not to say that again; it cuts my heart like a knife."

A fresh stream of tears flowed from her eyes.

The officer exchanged some words in French with his wife.
He told her that a ministerial order had come which gave the
colonels power to send the blind soldiers to their homes, with
unlimited leave of absence—there to wait for a final discharge from service. Although this measure was not to be
brought into operation for some weeks, he was yet ready
to make an attempt with the colonel to get an exception made in favour of the peasant girl's unhappy friend,
and to procure him his leave of absence on that very day.
His wife urged him to execute this plan. Trien did not
understand what they said, but she could perceive that

her protector was urging her husband to some good deed, and the half-consoled girl nodded her head beseechingly, as if she would thereby encourage him to his benevolent under-taking.

The officer turned to her, and asked—

"Would you be glad if your friend returned home with you?"

An indescribable expression of mingled joy and anxiety lighted up Trien's countenance. Her great wide-opened eyes seemed to wish to draw more words out of the officer's mouth. At last her feelings found vent—

"Be glad! be happy!" she cried. "The very question almost makes me mad. Oh, sir, sir, do not delude me with such a hope! I would creep in the dust before you, and kiss your feet with gratitude."

The officer quickly seized his cap, buckled on his sabre, and went out with the words—

"Keep up your spirits, my girl! Perhaps I shall succeed. At any rate, you shall see John again to-morrow, I'll take care of that."

Some unintelligible sounds of thankfulness followed the officer to the front court, and then Trien began earnestly to thank her benefactress; but the lady did not give her time to speak out all the feeling with which her heart overflowed. She went to the kitchen, and returned with a maid, who placed a little table before Trien with meat, bread, and beer, and said to her—

"Eat and drink, my girl! from my heart I give it."

"Ah! I know that well, my lady," sighed Trien; "but now have I deserved so much kindness? You act as if you were my mother. May God reward you!"

"Is it long since you ate anything?" asked the lady.

"I have eaten nothing since three o'clock this morning,"

said Trien, enjoying the food with genuine appetite. I have
walked seven hours; but now I thank the merciful God in all
my grief, that He has made you so good, my lady."

For a long time Trien evinced her gratitude, and for long the
noble-minded lady consoled her with sweet and sisterly words,
for the officer did not return for two hours. By this time
Trien had related the whole history of her life, and spoken with
deep attachment of the beautiful and much-loved Kempenland, where soul and body are pure as the air of the sandy plain,
where the odour of simplicity and honesty breathes round every
feeling of the soul—just as the ever-blooming flowers of the
heath are bathed every morning in rich and balmy vapours.
The lady found an inward pleasure in this peasant maiden,
whose artless talk betokened an intelligent mind, and richly
gifted heart. More than once had Trien stirred her soul and
made her eyes sparkle with emotion.

While she was sitting there waiting, and talking of a
country life, the officer had returned, and gone up into the
blind-room with the sergeant. After staying some time there,
he had come down again into the court, accompanied by
John, who, with knapsack on back and staff in hand, was
led by the sergeant to the door of the officer's house. Here
the latter took the blind man's hand, and said to him as he
opened the door—

"Trien is within; she waits for you."

John drew a paper from his breast-pocket, and holding it
up above his head, cried with a joyful shout—

"Trien, dear Trien! I may go home with you. I need be
a soldier no more; here is my discharge!"

"What he says is true," observed the officer, who perceived
that Trien did not dare to believe it.

Meanwhile, John entered the room with outstretched arms;
but Trien did not run to meet him. The poor girl, over-

powered by this unexpected kindness, sank from her chair upon her knees, and crept in that attitude to her benefactress, who sat at a little distance from her on a sofa. With outspread arms and many tears, and gazing with gratitude into her eyes, the maiden said—

"Oh, my lady! if *you* do not go to heaven, who then can hope for blessedness? I cannot speak! Ah! my heart is breaking—I shall die of joy! Thanks! thanks!"

In fact, she let her head sink powerless into the lady's lap, and embraced her knees in silence. All of a sudden she awoke out of this deep emotion, sprang up, and threw herself, with loud expressions of joy, in which nothing but the young man's name could be distinguished, into the arms of the blind soldier.

After they had quite exhausted their expressions of joy and gratitude, Trien and John left the hospital, accompanied by the good wishes of their benefactors.

It was a strange and interesting sight to see, walking through the streets of Venloo, this blooming peasant girl leading the blind soldier by the hand. The passers-by stood still to look at them—attracted, not so much by the appearance of the unfortunate youth with his knapsack on his back and the green shade over his eyes, as by the inexplicable expression of pride and joy which gave to the young girl's countenance an expression at once noble and wondrously beautiful. The good Trien was so happy, so proud at the unexpected result of her self-sacrifice and determination, that she stepped forward with elated head and exulting mien, far too happy to cast down her eyes before the curious looks of the wondering citizens.

She was in great haste to leave the city, and urged the

blind man to walk quickly. The unlooked-for success had surprised and astounded her, even yet she could scarcely believe it, and felt at intervals an anxious shudder creep over her, with the fear that it was still possible for some one to tear her friend from her.

At last she gained the city gate; she saw the free fields stretching away towards the distant horizon, and over these lay the way to her village. Now for the first time a loud cry of joy burst from her lips; she turned her eyes thankfully towards heaven, and exclaimed with a sweet rapture—

"Now, John, come; now we are free!"

CHAPTER V.

It was still oppressively hot, though the shadows of the trees were now considerably lengthened. Over heath and field still hovered the transparent summer air: no breeze whispered among the foliage; the birds sat panting and still among the motionless leaves; every voice of nature was silent; so far as the eye could reach, neither man nor beast was visible; the earth seemed to have fallen asleep with weariness.

By the side of a solitary road, overhung by the branches of some young oaks, lay a soldier asleep, with his head on his knapsack. His feet were bare, and his shoes lay on the ground near him. A young peasant girl sat by his side, with her anxious look fixed on him, while with a birch twig she drove the flies from his face and feet, and maintained the deepest silence.

The soldier lay on a bed of wild thyme, which emitted its sweet odours round him, while the blue-bell bent its little cups over his brow; lower down, beside his feet, the azure gentian raised to him its beautiful petals. He must have already slept long, for his companion looked uneasily towards the sun, as if she would measure by the progress of heaven's torch how far the day was spent. Perhaps her sadness had another cause. In truth, she was vexed to perceive that the sun had turned round the corner of the oak wood, and was already casting some of its beams in full glow on the body of the sleeper. Her annoyance increased. She rose, and endeavoured to bend the young oak branches and bind them together, to form a thicker shade overhead to protect the soldier's repose; but she soon gave up this, as the sun seemed to fall on the roadside almost horizontally. Advancing softly, and with the greatest caution, she crept into the bush and cut off two long straight twigs, and placing herself before the soldier and looking at the sun as if making a calculation, she stuck both sticks beside him in the earth. She next took her apron, and hung it like a broad wall of shade before his face, and then sat down again with an expression of satisfaction. For a considerable time she looked at him as he slept, and watched his breathing, as if she would count the very pulsations of his heart. She could not see his eyes, for a green shade concealed them.

At last the soldier moved, groped anxiously round him, and stretching out his hands, called out with a voice of alarm—

"Trien! Trien! where are you?"

The maiden took his hand—

"Here I am, John. Compose yourself. You are trembling; what is the matter?"

"Oh! I dreamt that you had left me," replied the young man, sitting up. "Heavens! what a fearful dream! The cold sweat still breaks from me when I think of it."

"What could make you think such a thing as that?" observed the girl with a kind of good-humoured indignation. "Only, it is so much the better that you have dreamt it, John; it is a sure sign that I shall not leave you,—dreams always go by contraries."

"It is true, dearest," said the soldier, pressing her hands "God will reward you in heaven for all this."

Meanwhile, Trien had unbuckled the straps of the knapsack, and taken out a piece of bread and meat. She cut the bread into little bits, laid them on the thyme, and then covered them with meat; at the same time saying affectionately—

"How are you now, John? Are you rested? Has your sleep refreshed you?"

"I am no longer weary, Trien dear; but, I do not know how it is, that hateful dream makes me quite melancholy."

"Oh, that will soon go away, John; it comes from sleeping on the hard ground. Will you eat something?"

"Yes, Trien, I feel hungry."

The girl put the bits of bread and meat one after the other into his hand. While he silently took the proffered food, she remarked a peculiar expression of dejection and trouble on his face. Believing, however, that the uneasy sleep was the only cause of this apparent melancholy, she made no attempt to enliven his spirits, but so soon as she had given him the last bit of bread, she drew on his stockings and shoes, and prepared to resume their journey. The soldier picked up the knapsack, but the girl took it from him.

"No, no, Trien," he said, "let me carry it now, I entreat you: you weary yourself too much. It is not proper, besides, that a young girl should walk with a knapsack on her back; it must already look singular enough to see a peasant maid travelling with a blind soldier. What will people think of it?"

"Why should people's opinions trouble us, John? You, who can't see, suffer a hundred times more fatigue than I do, for you are always making false steps. Besides, you are far from being well and strong yet. The knapsack is nothing to me."

So saying, she took it again upon her back, and being now ready to set out, led the soldier into the middle of the road, putting a staff into his hand and fastening the other end on her shoulder, that the blind man might walk securely in her footsteps. When setting out, she said—

"Should I walk too quickly, dear John, you must tell me. And let us talk a little as we go; it will shorten the way."

As she received no answer, she turned round, but without stopping, and said to her companion—

"John, you should not hang your head in that way; it fatigues your chest."

The young man silently raised his head; but after a few steps, let it sink again. He was evidently lost in earnest thought: so Trien saw; but although anxiety was expressed in her features, she said in a clear cheerful tone as if she would rouse him out of his despondency—

"Oh, John, to-morrow evening we shall be home! That will be glorious! Your poor mother thinks that you are still pining away in the dark sick-room. How happy she will be and with what joy she will embrace you again! And Pawken, who shed so many tears when you went away to be a soldier, how he will leap and dance!—and my mother, and grandfather! I seem to see them all coming out with open arms to meet you. And the ox, poor beast! when it hears you, will be as happy as the rest; for I could see every day in his eyes that he had not forgotten you. And then grandfather will kill the fat buck, and we shall all feast and rejoice together like kings. Ah, I wish that I were sitting there now!"

While chatting away in this style, she often looked round at the blind man, who walked behind holding by the leading-stick, in order to see the effect of her words on his face. A faint smile was the only change she perceived on it; but this indication of pleasure, slight as it was, encouraged her, and though her companion had made no reply, she proceeded—

"And when we once find ourselves at home again, John, I will stay by you, and never leave you. I will buy songs, and learn them by heart, to sing them to you in the evening by the fireside; when I am working in the fields, you will always be beside me, and we shall talk together during our work; and what you can't see, I shall let you feel with your hands, and in that way you shall know just as well as I how the crops are getting on—you shall see them grow in your mind. I will take you to church, too; and on Sunday evenings drink a can of beer with you at the 'Crown,' that you may have a chat with your old friends. Everything will be just as if you were not blind. What do you say to all that? Is it not all very delightful to think of?"

A few tears fell from under the green shade which covered the soldier's eyes, and rolled like rain-drops upon the road. He replied in a melancholy tone—

"Trien dear, your voice is so sweet that it makes my heart tremble with a kind of sadness. When I listen to your beautiful talking, I feel as if my guardian angel were walking on before me: I see you standing in front of me; you have wings, and your body is as bright as the sun. I believe it is our dear heavenly Father who lets me see with my poor blind eyes how you are to be afterwards rewarded in heaven for your inconceivable goodness."

"Ah, John, you must not speak in that singular way," replied Trien; "I desire only one reward for my labour, and that is to see you less melancholy. You were much more cheerful yesterday."

The blind man drew back the stick, and taking the maiden's hand that he might walk beside her, said—

"Trien, yesterday I was merry, because I was thinking of my return home. But since this morning, and especially since I slept yonder, I perceive how matters really stand. Something disturbs my heart which I will not hide from you —God himself would punish me were I to repay your love with selfishness."

"Well, John, what has come into your head now   You make me so anxious that I can scarcely walk on. Tell me what grieves you so; it must just be some fancy or other."

"Let us talk quietly and calmly over the matter, Trien," replied the young man, with a choking voice. "You are strong, pretty, and good of heart, and can do every kind of work; and is it proper that you should let your young life be wasted and lost out of love and pity for an unfortunate blind man? And then, when our parents lie in the churchyard, you will be old, alone, and destitute, and all for my sake."

The maiden, moved by the sad tones of his voice, wept bitterly, though the young man did not perceive it.

"Trien, even on my deathbed shall I think of that blessed moment by the linden-tree, when we took farewell of one another. I understood what your darling blue eyes then said, and it has made me happy in my sufferings. Even when the doctor was burning my eyes with the caustic so that I screamed with agony, you stood before me with the same blush upon your brow, and I still felt your hand tremble in mine. Ah! if the all-merciful God had left me but one eye to work for our daily bread, I would have fallen on my knees before you, Trien, to entreat that we should be united for life; and I would have worked myself to death to reward you for your kindness in granting my entreaty. But now, that is all over."

"But, for God's sake, John," cried the girl, full of despair, "what are you talking of? Do you say all this to torture me? I do not understand you. What in the world then do you wish?"

"Sorrow—and death!" sighed the youth.

"Death!" cried Trien with vexation. "Do you think I will let you die? What do you mean? Speak more clearly. I can't bear these mysterious words. I will go no further.

Sit down here for a little, that these hateful thoughts may be driven out of your head."

She led the blind man to the roadside, and taking off the knapsack, sat down with him on the thin grass, and said—

"Now, then, John, let me hear what you have got to say; and speak right out what you mean."

"Ah, dear Trien, you know what I mean; you will cast away your youth for my sake. Can I then desire that you should waste your whole life out of compassion for me? The very thought tears my heart in pieces. If you wish me to have an easy mind and be cheerful, then promise that you will be henceforth nothing more to me than a sister; that you will go to merry-makings as formerly, and be friendly to other young men."

Trien interrupted him with sobs and tears—

"John, John! how is it possible that you can be so cruel? You cut my heart in two like a butcher. All the reward for my kindness is, 'Go, seek other young men.' How have I deserved that, or what have I done wrong?"

John sought for the maiden's hand, and when he had grasped it, said with a melancholy voice—

"Ah, Trien, you *will* not understand me. Had I still six eyes I would let them all be burnt out just that I might love you, if I could do so without bringing you sorrow. And yet blindness is a calamity the bitterness of which no one can conceive so long as he has the light. But God would assuredly punish me were I to use your life for my own advantage."

"And were I to follow your hateful advice, I suppose you would forget me too?"

"Forget!" replied the blind man. "It is always night around me. My whole life long I must think and dream. On whom and on what? Only on your goodness, and on what your eyes said when we parted yonder."

"And even if you gained your wish, you would still continue to love Trien, then, would you?"

"Always, always—till death!"

The maiden wiped the tears from her eyes. A totally different expression now took possession of her features, and with joyful pride and a cheerful heart, she rejoined—

"And *I* in the meantime should forsake you? Go to merry-makings with other young men, while you sat all week long in your house, at the corner of the hearth, forsaken and alone, mourning and thinking of me? John, how could you even imagine such a thing? Were it not *you*, I should certainly be very angry. Do you think, then, that I have no heart, and would let you pine and waste away alone with nobody to care for you? No, no; you loved me dearly when you still had your two fine black eyes; and I will still love you when you have lost them, poor fellow! Speak to me no more of other young men—it vexes me; for it sounds as if you cared no more about me; and the very thought of that makes the tears roll over my cheeks."

John pressed the maiden's hand with mute and wondering gratitude; and, after a pause, said with a sigh—

"Trien, you are an angel upon earth. I feel that you alone can make me forget what God has taken from me; but it cannot, cannot be."

"Yes," she replied; "I understand you now: you would say that I should enter the order of St. Anna, and be an old maid for life. It shall not be so. I mean to make a happy marriage, and that before the winter corn is sown, I tell you."

"Marry!" murmured the soldier, secretly disquieted; "oh, Trien, now is my heart at rest. God grant that your husband love you as you deserve. You will be married, then? With whom? Is it a friend in our village?"

"John, have you lost your senses?" cried the girl, with

such emphasis that it re-echoed in the fir-wood behind. "I say that I shall marry, and you ask whom. Why, *you!*"

"Heavens! Me!—a poor blind man!"

"Yes, you; him who would give six eyes to dare to love *me*."

"Oh, thanks, thanks, Trien, for your inexpressible goodness. May God bless you for a love so great; but"—

Trien laid her hand on his mouth and arrested the *but*, saying at the same time—

"Silence; you spoke so earnestly just then, that my heart leapt in my breast when I heard you. Say no more; let me speak now. If Trien had become blind through some misfortune, would you have driven the poor forlorn sheep from you? And if she still continued to love you in her affliction, would you have given her a deathblow by looking after other girls? Answer me."

"I may not answer."

"You must, John; and answer directly, too."

"Ah, well, Trien, I would have done as you do now: but it cannot be, dearest: what would people say of *me?*"

"It *shall* be," said the maiden with decision. "Promise it here, on my right hand, that God may see it, and that it may be ratified in heaven, till the priest shall unite us in the church."

When the soldier heard this, he covered his face with both hands, and let his head sink slowly on the maiden's breast, overpowered and speechless with emotion.

"People!" exclaimed Trien with animation. "He who does rightly need not be ashamed of himself before any man. And when I go to church with you, and take your hand before the altar, then shall I hold my head proudly, and think that God alone knows what is good and what is bad. And when I have once done it, I shall soon show what one can accomplish where there is a stout heart and strong arms. You shall want for nothing, John dear; Trien will take care of that; and she will remain with you, and comfort and cheer you till death separates us. And so shall we live with our mothers and grandfather and Pawken in peace and happiness as we used to do. Is it not delightful to think of all this?"

With tears in his eyes, the blind soldier kissed her hands. He still murmured a few words of unwillingness to accept her affectionate sacrifice; but she spoke in an imperative tone—

"John, we cannot sit here any longer; we must go. It will be dark before we reach the farm-house where I slept four days ago. Rise and push on a little further with a cheerful heart. No more of this; what is said is said. Let us talk now of other things."

She took the knapsack on her back, gave John the end of the staff as before, and both trudged on over the heath in silence, but with joyful hearts.

CHAPTER VI.

On the following morning by daybreak, Trien was again on her way, with the knapsack on her back and the blind soldier behind her.

The grass by the road-side, and the herbs on the heath, glistened in the early rays of the sun as if they had been strewed with diamonds; while the tops of the firs, moistened with dew, seemed all arrayed in silver. The eastern heavens were lighted up with a golden and purple glow; and away towards the distant copse, the night-vapours rose and floated between earth and sky. The birds were awake, and filled the air with their songs; the bees hummed busily round the wild thyme, while beetles and butterflies flew cheerfully about. All nature smiled at the dawn of beautiful day; everything proclaimed the advent of light.

The good maiden, too, found herself in a pleasing though unconscious harmony with nature. From time to time she sang in lively tones snatches from various ballads, to give utterance to the joy which she felt; while the soldier walked on silently, but with a pleased expression which showed a heart at rest.

" How comes it, Trien dear," he said, after some time, " that you are so happy? It must be owing to the beautiful weather surely. I cannot see it, but I hear the merry song of the birds welcoming the day, and the joyful hum of the bees at my feet."

"No, John, that is not the reason," she replied; "come closer and I shall tell you what it is—something which will make you wonder. It is only a dream, to be sure, and I had almost forgotten it; but this fine fresh air has revived me, and it has all come to mind again. It is a pleasant thing to dream, is it not, John?"

"Sometimes."

"Yes; I mean when the dreams are beautiful. I do not know when I have been so happy as last night when asleep, and I would not give my dream for twenty crown-pieces, and that is a tremendous lot of money. It is vexing, John, that dreams are not true."

"What dream have you had, then, Trien, that was so very beautiful?"

"You, too, are concerned in it, John; *that* you may well suppose. Ah, it was so delightful! only listen: The farmer's wife—may God reward her for it, good woman!—had shown me into a little bedroom for the night. When I found myself alone, I knelt and prayed before the image of the Virgin which stood on the little house-altar. I do not know how long I knelt, but when I rose my head whirled round, and I almost lost the power of knowing where I was or what I was—so at least it seemed to me. The moon had in the meantime risen, and shone so brightly through the little window, that my room seemed all glorified with such a flood of light, that I could scarcely recognise it to be the same place. I laid my brow upon the window-pane to cool my head, and then threw myself half-dressed on the bed, that I might be ready early on the following morning. But still I could not sleep, for the moon seemed always right before my eyes; and I tormented myself to find out the man with the bundle of sticks in it.

Whether I fell asleep at last is more than I can tell; but it must have been so, for only hear what happened to me next. All of a sudden, the moon changed into a mouth and blue eyes of wonderful beauty; then a ruddy hue like that of a ripe apple came over it, and it looked at me with so friendly a smile, that I was quite enchanted. I have never in my life seen a woman so beautiful, and so like an angel in heaven; for if there were such a one on earth, everybody would certainly kneel down and worship her. I am quite sure of that; but listen to what followed. Gradually there grew out of the moon arms and legs, and a long robe adorned with great golden blossoms; and on its head there appeared a silver crown of seven bright stars. And now it was no longer the moon, but a woman who bore in her arms a little child more beautiful than the little cherubs in heaven. And, oh, John! it was our dear Lady out of the little room at home, who had become alive, and had our blessed Lord in her arms; and He smiled and beckoned to me. But there is more and better yet. How she came there I do not know, but I saw her next sitting on a chair outside the window, and *you* too saw her with your blind eyes; for we fell down together on our knees, and stretched out our arms from behind the window, as if calling upon the Holy Mother to come to us. Then she came gently, gently down, always nearer and nearer, and right through the window into the room. She said something to her child, Jesus, and the child touched your eyes with his finger, and you, John, exclaimed, quite mad with joy, 'I see! I see!' I, poor thing, was so overpowered by it all, that I sprang up in my sleep and fell out of bed; and oh, John, it was not true. I had only dreamt; for the moon, with the man in it, still shone in the sky, and the image of the Virgin still stood calmly on the little altar in the corner of the room. Is not that a charming dream?'

She was silent, and waited for a reply. After a short pause, the young man said—

"Trien, how beautifully you can tell a story. My heart beat with pleasure while you were speaking; I seemed to see it all happen. And when you said that our Lord touched my eyes, I felt something which I cannot describe; and I saw our dear Lady so clearly and distinctly, that I could draw on the sand the golden flowers which sparkled on her robe."

"What kind of flowers did you see, John?"

"Large roses."

"And so did I; that is strange."

"And lilies, like those which stood in the brewer's garden last year."

"I saw roses and lilies too. But how is that possible? It quite puzzles me."

"Ah, dearest," sighed John; "do not deceive yourself with a false hope. 'Dreams are bubbles,' says the proverb; it is only a little comfort which God has sent to cheer us on our way."

"Never mind," said Trien joyfully; "since last night, I seem to love the Virgin-Mother more than ever; and when we are at home, I shall go to the sexton's daughter, Marion, and beg some silver paper, in order to make just such a silver crown with seven stars, as I saw last night, to put on the image under the linden-tree; and if we are ever able to do it, we shall dress it in a robe adorned with golden flowers besides. Let us now make speed, before the sun rises higher; and take hold of the stick, John, for the footpath is growing narrow and rugged. I think we must have wandered out of our way when I was telling my dream."

"Trien dear, take great care to keep the right way, for my knees begin to grow weary already. I don't think I shall be able to manage ten hours to-day."

"Do not vex yourself, John," she replied, walking more slowly; "on a flat heath like this one can't go far wrong; and I see yonder in the distance, the two towers, Moll and Baelen, as we were told this morning."

"How far distant are they?"

"An hour and a half yet. Can you manage so far this morning?"

"Yes, if we take a rest now and then by the way."

"You must tell when you are tired. We shall not speak, for it will make you feel sooner fatigued."

———

The sun meanwhile had risen high, and began to pour its burning light over the heath like a stream of fire. The air was so sultry, that it was with difficulty our travellers could breathe, and the perspiration poured from their faces. Exhausted though he was, the soldier would not allow himself to complain of fatigue, but continued to walk bravely on behind his guide. He had broken the long silence only once, with the observation that his eyes pained him excessively, as if the burning rays had increased the inflammation.

After she had kept steadily on for an hour or more, Trien suddenly stood still. Surprised at the unexpected pause, he said—

"Trion, what is the matter? Why do you stop all at once in that way?"

"Well, John," she replied in a grieved tone, "here is a pretty business. Heaven knows how far we have wandered from the right road, and now there stands right before us, and running quite across the whole heath, a broad stream, and not a bridge of any kind to be seen."

"That is very vexing," sighed John; "for I am already quite worn out. Is the water deep, Trien?"

"Oh, no; it is a broad shallow stream; I can see the

bottom quite well, and it would not take me above the knees to wade across it."

"Let us venture it, Trien; and then we shall be saved going round."

"But it is impossible, John; for the banks are so high that you could go neither up nor down. But come, come, let us make a virtue of necessity."

She led her blind companion to the edge of the brook, and, first throwing the knapsack across, stepped down into the water; the young man heard her, and asked what she was going to do.

"Throw your arms round my neck, and take fast hold," she replied; and drawing the soldier towards her, she compelled him, spite of his objections, to obey her kindly order; then carrying the heavy burden through the water to the opposite side, she said—

"John, there stands a willow-bush on the bank, take hold of it and help yourself up, and I shall assist you."

He did as she told him, and gained the firm ground without any difficulty. Trien immediately joined him, shaking the water out of her clothes as she approached.

"Ah, Trien!" said the blind man, "you are goodness and love itself. How it grieves me to think that I can never reward you for so much pity and kindness."

"Now, John," she interrupted, "is it worth while to waste a word on such a trifle as my carrying you through the water? That is nothing; the sun will dry my clothes in a very short time. Try to go a little further at a slow pace, for in half an hour we shall reach the first tower, and that is Moll, as we were told. There we shall rest ourselves a little."

"Is the water of this brook pure?" he asked.

"As clear as crystal," she answered; "are you thirsty? Wait a moment—I can't get more than one wetting—and I shall get you a hearty draught of it."

While speaking, she had untied the camp-kettle from the knapsack, but the soldier said—

"No, Trien, I do not wish water to drink. My eyes pain me excessively; and I think if you were to give me water on a napkin to wash them with, it would refresh them a little."

She stepped down into the brook, and having filled the little vessel with the purest water, went up to the blind man, and, drawing a white linen cloth from her bosom, said to him—

"Sit down, and let me wash your eyes; for you could not do it yourself without wetting your clothes."

The soldier sat down on the grass with his back towards the sun, while Trien took the shade from his head and bathed his closed eyes with the wet cloth. And when he told her that this washing revived and refreshed him very much, she kept laving his face and brow copiously, till he held her hand and told her to stop. As she stepped a little aside to pick up the shade, the blind man suddenly sprang on his feet, with a singular cry, and stood trembling and stretching out his hands towards his companion, while unintelligible sounds escaped from his lips—

"Heavens, John! what is the matter with you?" cried Trien, running to him with alarm.

With an air of perplexity and confusion, he pushed her gently back, saying—

"Trien, Trien, go back again to the same spot, I beseech you!"

Astonished at the tone of his voice and the incomprehensible joy depicted in his countenance, the girl did what he desired, and placed herself some steps from him. He opened his dead eyes, and, with outstretched arms, exclaimed—

"Trien, Trien! I saw you! My left eye is not quite gone."

As if struck by lightning, the poor girl trembled all over, and with tottering steps approached the soldier—

"No, no, John, it cannot be! Do not kill me with joy. This bright sunlight must have deceived you, poor fellow!"

"I saw you," exclaimed the soldier almost mad with joy, "like a black mass. You passed before my eyes like a shadow. My left eye is not quite gone, I tell you. Oh, Trien dear, it is your dream of last night."

Trien uttered a cry as piercing as if it had escaped from some one in agony, and falling on her knees, with trembling and uplifted hands she offered up to God a calm and silent but deep and earnest thanksgiving. The soldier saw her in indistinct and shadowy outline, and knelt likewise beside the praying girl. She was so lost, however, in devout adoration, that she did not perceive him, and knelt for a long time absorbed and motionless. At last, calmed by her devotion, she turned her head and saw her friend also on his knees.

"John, John! did you see what I did?" she exclaimed.

"I saw it!—I saw it!"

"Oh, our dear Lady!" sighed Trien, while a torrent of tears now first burst from her eyes. "This is thy doing, holy Mother of God. I will never forget it; but every year make a pilgrimage barefoot to worship thee at Scherpenheuvel."

After this earnest declaration, strength seemed all at once to leave her; she threw her arm round the soldier's neck, and, leaning her head on his breast, wept in silence. The young man's emotion was equally great; words failed him to express the mingled feelings which overflowed his heart. A whole future of gratitude, of love and joy, had opened itself to his view, and uplifted his soul with the enchanting prospect of a useful and happy life. At last, Trien raised her head, and, every now and then uttering expressions of joy, she bound the shade over the soldier's eyes; and taking the knapsack on her back, and the young man by the hand, both set out again with light steps to finish their day's journey.

"Oh, John dear," said Trien, "I don't know how it is, but I could dance and leap with joy; *now*, I could walk twenty hours longer without feeling tired."

"It is the same with me," replied the soldier; "I feel as if I could fly. Oh, dearest Trien, if my left eye were to grow quite well again, what happiness! what joy! My heart feels oppressed when I think of it."

"Grow quite well! to be sure it will. Our dear Lady will take care of that. Do you not see that it is the hand of God? My dream last night."

"Trieny dear, Trieny dear," he cried, while he tremblingly pressed her hand; "ah, if it were to turn out so, how beautiful should our life on earth then be! We should then marry, as you have so kindly promised, and I should work like a slave—but oh, with what life and happiness!—while you, my dearest wife, should have nothing to do but take care of yourself and"—

"Not so, John," she interrupted, smiling; "do you imagine I could live in idleness? I would show you other things, I can tell you."

"It is all the same," he said; "you should do only what you chose to do, and nothing more. And our parents, Trien, how happy should we make their last days by our care and love! I would tear down the partition between the two huts and make one house of them, that all might live together. It would be quite a heaven of love and joy."

"Oh, how beautiful!" sighed Trien with emotion; "the partition must be taken down at once; and then grandfather, and our mothers, and Pawken, and you and I, and our cow too, shall be always together. What a life! Oh, what a life!"

Trien clapped her hands with joy, like a child.

"And then," continued John, "we farm too little land just now to give us enough to do, and enable us to make progress. I shall drive a trade with fir-cones, besides, and gradually add wood and bundles of twigs. Then we must look a little to the future ; if "—

He said no more, for the maiden had covered her face with her hands, and he heard her sobbing.

"Why do my words trouble you so ?" he asked.

"For Heaven's sake, speak no more of all these beautiful things. I feel as if my heart would break with joy at the thought of it all. John, I am so happy, that I shall go out of my senses if you go on talking about the paradise that awaits us on earth."

"And I too, Trien. But I cannot be silent for all that; my heart overflows. Let me go on, and do you speak also; and so we shall be at Moll without knowing it, so light and easy will the way appear; and there we are to rest, you know."

The soldier began anew to unfold his fine plans, and enchanted the maiden with his pictures of a blessed future in which both lived their whole life through by anticipation, and enjoyed pleasures in prospect.

At last, they reached their resting-place. Trien gave John the knapsack, and both entered the village hand in hand.

CHAPTER VII.

LATE in the afternoon, Trien, accompanied by her friend, might be seen wandering over the heath on the farther side of Casterlee, where they had crossed the Nethe. Both were silent and much depressed, but neither had courage to disclose to the other what each feared; on the contrary, the few words which they exchanged were attempts to appear as cheerful as possible. Notwithstanding this, however, they felt that they had been cherishing a delusion, and their hearts were filled with sorrow. Since they had resumed their journey, Trien had already washed the soldier's eyes five or six times; she did not pass a brook, indeed, without trying whether it possessed the wonder-working power of the stream on the heath. Alas! her loving solicitude became for herself and for the unhappy John a source of disappointment and despair.

Whether it was that the soldier had deceived himself when he imagined that he saw Trien, or that the cold water and the rubbing had increased the inflammation, he saw no longer, however much he strained his eyes to discern the outline of his companion's form. He could not even bear the light, and closed his eyes with intense pain whenever Trien took the shade from his head. Accordingly, the terrible conviction took possession of both their minds, that they had been the victims of a vain delusion, and that the blindness was total and incurable. A last ray of hope, to be sure, in

the form of a happy uncertainty, still lived in the bottom of
their hearts; but it was able to light up their quiet despair
with only a passing gleam, which by contrast with the sad
reality served only to make their sorrow greater.

They were sad and spiritless also on another account.
Since the morning they had walked for eight hours, and were
excessively fatigued; the soldier, indeed, felt quite exhausted
and powerless, and often stumbled as he crept along. Unconsciously and heedlessly he tottered on behind Trien, still
holding the stick, with his body bent forward and his limbs
relaxed and lifeless. His feet were blistered, and had he not almost lost consciousness he would have felt warm drops of blood
oozing out of his right heel into his shoe. Trien was no less
weary; but she pushed steadily on notwithstanding, without
saying anything—even without looking back at her companion. The poor girl was too dejected to speak. Her heart
was now bereft of consolation; her hopes had vanished, her
glimpse of happiness faded away. An inexpressible joy had
almost deprived her of her senses as she built up for herself
and family such a glorious future, and now when undeceived
her grief was all the deeper; and courageous as she was, she
felt quite overpowered, and bent like a slave under the yoke
of an intense depression. What could she say to her friend
to raise him out of his despair? Should she speak of his eyes
and of hope, and belie her own feelings? She could not do
so; it would have fallen on her own heart as well as his like
bitter mockery. She therefore walked on silently and heavily,
sunk in melancholy thoughts, and scarcely conscious of her
own condition.

When they had walked fully half an hour in this way, the
soldier suddenly stopped, and breathing with difficulty, said—

"Stop, Trien! I am able for no more."

"I am quite worn out too," replied the girl without looking

round; "we shall rest a little, and then sleep to-night in the village yonder."

"O stop, then!" said the blind man imploringly.

"We are quite near a country-house; only twenty steps farther, John, and we come to a beautiful beech-grove, and there we can sit in the shade."

"For Heaven's sake go quickly, Trien!"

Taking him by the hand she led him to the grove, and seated him with his back towards it. The young man fell like lead upon the grass, and sat with his head drooping on his breast.

Behind the spot where the soldier and his companion were seated, and in the centre of the beech-grove, there was an arbour. In it a man sat reading. He must have been very old, for deep wrinkles furrowed his countenance, and the scanty hairs which like a crown adorned his head were as white as snow. A frock-coat buttoned to the throat and an honorary badge on his breast gave him the appearance of a retired officer.

When he heard the noise which the two travellers made behind him, he turned, and saw through the foliage of the arbour a soldier and a peasant girl with a knapsack on her back. The sight of this surprised him at first; but he thought that it must be a sister who was conducting her brother home, and was carrying his burden out of affection. He wondered, nevertheless, at this simple token of love, and smiled with friendly sympathy as he looked at them while resting on the bank.

Trien, meanwhile, had sat down beside the blind man, and said to him—"John, you are so quiet and melancholy! What is the matter with you? You are weary—is that the reason? Your fatigue will soon pass away, and you will feel quite fresh again."

As she received no answer, she continued in an encouraging tone—

"Keep up your spirits, John, and think that we shall be home to-morrow. It has taken twenty hours to come from Venloo hither: three hours more, and we are in our own village. If we rise early to-morrow, we can get over it all just like a pleasure-walk. We have still great cause to be contented, for it is really a great piece of good fortune that I was permitted to bring you home from among the soldiers. And as to the rest, I shall take care that you do not have much to vex you in the course of your life, John dear.—Why do you not speak?"

The young man made an effort to draw breath, and then said with a sigh—

"My heart beats, and my eyes burn like fire; let me rest, Trien."

Some minutes passed in unbroken silence: gradually Trien began to think that it was grief more than fatigue which so oppressed her companion. So, with a noble effort, she repressed her own sorrow in order to pour consolation into the blind man's heart, and said cheerfully—

"But John, you are still certain that you saw me? That makes me believe that there must still be life in your left eye, although you are quite blind again in the meantime; that must just be caused by the heat, which has inflamed your eyes more than usual. Only have patience till we are at home; we shall then sell some new grain, and fetch the doctor from Wyneghem. There is no fear of his being able to cure you, for he has worked many wonders, even on men who for several days were thought to be dead. Only think, John, to-morrow we shall see your mother, and grandfather, and Pawken, and then I shall lead you round all your friends to see how they are. Then, when you have rested well, your eyes will not pain you any longer, and there is no doubt but you will see a little again. And then we shall pray together under the linden-tree, in order to thank our dear Lady for her compassion; for you may be quite sure, John, that she has heard me, and will——What is that? I see blood on your stockings! And you have said nothing about it, poor fellow!"

She hastily drew off his shoe and stocking, and wiped away the blood with her white neckerchief. She was then just about to tell him that the bruise was not serious; but scarcely had she raised her eyes to his face, when she trembled like an aspen leaf, saying at the same time in an anxious tone—

"John dear, what is the matter with you? You are so pale."

The young man sighed almost inaudibly—

"I cannot tell; my heart is breaking. I feel as if I were dying."

He trembled violently, his head sank powerless on his shoulder, and his arms fell lifeless by his side.

Trien screamed with anxiety and alarm, while she laid her hands on his pallid cheeks, and endeavoured to raise him up, calling out in despair—

"John! John! Poor, poor fellow! he is dead! Water! water! Help! help!"

With these words she sprang up, looked wildly round her, and ran from one side to another to see if she could find water. She then suddenly perceived an open gate, which was the entrance to a gentleman's house; and uttering a cry of joy, she ran towards it at full speed to beg assistance. As she approached the house by the winding path of the flower-garden, she saw two men come out of it and approach her. The one was an old gentleman with snow-white hair, and a countenance commanding respect; the other, though likewise advanced in years, seemed still to retain the strength of youth.

A broad scar, like a sabre-cut, ran down the face of the latter from the brow over the mouth and chin, giving a severe character to his features. He carried a jug, two bottles, and some linen. He must have been the old gentleman's servant, for he followed him at a little distance without speaking.

"Oh, sir," said Trien in a tone of despair, "give me some water or vinegar! yonder, behind the grove, lies a poor blind lad in a faint. For God's sake, sir, have pity! do a good work and go with me! Oh, if you would be so good!"

The old man smiled compassionately, and taking the maiden's hand, replied calmly—

"Be calm, my child; it is nothing. We are on the way to cure him. You need not be anxious, it is nothing but an ordinary faint. Your companion has exerted himself too much. Come along, and dry your tears."

Trien scarcely understood what he said; it seemed to her so wonderful that help should be at hand, when no one had told at the gentleman's house what had occurred, that in her simplicity she thought that she again discovered the kind interposition of the Virgin Mother. With mingled joy and surprise she gazed at the old man's friendly and consolatory face, which smiled on her protectingly.

"You are a brave girl, my daughter, to show such affection for a poor soldier," he said, as he walked hastily on. "From what place have you come with him? From Venloo?"

"Yes, from Venloo, sir; it is very far from this."

"And have you carried that knapsack on your back all the way?"

"Ah, sir," she sighed, quietly weeping, "the poor fellow is blind and cannot walk easily, not being able to see the road. We were in haste, and I am strong and healthy—— O God! see, there he lies, as pale as death!"

A fresh torrent of tears burst from her eyes, and folding her hands as if in prayer, she exclaimed in an anxious and beseeching tone—"He will not die yet, sir?"

With a smile the old man shook his head, and approached the lad. The servant set the bottles on the ground, and without waiting for an order, raised the soldier's head with one hand while he untied his neckcloth with the other and put aside the clothes which covered his breast. Meanwhile, the old gentleman bathed the sick man's face and hands. Trien knelt beside them, and beheld with tears the care and kindness with which the two strangers treated her unhappy friend.

She soon perceived that these men were accustomed to tend the sick, and had no doubt that the old gentleman was a physician. This thought consoled her, and raised her spirits. A mingled feeling of gratitude and anxious anticipation found expression on her countenance in a peculiar smile which glimmered through her tears. Her surprise increased when she heard the following words:—

"Major," said the attendant, "this is just as it was at Sabijana de Alba in Spain. It makes me quite melancholy to think of it."

"Our poor friend Captain Steens, you mean?" replied the gentleman with a sigh. "The faint is deep! Give me the bottle."

"Yes, I seem to see it still: the Captain lay just so, at the foot of a citron-tree; but he left his body at Vittoria, poor fellow! *That* was a slashing, and stabbing, and shooting, and mangling! Many a one we picked up, and many a wound we dressed that day. I was all blood from top to toe, and you too, Major."

"The heart begins to beat again: he will come to himself immediately," said the physician.

The attendant raised the young man's eyelids with his finger, and said—

"He is blind—the soldier's old disease; we know the pestilence well. But look at the left eye, Major, it seems to me not quite gone."

A cry of joy burst from the maiden's heart. She had watched for the return of life to her friend's pale face, and had perceived with beating heart a gentle colour suffusing itself over his cheeks. Now he moved. The moment he came to himself, the blind man touched the clothes of the two strangers who had been assisting him, and said anxiously—

"Where am I? what has happened to me?" And stretching his hand farther round him, exclaimed in a tone of alarm —"Trien! Trien! where are you?"

The girl seized his hands, and said exultingly—

"Oh, John, thank God that you are here! It is a great good fortune; good men are beside you. They say, too, that your left eye is not quite dead."

"Whoever you are, may our Lord God bless you for your goodness!" said the lad.

"Comrade," interrupted the attendant, "we shall try whether we can stand now. Only have courage, and you will manage it easily."

He seized the soldier under the left arm, while the old gentleman supported him on the other side, and thus they raised the blind man to his feet. Under the belief that the attention of the two strangers would end here, Trien smiled sweetly, and said, with a bright and cheerful look—

"Gentlemen, I am a poor peasant girl, and our John, too, is not rich; but be assured we shall our whole life long think of you in our prayers, and bless you for your kindness. Give yourselves no more trouble, pray; let him sit on the grass to rest himself, and I shall wrap cloths round his wounded feet.

We must then go to the village, where we shall spend the night. May God send you health and happiness on earth and afterwards eternal bliss in heaven!"

"No, no, not so," replied the old man; "follow me. You are stout-hearted both of you, but I do not wish you to fatigue yourselves on your journey home. The young soldier shall not go farther till he has regained his strength. We shall see whether I can do anything to reward your noble self-sacrifice, my child."

"We have still some bottles of old Spanish wine left," added the attendant, "which might restore a dead man to life and health. That is all the medicine he needs. Only wait a little, my daughter; in an hour you will scarcely know him again."

"Ah, sirs," stammered the girl, "do as your Christian hearts tell you. I can scarcely speak, I feel your kindness so deeply. A thousand, thousand thanks, good, dear men!"

Supported on both sides, by master and servant, John tottered on with slow steps. When they came into the garden, Trien went by the servant's side, and whispered—

"Tell me, friend, is your master a doctor?"

"Doctor!" replied the servant; "he was *Chirurgien Major* under Napoleon. We have cut off more legs and arms than could lie here on this path, and that is not few."

"Can he cure diseased eyes also, friend?"

"Yes, yes; and a great deal better, I can tell you, than the surgeons of the present day. There are very few, alas! now alive of the brave comrades of the Peninsula, else many would be going about who had to thank him for their eyesight."

"Ah, good man! you must beg him, very humbly, to look at our John's eyes; perhaps he may cure them! God knows."

"Keep your mind at ease, my daughter; he will do that

with pleasure. He loves soldiers. John will not go from this very soon."

"And if you can do anything in the matter, or put in a good word, I shall be very thankful to you."

"You need not ask me to do that; I shall not fail to do so. 'Where a soldier, there a comrade,' says the proverb. Do you see, he is somewhat better already; I am giving him scarcely any support."

They stepped over the threshold, and entered a beautifully furnished room. The old gentleman led the blind youth to a broad arm-chair, and made him sit down with his back to the light. He then gave a key to the servant, which he received with manifest pleasure, and quickly left the room, returning almost immediately with a bottle and some glasses. As he passed, he whispered in the maiden's ear—

"It is the wine which would raise the dead. You shall see the miracle immediately."

Trien did not rightly catch what he said, and with intense curiosity she looked at the old gentleman, who was now putting a glass of a clear red liquid to the young man's lips.

"Drink this—and take a hearty draught," he said; "it will refresh you."

"Heavens! what is that?" cried the blind man with astonishment, some moments after he had taken the drink; "how it warms me within! Thanks, thanks. I am hungry now."

"Gently, comrade; not so fast," said the old man; "we shall now dress your feet, and then examine your eyes. Come, daughter—I had almost forgotten you, my dear child—sit down on this chair, and, Charles, give the girl a glass of wine."

While the servant was engaged with Trien, and was praising to her the wonder-working qualities of the Spanish wine, the old man had bound up the youth's feet. He now washed his eyes with a liquid, and anointed them with a white salve. When he had done this, he went to the window and let the curtains down, to soften the light; and then approaching the soldier again, he said—

"Friend, open your eyes, and try whether you can distinguish anything."

John opened his eyes, and remained for a time silent; although the old gentleman asked him frequently whether he perceived anything. He seemed to be seeking an object with his dead eyes.

Suddenly he uttered a loud cry, and, rising from his chair, went with outstretched arms towards Trien, who had sprung from her seat, and, trembling with feverish hope, watched him as he approached. She would have rushed into his arms, but the servant held her back.

The blind man advanced, and held out his hand to her with an uncertain motion, saying at the same time, with a low and trembling voice—

"Trien, Trien, I am not blind! It is true this time; I shall once more see mother, grandfather, and Pawken. Yes, I see that you have your red neckerchief on."

The maiden embraced him, uttering unintelligible words, which sounded more like lamentations than expressions of joy. The old gentleman, however, took the young man from her, and made her sit down again calmly on the chair. He then immediately tied the shade before the soldier's eyes, saying—

"You said that you saw that your friend had a red neckerchief on. It seems to me impossible that you could distinguish the colour; you are surely deceiving yourself."

"I see nothing but a gray shadow," replied the soldier; "but when growing blind, I observed that red seemed much blacker in the dark than other colours; and in this way I know that her neckerchief is red."

"So I thought," the old gentleman remarked. "We shall now go prudently and carefully to work. Charles, take our comrade into the kitchen, and let him have a little bread and meat—half rations only, no more at present—then lead him into the back room, that he may go to bed and rest. Tell the maid-servant to bring some food for the girl at the same time."

So soon as the servant had left the room with the soldier, Trien fell at the old man's feet with loud sobs, and embraced his knees speechlessly, moistening them with her tears. He endeavoured to raise her up, but she resisted him, and, turning her bright blue eyes upon his face, she exclaimed—

"Oh, sir, sir, God will reward you for having shown such kindness to poor peasant people. I cannot say all I feel; but I would willingly die ten years before my time, if it would procure for you a longer life. And because you mean to cure our John's eyes, angel of God that you are! we shall pray every day for you, and make a pilgrimage besides, dear sir!"

The old gentleman raised the girl from the ground, and addressing to her kind and comforting words, he led her to the table, where the maid-servant had already placed a refreshment.

Either from over-fatigue or emotion, Trien could eat very little; she paused in a few moments, and then gazed at her benefactor with an earnest, calm, and grateful look. He was seated near her, and was trying to induce her to eat; but when he perceived that she would take no more, he took her hand and said—

"Now, tell me from what place you come, and how it happens that you are travelling alone with a blind soldier, and whether you have parents, and where they dwell?"

With a natural and simple eloquence, the young girl began to tell him about the mud-huts, the lot-drawing, the old mother, the grandfather, Pawken, and the separation. When she came to tell him, however, all that she had suffered in her efforts to find her blind friend in Venloo; how she had nearly fainted for joy when the officer gave her permission to take the unhappy man home with her; how she dreamt of our dear Lady, in the little room of the farm-house, and all that they had said to one another by the way; then the old man was overpowered by deep emotion, and now and then wiped a tear of sympathy from his eye. The sweet tones of the maiden's voice had an irresistible effect upon him, and he wondered at her rare self-sacrifice and love. She concealed nothing from him, but told him, honestly and openly, all her plans—her marriage with the blind man, and all which she had promised to him and expected to be able to fulfil, with a view to sweeten his bitter lot; she even told him what John had promised to do for her, if through God's goodness he regained his sight.

The affecting tale had lasted for a considerable time, and the old man had listened attentively without interrupting her. When the girl had concluded, with an expression of deep gratitude to him, and seemed waiting for some remark, he said nothing for some time, but sat with downcast eyes, sunk in deep reflection. In a few minutes he raised his head—

"You have done rightly, my daughter," he said. "You are a virtuous, noble-minded girl! So, your dream of future life was, that by working day and night you would get on happily together. Your ambition was to mitigate the misery of blindness to your friend—his to reward you for your great love; and the desire of both of you to make the last days of your aged parents peaceful and happy? It is well; God has heard your prayers. He it is who has led you hither, and has commissioned me to do a good work. I will devote all my experience to the cure of your friend's left eye, and I have good grounds to believe that I shall be successful. As to other things, keep your mind at ease. Your noble dream shall be realized. To-night you sleep here. To-morrow we shall see what is to be done. Meanwhile you may take repose, or walk in the garden, and if you wish anything, you have only to ask it from the maid-servant, or my attendant; they are good people who will be eager to serve you. I shall now leave you till the evening."

Trien gazed after the old man as he left the room, unable to utter a word in reply. After a time, she went out, and wandered about the garden with a cheerful mind, thinking on the occurrences of the day, and on what the old gentleman had said to her.

———

Next forenoon a carriage left the garden-gate of the country house. On the foremost seat sat the servant with the great scar on his face, whistling a merry air, and cracking a large whip. On the back-seat sat the young man, with the green shade over his eyes, and beside him, the now light-hearted Trien. She quietly pressed his hand, and whispered in his ear—

"Oh, John, we are happy—very happy, are we not? My beautiful dream is now come true. Oh, how joyful will your mother be now! And you, too, will soon be quite well again, for the old gentleman has assured us of it. How will they all wonder too, when they see us drive up in a beautiful carriage, like barons!"

"We shall go by Gierle and Wechel-ter-Zande," said the servant, "and so to Zoersel. Then *you* must show me the way; and now off we go."

He gave the horse the rein, calling out—

"Hopla, Marengo, forward! march!"

The dust of the highway rose like a cloud, and the carriage soon disappeared among the houses of the village.

CHAPTER VIII.

One day as I was wandering in perfect solitude over the heath, with my soul open to the poetic impresses of nature, a storm arose in the west.

It is a wonderful, a fearful thing, to find one's-self on a hot summer's day on an open plain, when lurid, lightning-laden vapours are slowly gathering into thunder-clouds in the limitless heaven. One would think that nature had been suddenly smitten with a mortal agony; the sun pales, and emits feeble rays; the air grows sultry; the birds fly home—and every animal skulks away with terror; the bees shoot like arrows through the air to reach their hives; every leaf is at rest, and the wind holds its breath for a time; the little herbs close their leaves and blossoms, and all Nature waits in still anticipation of some awful event. An indescribable feeling of mingled wonder, pain, and reverence, weighs upon the poet's heart; and, in the midst of the universal fear, his soul alone exults because it is given to him to behold this terrible wonder of nature in its full majesty.

But soon the clouds rush confusedly together; what has lain for hours calmly in the sky now gathers in wild career, and bursts into a storm. The hurricane rages and roars as if lashed into fury by the hand of the Almighty; it tears from the fir-woods a low howl of agony; whirls aloft clouds of sand and leaves, and breaks to pieces or uproots the solitary and unsheltered trees. Then comes the thunder and drowns every other sound with its mighty voice; through the spacious air the lightning shoots its flaming arrows; the heath seems to be on fire with the fiery serpents which are sweeping over its breast; torrents of water pour down upon the earth, and, in the intervals of the thunder's roar, the monotonous dull plash of the falling rain is heard.

On this day my soul was stirred to poetic contemplations; I had beheld with more than ordinary pleasure the grand spectacle of this fever of nature, till the frequent flashes of lightning reminded me that I must do what every living creature had already done—seek shelter, and hide my head in humility before the wonders of the Creator. Not far from the spot where I was, stood a farm-house, alone upon the heath, like an oasis in the desert surrounded by green fields and fresh woods.

Scarcely had the rain begun to pour down like another deluge, when I entered the door of the farm-house and asked permission to shelter myself under its roof. I found the inhabitants kneeling in prayer surrounded by the deepest silence. The farmer was the only one whom my entrance disturbed, and, as soon as he had pointed to a chair with a friendly smile, with bended head and folded hands he resumed his prayer. I know not how it was, but though the storm, as being a useful natural phenomenon, did not affect me with that mysterious terror which made these people tremble, it yet seemed to me so beautiful, so touching, and so heavenly—this calm family devotion, that an irresistible feeling constrained me to unite with these simple peasants in adoration of that God whose voice, high above us, resounded through the sky. I uncovered, and, with folded hands, I likewise knelt and prayed. It did my soul good to find once more this pure emotion of my childhood, as if the withering breath of the disenchanting world had never touched my heart.

After a time, the storm began to pass away. The inhabitants of the cottage, however, did not cease to pray, and thus left me time to look at them all attentively, as an observer of human nature, and above all an author, loves to do.

There was an aged grandfather who might have reached his ninetieth year or more, for his head and hands trembled continually as if he had an ague-fever. Beside him were two women, also advanced in years; further off, a powerful-looking man, who had lost his right eye, which rolled like a white ball under his black eyebrow, while the left sparkled with a genial kindliness and vivacity. By his side sat a young woman with a child on her lap, and at her feet a little boy and girl of seven or eight years; and at the extreme end of the table, a fine-looking young man, with blooming countenance and bright-blue eyes.

On a signal given by the one-eyed man, all rose. The grandfather went with tottering steps to the corner of the hearth and sat down, while the others directed their attention to me, requesting me to use their house as shelter while the storm lasted—for it still rained heavily. In a short time, I was on quite intimate terms with these good people, and chatted with them like a long-known friend. In the afternoon, I shared with them the nutritious rye-bread, and drank the coffee of welcome. And as I had nothing better to do at that time than to listen to the pleasant stories which the man with the one eye and his wife told me, I did not leave the farm-house till the following morning.

What I have related to you in this history, dear readers, I heard that night in that lonely farm-house, which formerly consisted of two mud-huts, but has now become a fine homestead, with four cows and two horses. John Braems and Trien, his noble-hearted wife, work for each other as they had vowed to do. And God has blessed their love; three children play around them, and lighten their daily toil with their affectionate caresses.

All are still alive; the grandfather, though with one foot in the grave, still smokes his little pipe by the fireside; both mothers are happy in the happiness of their children, and are still active in looking after the cattle and helping in the house-work. Pawken, a fine-looking youth, now takes care of the horses and plough, and works for his brother; but next Easter he is to marry the younger sister of the wooden shoemaker's Kate.

Every evening the whole family prays for the old doctor; for it was he who restored John's sight, and it was he who, by his benevolent aid, converted the mud-huts into a substantial farm-house.

May God grant to the Generous and the Grateful a long and happy life here below!

MINE HOST GANSENDONCK.

INTRODUCTION.

In a village between Hoogstraten and Calmpthout, in the Antwerp Kempen, dwelt Peer Gansendonck, mine host of the St. Sebastian.

I first became acquainted with him in 1830, when I was a soldier: at that time, however, I knew nothing more of him than that peasants and common soldiers were his aversion, and that he had a very weak side for officers. I remember he was excessively angry with the burgomaster because he had received the captain of the company into his house, while the other three officers were the guests respectively of the baron, the notary, and the doctor; leaving poor Peer Gansendonck no more important personage to entertain than your most humble servant the sergeant-major.

I was in the habit of filling up my idle hours with the manufacture of pretty toys of all kinds for little Lisa, mine host's daughter, a child of five. She was a delicate girl, and seemed slowly pining away; but there was something so lovely in her angel-eyes, something so pure in her marble features, and so sweetly plaintive in her small voice, that I found a kind of pleasure in comforting and delighting the sickly little lamb with games, and songs, and tales.

How bitterly did little Lisa weep, how fast flowed the tears over her cheeks, when the drums beat a last farewell, and her kind friend the sergeant-major, with knapsack on back, stood yonder in marching order, about to leave her for ever! But such sorrows pass quickly from a child's soul. From that time little Lisa never occupied my thoughts; and she, without doubt, had entirely forgotten me.

A short time ago my wanderings led me through the Kempen, and again I found myself in the same village.

I entered it without the slightest anticipation. Scarcely, however, had I observed the church, the houses, and the trees, than a smile of surprise overspread my face, and my breast heaved with a pleasing emotion. It was the old sign over the inn door which in an especial manner affected me. Overpowered, I hung my head, and stood for a while motionless to enjoy the flood of youthful memories which, like a warm beneficent stream, flowed through my brain.

How strong and impressible must be our soul in youth, making as it does all the circumstances of our earlier years an eternal possession, and surrounding them with a sacred halo of love! People, trees, houses, words—everything, living or lifeless, becomes a part of our own being; on every object we hang some memory, beautiful and sweet as youth itself. Our soul overflows with power—it beams the fire and lightning of its own life over all creation; and while we exult with unrestrained feelings at the happiness which awaits us as children or youths, everything in nature sings and rejoices in unison with us.

Ah! how I love the meadows, the lime-trees, the farm-house, the church, and all the other objects which greeted me when the roses of youth and the lilies of the purity and poetry of life adorned my head! You have enjoyed what I enjoyed then; I saw them luxuriate in green, blossom and smile in the sunshine, when I was light of heart, and was entering too confidently on the unknown path of human destiny. They are the old companions of my play—my familiar friends: each object has some charming tale to tell me; they speak the utterance of my heart, and the finest chords of my soul respond to their call with all the life of youth. And with a calm and holy emotion, I thank God that He has permitted the sweet wells of memory to spring fresh in the jaded heart of world-weary man.

Standing before the tavern door, I was charmed back into other and better times. Again I saw my comrades and officers; the distant drum rolled in my ear; I heard the loud word of command; the soldier's farewell song died away beyond the houses, and the trumpet resounded among the trees. But more vividly than all the rest, little Lisa's calm angel form seemed to smile to me out of the past.

The thought of man hastens more swiftly through the world of ideas than the lightning through space. For about one minute only had I yielded myself to these emotions, and already five beautiful months of my life had passed before my eyes.

With high anticipation and cheerful countenance, I entered the inn door. I would see Lisa. She could not recognise me, I well knew, for the child must be a beautiful woman now; the sight of *her*, however, I thought, would give me pleasure. But in the days when she first charmed me she was a sickly child, and perhaps, long ere this, she lies in the quiet churchyard. Away with such hateful thoughts, with which cold reason would destroy these warm memories!

But now sad and strange is everything to me here in the St. Sebastian! Everything is altered, people and things. Where is mine host? where is little Lisa? where the folding table, on which I and my companions so often played for a can of beer? All are gone!——Poor little Lisa! I see the corner of the window where you used to lie with your head on your mother's lap, and where I used to make you so happy with a carriage made of cards drawn by four cockchafers, and where your languid look seemed to me a prayer of thankfulness for my kindness.

I had entirely forgotten everything, never suspecting that I should ever revisit these scenes. But now forms and voices rise around me; I see, I hear everything again; everything is again young and smiling—even my heart, which returns into harmony with these well-known and beloved objects.

Sweet little Lisa! who would have thought, when I was delighting your little soul with childish tales, that I should one day narrate your history to my fellow-countrymen?

Life is like one of those gigantic streams of America, which for a long distance rolls calmly down between smiling banks. then suddenly precipitates itself from some high rock, and with noisy waves rolls on in its stormy and destructive course. Man is a straw which floats upon the stream: the calm progress between blooming banks is youth; human society is the roaring waterfall and the turbid current, in which the individual is swept along like a straw. He slips, he falls, rises and sinks again; is tortured, bruised, broken, worn to death. Who can tell on what coast the poor straw will be thrown?

CHAPTER L

" Nothing with something,
Makes nothing of something."

BAAS GANSENDONCK was a peculiar man. **Although**
sprung from the humblest villagers, he had early fancied that
he was made of quite other stuff than the rest of peasants;
that he alone knew more than a whole host of learned men;
that the affairs of the community had fallen into confusion,
and were fast retrograding, merely because he was not burgomaster: and many other things of this kind.

And yet the poor man could neither read nor write, and
had forgotten nothing because he had nothing to forget. But
he had plenty of money.

In this respect at least he was like many people of distinc-
tion, whose intellect lies in a chest at the back of the castle,
or whose wisdom is lent out at five per cent, and, with the interest, comes fresh into their head every year. The inhabitants of the village, feeling themselves daily insulted by this
ridiculous fancy on the part of mine host, had gradually acquired a deep hatred of him, and nicknamed him " Swaggering Jack."

The landlord of the St. Sebastian was a widower, and had
only one child, a daughter of eighteen or nineteen. She was
a slender and pale-faced girl; but with a countenance so
tender and refined, and a nature so lovely and sweet, that
she attracted the eyes of many a young man. Her father

in his folly considered her far too good, too refined, and too
beautiful to marry a peasant's son. He had sent her for
some years to an educational institution to learn French and
fine manners, as became her high destiny. Happily Lisa,
or Lieschen, as the peasants called her, returned as simple as
she went. The seeds of vanity and levity, it is true, had
been sown in her mind, though happily in small measure;
but the natural purity of her heart did not permit the dangerous seed to take root and grow up, while her maiden innocence gave a charm even to the indications which occasionally
appeared of the training she had received, and indeed made
everything in her loveable. As usual, she had received only
a half education: she understood French pretty well, but spoke
it very imperfectly. On the other hand, she could embroider
very prettily, make beautiful slippers and cushions, knit with
beads, cut out flowers in paper, say a very charming good-day,
courtesy and bow, dance very artistically, and had many other
fancy accomplishments, which suited her father's peasant
home as well as, according to the proverb, a lace collar does
a cow's neck.

From childhood it had been understood that Lisa was to
marry Charles the brewer's son, one of the finest-looking young
men far and wide. For a villager, he was wealthy and well
educated, for he had attended the gymnasium at Hoogstraten
for some years. Study, meanwhile, had little altered him: he
loved as much as ever the unrestrained freedom of country life;
was as merry as a bird; drank and sang with everybody, but
always in moderation and with propriety; was full of genial
life, and conducted himself towards his acquaintances like a
right steady friend and comrade. On account of the early
death of his father, he had left the gymnasium to help his
mother in conducting the brewery; and the old woman
thanked God daily that He had given her so good a son to

comfort her; for a more industrious and regular young man could nowhere be found.

Only in Lisa's presence did Charles lose his customary ease, and sink into vague poetic dreams. When sitting by the beloved girl he became little better than a child, found pleasure in the most insignificant of her occupations, and adapted himself to her smallest wishes with a kind of religious obedience: she was so tender, so weak, so beautiful,—and *his* bride. He, the vigorous and manly youth, treated this gentle being with such jealous attention and anxious care, that one might have thought he had been intrusted with the life of a fading flower.

For five or six months Host Gansendonck had offered no objections to his daughter becoming Charles's wife. His pride, to be sure, was not satisfied with it; still, a rich brewer's son was no mere peasant, at any rate, he thought. Besides, he did not wish to break his long-given promise, and accordingly agreed that preparations should be made for the approaching nuptials.

Everything was going well with the young people, when our host's unmarried brother died of a fever and left a fine property behind him, which soon after became added, in the shape of hard cash, to other money-sacks in the strong room of the St. Sebastian. Peer Gansendonck shared the belief of many people, that the intellect, the worth and excellence of a man, is to be measured by his wealth; and although he knew no English, he had yet stumbled on the elevated and peculiarly English notion-implied in the question, "How many pounds sterling is he worth?" The reply is irresistible in the words of the old Flemish rhyme—

In dumb gold
What virtue lies!
Makes young the old,
The crooked straight,
And blockhead wise."

It stands to reason, then, that with such a notion of life his pride, or I should rather say his insanity, was likely to increase with his wealth. He now considered himself as good at least as the baron of the village, for he imagined that he was worth quite as many pounds as the noble proprietor.

From this day forward our host's brains became more disordered than ever, and he considered himself the first man in the country. He often dreamt all night that he was of a noble race; and even by day, flattering thoughts passed through his head perpetually. In order to bring his fancied excellence to a sober test, he laboured at times to bring out the precise difference between himself and a nobleman, but could never find any. He was conscious, to be sure, that he was too old to learn French, or alter his way of life entirely and enter into higher circles of society; at the same time, if *he* could not do that, he was determined that his daughter at least should look higher, and marry the first baron who came in her way. What a charming prospect for Peer Gansendonck! Before he died he should have the pleasure of hearing his daughter addressed as My Lady Baroness! Nay, he himself would actually be the grandfather of little barons!

On this account Charles the brewer's attachment to Lisa began to give him serious uneasiness; and indeed he looked upon the fine young fellow as standing in the way of his daughter's prospects. Already, in Lisa's presence, he had more than once uttered words of depreciation about Charles, and on one occasion said things which hurt the poor child's feelings so much, that for the first time in her life she boldly contradicted him, and then for full two hours shed bitter tears.

After this, he gave up all direct opposition to the brewer's love, but he determined to postpone the marriage till Lisa should of her own accord open her eyes, and see that Charles was only a coarse peasant like the rest.

CHAPTER II.

*"Whose bread I eat,
His song I sing."*

In the courtyard of the St. Sebastian, the domestics and lay-labourers had been busy with their usual occupations since daybreak. Trees the dairymaid stood at the trough washing turnips for the cattle; in the open barn was heard the measured beat of the flail, and the stable-boy sang a rude song while currying the horses.

One man alone walked idly up and down smoking his pipe, and stopping now and then to observe the others at work. He was clothed like a day-labourer, and wore a jerkin and wooden shoes. Although his face when at rest expressed a lazy indifference, there looked from his eyes a certain shrewdness and cunning. For the rest, one could easily see from his plump cheeks and red nose that he was in the habit of sitting at a good table, and knew the way to the cellar.

The dairymaid stopped washing her turnips, and went towards the barn, where the threshers were spreading some fresh sheaves, and took advantage of the opportunity to have a little chat. The man with the pipe was by.

"Kobè! Kobè!" cried the dairymaid to him, "you at least have drawn a lucky number. Here we are, working ourselves to death from morning to night, and instead of reward get a scolding for our pains when all is done. You have the wind behind you: you walk about at your ease smoking your pipe, are the landlord's friend, and get the best food that's going You must confess that your bread has fallen in honey."

Kobè smiled roguishly, and answered—

"To have is to have, and to get is the art: fortune has wings and flies, and he who catches her has her."

"To flatter is to lie, and a fawning fellow is little better than a knave," muttered one of the day-workers sharply.

"Words are not knives," laughed Kobè. "Everybody in the world is bound to do good to his father's son; and he who finds anything let him pick it up."

"I would be ashamed of myself," cried the enraged worker. "There is no great art in cutting thongs out of another's eather, and a sucking pig grows fat without working!"

"It makes one dog angry to see another go into the kitchen," said Kobè jestingly. "Dishes, that are not alike, make bad brothers, and it is better to be envied than pitied. And since one must sit down in this world, I had rather sit on cushions than on thorns."

"Hold your tongue, you shark, and remember that it is on our sweat that you fatten!"

"Tisty, Tisty, why so sharp with me? You can't bear to see the sun shining on my pond. Do you not know the proverb, 'He who envies another tears his own heart, and wastes his time'? If I were anything less, would you be anything more? Am I proud? do I ever do an ill-natured thing? On the contrary, when the landlord is coming, I smuggle off many a good can of beer into the cellar for you. You are seeking where nobody has lost, Tisty."

"Yes, yes, we know the worth of your benevolence. You are like the minister who blessed everybody, but himself first."

"He was quite right, and I too. He who serves the altar, must live by the altar."

"Quite true," cried another worker. "Kobè is a good fellow, and I wish I were in his shoes; then should I too earn my bread while blowing smoke to the crows. 'A full belly is a heart at ease.'"

"Ay, thick-paunch, sleepy-feet! A full stomach, an empty head."

"Let them talk on, Kobè. It is not every one that has a lucky star; and *I* say that you are a very clever fellow."

"I have no more cleverness than the mushroom yonder on the cherry-tree," said Kobè, with feigned modesty.

All looked surprised at a great fungus which grew between the largest branches of a cherry-tree, and then as quickly turned to Kobè to receive as usual some waggish interpretation.

"O ho!" cried the dairymaid, "no more cleverness than the mushroom yonder! Then you must be a fearful blockhead."

"It does not follow, Mieken. What says the proverb?— 'Work is for blockheads.' I don't work, do I?"

"But what has the mushroom to do with that?"

"Why, you see it is a riddle: the fine large cherry-tree is our landlord."

"O you fawning fellow!" cried the dairymaid.

"And I," continued Kobè, "am the poor, humble mushroom."

"Hypocrite!" muttered the irritated day-worker.

"If you could but guess it, you would then know what little dogs must do if they would eat with big ones out of the same dish without being bitten."

It was Kobè's intention to puzzle them still longer with his double meanings; but he heard the landlord's voice in the house, and said to the workers, at the same time resuming his pipe—·

"Let the men go on with their threshing, good people. Our good kind landlord comes to see how the work goes on.

"We shall get our breakfast now, and no small uproar will there be," cried the dairymaid, running to the trough to re-commence her work.

"If he snaps at me again, and insults me by calling me Lazy-bones and Looby, I'll bring the flail down on his pate," said one of the day-workers angrily.

"When the mug fights with the stone, the first knock snaps the mug in two," said Kobè jestingly.

"What matters it to me?" remarked a second workman. "I laugh at his scolding, and let him rage on in peace."

"That is the best way," interrupted Kobè; "just keep your ears wide open, and it will go in at one and come out at the other. Our host must have something for his money; give him what he has a right to, and do what he tells you."

"Do what he tells us! And what if one can't do it?"

"Then still give him what he has a right to, and don't do it; or, what is better, say nothing, but hold your tongue, just as if you heard nothing of all his blowing and blustering;— think that silence is the best policy."

"Men are men. *I* laugh at his brutal way of treating me! Just let him begin, and I will show my teeth for once. He has no right to treat me like a beast, though I be only a day-labourer."

"It is quite true what you say, and yet you do not quite hit the nail on the head," remarked Kobè. "Every one must know his place in the world. What says the proverb? —'If an anvil, bear like an anvil; if a hammer, strike like a hammer.' Besides, a little word, though good in itself, often brings trouble; and if you wish the thing put in a stronger light, consider that you can't catch flies with vinegar, or hares with drums."

"Kobè! Kobè!" called a voice from within, with manifest impatience.

"Only see what a hypocritical face he is putting on now!" said another thresher jestingly.

"That is precisely the art which you will not learn," replied Kobè; and immediately turning towards the house, he shouted out in a humble tone—

"I am coming! I am coming, my dear host. Don't be angry, I come on wings. Here I am already!"

"He earns his bread by acting the lap-dog!" muttered the angry day-labourer contemptuously. "I would rather thresh all my life. He is one of those washed in all waters."

"He has served ten long years to learn to play the innocent in the play, and get his bread for nothing. After one has become a gentleman's servant, one's hands don't grow hard with labour. But what a clever riddle he gave us! Do you understand it?"

"Oh, it is easy to explain," replied the first; "he means that he sits and feeds on our landlord's neck, as the fungus does on the cherry-tree. Come, come, let us go on with our threshing."

CHAPTER III.

" Great cry, but little wool."

"Now, then, Kobè," said mine host Gansendonck to his
servant, "how do I look with my new cap?"

Kobè stepped two paces back, and, rubbing his eyes like
some one who must prepare himself to wonder at something
incredible, he exclaimed—

" O mine host! tell me at once, and truly, whether you
are really yourself. I thought I saw the lord Baron standing
before me. But, heavens! how can it be? Hold your head
up a little. Baas, Baas, turn round; walk forward a little,
Baas, that I may make quite sure. Why, you see, you are
as like the lord Baron as one drop of water is like"—

"Kobè!" interrupted Baas, with assumed seriousness,
"you mean to flatter me; and I have a particular aversion
to that."

" I know well that you dislike it, sir," replied he.

" There are few men who have less pride than I; though
some, out of mere envy, say that I am haughty, because, forsooth, I cannot endure peasants."

" You are quite right, Baas. But I still have some doubts
whether you are not really the Baron."

Peer Gansendonck's eyes beamed with pleasure; throwing
his head back, and standing in a proud attitude, he looked

with a benignant smile at Kobè, who continued to make all
sorts of gestures expressive of wonder. He had not, indeed,
quite told his master a falsehood. In outward appearance—
not taking the absurdly stupid face into consideration—Peer
was very like the Baron. And no wonder, as for several
months he had worn imitations of the Baron's clothes, though
the fact generally escaped observation, as the latter lived on
his estate in a free and easy way, and generally wore a very
ordinary dress.

Some weeks before this conversation, however, the Baron
had taken a fancy—who does not at times? A very beautiful water-dog had died, and he had got a cap made of its
skin. This fine cap took such entire possession of poor Peer's
mind, that he had no rest till he got a similar one made in
the city; and now, with its thousand curls, it was adorning
the head of mine host of the St. Sebastian, who could not
sufficiently admire himself in the mirror since he had heard
the flattering remarks of his servant.

At last, he prepared to go out, and said—

" Kobè, take a staff, and let us walk through the village."

" Yes, Baas," replied the servant, following at his master's
heels with an assumed aspect of grave humility.

On the broad path which ran between the lines of houses,
they met many villagers who gave a friendly hat to mine
host; but burst into laughter as soon as he had passed.
Many of the inhabitants also came running out of their houses,
curious to see and wonder at Baas's hairy cap. Our host
greeted no one at first, but walked forward in a stately way,
with uplifted head and slow steps, keeping steadily on at a
uniform pace, as the Baron was accustomed to do. Kobè
walked silently behind his master, with a face of mock innocence, following all his turnings and windings as accurately
and faithfully as a dog.

Everything went well till they reached the smithy. Some young folks stood there talking together, and so soon as they observed Baas approaching, they began to laugh so loudly that it resounded through the whole street. Sus, the smith's son, who was well known as a jesting fellow, walked up and down before the smithy with head thrown back and measured steps, and imitated mine host Gansendonck so excellently, that he almost burst with vexation. As he passed, he directed a look of anger towards the young smith, putting so severe an expression into his eyes that they almost cracked with the effort. The smith replied with a defiant and mocking laugh, so that mine host, boiling over with wrath, found his only refuge in passing rapidly on, and then struck into a by-path to escape the general observation, muttering to himself as he went.

"Swaggering Jack! Swaggering Jack!" they shouted after him.

"Now, Kobè, what do you say to the pack of boors?" he asked, when his wrath was somewhat allayed. "*They* would dare to despise me!—make sport of me!—a man like me!"

"Ay, Baas, flies bite a horse, and yet a horse is a great beast."

"But I will know how to get at them, the clowns! Just let them wait a little; they shall pay dear to me for this! Hills cannot come near each other, but men can."

"True, Baas; forbearance is no acquittance."

"I should be a perfect fool if I allowed my horses to be shod by the ill-mannered clowns, or let them do my other work."

"To be sure, Baas; to be too good is to be half a fool."

"And not one of my people shall ever again set foot in his smithy."

"No, Baas."

"*Then* w'll the mocking fellow be sorry enough, and bite his nails with vexation."

"Without doubt, Baas."

"It is my belief, Kobè, that that rascally smith is paid by some one to persecute and annoy me. The watchman thinks that it was he who last May-night wrote something on my sign."

"'*The sign of the Silver Ass,*' do you mean, Baas?"

"It is not necessary to repeat the cursed insolence, is it?"

"No, Baas."

"Between ourselves, you must give him a sound thrashing when nobody sees you, and then give him my compliments."

"Yes."

"Will you do it?"

"Give him your compliments? oh, to be sure."

"No; give him a sound thrashing, I mean."

"If you would see me come home without either arms or legs! I am not very strong, Baas; and the smith is not a cat to be caught without gloves."

"And are you actually afraid of the cowardly braggart? I would be ashamed of myself."

"It is not pleasant work fighting with one who is weary of his life. 'Better a timid Jack than a dead Jack,' says the proverb."

"Kobè, Kobè, I believe *you* will never die of courage."

"I hope not, sir."

While they talked in this style, mine host's rage began gradually to die away. With many faults, he had still one good quality—although he quickly flew into a passion, he as quickly forgot the injury he had received.

He had now come to a plantation, and passing behind it through his own fields, he found objects of every kind on which

to vent his exaggerated notions of the rights of property, and
make him scold and rail at God and all the world. Here
a cow had strayed from the road upon his land; there a
goat had eaten the foliage from some of his young trees; and
further on, he believed that he perceived the footsteps of
hunters, and the tracks of their dogs. This last discovery
roused him to such fury, that he stamped his feet. He had
erected high posts on all parts of his fields, with the inscrip-
tion—"Hunting prohibited;" and, spite of that, some one
had actually been bold enough to intrude, and contemptuously
trample under foot his rights in his own property. A storm
of vituperation burst from him, and, in his rage, he struck a
beech-stem with his fist.

Kobè stood behind a little, and thought of his dinner. He
knew that they were to have a hare that day, and imagining
to himself that the cook might possibly spoil the sauce, he
likewise stamped his feet in apparent sympathy with his
master. Meanwhile he never gave any other answer than,
"Yes, Baas," and "No, Baas," without paying any attention
to what his master was saying.

All of a sudden, Peer Gansendonck heard a voice shouting,
in a loud and mocking tone, "Swaggering Jack! Swaggering
Jack!"

Foaming with rage, he looked round, but saw no one except his servant, who was looking intently on the ground, and
moving his lips as if engaged in the act of eating.

"What! villain, was it you?" cried Baas wrathfully.

"Yes, it is I," replied Kobè; "but, Lord preserve us!
what has come over you, Baas?"

"I ask you booby, if it was you who spoke then?"

"Did you not hear me, Baas?"

The enraged Gansendonck tore the staff out of his hand,
and was about to beat him with it; but as soon as Kobè per-

ceived that things were taking a serious turn, he sprang back, and, with uplifted arms, cried out—

"Alas, alas! now is our good landlord quite out of his senses!"

"Swaggering Jack! Swaggering Jack!" again screamed some one from behind Peer.

He now for the first time perceived that a magpie was perched among the branches of the beech, and kept repeating the opprobrious epithet.

"Kobè, Kobè," he cried, "run and fetch my rifle. It is the smith's magpie; the cursed brute must die!" But the bird left the tree and flew home.

Kobè burst out into such violent laughter, that he sank on the grass, and rolled there helplessly for a considerable time.

"Stop!" screamed Baas, "stop, or I shall drive you from my house. Stop laughing, I tell you."

"I can't, sir; I can't."

"Stand up."

"Yes."

"I will forgive your unmannerly conduct on one condition; and that is, that you kill the smith's magpie."

"With what, Baas?"

"With poison."

"Certainly, Baas, if it will eat it."

"If not, then shoot it dead."

"Very well."

"Come, let us go. But, hallo, what is that I see there in my fir-wood? One may as well not be a proprietor at all, if one is to be plundered by whoever pleases in this fashion."

With these words, he hastened on, accompanied by his attendant, railing stormily as he went.

He had seen from a distance a poor woman and two children busy breaking the withered branches of the firs, and tying them into large bundles. Although an ancient custom permitted the poor to gather withered branches in the fir-woods, Baas Gansendonck would never permit it. The dry wood was as much his possession as the green, he said, and no one was to dare to touch his property. Besides, it was only a poor woman, and he had therefore no resistance or insolence to fear. This inspired him with courage, and gave him an opportunity of wreaking his whole wrath without the dread of retaliation.

Seizing the poor woman by the shoulder, he cried out—

"Shameless thief, begone! Off to the village with me—to the police! To the lock-up, you pilferer!"

The trembling woman let fall the wood she had collected, and was so overpowered by the suddenness of the attack and the violence of Baas's threats, that she lost the power of speech, and began to weep; while both the little children clung to their mother's clothes, and filled the plantation with their terrified cries.

Kobè shook his head with vexation; the expression of careless indifference had left his face, and a feeling of compassion for the poor woman had evidently taken possession of him.

"Here, you idle good-for-nothing!" exclaimed Baas to him; "stretch out your hands and take this brood of thieves to the police."

"Dear man! I will never do it again," said the woman imploringly. "Think of my poor children; they will die of terror."

"Silence, vagabond!" thundered Baas; "I will teach you to rob and steal."

Kobè took hold of the woman's arm with assumed anger, and shook her with seeming violence; but at the same time whispered in her ear—

"Fall on your knees, and say, 'Gracious sir.'"

The woman fell down on her knees before Baas Gansendonck, and, stretching out her arms, said—

"Ah, gracious sir! gracious sir! pardon me, I beseech you. O do so, for the sake of my poor little children, I beseech you!"

Some secret influence seemed now to be at work in mine host; he stood back a little from the woman, and looked at her in a dreamy way, and with a mild, friendly expression. Yet he did not bid her stand up. Some one on her knees before him with uplifted hands, and praying for mercy! Was it possible? Oh, it was kingly.

After he had enjoyed for a time this intense pleasure, he raised the poor woman from the ground, and wiped a tear of emotion from his eyes, saying at the same time—

"Poor mother! I have been too hasty. It is all past now. Take up your bundle again; you are a good woman. In future, you may break the withered wood in all my plantations; and if a little bit of green should now and then find its way into your bundle, I shall say nothing. Compose yourself; I grant you my full pardon and favour."

With great surprise, the woman gazed alternately at these two peculiar men who stood before her; Baas with his patronizing countenance, and the servant, who was making violent efforts to keep himself from laughing.

"Yes, good mother," repeated Baas, "permission is granted you to gather wood in all my plantations." As he said this, he moved his hand round in a circle, as if the whole parish belonged to him.

The poor woman moved back a few paces to pick up her bundle, and sighed, as she said with gratitude—

"God bless you for your kindness, my lord Baron!"

Mine host Gansendonck felt a thrill of delight run through

his frame, and his countenance lighted up as if irradiated by
the sun of happiness.

"Woman, woman!" he cried, "come hither. What is
that you said? I did not understand you."

"I said that I thanked you a thousand times, my lord
Baron."

Baas Gansendonck put his hand in his pocket, and, drawing out a silver coin, handed it to the woman, saying, with
tears in his eyes—

"There, good mother; make a happy day of it; and in
winter, come every Saturday to the St. Sebastian, and you
will get wood and bread in abundance. Now you may go
home."

With these words, he left the woman and the plantation.
He wept, and the tears rolled over his cheeks. Kobè, who
perceived it, also wiped his eyes with the sleeve of his jerkin.

"It is a singular thing," at last sighed Baas, "that I can
see no one in suffering but it goes to my heart at once."

"It is the same with me, Baas."

"Did you hear it, Kobè? The good woman took me for
the Baron."

"With good reason, Baas."

"Be silent for a little, good Kobè; and let us go slowly
home."

"Certainly, Baas."

With the greatest submission, Kobè followed in his master's
footsteps, and both went dreamily on. Mine host thought of
the beautiful names by which the woman had addressed him
—Kobè, of hare and wine-sauce.

Three hunters meanwhile had come out of an oak-wood,
and stood at a little distance laughing and joking at mine
host and his attendant. They were three young gentlemen,
dressed in elegant hunting suits, and with rifles in their hands.

One of them seemed to know the host of the St. Sebastian
well; for he was relating to his companions by what a singular demon of pride the man was possessed, and spoke at the
same time in warm language of his daughter Lisa.

"Come, come," he cried at last, "we are fatigued with our
sport; let us have some amusement. Follow me; we shall
go to the St. Sebastian and empty a bottle. But remember
to address him with great respect, and compliment him
largely—the more absurdly the better."

After saying this, he and his companions leapt the dry
ditch before them, and he hastened to Baas a little in advance, bowing low as he approached, and greeting him in the
most courtly style. Peer Gansendonck took his fur-cap in
both hands and made great efforts to imitate the actions of
the young gentleman. The two other hunters took no part
in these compliments, but, sheltering themselves behind the
attendant, made violent efforts to restrain their laughter.

"Now, Herr Adolph, my friend," said mine host, "how
goes it with your papa? Still stout and thriving, I hope. He
never pays us a visit, now that he lives in the city. But,
'Out of sight, out of mind,' says the proverb."

Adolph took one of his laughing friends by the hand, and
drew him forcibly towards Baas.

"Herr von Gansendonck," he said solemnly, "I have the
honour to present to you the young Herr Baron Victor of
Bruinkasteel; but you must excuse his malady, it is a nervous
affection—the remains of an attack of convulsions; he can
see no stranger without bursting into laughter."

Victor could restrain himself no longer; he threw back his
head, stamped his feet, and laughed till he was black and blue.

"You are spoiling the sport," whispered Adolph to him,
"stop, otherwise he will perceive it."

"As you please, Herr von Bruinkasteel," said mine host.

" ' Better be blithe with little than sad with nothing,' as they say."

Taking his friend a second time by the hand, Adolph repeated the presentation.

" Herr von Bruinkasteel has the honour not to know me," said mine host with a bow.

" Indeed," replied Victor, " I have the honour not to be known to you."

" The honour is not great, gracious sir," said Baas, again bowing. " The Herr means, I suppose, to spend the hunting season at our friend Adolph's little country-seat ?"

" Yes, at your service, Herr von Gansendonck."

" His father has bought the hunting-box from us," said Adolph. " Herr von Bruinkasteel will be your neighbour every winter after this, and will probably be a frequent visitor at your house, Herr von Gansendonck."

" But Adolph, my friend, why does the other gentleman stand behind Kobè, there ? Is he afraid of me ?"

" He is very shy, Herr von Gansendonck. What can one make of it ? It is the unspotted innocence of youth. But, Herr von Gansendonck, you possess a fine shooting-ground ; you too are a huntsman, I perceive."

" I am a great amateur, am I not, Kobè ?"

" Ay, Baas, of hares ; and I too ;—only they must not be overdone," he added in a lower tone.

" What did you mutter there ?" cried mine host with anger, to show the gentlemen that he governed his household as a great man ought. " What did you mutter there, you shameless clown ?"

" I ask if you do not think it is time to go home, Baas ; and I was just saying so to myself : fishing and hunting make hungry stomachs."

"When a sucking pig dreams, it dreams of husks. It is your part to be silent; be so good as to remember *that*."

"Very well, Baas; to think and say nothing, does harm to nobody."

"Not a word more, I command you."

"No, Baas."

"Will the gentlemen do me the honour to drink an early glass of wine in my house?" asked Peer Gansendonck, again addressing the strangers.

"It was our intention, sir, to visit you for that purpose."

"Indeed! come along then; you shall have wine worth speaking of. Is it not so, Kobè? You tasted it once in your life. If you do not lick your lips after it, gentlemen, then call me *peasant*."

"That is quite true, Baas," replied the servant.

Mine host now strode majestically on, talking in a friendly way with Adolph, whose two companions hung back a little to give free scope to their fun. Kobè looked at everything with a singular and undefinable expression, and would have laughed too, had his head not been so full of the spiced hare that he almost took a spasm in his stomach with thinking of it.

Slow y the company moved towards the St. Sebastian.

CHAPTER IV.

"Bring not the wolf into the sheepfold."

IT was a glorious morning. The sun shone in the eastern horizon, glowing like burning gold, and shooting dense masses of dazzling radiance through sky and air. Its sparkling beams penetrated half-playfully the window of the St. Sebastian, and fell with a roseate light on a young girl's brow.

Lisa Gansendonck sat at a table by the window. She was dreaming; for her long dark eyelashes hung over her eyes, and a gentle smile played round her mouth, while now and then a slight blush on her pale cheek betokened some secret emotion of the heart. Suddenly she raised her head; her eyes sparkled, and she smiled as if some pleasing idea had struck her.

She took up a French paper from Antwerp, which lay open before her, and after reading a few lines, laid it down again, and relapsed into her former reverie.

How charming she looked as she sat there, like a lovely dream, surrounded by the deepest silence and with the warmest ray of the morning sun upon her!—pale and tender, young and lovely, like a white rose half-blown.

Sounds tender and tremulous, like the dying breath of a distant harp, escaped her lips, as with a sigh she murmured—

"Oh how happy one must be in the city! Such a ball!

All the rich dresses, diamonds, flowers in the hair, and clothes so costly that one might buy half a village with them ; everything dazzling with gold and light ! and then the fine manners ! and the beautiful conversation ! Oh, if I could but see it once, were it only through a window !"

After she had dwelt long upon this subject in her thoughts, the charming idea of a city ball seemed to leave her at last ; and standing up, she approached a mirror, where she looked at herself attentively, arranging a fold in her dress here and there, or smoothing down her beautiful black hair till it shone with more dazzling brilliancy than ever. Her dress was very simple, and one would have found nothing to blame in her ornaments had not the smell of the byre, the smoked walls of the inn, and the tin cans on the shelf, proclaimed from every side that young Lisa was not in her place.

Her black silk gown was plain, and had only a single flounce ; her neckerchief was of a rose-colour, and both suited her pale face beautifully. Her head was uncovered, and her hair lay simply down in front, and was tied up behind like a little coronet.

After she had spent some time at the mirror, she returned to the table, and sitting down, began half-idly to embroider a lace collar, while her wandering looks betokened that her thoughts were busy with something far removed from her work. Immediately after, she said in an almost inaudible tone—

"The hunting season has begun ; the gentlemen will leave the city again. Father says I must be friendly to them. He will take me to town to purchase a silk hat for me. I am not to sit with downcast eyes. I am to laugh and look the the gentlemen in the face when they speak to me. What does father mean by it ? I don't know what good purpose it could serve, he says to . . . . . but then Charles ? It seems to be disagreeable to him when I change my dress frequently, and it annoys him when strangers talk too much with me. What am I to do? Father *will* have it so; and I cannot be unkind to the people who come about. Yet I will not vex Charles either."

Just at this moment, her father's voice was heard at the door; looking through the window, she saw him bowing and showing great politeness to three young gentlemen in hunting clothes. A deep blush overspread her brow. Was pleasure or perplexity the cause of it? She once more smoothed down her hair, and remained sitting as if she had heard nothing.

Mine host entered with his company, and in a fond and complacent tone, said—

"See, gentlemen, here is my daughter! What say you to such a pretty flower as that? She is well educated, and knows French, gentlemen; between my Lisa and a peasant girl, there is as great a difference as between a cow and a wheel-barrow."

Kobè burst into a loud laugh.

"You scoundrel!" cried mine host in a fury; "what are you laughing at? Get along with you, you villain!"

"Very well, Baas!"

Kobè sat down at the hearth corner, and with intense pleasure inhaled the smell of the hare, whose rich steamy odour found its way into the room from a back kitchen. Meanwhile he gazed into the fire, and seemed or feigned to become quite unconscious of everything that was going on around him.

While Lisa was engaged in exchanging some French politenesses with the gentlemen, mine host Gansendonck had betaken himself to the cellar, and returned with a bottle and glasses, which he placed on the table before his daughter.

"Seat yourselves, seat yourselves, gentlemen," he said,

" we will drink Lisa's health. She shall pledge you. Ah!
you are speaking French with her, are you? Singular fact,
that I always hear French spoken with so much pleasure; I
could listen to it the whole day long; it always sounds to me
as if some one were singing a song."

He took Victor by the arm, and forced him down beside
Lisa.

" Not so much ceremony, Herr von Bruinkasteel," he cried;
" pray act as if you were in your own house."

Lisa's beautiful, gentle face had at the first glance inspired
two of the young hunters with a kind of respect; they sat on
the opposite side of the table, and looked in silence at the
simple girl, who evidently exerted herself to be as agreeable
as possible, while her bashfulness and timidity made her brow
glow as if with fire. Victor von Bruinkasteel, however, was
far from being so respectful or reserved. He began boldly to
flatter the young maiden, praising her beauty, her embroidery,
and her French; but was at the same time so skilful in dis-
posing his words, and mingling his flatteries with the rest of
his conversation, that all appearance of anything forced or unbecoming was taken away; and Lisa dreamily listened to his
talk as if it were a sweetly-sounding song.

Mine host, whose hopes rose higher with every word, and
who cherished a predilection for Herr Victor, rubbed his hands
with pleasure, while he said to himself :—

" No one knows how a penny-piece can roll, and everything
is possible, except falling upwards. It would make a beautiful pair, it would.—Now, then, gentlemen! drink another
glass. Your health, Herr von Bruinkasteel! Go on speaking French; you do not need to trouble yourself about me;
I see in your eyes what you would say."

The young hunters seemed to enjoy themselves amazingly.
Lisa's French, to be sure, was not the best; but in her mouth

everything sounded so charming and beautiful. The perpetual blush upon her cheeks had something in it so graceful and attractive; and there was something so fresh and loveable about her whole nature, that the very tones of her voice alone roused a sweet feeling in the heart.

Victor, an experienced gallant, had soon discovered the weak side of Lisa's virgin soul. He spoke to her of the newest fashions, of beautiful dress, of city life; described festivals and balls in glowing colours; and knew so well how to engage her attention, that the poor girl became almost unconscious of everything around her. Gradually he grew so bold as to seize Lisa's hand, while speaking, in a seemingly casual way.

Now, for the first time, the poor girl seemed to awake out of her dream. Trembling she withdrew her hand, pushed back her chair, and looked at her father with an anxious and inquiring expression. He, however, delighted above measure, looked at her reproachfully, and nodded to her to keep her seat. Lisa's modest withdrawal of her hand took Victor by surprise, and he turned aside his face to conceal his confusion. He now perceived that the servant, who had sat down by the corner of the hearth, was on his feet, and had his eyes fixed on him with a threatening expression, mingled at the same time with a bitter and sarcastic smile.

Turning to mine host, he said with some annoyance— " What has that looby to say here, that he stares and laughs at me so impudently ?"

" He anything to say !" screamed Baas, " you shall soon see that."

" Kobè !"

" What do you want, Baas ?"

" Is it possible that you looked at Herr von Bruinkasteel in a disagreeable way ? Did you dare to laugh at him, you earthworm ?"

"I laughed as a dog does who has eaten mustard. I have burnt my hand, Baas."

"Foh! you are too awkward to dance before the devil. Get out of the house at once."

"Very well, Baas."

Kobè then left the room with slow steps, taking off his cap awkwardly and sheepishly as he went, as if he had been incapable of observing anything.

Soon after, Victor's impudence was forgotten: the young gentlemen talked French with Lisa agreeably, while mine host encouraged them to visit his daughter often, by telling them that a bottle of the best wine was always at their service. Victor's French talk, frivolous though it was, seemed to please Lisa, and she quietly made the observation to herself, that such fine discourse was a thousand times more delightful than the ordinary every-day conversation of the peasants.

At this point, a young man opened the back-door, and entered the room, accompanied by Kobè.

"A glass of beer, Kobè, and draw one for yourself at the same time," he said with a manly voice.

He was a vigorous youth, and wore a smock-frock of fine blue linen, a silken neckerchief, and a cap of otter's skin. His fine and well-formed face was deeply sun-burnt; his broad hands bore the marks of daily toil, while his large blue eyes, full of fire and life, gave the impression of one whose mind and heart were as richly endowed as his body.

At his entrance, Lisa stood up and smiled to him such a kind and friendly welcome, that two of the hunters looked at him with surprise; the third, Adolph, knew him of old. Mine host muttered some grumbling words, and put on a sour expression as if Charles the brewer's presence was particularly disagreeable to him at the present time; he even stamped his foot irritably, and made no effort to conceal his vexation.

The young man affected not to observe anything unusual, but kept his eyes fixed on Lisa's, as if he would ask her something; she smiled to him still more kindly and openly than before; and now, for the first time since the strangers had entered, her face assumed an expression of freedom and satisfaction.

"Father!" said Lisa.

"That boor's word again!" cried Baas.

"Papa," resumed Lisa, correcting herself, "Papa, is Charles not to drink a glass of wine with us?"

"He may get a wine-glass out of the cupboard himself," was the rude reply.

"Thank you, mine host Gansendonck," said Charles with a bitter smile. "I do not like wine in the morning."

"No, I daresay not; drink your beloved beer! That is the way to get thick brains," said Baas jestingly, and smiling complacently like one who thought he had said a good thing.

Charles was accustomed to Gansendonck's coarse way of talking, and so thought no more of it now than on any other occasion. He was about to sit down by the fire opposite Kobè, but Lisa called out—"Charles, here is a chair! come and sit beside me, and chat a little with us!"

Peer Gansendonck looked at his daughter with an irritated countenance, and bit his lips with impatience. This did not prevent Charles accepting Lisa's friendly invitation, however, although he perceived very clearly the insulting and contemptuous conduct of her father.

"You will have capital sport this year, gentlemen," he said in the Flemish tongue, sitting down beside Adolph; "there is abundance of hares and partridges."

"So I believe," replied Adolph, "but we have not succeeded in shooting anything this morning; the dogs have no nose to-day."

"I thought so," said mine host, in a mocking tone. "I thought he would put a clog on the wheels with his everlasting Flemish! Now, you will hear of nothing but dogs, cows, horses, and potatoes. Just let him talk away, Herr von Bruinkasteel, and do you go on speaking French with our Lisa. I have such pleasure in hearing it—I cannot tell you how much pleasure."

Charles smiled and turned his eyes towards Victor with a free and manly look. The latter seemed all at once deprived of his light smooth talk, and showed evident signs of disinclination to continue his flattering conversation with Lisa in the presence of Charles. An interval of painful silence followed. With a kind of despair, mine host saw that Herr von Bruinkasteel felt annoyed. He cast a reproachful look at Charles and said—

"Herr Victor, do not mind him; it is only our brewer, and an acquaintance of our family; but he has nothing to say here, though he fancies he has drawn Number One. Go on, Herr von Bruinkasteel! I should like my daughter to be on good terms with you, and smile and enjoy herself, if you will have the goodness to speak with her. If the brewer means to make wry faces at it, he may go out and do it on the street."

Encouraged by these words, and perhaps with the intention of annoying the young brewer, Victor turned to Lisa, and, while talking, looked at her with that tender glance which some men allow themselves in fashionable society, when they have not the highest opinion of a lady's honour. Charles grew pale, trembled, and ground his teeth violently; and though he immediately restrained this expression of sorrow and anger, it did not escape notice. Victor was alarmed when he saw it. He was not afraid, but notwithstanding it made so deep an impression on his mind, that pleasantry and merriment

lost all their zest. Mine host, on the contrary, was more
furious than ever, and stamped his feet, at the same time
muttering to himself. Lisa, again, who thought that it was
her father's harsh words only, which had pained the young
man, looked to the ground, and was on the point of bursting
into tears. Charles sat calmly on his chair, somewhat pale
and trembling, it is true, but in outward appearance sufficiently composed.

Suddenly Victor rose, and, taking his rifle, said to his companions—

"Come, let us continue our sport.—Miss Lisa, I hope, will
pardon me if I have unwittingly said anything which was disagreeable to her."

"What! what!" cried her father; "everything which
you have said has been beautiful, and could not have been
better; and I hope, sir, that she has not seen and heard you
for the last time."

"Miss Lisa perhaps thinks otherwise; though my intention
has been to show her all respect and kindness."

When he saw that his daughter made no reply, mine host
continued with some irritation—

"How now, what does this stupid boor's-play mean? Lisa,
why do you sit there like a 'Kate touch me not?' Answer the
gentleman, and quickly too!"

Lisa rose, and said in Flemish, and in a cold but polite
tone—

"Herr von Bruinkasteel, you will not take it ill if I have
been a little absent. Your conversation has been very agreeable to me, and if you should again do us the honour to visit
our house, you shall always be welcome."

"That's right! that's right!" cried Baas, striking his
hands together. "Ah! Herr von Bruinkasteel, she is a jewel
of a girl. You do not know her yet; she can sing like a

nightingale. Will you not take your seat again? I shall
fetch another bottle."

"No; we must away; the day is passing. We thank
you for your kind reception."

"I shall go a bit of the way with you, if the gentlemen
have no objection," said Baas. "I have a little plantation
off the highway which I wish to look at. 'The master's eye
makes the horse fat,' says the proverb."

The young gentlemen all declared that Herr von Gansendonck's society would give them the greatest pleasure. They
then left the house together, talking in the politest way im-
aginable, with Kobè at their heels.

So soon as the young people found themselves alone, Lisa
said in a kindly way—"Charles, you must not vex yourself
on account of the coarse way my father talks; you know he
does not mean anything by it."

The young man shook his head, and replied—

"It is not that, Lisa, which pains me."

"What, then?" asked the maiden with surprise.

"I feel it difficult to explain to you what I mean, Lisa.
Your pure unspotted soul would not understand it. It is
better to say nothing about it."

"No, Charles; you must let me know what you mean."

"Well then, the truth is, I do not like to see young gal-
lants come out of the city to make a display of their flat unmeaning compliments and phrases before you. Something
improper may easily arise from all this; and in any case,
their fine French manners and tender glances of the eye show
that they do not approach you with that respect which is due
to a lady."

Impatience, and perhaps a slight irritation, were depicted
on the young girl's face.

"You are wrong, Charles," she said; "the gentlemen have

said nothing improper to me. On the contrary, when I listen to their conversation, I learn how one must talk and act, if one would not pass for a mere peasant girl."

At this, Charles hung his head in silence, and sighed anxiously—"Yes, I know it," continued Lisa; "you hate city men and city manners; but whatever you may think about these things, it is not my part surely to act unkindly towards the gentlemen who visit my father. You are very wrong, too, Charles, in wishing to make me hate people who deserve esteem more than any others."

The young girl had spoken these words with considerable irritability. Charles sat in silence, and looked into her eyes with a strange expression. Lisa felt that he was not a little distressed, though she could not understand how it should happen that what she had said could annoy him so much. She took his hand affectionately, and continued—

"But, Charles, I do not understand you; what, then, am I to do? If you were in my place, how would you act when strange gentlemen came and spoke with you?"

"Feeling can alone determine that, Lisa," replied he, shaking his head. "I do not know what to advise you; but if, for example, they were such manufacturers of compliments and pretty things as the visitors who have just left, I should answer them, it is true, politely, but I would not permit three of them to plant themselves round me, and blow their empty phrases into my ears."

"But then my father, who compels me to do it?" said Lisa perplexed.

"One finds a hundred reasons for standing up, if one *will* not sit still."

"Then I have not acted properly in your eyes?" said the poor girl, sobbing and shedding tears. "I have not conducted myself rightly?"

The youth drew his chair nearer to Lisa, and answered in a supplicating tone—

"Lisa, forgive me. You must be indulgent to me; it is not my fault that I love you so much. My heart quite overpowers me; I have no command over it. You are fair and unspotted as a lily: I tremble at the thought of a word of double meaning being uttered in your presence—of a breath of impurity touching you. I love you with a deep and anxious reverence: is it then surprising that the forward looks of these young fellows should alarm me? Oh, Lisa, you think that my feeling towards them is blameworthy. Perhaps it is so; but oh, my best friend, could you but know what agony shoots through my soul when I see their light conduct, and what sorrow it prepares for me, you would have compassion on my too great love. You would forgive these fears, and console me in my anxiety."

These words, which he uttered in a low tone, had a deep effect on the girl. She replied kindly, with tears in her eyes—

"Ah, Charles, I do not know what kind of fears you may have; but let them be what they will, since it vexes you, this shall not occur again. In future, when gentlemen come, I shall rise and go into another room."

"No, no, Lisa, I do not mean that," said Charles, half ashamed of the consequences of what he had said. "Be polite and friendly with every one, as is becoming, as well as with the gentlemen who have just left. You have not rightly understood me, dearest. Act as before; but think that certain things pain me; do not forget, when placed in these circumstances with visitors, that your father is sometimes deceived, and is regulated by the estimate you put on yourself, in telling you what you should do. I know the purity of your heart, Lisa; it is all the same to me who comes heie, but I wish that you should always be treated respectfully; the smallest slight—the very appearance of disrespect—pains me most deeply."

"But, Charles, you have heard that Herr Adolph and his friends will be often here; I must listen to their conversation if I stay in the room. Will you be offended and annoyed every time *that* occurs?"

Charles blushed, and immediately reproached himself for the remarks which he had permitted himself to make; while at the same time he admired the simplicity and goodness of heart of his betrothed. Taking her hand, he replied, with a smile—

"Lisa, I am a fool. Will you grant me a favour?"

"Certainly, Charles."

"Well, then, in sober earnestness, will you forgive this humour of mine? In fact, it would annoy me now, were you to alter your conduct in the least. Why should I even desire it, when your father is master here, and would constrain you to act as he wished, whether it was agreeable to you or not?"

"Now, you are good, Charles," replied Lisa. "I must still continue to be friendly with these strangers—is it not so? My father is master here. Besides, you are in the wrong in the other way too. Herr von Bruinkasteel talked with me for a long time, to be sure, but all he said was very proper; and I know, for my own part, that I listened to him with great pleasure."

Charles again felt a weight upon his heart; but he repressed the rising feeling, and answered—

"Let us forget, dearest, what has happened. I bring you good news. My mother has at last consented to enlarge our house considerably; the alterations will begin next Monday. You shall have a fine room for your own use, handsomely furnished. Our house shall have an entrance of its own:

and a coach-house for a little carriage. So, Lisa, you will not have to go through the brewery, or sit at the common fire. You will lead a quiet and peaceful life, and get everything your heart can wish. Does that not give you pleasure, dearest?"

"You are too good, Charles, and I am thankful in my heart for so much love and friendship; but I believe father has something better to propose to you, which will probably please you too. He is very desirous that we should rent the farm-house which stands empty behind the castle. The thought appears to me not a bad one. Then we should have no occasion to mix with the peasant people, and could gradually make the acquaintance of respectable families."

"But, Lisa," interrupted the young man, rather impatiently; "how is it possible that you can think of such a thing? *I* leave my mother! She is a widow, and has no one in the world except me. And even were it not so, I would not do it; from childhood upwards I have worked, and I must continue to do so, for my own pleasure and health, for my mother's welfare—for you, Lisa, to make your life easier and happier; and that I may have the feeling that the fruits of my labour are contributing to your happiness."

"Oh, that is not necessary," sighed Lisa; "our parents already possess sufficient money and property."

"And then, Lisa, we stand now in the foremost place among those of our own station. Your father is one of the largest proprietors in the whole district, and our brewery stands second to none. Shall I, then, consent to act the upstart purse-proud millionnaire—humble myself to procure the friendship of proud people, and allow myself to despise my former companions, like one who would fain play the fine gentleman? No, Lisa, that might flatter many a one's self-love—it would make *me* feel mean and miserable. It is better to be respected and loved by peasants, than have people of rank look askance and laugh at you."

Lisa was about to reply to Charles's warm speech, but just at that moment Kobè opened the door with visible haste, and advancing to the young man, said quickly—

"Charles, have you a desire to quarrel for a couple of hours with our respected landlord?—No? Well, then, make haste off, for he is furious at you. You must have trode on his toes most cruelly. If you do not go, he will turn the house upside down."

"O Charles!" said Lisa anxiously, pressing his hand, "go, till my father's anger is past. This afternoon he will have forgotten all about it."

The young brewer shook his head, and, with a troubled look, took leave of his betrothed, and hastened out of the house by the back-door.

Kobè followed, and said, as he parted from him—

"Fear nothing, Charles; I will keep an eye on the sails, and give you a hint if I see the vessel going out of the right track. There's a screw loose about our Baas. But do you keep your mind at ease—the humour will soon pass. The weathercock on the steeple turns with every breath of wind, like a fool; but for all that it shows what kind of weather we are going to have."

CHAPTER V.

"Honour is woman's glory;
Beauty but a tender flower."

Two months had passed. Early one morning three or four young peasants stood in the smithy and chatted of various things. Sus held a piece of iron in the fire with one hand, and worked the bellows with the other, slowly enjoying his pipe the while.

"Well, who has heard the news?" cried one of the young men. "Lisa Gansendonck is going to marry a Baron."

"O ho!" laughed the smith; "next year Easter falls on a Friday. Go and sell your wares at another market."

"Yes, but it is true; she is to marry the young fellow who has been staying these six weeks in the St. Sebastian."

"The ox will calve if all goes well," cried Sus.

"You do not believe it? Swaggering Jack himself told it to the notary."

"Then I believe it less than ever."

"Do you know what I think? Baas Gansendonck is brewing bitter beer for himself. Strange reports are already abroad about young Lisa. Folk speak of her as the Jews of pork."

"Swaggering Jack only gets what he deserves, and the light-headed girl too. 'He who plays with the cat must bide scratching,' says the proverb."

"And the unfortunate Charles!—he is a fool to be vexed

about it. I'd see her to the deuce first, with her fine Herr Baron."

"There comes Charles himself," said one of the peasants who stood at the door. "Even at this distance, one can easily see that he is out of spirits. He hangs his head on his breast as if he were searching for a needle. He looks as if he had already ordered his coffin."

All turned their heads and looked towards Charles, who was coming along slowly and carelessly, with downcast eyes and dreamy look.

Sus brought his hammer down upon the anvil with a tremendous blow, and muttered to himself, as if some great vexation had suddenly had the effect of paralysing his voice.

"What is the matter with you?" asked the others.

"When I see Charles, my blood boils," cried Sus. "I would bind myself not to taste a drop of beer for a whole year, if I could just come down once on Swaggering Jack's back—so. Ah, the proud booby! He will bring his daughter into disgrace through his silly fancies—he knows that well enough; though indeed the light-minded girl deserves no better. But when I see him make my good friend Charles pine away with grief in this fashion, hunting him into the grave—a young fellow like a tree, well-to-do, clever, and good-hearted, worth more than a hundred such Swaggering Jacks and fashionable fops—it makes me almost mad. Why, you see, I wish no man harm; but if Gansendonck should break his neck accidentally some of these days, I should say it was well done, and a judgment of God!"

"Keep your mind at ease, Sus. Pride goes before a fall. If the ant gets wings, it soon dies."

"Don't be too free with your threats, Sus. Swaggering Jack has said that he will never rest till he has you in the lock-up.'

"Pah! I care no more for the boasting fool than if he were painted on the wall."

"But could you not persuade Charles to let her go for what she is worth?"

"Ah, *there* no medicine will work a cure; the more they treat him like a fool in the St. Sebastian, the more vexing it is. They make him believe there that the cat lays eggs; he is quite out of his senses, I think. There is no more spirit in him. If one speaks to him about it, the tears come into his eyes; he turns away, says good-bye, and you see no more of him till the next day."

"Can Kobè then not make his master understand, that if a crow will fly with swans' feathers, it is sure to fall and be drowned in the sea?"

"Why, Baas and his servant are of the same stamp; two wet sacks won't dry one another."

"Be quiet, Sus; here he is. I think he is coming to the smithy."

Charles advanced, and greeted the peasants with a forced smile. Without saying a word, he went to the working-bench, and kept turning the screw in a dreamy way, or carelessly taking up some tool, while the young peasants looked at him with curiosity and compassion.

In truth, a ceaseless suffering must have been gnawing at the young man's heart—so altered was he in a short time. His face was pale and ashy; his eyes wandered from object to object with a dull, lifeless expression, or stared in a fixed and peculiar manner at some trifling object; his cheeks were sunk and haggard. His whole appearance betokened indifference and negligence; his clothes were scarcely clean, and his hair fell uncombed upon his neck.

"Now, Charles," cried Sus, "here you come again like the sweet sunshine, without uttering a word. Come, come, throw

hateful thoughts over the hedge, and think that you are a
better man than those who are the cause of your grief. Make
the sign of the cross and have done with it, and then drink a
good draught of beer. Vex yourself as you may, you will not
drive sense into Swaggering Jack's pate. And of his dainty
daughter you will make nothing but a "—

Charles trembled, and his wild look made the word stick
in Sus's throat.

"Yes," he continued, "I know well that I must not open
the cask. Kill poor patients first, and then push the medicine after them into the grave. But it does not do to suffer
too long from foolish fancies. Do you know what Swaggering Jack has said? Ma'mselle Lisa is going to marry Herr
von Bruinkasteel before notary and priest."

"Rather him than me," said another. "He will have a
precious piece in her—a vagabond peasant girl, who sees no
other way of saving her virtue."

Charles had grasped the stock of the screw convulsively,
and directed a fierce look at the speakers.

"Lisa," he said with a hollow voice, "is innocent and
pure. You slander her, you speak unjustly."

After speaking these few words, he turned and slowly left
the smithy, without paying any attention to his friend Sus,
who had again addressed him. He went unsteadily across
the road, and struck into a footpath which led through the
fields. On the way he spoke aloud to himself, at one time
standing still and stamping his feet, at another hastening on
with increased speed; and so he dreamily wandered on, till
he found himself a considerable distance from the village,
and suddenly heard his name called at the corner of a fir-
wood. There he saw Kobè sitting on the stile, with a bottle
in one hand and a bit of meat in the other; a rifle lay near
him.

"Ha, Kobè!" cried the young man with pleasure; "what are *you* doing here?"

"A new whim of our respected landlord," he replied. "Whenever he can want me, he packs me off here to act as a kind of wood-bailiff. I sit here and take care that the trees don't fly away."

"Come a bit with me," said Charles.

"I have just finished my dinner," he replied, rising. "Look, Charles, that is a fine rifle. The cock is so rusty, that one could not pull it were he to yoke a horse to it; and the barrel has been loaded for twenty years and three months. Like master, like weapon."

"Come, Kobè," replied the brewer, "tell me something which may ease my mind a little. How goes it at home?"

"I don't know on what side I shall attack the rotten apple. In that quarter everything goes wrong. Mine host does not know what to do for joy: he dreams aloud of barons and castles. He is at the notary's thrice a day."

"Why, what does that mean?" asked Charles, alarmed.

"He says Lisa is to be married in a short time to Herr von Bruinkasteel."

The brewer grew pale, and looked sadly and anxiously at his companion.

"So he says," continued Kobè. "But the young Baron knows nothing about it, and thinks of everything but that."

"And Lisa?"

"Nor Lisa either."

"Ah!" sighed Charles, as if a load had fallen from his heart. "This matter pains me deeply."

"Were I you, I would see into the matter at once: let weeds grow too long, and they will eat up the finest corn. You never come to the St. Sebastian but when Herr von Bruinkasteel is gone out; and there you sit for half a day, bemoaning yourself in a way that would draw pity from a stone. Lisa inquires into the cause of your distress, and you make her understand that you are ill, and she believes you."

"But, Kobè, what can I do? When I give the slightest hint of the truth, she at once bursts into tears. She does not understand me."

"Woman's tears are cheap; I would not place much importance on them. If the calf is drowned, 'tis of no use emptying the well. A dog makes short work of a sausage."

"What do you mean by that?" muttered Charles with alarm. "Do you suspect Lisa? Do you fear that she"—

"If I knew that a hair of my head thought any evil of Lisa, I would tear it out. The poor thing fancies that all this fooling and French talking are fine manners. And if at any time, out of love for you, she dismisses the Baron rather coldly, then down comes mine host upon her and compels her to treat him kindly. Herr von Bruinkasteel must surely be an excellent man! Mine host throws Lisa into his arms ten times a week!"

"What! into his arms?" cried Charles fiercely.

"That is only a mode of speech," continued Kobè; "if you do not understand me, so much the better."

"What shall I do?" cried Charles, stamping his feet in despair.

"It does not lie concealed under the earth, Charles. Were it my affair, I should go boldly through with the matter; better a window broken than the house destroyed."

"What do you mean, for Heaven's sake? Speak more clearly."

"Why,—quarrel with Herr Victor. If there were to be a regular commotion, it would at least bring about a change; and the bad generally becomes better when it changes."

"If he would only give me an opportunity," cried Charles; "but everything he says is so cunningly calculated, that I cannot take hold of it and chastise him, even if I were bursting with revenge."

"Come, come, he who wishes to find, need not seek long. Tread on his foot unintentionally; his shoes, you know, are none of the thickest. That will set the game agoing."

"Ah, Kobè, what would Lisa say to that? Shall I damage her reputation by an act from which one would infer that I suspected something amiss?"

"You dear innocent! and do you think Lisa is not already in the people's mouths? The most dreadful things are said of her daily. The whole thing hangs on the church bell-rope, and everybody hangs something on that."

"By Heaven! she is innocent, and yet every one accuses her of acting badly!"

"Charles, Charles, you have no more blood in your heart! You see the evil growing daily, and bow your head to it like a feeble child. You see everything combining to bring your innocent bride to ruin—Victor's seducing conversation, her father's insane pride, and her own liking for everything that smacks of city life. Nobody can rescue her but you; and you are like a guardian angel who sleeps while the devil is laying a trap for the soul. By your timid compliance you expose Lisa helpless and unaided to this threatening danger. If she unhappily stumbles, who is to blame? Heaven helps those who help themselves; have some spirit, act, be a man! Says not the proverb, 'While they look about to find the way, the wolf carries off the lamb'?"

After a pause Charles replied—

"Alas, alas! everything alarms me. What can I do? The moment Lisa looks at me, my courage is all gone. Kobè, my heart is sick; I must bear with patience my bitter lot."

"Defend her at least from the slander and insult of the Baron."

"Insult! Has he insulted her?"

"Do you know what Herr von Bruinkasteel jestingly said to his comrades the day before yesterday? Adolph's gamekeeper was present at the time."

He approached the brewer, and whispered some words in his ear.

"You lie! you lie!" cried Charles, throwing his companion from him. "He did not say that."

"As you please, Charles," grumbled Kobè; "it is all the same to me. I lie, and the gamekeeper lies; it is not true, it cannot be. Herr von Bruinkasteel loves Lisa far too much to say anything of the kind!"

Charles had grasped a fir-stem for support; his breast heaved violently, he breathed hoarsely, and his eyes sparkled with a singular glow under his knitted eyebrows. What Kobè had whispered to him must have inflicted a deep wound, for he stood there trembling like a reed, and furious as a roused lion. Suddenly he closed his fist, and approaching his companion like a man insane, said—

"Ha! Is it a murder you would have me commit, devil?"

Kobè retired a few paces in terror, and stammered out—

"Charles, is it in jest or earnest that you put on a face like famine? I have done you no harm. If you would prefer to see my back, you have only to say so; with a 'good-day' everything is over, and each goes his own way."

"Stay where you are!" exclaimed the brewer.

"Then open your hands," replied Kobè. "I don't like to see closed fists."

Charles looked to the earth again, and stood for a long time motionless, without looking at his companion. At last he raised his head, and asked with a tremulous voice—

"Kobè, is Victor von Bruinkasteel at present in the St. Sebastian?"

"Yes—but," cried he anxiously, "you are not to go there, Charles; I will not permit you, were I to wrestle with you till every bone in my body was broken. I do not understand you; you are, as the proverb says, now too wise and now too stupid, but always queer and crooked. You would do fine things at the St. Sebastian just now! You are like a mad bull."

Without paying any attention to Kobè's remarks, Charles turned round and struck hastily into a path which led towards Baas Gansendonck's dwelling. Kobè threw down his rifle, and springing forward, planted himself in front of him, and held him back by main force.

"Let me go!" said Charles, while he looked at Kobè with a bitter laugh; "you shall not hinder me. Why will you compel me to do you harm?"

The coldness with which he said these words astonished Kobè not a little; he did not let him free, however, but asked him—

"Will you promise me to be patient, and to keep your hands in your pockets?"

"I mean to do harm to nobody," said the young brewer.

"What is your intention, then?"

"To follow your advice, Kobè; call them to account about everything, and speak out openly what lies so heavily on my heart. Fear nothing, Kobè; I do not forget that I have a mother."

"Aha! your senses are restored, I see. You could give a lecture to the weathercock on the church-tower now! You do not dissemble, do you? Well, then, I shall go with you. Be cool and firm, Charles; bold speech is half the battle. Make some stir, show your teeth, and read gospel truth to

mine host for once in his life; he is not likely to take a fever
from excess of courage, I assure you. Heaven knows, if you
take the proper way with him, whether he may not request
the Baron to pass by his door henceforth! After pain comes
pleasure! I think I see the fiddler sitting on the roof already."

Both of them went along the path with measured steps.
By the way, Kobè opened up a consoling prospect to the
young man, and encouraged him gently, at the same time
counselling him to be collected and determined, and not to
heed Lisa's tears this time, till he had quite attained the object
he had in view. As they approached the St. Sebastian, he left
his melancholy companion with the remark, that it was still
too early for him to return home—he must still play the wood-
bailiff for an hour. Charles pressed his hand gratefully, and
promised to follow his advice.

So soon as the young man found himself alone, he felt
as if a bandage were taken from his eyes; he saw clearly
how matters stood, and what he ought to do. He resolved
to demand from Baas Gansendonck an explanation of his
conduct, and to convince him—whether he took it well or ill
—that his folly not only damaged Lisa's good name, but even
seriously endangered her honour. As he approached the
house, the young man's countenance expressed calmness and
determination.

So soon as he had reached the back-door of the St. Sebastian, however, this resolution was suddenly altered. For
within, the seductive voice of the Baron was heard singing a
French romance, whose tone and music breathed love and
tenderness.

When Charles heard the song, he stood trembling, and
listened with feverish attention to the words—

> "Pourquoi, tendre Elise, toujours vous défendre?
> A mes désirs daignes vous rendre."

The brewer's hands were violently convulsed; a fearful storm began to rage in his tortured soul.

> "Ayez moins de rigueur;
> Si mon amour vous touche,
> Qu'un mot de votre bouche
> Couronne mon ardeur."

Lisa's voice timidly mingled itself with the Baron's: she too sang the tender words.

The blood boiled impetuously in the youth's veins; his eyes sparkled, he gnashed his teeth, and as the closing verses of the romance fell from Lisa and the Baron, like a consuming fire upon his heart, his very hair stood on end—

> "Pitié! mon trouble est extrème—
> Ah! dites ' Je vous aime!'
> Je vous aime!"

"Bravo! bravo!" cried mine host, clapping his hands. "Ah, how beautiful!"

A heavy groan escaped from the young man's bosom, as he just at that moment entered the room. At his appearance, all sprang from their seats with alarm or surprise; Lisa uttered a shrill cry of pain, and imploringly held out her arms towards Charles; the Baron assumed a proud and inquiring look, while mine host stamped his feet with impatience, and muttered some insulting language.

For a time, Charles stood as if unconscious, his hand resting on a chair; he trembled so violently that his knees almost knocked together under the weight of his body; his countenance was as pale as death; his cheeks and brow seemed convulsed. His whole appearance must have been something frightful, for the Baron, courageous as he was, grew pale likewise, and retreated a few paces to get out of the reach of the raging brewer. Mine host alone treated the thing mockingly, and looked at Charles with a contemptuous laugh. Suddenly the young man threw a fierce look at the

Baron, full of hate and revenge. The latter felt himself insulted by it, and exclaimed haughtily—

" Well! what means all this child's-play here? Do you know who I am? I beg you to put an end to that insulting stare."

Furiously the brewer seized the chair, and was about to raise it to fell the Baron to the earth, when Lisa threw herself on his neck, screaming and weeping bitterly. She looked at him so imploringly and so affectionately, and called him by such sweet names, that he at once let the chair fall as if deprived of power, and said with a deep sigh—

" Oh, thanks, thanks, Lisa! You have saved me. Had it not been you, the deed would have been done."

The maiden still continued to hold both hands, and to calm and console him with words of affection; she perceived clearly, from his whole aspect, that wrath still blazed furiously in his heart, and exerted herself to allay his passion.

Meanwhile the Baron approached the door, and was about to leave the house, but mine host called out—

" How now, my lord, are you afraid of a mad boor? Stay where you are—my servants will turn him out of the house."

" I fear no mad boor in the whole world," replied the Baron, " but it does not become me to enter into a contest with a mad boor."

At these insulting words, Charles tore himself from his beloved, and hastened towards the door, to follow the Baron into the street; but mine host seized him, and exclaimed in a violent passion—

" Hold, fellow! you would insult both of us now! This lasts too long. What! you would hunt people out of my house, and play the landlord here! Throw chairs at the Herr Baron von Bruinkastee.! What prevents me sending for the police? Come, I will tell you things which it is unnecessary my daughter should hear; and so we shall bring matters to a conclusion once for all. If not, I shall show you who is master here."

A bitter smile played round Charles's lips as he followed mine host into another room. The latter bolted the door, and then, with a threatening look, stood silently before the brewer, who was evidently making great exertions to restrain his anger and be composed, as was necessary in this long desired conversation, if he would attain his end.

"Make as many faces as you please," said mine host; "I laugh at your absurd whims. Come, tell me quickly, who gives you permission to come to my house and act in this boorish way to everybody? But perhaps it is your intention to purchase my daughter?"

"Do not rouse me, for Heaven's sake! Just give me liberty to speak, and I will come to an explanation with you; and if you do not choose to understand me, I shall leave your house and never cross your threshold again."

"Well then, go on, for I am curious to hear what you have got to say; I know quite well what song you will sing; but I assure you, you will get nothing by it—you knock at a deaf man's door."

"My father once befriended you, and rescued you from ruin. You gave a promise to him when on his deathbed, that Lisa should be my wife. You have encouraged our love."

"Times change, and so do men."

"And now that you have inherited a bit of dirt—dirt, that is called gold, you will not only break your sacred word like an ingrate, but you stain the reputation of my betrothed. For the vain hope of a rank, which you can never attain, you sell her good name, drag her honour through the mire, and "—

"O ho! what tone is this to take? and to whom do you think you are speaking?"

"—and me you are killing with grief and despair. Not because you will rob me of Lisa; no! that you cannot do, for she loves me. But can a man suffer a greater agony of soul than to see his beloved, his bride, ruined before his eyes —to see her stained with all the frivolity and wantonness which a city breeds? To be compelled to lead her to the altar, clothed with the rent garment of a violated purity."

"Where have you picked up this stuff? To the devil with all that. I am master, and what I do is well done; do you imagine that you have a better head than Baas Gansendonck?"

"Oh! blind man! you compel your daughter to listen to the Baron's poisonous words. Every one of his flattering lies is another stain on her pure soul. You force her into destruction, and should she fall, ah! then, the father has dug the grave in which the honour of his child is to be buried. What do you expect? That she will marry Herr von Bruinkasteel? It is impossible. Even were there no father and relations to prevent him, he himself would reject a woman who was already dishonoured, in his eyes, by your indecent invitations and his own base designs."

"Go on," said Baas Gansendonck mockingly; "I did not know you had so many notes to your song. She is not to marry the Baron, say you? We shall see that. If you behave yourself well in the interval, you may come to the wedding. Drive love out of your head, Charles; that is the best thing you can do; otherwise, you may choke with it! Stay away from our house in a friendly way—for you see the Baron is here almost all day long, and you only run between his legs. He is not the man to have anything to do with peasants."

"Then my mortal agony has no power over you? He is to come here as formerly, to flatter her, to betray her with shameful words, to sing of wantonness and passion, and fill my Lisa's heart with a poison which will infect her whole nature?"

"Poison! what kind of language is this? Because you, forsooth, cannot rival him! That is the way boors always speak of city people; they burst with envy when they see any one who has good manners and is accomplished. But ease your heart, my good friend—go on, but it will do you no good. The Baron shall visit here as formerly, and Lisa shall become a fine lady. And if you were to split your head in two about it, it will be of no more assistance to you than a fly in your brewing-vat. I have a right to do what I please with my house and daughter, and no one has a right to intrude—you as little as another."

"The right!" cried Charles with a bitter laugh. "The right to ruin your child's honour! To expose her, pure and innocent as she is, to the defamation of every tongue! To make her the object of universal contempt and universal mockery, as the wanton paramour of a dissolute young man! No, you have not the right. Lisa is mine. If her father will force her down into the mire of shame, I will rescue her triumphantly. I had forgotten my duty—but now I see it. Your Baron shall never return. Lisa shall be cared for against your will. No, I respect your unhappy ambition no more."

"Is that all you have got to say?" asked Baas with the greatest indifference. "Then I just inform you, that I forbid you my house; and if you venture to come here again, I will get you turned out of doors by my servants and the police."

"An inn is open to every man."

"There are rooms enough in my house where the Baron can speak with my daughter"

Exhausted and dejected, the young man sank into a chair, let his head sink on his breast, and remained speechless with his eyes fixed on the ground.

"Come, come," said mine host, "hold up your head. Your grief will soon be healed. Go home and keep away from the St. Sebastian, without troubling yourself more about Lisa. On that condition we shall still be good friends. I will forget your pride and your strange humours. Good sense, though long of coming, is still wisdom. Well, are you going?"

Charles rose. His countenance had undergone a complete change. The excitement, in which he had been, had disappeared; the feverish impulse to do something had exhausted itself. The fruitlessness of his expostulations and defiances had robbed him of all courage. With folded hands and an imploring look, he approached Baas, and with tears in his eyes, said—

"O Gansendonck! have compassion on me and on Lisa! Be assured, I must die. By the memory of my father, I conjure you to open your eyes, and give me your daughter to wife before her reputation is quite blasted. I will make her happy, love her, care for her, and work for her like a slave. I will love and honour you like a son, and obey you like a hired servant."

When mine host saw Charles humble himself before him, he felt some compassion for him, and replied—

"Charles, I will not say that you are not a good young man, and that my Lisa would not have a good husband in you."

"Oh, Baas! for God's sake," entreated the young man, looking into his eyes full of hope; "for God's sake, pity me, and give me Lisa! I will fulfil your smallest wishes with childlike submission—sell the brewery, dwell in a fine house, even abjure the rank of peasant, and alter my whole way of life."

"It cannot be, dear Charles; it is too late."

"And if you were to know assuredly that it would be my death, what then?"

"I should be very sorry to hear it; but I cannot force you to remain in life."

"Oh, Gansendonck!" cried the youth, falling on his knees and stretching out his arms, "give me some hope—do not, do not kill me."

Mine host raised him, and said—"Have you lost your senses, Charles? I can do no more. Think for a moment how matters stand. To-morrow we dine at the hunting-box with the Baron. He gives a feast in honour of Lisa."

"She! she! my Lisa, at the hunting-box with the Baron? Oh, you will ruin her honour for ever, irretrievably. There is not a single lady in his house."

"She is to become acquainted with the hunting-château of her future husband."

"So, then, all hope has vanished. For her, dishonour—for me, the grave!" cried the brewer in despair, while he covered his eyes with both hands, and a flood of tears rolled down his face.

"I pity you, Charles," said Baas, coldly; "Lisa is about to become 'my lady!' It is written above, and it shall be accomplished."

He took the sorrowing Charles gently by the shoulder, and pushed him towards the door, saying—

"Come, this has lasted long enough, and no good comes of it. Go home; and never speak with Lisa again."

Charles let himself be taken out without uttering a word, and as if all strength had left his body. He let his head sink upon his breast, and his tears fell upon the ground. Passing through the room where Lisa sat, he paused for a moment and gave one last look—an eternal farewell.

The maiden, who for a long time had listened with intense anxiety to the unintelligible sounds which had proceeded from the adjoining room, was waiting with fearful anticipation and alarm till the door should open.

Her betrothed now appeared before her, weeping and silent, like a patient sacrifice which was being led to the altar. She uttered a loud shriek, and, running to the young man, threw her arms round his neck, forcibly tearing him from the door. Charles looked at her kindly, but with such a strange and troubled smile, that the expression of his countenance forced from her another cry of agony.

With threatening words Baas Gansendonck tore his daughter's arms from Charles's neck, and showing the young man out of the house, shut the door behind him.

CHAPTER VL

"The self-conceited fool is a laughing-stock to all."

MINE host Gansendonck ran up and down his room like a
fool; set the mirror down before him, that he might be able
to see his legs, and went now backwards, now forwards, lost
in self-admiration. He was in his shirt sleeves, and had a
new pair of trousers on, adorned with stripes. On a chair by
the wall lay a pair of yellow gloves, a white waistcoat, and a
shirt front with lace frills. Kobè stood in the middle of the
room, and had a folded neckcloth over his arm. He looked at
Baas calmly; only, from time to time, an almost inexplicable
smile of mingled pity and restlessness played round his mouth.

"Now, Kobè," said mine host with delight, "what do you
think? Don't they fit admirably?"

"I don't understand these matters," said Kobè, rather
annoyed.

"Why, you can see surely whether I look well or ill?"

"I would rather see you without straps to your trousers
than with legs as stiff as broomsticks."

Gansendonck heard this bold remark with considerable surprise; and, looking fiercely at his servant, exclaimed—

"What do you mean by that? Do *you* begin to show your
horns? Do you think that I pay and feed you to say disagreeable things? Come, let me hear. Do they fit me well or
not?"

"Yes, Baas."

"What? 'Yes, Baas!'" screamed Gansendonck, stamping his feet. "I ask you whether they fit me well or not?"

"They could not fit you better, Baas."

"You are a thickhead! Do you wish your reckoning made up, and yourself packed off to seek another service? Or are you not well enough off here, you scoundrel? You wish perhaps better bread than home-made? So it is that a man leaves clover for weeds; but there is truth in the proverb, when it says, 'Give an ass oats, and he leaves them for thistles.'"

Kobè said imploringly, with a hypocritical or genuine anxiety, it would be hard to say which—

"Ah, Baas! I have the colic, and don't know what I say. You must pardon me. Your trousers fit so admirably, that one would think they were painted on your legs."

"Oh, so you have the colic?" said mine host, sympathizingly. "Open the little cupboard yonder, and take a little wormwood brandy. What is bitter in the mouth does the heart good."

"Oh, Baas; you are so good, Baas!" said Kobè, going to the cupboard.

"Give me my neckerchief now; but carefully, so as not to crease it."

While he proceeded slowly with his dressing, he said, half musingly—

"Ah, Kobè, how the boors will gape when they see me pass with a white waistcoat, lace ruffles, and yellow gloves! Heaven knows, they have never seen such a thing in their lives before. I very slily asked Herr von Bruinkasteel how fine gentlemen dressed when invited to dinner, and within four days I had procured a supply of what I wanted. One can do more than conjure with money—one can work miracles with gold. And Lisa, too, will attract the people's eyes quite as much, with six flounces on her silk dress."

"Six, Baas! why, my lady at the castle never wears more than five, even on a Sunday."

"If Lisa would do what I wish, she would wear ten. He who has may use, and he who can pay may buy. You should see her, were it only for once, appear before the peasants as 'my lady' ought, Kobè, with a satin hat adorned with flowers, like those that blossom at the castle in winter."

"Camellias, Baas?"

"Yes, camellias. Just conceive, Kobè; they had ornamented her hat with imitations of corn and buckwheat! But I quickly ordered the peasant-emblems to be torn off. Give me my waistcoat; but do not let your hands come too near it."

"That is an art I have not learned, Baas."

"Blockhead! I mean, take it up with your handkerchief."

"Very well, Baas."

"Tell me, Kobè, do you fully realize to yourself me sitting at the table in the château? Lisa between me and the Baron. Do you hear what pretty compliments we pay to each other, and what fine things we say? And then drinking all sorts of foreign wine, and eating game prepared with sauces, whose very names the devil himself could not remember; in golden dishes, too, with silver spoons!"

"Oh, Baas, say no more, if you will be so good! I feel as hungry as a dog with the very thought of it all."

"And you have good reason too, Kobè. But I do not wish to be happy while others are not. There is still half a hare which was left yesterday—you can feast upon that; and take two glasses of ale in addition."

"You are very kind, Baas."

"And in the afternoon, you may come to the hunting-box to see if I have any orders for you."

" Very good, sir."

" Tell me, Kobè, is Lisa dressed?"

" I don't know. When I fetched fresh water, not long ago, she was still sitting at the table."

" What clothes had she on?"

" Her ordinary Sunday clothes, I think."

" Did she tell you that I showed the brewer to the door yesterday?"

" I saw that she was very desponding, Baas. But I never inquire into matters which do not concern me. He is a fool who burns his finger in another man's pot."

" You are right there, Kobè; but I am master, and may tell you all about it, if it pleases me to do so. Could you believe it? she has still so great a love for that mad Charles as to refuse to go to dine at the hunting-box, because she saw the milksop shed tears as he went out of the house. I have had to talk with her the whole night to overcome her obstinacy."

" Has she at last consented to go, then?"

" What! she has no right to say yes or no in the matter—I am master here."

" True, Baas."

" Why, what do you think? she has had the impudence to say she will not marry the Baron."

" So!"

" Yes; and that she will remain unmarried all her life, if she cannot get that awkward Charles for a husband. She would look very fine sitting there in the dirty brewery, beside the kitchen pot, with a spinning-wheel before her! And if she wished to go to town at any time, she could mount the beer-cart, eh, Kobè?"

" Yes, Baas."

" Come, give me my gloves, I am ready. But now to see after Lisa: perhaps she has still some fancies that require to be driven out of her. Yesterday evening, at any rate, she refused to have anything to do with the six flounces which were attached to her new dress. Like it or not like it, she shall clothe herself as I think best."

Lisa was sitting at the window of the front room. There was a sad and anxious expression on her pale face; she held a needle in one hand and a piece of embroidery in the other, but her thoughts evidently wandered far from her work, for she sat idle and motionless.

"What does this mean?" cried mine host, with no small annoyance. "Here am I, dressed from head to foot, while you sit there as if nothing were going on at all."

"I am ready, father," replied Lisa, in a tone at once kind and cold.

"There again; 'Father!' 'father!' Do you wish me to jump out of my skin?"

"I am ready, papa," she repeated.

"Stand up," said Baas Gansendonck, with a stern countenance. "What dress is that you have on?"

"My Sunday dress, papa."

"Go quickly, and put on your new clothes, and your hat with the flowers."

Lisa hung her head; but made no reply.

"How now, how long is this to last?" screamed Gansendonck. "Will you speak, or will you not?"

"Ah, papa!" entreated Lisa, "do not force me to put on such clothes. The dress and the hat do not suit our station. I have not courage to go through the village with them. You insist that I should accompany you to the château, though I have begged on my knees to be left at home. Well then, I consent to go, since it must be so; but, for Heaven's sake let me go in my usual Sunday clothes."

"With a peasant's hood on! and with only one flounce on

your dress !" said mine host Gansendonck, contemptuously.
"You will look very beautiful with such a dress, sitting at a
table with golden dishes and silver spoons! Come, come,
make no more words about it. On with your new dress and
your hat. I *will* have it so."

"You may do what you think proper, papa !" sighed Lisa,
hanging her head with a look of deep vexation. "You may
rail at me, punish me, but that new dress I will not put on—
that hat I will not wear."

From the corner of the fireplace, Kobè nodded his head
approvingly. Mine host turned sharply to his servant, and
said with fury in his face and voice—

"How now, what say you to a daughter who dares to
speak so to her father?"

"Possibly she is right, Baas."

"What do you say? you too? Have you plotted together
to make me burst with vexation? I will teach you manners,
you ungrateful scoundrel! To-morrow you pack off."

"But, my dear host, you don't understand me," replied
Kobè with an assumed fear. "I mean to say, Lisa might be
right—if she were not wrong."

"Ha! then be good enough to speak more plainly another
time."

"Yes, Baas."

"And you, Lisa, make haste! Whether it pleases you or
not, you *shall* obey me, even if I have to dress you by main
force."

The poor girl burst into tears, but this only annoyed her
father more—for he muttered passionately to himself, and
knocked the chairs about.

"Better still!" he cried. "Cry away there for an hour or
two, and then you will be a beautiful object, with a pair of
eyes as red as a white rabbit's! I will not permit you to

shed a tear, I tell you—for it is merely a trick to be allowed to stay at home."

Lisa said nothing, but wept on.

" Come," said Baas with impatience, " if it cannot be otherwise, dress yourself as you please ; but stop crying, I beseech you. For Heaven's sake, Lisa, make an end of it."

She rose and went down stairs without saying a word, to prepare for the visit.

She had scarcely left the room when Herr von Bruinkasteel entered, and said to Gansendonck—

" Why are you so long of coming, Herr von Gansendonck ? I was beginning to fear that something had occurred to prevent you. We have been expecting you this hour."

" It is Lisa's fault," replied mine host ; " I had ordered a new dress and satin hat for her ; I don't know what has put it into her head, but she refuses to put on any of her new clothes."

" She is quite right, my dear Herr von Gansendonck. She is pretty enough without them."

" Fine clothes won't make her look worse, my dear Herr Victor."

Lisa returned and greeted the Baron with a quiet friendliness. One could read her misery in her eyes ; and it could easily be seen that she had been weeping. She wore her ordinary silk dress, with the simple border, and had a clean and very fine lace hood over her head. She took her father's arm, purposely to avoid walking with the Baron ; but mine host took away his arm, and kept at a little distance from her, as if he would compel the Baron to offer his. Herr Victor affected not to perceive it. Perhaps he thought that it was unbecoming for him, as well as for her, to go arm in arm through the village. After some polite words, as to who should go first out, they left the house, mine host making a virtue of necessity and giving his arm to his daughter. On the way, he said sharply—

" Do you see now, you self-willed girl, that if you had put on your beautiful new dress and fine hat with the flowers, the Baron would have given you his arm ? Now he will not do it ; you are too poorly dressed—that is what comes of it all."

It was necessary to pass the brewery. There, behind the stable-wall, Lisa saw Charles standing. With folded arms and sunken head, he looked at her sorrowfully, but without manifesting either vexation or surprise. One could read in his countenance nothing but exhaustion, dejection, and calm despair. Lisa uttered an exclamation of surprise, and tearing herself from her father, ran to Charles, and took his hands tremblingly in hers, addressing to him a few confused but affectionate and consolatory words. Gansendonck hastily approached the two lovers, and looking fiercely at the brewer, dragged his daughter forward.

Silently and full of melancholy forebodings, Lisa went to the **hunting-box of Herr von Bruinkasteel.**

CHAPTER VII.

" Pride is the source of all evil."

LATE in the afternoon, Charles might be seen standing among some high copse, leaning his back on a birch-tree. There before him, on the other side of the ditch, lay the hunting-box of Herr von Bruinkasteel.

The young man had stood long in this solitary spot; he did not himself know how or why he had come there. As he sauntered carelessly through the fields, his soul full of horrible fancies, his heart had led him to this place, where he was to drain a cup of sorrow more bitter than any he had yet tasted. There he stood now, like an insensible statue, with his eyes fixed immovably on the Baron's dwelling; and the only sign of life which was visible, was from time to time a smile of despair, or a trembling of his limbs. His soul was on the rack, and his self-torturing imagination penetrated through the walls, on the other side of which he knew Lisa was sitting. He saw her by the Baron's side, and heard his expressions of love and his seductive flatteries; he caught him in the act of directing fond glances to his bride; and saw Baas Gansendonck frowning down his daughter's modesty, and then—the weak Lisa knew no longer what to do. She let the Baron take her hand, and did not resent with indignation those immodest glances of the shameless wanton, themselves sufficient to stain the purity of a virgin soul.

Poor Charles! inflicting a thousand wounds on his heart,

and compelling his over-excited fancy to revel in its own horrible pictures, that he might drain the cup of sorrow to the very dregs !

After he had given himself up for a long time to these terrible thoughts, he gradually became quite unconscious of out ward objects, and fell into a deep reverie. The mental tension from which he had been suffering was relaxed ; his face now had only the calm expression of weariness, and, with sunken head and half-shut eyes, he gazed intently on the ground.— Suddenly the distant tones of a harp struck his ear, accompanied with the almost inaudible sound of a man's voice. Unintelligible as the song was at such a distance, it had a powerful effect on the young man's soul. Trembling like a leaf, and vengeance depicted in every feature, he sprang up as if a snake had bitten him. His eyes shot fire, he ground his teeth, and convulsively clenched his fist. He knew the accursed song ; that morning already he had heard it like a voice from hell speaking to Lisa its wanton and shameless sentiment. Those debasing words which Lisa had sung with that traitorous noble, still burned agonizingly in his heart. In his despair, the young man broke the oak branches in pieces, and muttered horrible things. The tones of the song became clearer.—" *Je vous aime !*" resounded through the oak-trees ; and sung by the Baron with such fire, with such earnest feeling, that it was impossible that it could be directed to any one but Lisa. Quite beside himself, and scarcely knowing what he did, Charles ran through the ditch, and clambering up the other side, disappeared among the thick foliage of some hazel-bushes which lined a broad path. Carefully concealing himself, he crept like a wild beast through the bushes till he had reached a dark arbour. There were here two beech-trees at a short distance from each other, and their branches had been carefully intertwined, so as to form a deep shade overhead. Although the last rays of the sun were still falling on one side of the trees, and a few leaves here and there lay like gleaming points of light among the deep green of the rest, this retreat was dark and gloomy. The young man slipped across the avenue, and approached the house and the room in which the Baron and his guests were sitting. Three or four paces from a window of this room, stood several large shrubs, whose blossoms in summer must have filled the whole house with their delicious odours. In this place of concealment stood Charles, and saw from it into the room where the Baron's party was assembled.

How his heart beat and his blood boiled! He could observe everything and hear everything, for the calm air without and the gaiety within united to render everything audible.—It appeared as if one of the company was forcing Lisa to do something against her will. It was the Baron, who drew her with gentle force to the piano, while her father pushed her on without any consideration for her feelings, at the same time saying half-angrily—"Lisa! Lisa! your obstinacy will make me leap out of my skin yet. What you have done once to-day already, you can surely do again. The gentlemen beg you very kindly to sing that little song once more, and you are so disobliging as to refuse. You have no occasion to hide your voice, girl! it can afford to let itself be heard."

The Baron again entreated her; the father angrily commanded, and Lisa obeyed. She began to sing with the piano accompaniment, and along with the Baron—

> "Pitié! mon trouble est extrême—
> Ah! dites ' Je vous aime !'
> Je vous aime !"

—The branches of the shrubs moved restlessly, as if the wind had stirred them.—

Mine host Gansendonck almost lost his senses with exultation. His face beamed and grew red with self-complacency. He kept rubbing his hands, and spoke so freely, boldly, and so unceasingly, that a stranger would have taken him for the owner of the castle. Standing beside the piano, he nodded his head and kept wrong time with his heavy foot, calling out to his daughter in the pauses—

"Louder—quicker! Ah! that is good. Bravo!"

Adolph and his companions, and even Victor himself, made fun of him, but he did not perceive it. He considered their loud laughter, on the contrary, a sign of good feeling and friendliness on their part. Scarcely was the song finished when Adolph ran his fingers over the notes, and then began a quick waltz; and of so alluring a kind, that mine host, as soon as he heard it, felt a great desire to dance, and, in fact, had erected himself on his tiptoes, as if he meant to hop round the room.

"A dance! a dance!" he cried. "Our Lisa is a capital dancer. One would think she was actually gliding along the moment she raises her feet."

The poor girl, who had already been compelled to sing much against her will, began to move as far from the piano as possible, that she might escape her father's order this time. But he led her back into the middle of the room, and gave the Baron an inviting nod.

Briskly and joyfully he sprang forward, and throwing his arms round the girl, forcibly whirled her along five or six steps.

—From among the shrubs, there issued a deep groan, painful and horrible, like the last sigh of a dying lion; within, all were too much occupied to pay any attention to this voice of anger and sorrow.—

As Lisa resolutely refused to dance, and let herself be dragged along without making any effort herself, Herr Victor had to give it up. He begged pardon of the blushing girl with a profusion of fine phrases, and neither her visible annoyance nor her refusal seemed to make any impression upon him. The light-headed young man seemed to be merely amusing himself; to all appearance he saw in Lisa nothing but a pretty innocent young girl, with whom he could pleasantly pass the time. Had a deeper feeling attracted him towards her, one would have expected to see him hurt or annoyed by her coldness; but he seemed not to heed it in the least. With a slight bow, he offered Lisa his arm, which she dared not refuse, and then said to the others—"Come, let us have a walk in the garden till the lights are brought in! Do not take it ill, friends, that I act the cavalier to Miss Lisa."

All left the room and the house, and betook themselves to the shadiest parts of the garden. Many ways presented themselves to them. The Baron led Lisa towards a bed of dahlias, while Adolph and his companions immediately struck into another path. With terror and anxiety, the young girl saw her father likewise taking a different road. She threw an imploring look towards him, and would have left the Baron; but Baas Gansendonck ordered her, with assumed anger, to follow her companion, and then ran laughing to Adolph, as if he had done something very fine. Lisa trembled; her maiden conscience told her she was doing wrong in walking alone through solitary paths arm in arm with the Baron. Meanwhile, he said nothing unbecoming, and at the other end of the path she met her father again. Would it not be a coarse and awkward thing to let the Baron stand, and run away from him like an ill-bred peasant girl? With these thoughts, she accompanied the young man without resistance—giving him, however, nothing but monosyllabic and confused replies. Immediately after, they all disappeared down a deeply-shaded and winding path.

The unhappy Charles was in a fever of excitement, and suffered inexpressible torture. More than twenty times already had the revenge which burned so fiercely in his bosom

urged him to spring out of his hiding-place and strike down the
seducer; but then the image of his mother on her knees presented itself to him. And thus driven hither and thither—on
the one hand by his rising revenge, and on the other by the warn-
ing feeling of filial love—rage, grief, despair, and duty roused
a tempest of tumultuous feeling in his soul. Such a madness,
indeed, had taken possession of him, that his very breath felt
like a glowing flame upon his face. Suddenly he heard, only
a few paces from him, the Baron's insinuating voice, and saw
Lisa walking with hold of his arm with a calm and melancholy countenance. Both struck into the path that led towards the shrubbery, and then passed down the dark avenue.

When only a few paces from the spot where Charles stood
watching their movements with repressed breath and intense
anxiety, Lisa perceived the gloomy solitude which they were approaching. She requested the Baron to take her back to her
father; but he only held her all the more tightly by the arm,
and laughed at her fear to go with him through the avenue.
When she felt that he insisted on her accompanying him, she
trembled like a leaf, and grew pale with alarm. The nobleman, however, paid no attention to it; perhaps he believed it
was only affectation, and even began to drag her towards the
avenue with a mixture of jest and force, and partly succeeded
in his object.

"Father! father!" cried Lisa quickly with a piercing cry of
alarm. More quickly still, she uttered another and more
terrible cry; for before she could say a word, two powerful
hands were laid on the Baron's shoulder, and he was hurled
to the ground.

Raging, the Baron rose, tore a dahlia-pole from the ground,
and rushed upon Charles, who stood waiting his attack, his
breast heaving with revenge and fury. The Baron succeeded
in striking Charles such a blow upon the head, that the blood

ran down his face; and this was the signal for a violent struggle. Charles seized his enemy by the legs, lifted him into the air, and threw him to the ground like a stone. Notwithstanding this, the Baron offered a stout resistance to the young man, till the latter, lifting him in his arms, threw him a third time on the ground, and planting his knee on his breast, beat him violently about the face.

Lisa had stood for a moment screaming, till she saw the first drops of blood; she had then taken flight, and had fallen to the ground in a swoon a short distance off. Her cries for help, however, had fortunately been heard by the guests, and even by the servants, and had filled them with alarm. They all now arrived on the scene of combat from various directions, and tore the young man from the Baron's body. Adolph ordered the servants to arrest him, and five or six of them went up to him and took him by the arm, while he looked at his enemy whom he had handled so severely with a wild confused expression, and a half-unconscious smile.

Gansendonck, now tearing his hair wildly, thinking that his daughter had been murdered, hastened towards her.

Adolph and his friend assisted Herr von Bruinkasteel to rise. He was sadly disfigured in face and person; still he had strength enough left to express his indignation passionately, when he saw the brewer standing before him.

"Villain!" he cried, "I could have you beat to death by my servants; but the scaffold will avenge me on my assassin. Lock him up in the cellar; and you, Stephen, run for the gendarmes!"

The servants were about to drag the young man along, in order to execute their master's order; but so soon as he perceived their intention, he tore himself loose from them, knocked down one who tried to intercept his progress, and dashing through the water, vanished round a corner of the fir-wood.

CHAPTER VIII.

"Smooth water runs deep."

On the morning of the following day, Lisa Gansendonck sat behind the window-curtain in a side-room of the St. Sebastian. The excessive paleness of her face, and the flush upon her cheeks, showed that she was exhausted with weeping.

Wearied though Lisa was with anxiety and grief, her teatures yet indicated a restless excitement of mind, and her convulsive movements betrayed the secret tumult of her soul. It was as if some overpowering terror or agonizing expectation oppressed her heart, for now and then she looked anxiously through the window, and kept her eyes fixed on the road with visible fear, till some passer-by stood still and looked up at the house. Then although she could not be seen from without, she instinctively drew back her head, and a deep blush overspread her face. She looked down ashamed, as if she would fain flee from the accusing glances of the people; and then sat for a long time in the deepest silence, only again to approach the window and look into the street with a painful curiosity.

What was she expecting? She herself did not know; but her conscience gnawed like a worm at her heart. Charles's form hovered continually before her, and called loudly out to her that she was the guilty cause of all the agony which his too fond heart had endured. Her excited and terrified imagination seemed to hear all that the villagers said about her; and now, for the first time, she saw clearly that her reputation was gone, and that Charles would with good reason cast her from him for ever. Therefore it was that she trembled and blushed before the looks of the passers-by; for she saw in their faces that they spoke of the event of yesterday, and that mockery, contempt, and anger accompanied their remarks. Yes, she had even seen some peasants shake their fists threateningly at the house, as if they had sworn to take revenge for the disgrace which had been cast on the whole village by Gansendonck's daughter.

While Lisa sat in the side-room, drinking deep draughts of the cup of shame and remorse, Kobè crouched quietly and alone by the inn hearth. He held his pipe in his hand, but did not smoke. He appeared to be full of anxiety, and lost in deep reflection, and a very unusual expression was depicted on his face. One could read in it condemnation, sternness, and even indignation; his lips moved as if speaking, and his eyes sparkled with vexation and anger.

Suddenly he thought he heard Baas Gansendonck's voice. A smile of compassion played round his mouth for a moment, but as quickly disappeared, and gave place to his former anxious and troubled look.

So soon as mine host approached the back door of the house, Kobè heard him blustering and railing at some people who had evidently been abusing him, but could not make out who or what had put him in such a fury; and indeed it seemed all one to Kobè, for without disturbing himself, he sat by the hearth corner, calmly awaiting his master's entrance. In less than a minute mine host came tumbling rather than walking into the house, stamping his feet like a maniac, and striking the chairs right and left with his staff, as if they also had insulted him.

"This is going too far! yes, too far indeed!" he exclaimed.
"What! a man like me! What! they will dare even to
shake their fists at me in the open street! Call after me!
insult me! dare even to reproach me!—call me villain! ass!
Think of that, Kobè! Must they not be possessed by the
devil? The shameless boors actually ran after me out of the
smithy, shouting, 'A scandal! a scandal!' Had I not restrained myself, just because I did not wish to defile my hands
on the rabble, I would have broken two or three of their
heads. But Sus shall pay for all these lubberly scoundrels
at once. *I'll* teach him to throw mud at Baas Gansendonck!
We shall see if I can't make him laugh on the wrong side of
his mouth; if it were to cost half my wealth, I'll make him
pay terribly for this. I shall call in the gendarmes; and if
any one ventures even to make a face at me, I shall summon
the whole village to court. I have money enough to manage
that, thank Heaven; and Herr von Bruinkasteel, who is a
friend of the Attorney-general, will know how to give them a
few weeks in the lock-up. Then, perhaps, they will learn
manners, and find out whom they have to deal with, the
clowns! This thing must have an end. Since they have
insulted me so barefacedly, I will have no more pity, but let
them feel what Baas Gansendonck can do. Now that this has
once occurred, there's an end to everything like mercy!"

The raging Baas would apparently have raved on for a
long time in this abusive style, had not breath failed him.
Panting with his exertion, he threw himself on a chair, and
looked with surprise and irritation at the indifferent way in
which Kobè looked into the fire, as if he had heard nothing,
his face expressive only of annoyance.

"What do you mean by sitting idly and stupidly there,"
cried Baas, "like one who could not count three? An idle life is
the ruin of you, Kobè! I don't know how it is, but you are

growing as lazy and stupid as a pig. Now, this is not agreeable to me. My servant must have some spirit in him, and not remain as cold as ice when I am angry!"

Kobè looked at his master with an expression of sadness and pity.

"Ah, you have the colic again, have you?" cried Gansendonck. "It pains me very deeply to hear it. Do you think the St. Sebastian is an hospital? You *shall* not have the colic, I tell you; you must eat less, you glutton! How now, do you mean to speak or not?"

"I would speak with pleasure," replied Kobè, "if I did not know that, at the very first word, you would make me shut my mouth, and then break out as usual and sing a long litany."

"Ha! what way of talking is this? You had better say at once that I am a babbler; do not beat about the bush; everybody must now have a hit at Baas Gansendonck's back, it seems. You had better take up a stone and throw it at him who feeds you."

"There, you see!" said Kobè, with a smile of annoyance; "I have said only six words, and already you have mounted your high horse. I will avoid saying any harm of you, Baas; but you must grant that it would be an active spider that could spin a web across your mouth."

"I am master here, and may have all the talk to myself if I please."

"Indeed, Baas! then let me be silent, were it to choke me."

"Silent! no, that I will not. You *shall* speak. I am curious to see what good can possibly come out of such a blockhead."

"Smooth water runs deep, Baas."

"How now—explain; but do not speak too long; and bear in mind especially that I do not pay my servant to be instructed by him."

"There is a proverb, Baas, which says, 'The wise man goes to take counsel of the fool, and finds truth there.'"

"Now, then, let me hear what advice the fool can give to the wise man. If you will speak rationally, I will perhaps listen to you a little."

The servant turned his chair in front of his master, and said, with a free and bold bearing—

"Baas, during these two months, things have happened here which even a stupid servant cannot see without feeling his blood boil."

"I believe you; but it shall not last long, Kobè; the gendarmes are not paid to catch flies."

"As for me, Baas, I am a good-for-nothing idler, I confess; but my heart is good. I would do much to rescue our brave little Lisa out of misfortune, if I had the power; and I do not forget, Baas, that you, with all your pride, have been kind to me."

"That is true, Kobè," said Baas, a little moved. "I am glad to hear that you are grateful to me. But what is the particular object of all this seriousness?"

"Do not put the cart before the horse, Baas. I shall draw the painful thread soon enough."

"Make it short, or I shall run out of the house."

"Now, then, if you will but listen to me for a moment: Lisa has been long betrothed to Charles, who is a good young man, spite of this imprudent act."

"A good young man!" screamed Baas; "how can you call *him* a good young man, who, like an assassin, attacked Herr von Bruinkasteel in his own house?"

"The best horse will make a false step."

"So! you call that making a false step, do you? He is a good young man, is he? That word will cost you dear. There is an end to your living here; this very day pack off."

"As you please, Baas; my things are already packed," replied Kobè drily. "But before I go, you must hear what lies on my heart; you *must* hear it, were I to chase you into the fields, or the street, or even into your own bedroom. It is my duty, and the only thanks I can give you for your kindness. Your expelling me from the house does not surprise me in the least; truth finds harbour nowhere."

Mine host beat his feet impatiently on the ground; but he said nothing, for the earnest and self-possessed tone of his servant surprised and overpowered him.

"Our Lisa," continued Kobè, "would have been happy with Charles; but you, Baas, have brought the fox to your own geese—invited a frivolous young man into your house, and encouraged him to utter his pernicious sentiments in your daughter's ears, to talk to her of a feigned passion, and sing love-songs which run right in the face of all that is delicate and honourable."

"It is false," muttered Baas.

"It has been your wish that he should speak French with your daughter; and could you know what he said without understanding a word of the language?"

"And you, you thick-skulled booby, do you understand it so marvellously well as to dare to give your opinion so impudently?"

"I understood enough to perceive that the devils of wantonness and mockery were both at work. What has been the result of all your imprudence? The honour of your daughter stained—if not in fact, at least in the thoughts of the people —to such an extent that she can never again entirely regain her character. Charles, the only man who honestly loved her, and could have made her happy, dies of grief and despair; and his poor old mother is laid on a bed of sickness through sorrow for the sufferings of her only son. And you, Baas, you

are detested and despised by everybody; all say that you are
the guilty cause of Charles's death, your daughter's shame,
and your own misfortune."

"Yes, when one wishes the dog dead, it is easy to get up
the cry that he is mad; but what has all this to do with the
matter?" screamed Baas in his fury. "It has nothing to do
with it; I shall do what I please. And you, you shameless
scoundrel! will get what you deserve for putting your nose
into a business that does not concern you."

"It matters little to me whether my words please you or
not; they are the last which I shall speak in the St. Sebastian."

Baas Gansendonck, spite of his threats, was evidently excessively fond of his servant, and was very unwilling that he
should leave him; for the moment the latter had announced
his intention to leave his service, mine host's anger was suddenly allayed, and he listened to him without interruption.

Kobè therefore continued—

"What is to come of all this? Is one to say with the proverb, 'The pitcher goes long to the well, but is broken at
last'? No; your daughter's chastity will protect her from
any deeper shame. The Baron will grow weary of Lisa's
society, and seek other pastime; Lisa will remain where she
is, avoided in future by every right-thinking person; you will
be the people's butt; and all will rejoice at your disappointment and confusion."

"But, Kobè, who can please everybody? He who builds
in the street has many critics. I do not understand your stu-
pidity; or do you not know how matters actually stand? The
Baron means to marry Lisa; there is not the slightest doubt
about that—a child might see it; and then shall all the ill
tongues in the village, and you with them, stand gaping, their
eyes wide open, like a heap of owls in the sunshine. Yes,

were I not sure of that, the people might have some reason on their side; though, in any case, they need not trouble their heads about it, for I am master in my own house."

"So! the Baron will marry Lisa, will he? That would be all very well, and you would have a fine feather in your cap, Baas. But *will* and *ought* are different words. Will you let me ask you a question?"

"Well?"

"Has the Baron spoken to you of marriage yet?"

"That is not necessary."

"Indeed! Then have you inquired what his intentions are?"

"That is not necessary either."

"Has the Baron spoken to Lisa of marriage?"

"What a childish question, Kobè! He would require to ask Lisa for her consent, forsooth, when he knows that I alone am master here, and that it is I who must determine; that would never do."

"No! But perhaps you are not aware that the Baron laughed at you and your daughter, when the doctor asked him in the churchyard, in the presence of more than ten people, whether he intended to marry Lisa?"

"What is that you say—Herr von Bruinkasteel laughed at me?"

"He asked the doctor whether he could believe that he, a Baron, would marry a girl out of a country tavern; and when some one said that you had already spoken with the notary about the marriage-contract, he exclaimed, ' The daughter is a fine girl; but the father is a completely-developed fool, and should have been in bedlam long ago.' "

The moment Kobè said this, Baas sprang up from his seat as if some one had suddenly trod on his toes.

"What do you say there?" he exclaimed, with a threaten-

ing mien. "*I* should have been in bedlam? **What has**
come over you? Have you lost your senses entirely? It is
true, after all, 'A mad dog bites even his own master.' "

"I am only repeating to you what ten men heard as well
as myself. Believe it or not, as you please, Baas. What is
the use of "—

"Yes, say it all out. What is the use of spectacles, if the
owl *will* not see? I can't understand why I do not pitch you
out of doors."

"What is the use of the light to him who keeps his eyes
fast shut?" continued Kobè. "The Baron made some other
observations on your character, beside that."

"No, no; it is not true, cannot be true. You believe like
a simpleton all the slanders which people retail, who are bursting with envy because I have more money than they, and because they foresee that Lisa will be a fine lady, to the vexation of every one who grudges her the good fortune."

"When the blind man dreams that he sees, he sees only
what he wishes to see," sighed Kobè. "For your wound
there is no salve, Baas; therefore I cannot help you; and
so I say with the proverb, 'As you brew, you must bake.
Act as it pleases you, and marry your daughter to-morrow."

"Everything you have told me is only the invention of envious people, and nothing more."

"The doctor does not envy you, Baas; he is a quiet, prudent man—perhaps the only one in the village now who continues friendly to you. He himself urged me to open your
eyes, even against your will, to the danger to which you were
exposing yourself."

"But the doctor has been deceived too, Kobè; they have
told him lies of all sorts. It *can't* be otherwise, I tell you.
It would be a fine story, to be sure, if the Baron were not to
marry Lisa!"

"You can't be sure of your chickens till the eggs are laid, Baas."

"I am as certain of being right as I am of knowing my father's name."

"You are riding the horse before you are in the saddle. I tell you, Baas, the Baron makes sport of you, and laughs at you, and accounts you a blockhead at best. I tell you, you are blind! I pity you and Lisa from my heart. I leave this early to-morrow morning, that I may not see the end of the melancholy story; and if you would but open your ears, Baas, I would give you a parting advice as my farewell—very valuable advice."

"As your farewell? We shall see about that. Let me hear your precious counsel in the meantime."

"Why, you see, Baas, the credulous are easily betrayed. Were I in your place, I should know this very day precisely how I stood. I should go straight to the hunting-box, see Herr von Bruinkasteel, and ask him what his intentions are with regard to Lisa. Fine words and evasive phrases should have no effect upon me. I should meet everything with the plain, decisive question—'Do you mean to marry her or not?' I should compel him to deal openly with me, and give once for all a clear and decisive answer. If he refused, which is very probable, I should then forbid him ever to address another word to Lisa; on the contrary, I should bring things back into the old track—clear myself with Charles, call him back and hasten his marriage with Lisa. That is the only way left you of warding off great suffering and great shame."

"Well, then, if Herr von Bruinkasteel does not speak with me soon about the marriage, I shall be bold enough to question him; but there is no haste."

"No haste! From hand to mouth is hazardous work. This very day you ought to know what the Baron's intentions are."

"Well, well," cried Baas, "this very afternoon I shall go to the hunting-box, and demand from the Baron a final explanation. But I know quite well already what his answer will be."

"I wish you spoke the truth, Baas; but I fear you baked dough in your New-year's cake."

"What! that I spoke the truth?"

"Yes, if it were only for this once."

"The world has turned upside down," sighed Baas, with no little irritation; "the servant treats his master as a fool, and I must swallow it too! Play with the ass and he flings his tail in your face. But wait a little, my revenge is at hand. This very afternoon I shall go to the hunting-box. And what will you say, you impudent scoundrel, when I bring back the reply that the Baron means to marry Lisa?"

"That you alone have sense, Baas, and that every other person, myself not excepted, is an empty blockhead. But what will *you* say, Baas, if Herr von Bruinkasteel laughs at you?"

"It is impossible, I tell you."

"But if it should be so, what then?"

"*If, if!* If the sky should fall, we should all be dead men."

"I repeat my question, Baas. If the Baron laughs at you, what then?"

"Ha! Baron or not Baron, I shall show him who I am, and —

A loud and terrible scream of agony made the word die on his tongue. Both sprang up, alarmed and anxious, and hastened to the room in which Lisa was.

The maiden stood at the window, and looked into the street. She must have seen something fearful, for her lips were convulsed, and her teeth were pressed convulsively together. Her strained eyes seemed as if they would leap out of her head, and she trembled in every limb. Baas Gansendonck had scarcely entered the room, when a cry of agony more piercing than the first resounded through it; and Lisa, throwing up her arms, fell back lifeless on the floor. Baas knelt down beside her, crying for help.

Kobè went to the window and looked out. He, too, grew pale and trembled; tears burst from his eyes; and he was so overwhelmed by what he saw, that he did not hear his master's call for assistance: for, going along the road which led to the city, Charles might be seen between two gendarmes, with his hands bound at his back. An old woman tottered weeping behind him, and dropped her burning tears in the footsteps of her unhappy son. Sus, the smith, tore his hair, and stormed with rage and grief; and behind there followed a troop of peasant men and women, with downcast eyes and sorrowful faces. More than one handkerchief was in requisition to dry the tears of pity which flowed from many an eye. One would have supposed that it was a funeral procession accompanying some beloved friend to the grave.

CHAPTER IX.

"If the ass is too happy, it is sure to go on the ice and break a leg."

BAAS GANSENDONCK, following his servant's advice, set out immediately after dinner to inquire into the Baron's intentions. As he did not wish to pass the smithy, he left his house by the back-door, and struck into a by-path which led through fir-woods, and over a lonely field, to the hunting-box of Herr von Bruinkasteel.

No melancholy was visible in the countenance of mine host Gansendonck, although his daughter had lain in a violent fever since morning. On the contrary, it expressed an assured self-complacency; and every now and then he smiled—a smile as bright and cheerful as if he had gained some great victory. From the movements of his features, and their varying expression, one could easily see that his mind was occupied with nothing but pleasing fancies, and that he was heedlessly letting his thoughts flow down the stream of hope and delusion. He had for a long time muttered to himself in a low tone, and betrayed his inner feelings only by his gestures and expressions; but at last his imagination became too powerful for him, his voice became gradually louder, and he spoke aloud—

"Oh! they all conspire against me, and believe, forsooth, that I will yield one foot to their stupid outcry! Baas Gansendonck will soon show them what he is and what he can do. Some men might say, 'Better to have friends than enemies;' but I say, 'Better to be envied than pitied. Everybody's friend is everybody's fool.' The Baron will not marry Lisa? And he has this very day sent his servants twice to inquire how she is! If I can see anything at all, there is no room for doubt *here*. Has he not himself often said to me that Lisa is much too good and too refined to be the wife of a coarse peasant? Has he not added, too, 'She must make a better marriage, and render some man happy who can understand her worth'? To me it all seems clear enough. I dare say the rascally boors imagine that a Baron manages these matters like them, and without farther ado says, 'Betty, shall we be married?' No; that is not the way such things are managed in high life. How? Herr von Bruinkasteel refuse to marry Lisa? I bet five acres that he will fall on my neck the moment I begin to speak of her. Herr von Bruinkasteel not marry Lisa! not marry her! As if I had not perceived why he was always so kind to me, and treated me with such politeness that everybody noticed it! And it always was 'Herr von Gansendonck' here, and 'Friend Gansendonck' there. And then the hares which he sent! and the partridges he brought! And Lisa never eats game either; from which it is clear that he meant to curry favour with me. Why? certainly not for the sake of *my* beautiful eyes. No, no, he only wished to smooth his way before taking the great final step. I shall make the thing easy for him; he shall be very merry over it."

Mine host rubbed his hands in his great self-complacency, and was silent for a time, apparently only the better to enjoy his sweet fancies. Suddenly he burst out into a loud laugh and said—

"Aha! I think I see them all standing in the village, with noses as long as my walking-stick. There walks the Baron

with Lisa on his arm—clothed so gorgeously, that the peasants
have to shut their eyes before the splendour! Four servants,
their hats all covered with gold and silver lace, follow him;
and a little behind, the coach and four! I, Peer Gansendonck, I—walk by the side of Herr Baron von Bruinkasteel,
with head elate, and look at the slanderous and envious crea-
tures as it beseems a Baron's father-in-law to look at the common herd. Then we walk on in state till we reach the church;
fine carpets and cushions are all prepared for our use; the
organ plays till the window-panes rattle; the 'I do' is pronounced before the altar, and Lisa is off with her husband,
dashing and clattering through the village by special post, so
that sparks fly out of the stones. Next morning, at least
twenty peasants lie a-bed with vexation and envy. Meanwhile, I sell or let the St. Sebastian, and when my son-in-law
returns with my daughter, I remove to the Castle. Baas
Gansendonck—that is, Herr von Gansendonck—has feathered
his nest indeed: he never does anything afterwards but order,
eat, hunt, and take the air on horseback. But while I am
thinking of all these glorious things, I am running my nose
right on the door of the hunting-box!"

So saying, mine host pulled the bell. After waiting for a
time, a servant came to the door, and said while opening it—

"Oh, good-day, Baas! You come, I suppose, to visit his
lordship?"

"I do, fellow," said mine host in a tone of superiority.

"He is not at home."

"What! not at home?"

"That is, he will see nobody."

"What! he will not see *me!* That were fine, to be sure!
He is in bed, perhaps?"

"No, but he will receive no one. You may guess why: a
black eye, and a face all scarred"—

"What of that? He does not need to conceal his face from me; we are intimate enough, the Herr Baron and I, to admit of my seeing him although he is confined to bed. I shall go in; his order is not meant to apply to me."

"Come in, then, if you will," said the servant with a cunning smile. "Follow me, I shall announce you."

"That is quite unnecessary," said Baas; "forms between us are superfluous."

The attendant led him into an ante-chamber, and compelled him, spite of his expostulation, to sit down and wait the Baron's reply. More than half an hour had already elapsed, and the servant had not yet returned. Mine host's choler gradually rose, and he muttered to himself—

"This fellow means to make sport of me, I see. Very good; I shall take a note of it. He shall not get gray hairs in our service: he must pack! This conduct will get him a reprimand as it is. . . . Were I to listen till I was deaf, I believe I should hear nothing moving in the whole house! Is it possible that the fellow has pretended to forget that he has left me waiting here? He could not carry his boorishness so far surely! At all events, I cannot sit here till morning. Aha! there I hear the villain! He laughs. With whom does he laugh, I wonder?"

"Baas Gansendonck," said the servant, opening the door, "please to follow me. The Herr Baron has the goodness to receive you; had it not been for my good word, you should have had to go home again without doing your errand."

"What is that you say, you ill-mannered rascal?" cried Baas, with irritation. "Do you know whom you are speaking to? I am Herr Gansendonck."

"And I am Jack Miermans, at your service," replied the servant coldly and contemptuously.

"I shall know where to find you some other time, fellow!"

said mine host, as he went up stairs. "You shall know what
it is to have kept me waiting half an hour in an ante-room.
Pack up as quickly as you please; you shall not stay much
longer here to make sport of men like me."

Without replying to the threat, the servant opened the door
of the drawing-room, and called out with a loud voice—

"Mine host from the St. Sebastian," and immediately ran
down stairs, letting the enraged Gansendonck stand where he
was.

Herr von Bruinkasteel sat at the upper end of the room,
leaning with his elbow on the table. His left eye was covered
with a bandage, and his brow and cheeks bore marks of the
struggle of the preceding night. The object, however, which
most of all attracted Gansendonck's attention as he entered,
was the Baron's splendid Turkish dressing-gown. The varie-
gated velvet-like dress arrested his eyes so powerfully that,
with a smile of surprise, he exclaimed, before even greeting
the Baron—

"Heavens, Herr Baron! what a beautiful dressing-gown
you have on!"

"Good-day, Herr Gansendonck!" said the Baron, without
paying any attention to him. "You are desirous, I suppose,
to learn how it goes with me. I thank you for your kindness."

"Do not be offended, Herr Baron; but before I inquire
after your health, I should like much to know where you had
that dressing-gown made—I cannot get it out of my eyes."

"Do not make me smile, Herr Gansendonck; it pains my
face very much."

"I am not joking, Herr Baron; no, no, I am in solemn
earnest."

"Your question is a singular one. This dressing-gown
was purchased in Paris."

"At Paris? That is very vexing, Baron."

"Why so?"

"I should have ordered one to be made precisely the same."

"It cost two hundred francs."

"Never mind that."

"It would not be suitable for you, Herr Gansendonck."

"Not suitable! If I can pay for it, it will become me well enough, I should suppose. But leaving that subject, how is it with your health, Herr von Bruinkasteel?"

"You see—a black eye, and a body literally covered with bruises."

"The villain has been captured by the gendarmes, and is on his way to the city now. You will make him pay for his brutal attack as he ought?"

"Certainly, he must be punished. He has waylaid me with malice prepense, and attacked me on my own property. A heavy punishment is attached to such crimes; still, I do not wish that the law should be enforced with the utmost rigour; for in that case he could not escape with less than five years' imprisonment. His old mother was with me this morning, beseeching and imploring me to have mercy. I am sorry for the poor woman."

"Sorry!" cried Baas, with irritation and surprise; "sorry for such a wretch!"

"Though the son be a fool, in what respect is the old mother to be blamed?"

"She should have brought up her son better. The low scoundrel will get only what he deserves. And what would the peasants think, if they found they could treat men like us as if they were our equals? No, no, respect, honour, subjection, must all be kept up. Already they are carrying their heads too high. Were I in your place, I should spare no money to make the brewer, and the whole village with him, suffer for this."

" Well, that is my affair."

" I know that well, Herr Baron. Every one is master in his own concerns."

This direction of the conversation was apparently disagreeable to the Baron; for he looked aside, and sat for a moment without saying a word. Mine host, who was also at a loss for something to say, looked round the room with a perplexed air in search of something which might naturally introduce the subject of his daughter's marriage. He scraped his feet and cleared his throat several times; but nothing would come.

" And our poor Lisa!" said the Baron at last; " the sight of the brewer's capture must have shocked her very much. I can easily understand it; she has loved him since she was a child."

Mine host seemed to awake out of a dream the moment Lisa's name sounded in his ears. He thought that now the way was smoothed for carrying out his plans, and accordingly replied with a smile—

" She love him, do you say, Baron? No, no; it was a premature calf-love, as people call it; but that is all past long since. I showed the brewer to the door, and bolted it behind him. You think, I daresay, Baron, and with good reason, that the coarse beer-cask would fain have married our Lisa?"

" There are other people, Baas, who were able to perceive their mutual affection."

A beam of joy lighted up mine host's eyes; and, leaping from his seat, he said, with a stupid, cunning smile—

" Oh, I know what you are after. A shrewd man can easily tell where the cow lies when he sees its tail."

" A clever comparison."

" Is it not so, Baron? No, I should think I am not so

stupid. But let us take the cow by the horns; there is no need of roundabouts between us."

The Baron looked at Baas with a suppressed smile.

"Then does the Herr Baron think seriously of marriage?" asked Gansendonck confidently.

"From what quarter have you learned that? I have concealed it even from my own friends."

"I know all about it, Baron; ha! ha! I have more in my pocket than you suppose."

"Indeed! why, you must be a fortune-teller; or you only guess it: you hit the nail on the head, however."

"Well, then, Baron," said Baas, rubbing his hands, "we shall make short work of all that remains to be done. You see, I shall make a sacrifice; I shall give my Lisa a dowry of thirty thousand francs in money and property. When I die, she will get thirty thousand more. I shall sell the inn, that I may cut the society of awkward boors for ever—and I shall live in the castle with you. So in that way, you will in fact get the sixty thousand from the first."

At these words, he rose, offered the Baron his hand, and said—

"You see, my friend, I do not make many difficulties. Now, Herr von Bruinkasteel, let us shake hands on this marriage. —Why do you draw back your hand?"

"'On this marriage!' On what marriage?" asked the Baron.

"Come, take your father-in-law's hand, and within fourteen days the banns will be proclaimed! Do not be shamefaced, Baron; we are not children now. Give me your hand, and the matter is settled."

The Baron burst into a loud laugh. At the sight of this, consternation and anxiety were depicted on mine host's face.

"Why do you laugh, Herr von Bruinkasteel?" he asked in perplexity. "Perhaps from joy?"

"What! Herr Gansendonck," exclaimed the Baron, so soon as he could control himself, "are you out of your senses? or what is the matter with you?"

"Have you not said yourself that you mean to be married?"

"Yes, with a lady in Paris! She is not so beautiful as your Lisa; but she is a countess, and the possessor of an old and distinguished name."

This cut Baas to the quick; he trembled from top to toe; and said, in imploring accents—

"Herr Baron, no jesting; pray, if you will be so good! you intend to marry my Lisa, do you not? I know you are fond of a laugh, and like a joke of all things; but consider, Baron, that girls like our Lisa are not to be found everywhere. Beautiful as a flower in the field, well educated, amiable, of good birth, with thirty thousand francs down, and as much in expectation : all this surely is not to be laughed at; and I do not know a single countess who offers so many attractions. A good opportunity flies over the sea with the stork, and one never knows when it will return."

"Poor Gansendonck!" said the Baron; "I pity you! You certainly cannot have your five senses! There must be a screw loose in your head somewhere."

"What! what!" exclaimed Baas, somewhat excited;—"but I will control myself; it is perhaps only a jest. Our misunderstanding must have an end, however. I ask you directly, Herr von Bruinkasteel, will you marry my daughter, or will you not? Have the goodness to give me a short and clear answer."

"It is as impossible for me to marry Lisa, Baas, as it is for you to marry the morning-star!"

"And why so, then?" cried Baas, now at length raging; "why so? Perhaps you are too good for us? The Gansendoncks, let me tell you, are respectable people, sir; they have many a pretty bit of land under the blue sky. Say, in a word, will you marry my daughter, or will you not?"

"Your question is ridiculous; but I shall answer it—No! I shall marry Lisa neither to-day nor to-morrow, nor ever. And now, leave me, with your amusing madness!"

Trembling with rage, and red as a turkey-cock with shame and wrath, mine host stamped his feet on the carpet.

"So my question is ridiculous, is it? I am a fool, am I? You will not marry Lisa! We shall see about that! Justice is for every man—for me as well as for a Baron! And if it were to cost me half my wealth, I shall find a way to force you. What! you will force yourself into my house with hypocritical face, tell my daughter a heap of lies, bring her good name into disrepute, make sport of me!—and then dare to say, 'I will not marry her; I will marry a countess!' It will not do, Baron. No one shall trifle thus with Baas Gansendonck. After what happened yesterday, you dare no longer refuse me. You must repair my daughter's honour, or I shall bring you to law, and push the suit even to Brussels. You must marry her; and if you do not immediately say 'Yes,' I forbid you ever again to set foot across my threshold."

During this outbreak, the Baron had looked at Baas with a quiet smile of pity, and with great calmness. But as the latter began to threaten, the sudden flush on his face indicated anger or indignation.

"Herr Gansendonck," he said, "out of respect for myself I ought to pull the bell and order my servants to turn you out of my house; but honestly, I pity your insanity. If you please, I shall once for all clearly and decidedly reply to all you have said, and can say. In what has occurred, lies a lesson for you as well as for me. We shall both do well to make good use of it."

"I wish to know," interrupted Baas, "whether you will marry Lisa or not?"

"Have you no ears, that you ask me the same question so often? Attend, Herr Gansendonck, to what I am going to say; and do not interrupt me, otherwise my servants will bring our interview to an abrupt termination."

"I am listening, I am listening," muttered Baas, grinding his teeth. "If I should die, I shall not speak a word till my turn comes."

"You accuse me of forcing myself into your house," resumed the Baron; "and yet you are quite aware that you yourself invited me, and forced the acquaintance of your daughter on me. What have I done, then, which was not done with your full concurrence? Nothing. On the contrary, you considered that I did not treat your daughter with sufficient boldness. Now, you desire that I should marry her. So it was a trap you were laying for me, and you had your secret designs in it all! Judge yourself whether I ought not to look with abhorrence on such detestable plans. I came to Lisa because her society was agreeable to me, and because a genuine feeling of friendship attracted me to her. If this intercourse, by which I meant to honour you, has had a sad end for us all, it has arisen from neglecting the proverb, 'Keep with your like.' We have both acted imprudently, and are both punished. I was, to my great disgrace, almost beaten to death by a peasant; you have become the jest of the village, and now see crumbling into ruins all the air-castles which you have been building. Better confess at the gallows than never. I know that I did wrong in visiting a country inn, and acting as if I were your equal; and now I see clearly that if Lisa had not had a strong defence in her own pure nature, my conversation and behaviour would have done much to ruin her beautiful character."

"What is that you say?" interrupted Baas. "Have you ever uttered anything immoral to my daughter, you seducer?"

"I laugh at your folly," continued the Baron coldly; "and will still for a moment forget who it is who dares speak so to me. I have said nothing to your daughter but what is regarded among the higher classes as mere compliments of the day—things which are peculiar to the French language, and do little harm, perhaps, to people who from youth up have heard nothing else, but which corrupt the heart and morals in a lower rank of life, because there they are received as truth, and rouse passion, empty compliments though they be. Therein have I erred. It is the only fault—the only mistake which any one can charge me with; but which *you* certainly cannot accuse me of, for you have made me do and say even more than I myself desired. You have just threatened to forbid me your house; that is not necessary. I had already determined to put to good use the lesson I had been taught, and never again to visit you as a friend, but henceforth to conduct myself towards every peasant as beseems my rank."

"Peasant!" exclaimed Baas with impatience, "I am no peasant! My name is Gansendonck. What resemblance is there between a peasant and me? Tell me."

"Unhappily for you, no great outward resemblance," replied the Baron. "Your pride has misled you; now, you are neither fish nor flesh—neither peasant nor gentleman; you will your whole life long meet with nothing but enmity and mockery on the one hand, and contempt and pity on the other. You should be ashamed of despising your own condition so foolishly. A peasant is the most useful man on earth; and if he only be an honest and honourable man, who fulfils his duty in his position, he deserves above every other to be respected and beloved.   Do you know who degrade the condition of a peasant?   Persons like you, who imagine that a man exalts himself by looking with disdain upon his brother—who think that they are no longer peasants if only they speak of peasants with contempt, and that it is sufficient to hang eagle's feathers on their body in order to be an eagle."

"Have I now listened long enough?" cried Baas, leaping up, "or do you imagine, Herr Baron, that I have come here to let myself be dragged through the mud in this way, without answering a word?"

"One word more," rejoined the Baron; "I will give you a good advice, Herr Gansendonck.   Write over your bedroom door the proverb—'*Shoemaker, keep by your last.*'   Dress like other peasants, speak and act like people of your own rank.   Seek some good peasant's son for your daughter's husband, smoke your pipe and drink your beer in friendship with the villagers, and give yourself no more trouble to appear what you are not.   Consider, that if an ass wears a lion's hide, its ears peep through.   And now go home in peace with this lesson; you will thank me for it some future day.   If you think, however, that you must still say something, speak, and I shall now listen."

Mine host sprang up from his chair, and crossing his arms upon his breast to repress his rage, said—

"Oh, you imagine that you can deceive me with your assumed coldness and apish tricks!   No, no, it shall not end so.   We shall see whether there is no law in the country to compel you, Herr Baron!   I shall go to your father in the city, and tell him how you have stained the honour of my house.   And even if I have to write to the countess in Paris, whose name you conceal through fear, I will do it, put a stop to your marriage, and inform the whole world what a vile traitor you are."

"Is that all you have to say?" asked the Baron with suppressed anger.

"Will you marry Lisa, or will you not?" screamed Baas, shaking his fists threateningly.

The Baron put out his hand and pulled the bell twice violently. In a moment the steps of approaching servants were heard upon the stairs. Baas Gansendonck trembled with rage and shame. The door opened, and the servants appeared in the room.

"Did not the Herr Baron ring?" asked all at once, perplexed.

"Accompany Herr Gansendonck to the door," he ordered, with as much coolness as he could command.

"What! you will cast me out of your house!" screamed Baas, choking with fury. "You shall pay dearly for that, tyrant! traitor! seducer!"—

The Baron gave the attendants a sign, stood up, and left the apartment through a side door.

Mine host Gansendonck looked thunderstruck, and seemed not to know whether to rail or weep; while the servants pushed him gently but irresistibly towards the door, heedless of his exclamations. Before he had got a clear conception of what was going on, he found himself in the open air, and saw the door of the hunting-box shut behind him.

For a time he walked straight on dreamily, like a blind man, till he struck his head against a tree, and was roused to consciousness by the blow. Then he strode on rapidly, giving vent to his vexation and wrath by abusing the Baron mercilessly. He paused at the corner of a wood to think; after ten minutes of the most painful reflection, he began to beat himself with his fists, and strike his brow with his open hand, at every blow exclaiming—

"Ass that you are! dare you show face at home, you owl?

The whip is too good for you, you stupid clod! This will teach you to hunt after barons and fine gentlemen! Yes, go and put on a white waistcoat and yellow gloves! A fool's cap would suit you better. Simple and stupid enough to be drowned in a windmill! Hide yourself—creep into the earth for shame, you thick-headed boor!—thick-headed boor!—thick-headed boor!"

At last, after he had exhausted his vexation on himself, the tears gushed from his eyes; and weeping and sighing, ashamed and grieved, he walked on towards his dwelling.

Suddenly he perceived at a distance his servant hastening to meet him, and shouting out unintelligible words with great apparent excitement—

"Baas, Baas! come quickly!" cried Kobè as he approached his master. "Our poor Lisa lies in the agonies of death."

"O God!" sighed Baas Gansendonck. "Everything overwhelms me at once, and every one forsakes me!—You too, Kobè!"

"Forgive and forget," said Kobè, with deep compassion. "You are unfortunate; I will stay by you so long as I can be of use. But come, come quickly!"

Both hastened towards the village with rapid strides, and with anxious and sorrowing hearts.

CHAPTER X.

"Shame is the daughter of pride."

THE winter is past. Already the trees and herbs **begin** to unfold their tender green in the mild sunshine; the birds **are** building their nests, and have begun their sweet May songs; everything exults in its young energy—everything smiles hopefully towards the future, as if a gray cloud could never again darken the beautiful blue sky.

In a side-room of the St. Sebastian, a sick girl was reclining, her head supported upon pillows. Poor Lisa! a worm was gnawing at her heart, and wearing her life away! Yonder she sits, motionless, and yet panting with exhaustion; the slightest movement is a painful effort to her. Her countenance is pale, and transparent as glass; but upon each of her wasted cheeks a hectic flush glows faintly—a sad sign! Sunk in a deep reverie, her thin fingers carelessly strip some daisies of their leaves—little flowers which have been gathered to please her, as one would please a child. She lets them fall to the ground, her head sinks back powerless upon the cushion, her glassy eye gazes heavenwards, into the infinite; already her soul mingles itself with the Eternal.

At a little distance behind the maiden, and near the window, sat poor Baas Gansendonck, his arms folded on his breast. His sunken head, his half-closed eyes fixed intently on the ground, and his melancholy features, expressed repentance, shame, and bitter sorrow.

Of what nature were the thoughts of the unhappy father, who saw his only child wasting away, a martyr to his folly? Did he know that his pride was the executioner who had brought the innocent sacrifice to the altar? Be that as it may, he, too, evidently concealed in his heart a torturing snake; for the deep wrinkles of sorrow which furrowed his face, his wan cheeks, and slow motions, showed too clearly that the last sparks of self-confidence, energy, and hope, were quite extinguished in his breast.

The gentlest sigh of his sick daughter made him shudder; her painful cough tore his heart in pieces. If she directed a suffering look towards him, he trembled, as if in her lifeless eyes he read the terrible word—*child-murder!* Now, when the feeling of love within him had been freed from the pride which had obscured it, and was experienced in all its purity and strength, he would cheerfully have endured the most painful death to prolong his child's life but a single year.

Poor Gansendonck! Everything in the world had so smiled upon him. Beautiful dreams of fortune and greatness had all his life long played with him. And now he sat there like a dumb ghost beside his dying child; anxious and trembling, like a malefactor at the bar of Divine justice. If, on the one hand, the perpetual gnawing of conscience, and continual reflection on the past, had made his body old; it had, on the other hand, led his soul out of the darkness of pride and presumption, and softened his whole nature. Now, his dress was poor, his speech friendly, and his bearing modest. Patiently enduring his heavy lot, his whole life was now devoted to soothe his daughter's affliction, and obtain Charles's freedom.

Baas Gansendonck had sat for half an hour in the same

position; he held his breath, and did not stir a limb, for fear of disturbing his daughter's repose. At last, Lisa raised her head, with a sigh of restlessness and pain. Baas approached her with deep feeling—

"Lisa, darling, it distresses you, does it not, to sit always in this room, and alone? See how brightly the sun shines out there, and how soft and fresh the air is. I have put a chair in the garden—shall I take you into the sunshine? The doctor said that it would do you good."

"O no, father, let me stay here," she sighed.—"This pillow is so hard."

"The perpetual stillness of this room is painful, Lisa. Your heart needs something to revive it."

"'The perpetual stillness!'" repeated the maiden, musing; "ah! how still and sweet it must be in the grave!"

"Oh, Lisa, leave these sad thoughts! Come, shall I help you? No one shall see you, for I shall keep the garden door shut; and you shall sit in the beautiful ash-grove, and see how gloriously the flowers blossom, and hear how charmingly the birds sing! Do it to please me, Lisa."

"Well then, father, from love to you, I will try whether I can still go so far."

Supporting herself on the table with both hands, she raised herself slowly up; hot tears streamed down her father's face, when he saw how she tottered, and how all her limbs shook, as if her body were a burden too heavy for her. Silently he put his arm round her, and almost carried her along. In this way, father and daughter went step by step through the house —standing still to rest more than once on their way—and reached the garden with difficulty, where Lisa, exhausted and coughing painfully, sank into the arm-chair. After Baas had placed the pillows comfortably behind her, and under her head, he sat down by her side and waited till she had somewhat recovered from her exhaustion. At last he said, while the tears flowed fast, and his voice sounded sadly on the ear—

"Have good hopes, Lisa dear; the beautiful summer has begun—the sweet, pure air will strengthen you. You will grow well again."

"Ah, father, why deceive me?" sighed the dying girl, faintly shaking her head. "Whoever sees me—and you too, father—sheds tears, and weeps over my fate! There is no hope now! Is it not so? Before the Church-fest* comes, I shall lie in the grave!"

"My child! do not grieve yourself with such dreadful thoughts."

"'Dreadful thoughts!' In the world there is no good thing, father. Would that I were now in heaven! Yonder there is health, bliss, and eternal life!"

"Charles will soon return, Lisa. Have you not said yourself that you would soon be well again? He will comfort you; his friendly words will breathe new life into you, and deliver you from your heavy sufferings."

"Still six months!" sighed the maiden despairingly, looking towards heaven, as if asking something of God; "still six months!"

"Perhaps not so long, Lisa; Kobè went yesterday to Brussels with a letter from our burgomaster to the gentleman who is our intercessor with the Minister; and everything encourages us to hope that we shall get a diminution of Charles's punishment. Then he will be set free at once. If God so wills it, Kobè will bring us this very afternoon the joyful news of his early release from prison. Lisa, my child, do you not feel already the beginning of a new life?"

"Poor Charles!" sighed Lisa, musingly; "already four long months in prison. Oh, father, I have sinned grievously;

* The annual celebration of the consecration of the local church.—Tr.

but he, who is innocent, what must he suffer in his gloomy dungeon!"

"Not so, Lisa; I visited him the day before yesterday. He bears his fate with patience; if your illness did not make him sad, he would count himself happy."

"He has suffered so much, father. You will love him, will you not? and no longer drive him unkindly from you? Oh, he is so good!"

"'Drive him from me!'" cried Baas, with a trembling voice; "on my knees, I have implored his pardon; and I have wet his feet with my tears!"

"Heavens! And he, father?"

"He fell on my neck—kissed, and consoled me. I would have accused myself—told him that my pride alone was the cause of his misfortune—vowed that my whole life should be an atonement; but he closed my mouth with a kiss!—a kiss which, like a heavenly balsam, breathed hope and strength into my heart, made me strong again, and able to wait with less anxiety for God's decree. Blessed is the merciful, who repays evil with love!"

"And he has forgiven me too, father, has he not?"

"Forgiven you, Lisa? In what have you sinned? Ah! if you suffer—if a punishment from on high seems to afflict you—it is for my sins alone that you are atoning, my poor child!"

"And I, am I not guilty, father? Was it not my levity which from the first tore his heart, and drove him to despair? But he has forgiven me all, I know, for he is very good."

"No, no; Charles has had nothing to forgive you. In his eyes you were always pure and chaste as a lily! Even then, when my insane pride had compelled you to do what was imprudent, and when everything concurred to cause mistrust on his part, he never cherished the smallest suspicion of you;

but said proudly, My Lisa is pure, and loves me alone upon
the earth!'"

A sweet smile played round the young girl's lips, while she
said—

"Oh, this assurance will make the kiss of death so soft and
pleasing! When I go there, I shall pray to God for him; and
from heaven I shall smile upon him wherever he is, till he
also comes."

The cheerful tone of Lisa's voice encouraged her father to
make an attempt to divert her thoughts to more pleasing subjects; and he said joyfully—

"And you do not know, Lisa, all that he said to me the
day before yesterday, about a beautiful garden which he means
to lay out for you when he is free; with its beautiful flowers,
its winding paths, its arbours, grassy plots, and little ponds.
And while they are making it, he will take you to Paris, and
show you the most beautiful things in the world; and put new
life into you, my darling, by his watchful love, and by giving
you every kind of pleasure and happiness. Oh, Lisa! only think
—you will be Charles's wife then.   Nothing on earth shall
ever separate you—your life will be a heaven of bliss! And
Charles wishes that I should live with you and his mother in
the brewery. He is to be my son; and you, Lisa, will have
a tender mother again to love you. I will regain the good
will of the villagers through gentleness and kindness. Every
one will respect and love us; and we will love one another;
and our lives on earth shall be spent in peace and joy. But,
Lisa, child, what is the matter?—you tremble! Are you
not well?"

The young girl made an effort to smile; but one could see
clearly that she had not the power. She feebly sought her
father's hand, and when she had found it, spoke, with a weak
and gradually failing voice—

"Father, had God in heaven not called me, your cheering words might have restored me to health; but, ah! what can now deliver me from the death which I have always before my eyes, like something—I cannot say what—a cloud—something which beckons to me. There! there! again I feel it. It runs through my body, oh, so cold! The air is too keen. Water!—water for my brow! Oh, father, dear father, I think—I must die!"

With these sad words she closed her eyes, and sank lifeless to the ground.

Baas Gansendonck fell on his knees before his daughter, and raised his hands to heaven in earnest prayer, while tears gushed from his eyes. But he soon recollected himself, and sprang up with feverish haste; rubbed the hands of the unconscious Lisa, raised her head, called her by her name, kissed her stiff cold lip, and moistened her brow with tears of penitence and love. In a short time, the sick girl revived. While her father, half mad with joy, watched in her face the signs of her awaking out of her death-like sleep, she opened her eyes slowly, and looked round with an expression of disappointment and surprise.

"Not yet?—still on earth?" she sighed. "Oh, father! lead me in; my head whirls round; my breast glows as if on fire; the air burns my lungs; the sun pains me."

The father lifted her up with a jealous care, as if he would carry his child out of the reach of the death which threatened her, and bore her into her apartment. There Lisa lay down again by the table, and silently laid her languid head upon the pillow. Baas would have uttered some words of comfort, but she said imploringly—

"Do not speak, dear father: I am so weary. Let me rest."

Baas Gansendonck resumed his seat without saying a word,

and wept in silence as he thought on the approaching death of his darling child.

A half-hour had elapsed without a motion, a sound, or a sigh having indicated the presence of living beings in the room, when suddenly a vehicle drew up before the door.

"There is Kobè! there is Kobè!" cried Baas Gansendonck joyfully. "I know our horse's tread!"

A feeble glimmer of hope lighted up the dying maiden's eyes.

Kobè entered the room. Lisa seemed to exert all her remaining strength to learn the joyful intelligence. She raised her head and turned towards Kobè. Mine host sprang up—

"Well, Kobè, well?"

"*Nothing*," he replied, while tears filled his eyes. "The gentleman who was to have spoken for Charles to the Minister of Justice is gone to Germany."

A low but painful cry of anguish burst from Lisa's lips, her head fell back on the pillow, and a few quiet tears rolled over her wan and melancholy face.

"Ah!" she sighed, almost inaudibly. "He shall see me no more on earth!"

CHAPTER XL.

" Thistles sown—thorns mown."

ONE beautiful morning, a young peasant walked with rapid strides over the highway which led from Antwerp to Breda. His breath went and came quickly, and drops of perspiration stood on his brow. There beamed from his eyes, notwithstanding, an inexpressible rapture, and in the quick glances which he cast over green field and dark blue sky, there sparkled gratitude to God, and love for life-quickening nature. His steps were light, and at intervals an involuntary exclamation of joy escaped from his over-excited breast. One would have said that he was hastening with burning impatience towards a spot where some great good fortune awaited him.

It was no other than Charles the brewer, whose term of punishment had been shortened, and who was now on his way to his native village with his heart full of happy dreams. He would see his Lisa again—console her and bring her new life! Was it not his condemnation, his imprisonment, which had overwhelmed her with sorrow, and made her ill? and would not his release and return therefore infallibly restore her to health? Yes, he returned to her with a heart as fresh and loving as ever; he would surprise her by his sudden appearance; he would say, " Rise up out of your sorrow, my Lisa. Here am I, your true, unaltered friend! Draw strength from my love! Raise your head hopefully again, for all our sorrow is over! Look calmly and cheerfully into the future! Welcome life! a life which promises us so many beautiful years." And his good old mother—how he would reward her now for all that her rich maternal love had endured! He saw already in imagination how she hastened out to meet him, weeping for joy—felt her arms round his neck, her warm kiss glowing on his cheek, and her tears moistening his brow. Pleased with this sweet imagination, he laughed with delight, and, "Mother! mother!" fell in fervent accents from his lips.

Oh happy, happy was the youth! The once more tasted freedom made his bosom swell with emotion. The rich and odorous air of the fields surrounded him, and infused the fire of life into his breast: the vernal sun gilded the lovely green of the firs, and clothed nature in a gorgeous festal robe. Dreaming of a beautiful future, thanking God with overflowing heart, enchanting his soul with fond pictures of all that was most dear to him, now sighing when he thought of love, and again laughing for joy, the youth strode rapidly on till he found himself about half an hour's walk from his native village.

There all of a sudden he stood still, trembling as if some unexpected and hateful sight had filled him with fear and perplexity. Three young gentlemen had just issued from a side-path; one of them was Herr von Bruinkasteel. It was difficult to say whether they had perceived the young peasant or not; however it might be, they did not look at him, but struck into the road which led to the village.

Charles was at a loss what to do. He did not wish to enter into conversation with the Baron yet, for he felt by the palpitation of his heart, how dangerous it would be for him if his enemy were to address to him one insolent or contemptuous word. At the same time, he could not remain where he was, for his impatience to see his beloved, and embrace his mother, bore him too powerfully on. After short consideration, he quickly came to a resolution; and springing upon a by-path, he ran towards the village, making a circuit through copses and fields.

———

Over the village hang the slow and melancholy tones of the bell of death. In the churchyard a freshly-made grave yawns for its destined occupant. Every tone of the death-knell is repeated in the expectant grave. It is as if a hollow voice rose from out the ground, as if the dark earth, full of longing, sighed, "Come, come, come!" The animals even seem painfully affected by the solemn call of death. The dogs are howling, and the oxen at intervals reply with a deep and troubled low; and yet a profound stillness pervades the whole neighbourhood. No moving object is visible, save a few solitary old people, who here and there may be seen, prayer-book in hand, tottering like dumb shadows towards the church.

Soon after, a melancholy procession approaches. But how beautiful, how very beautiful, is this funeral procession to the final resting-place! Four young maidens in snow-white garments bear the body of their friend, who died in the flower of her youth; other maidens, similarly clothed, walk beside them, to take the dear burden on their shoulders in their turn. Behind, come all the daughters of the parish with flowers or branches of consecrated poplar in their hands—even the little children who do not yet know what "to die" means. Many are in tears, and all walk with downcast eyes, and mourn the poor, poor Lisa, who, alas! has expiated where she surely was not guilty. On the coffin are strewn roses and lilies, emblems of virgin purity. They emit so fresh an odour, and look so lovely on the white pall! In the coffin, too, there lies a flower, a lily, which the gnawing worm of sorrow has destroyed, cold and pale, a sin-offering, a sacrifice to pride and arrogance.

Only three men follow close to the corpse. On one side Kobè, on the other, Sus the smith, shedding tears of sorrow. Between them they sympathizingly support a third, who totters feebly along. His hands cover his face; through his fingers, the hot tears force their way, and his bosom heaves visibly with painful sobs. Poor Gansendonck! guilty father! Turn not thine eye on that bier! At every timid glance, thou art conscience-stricken—is it not so? Thou art trembling with grief and remorse—but I will not look into thy heart. I respect thine agony. Forgetting thy ill-fated pride, I would rather weep tears of sympathy for thy present anguish of heart.—They approach the field of the dead; and yonder stands the priest who is to utter the last prayer over the corpse.

But what is this which fills every heart with astonishment and terror? Why this agonizing cry which bursts at once from every breast? What dreadful apparition makes the maidens tremble? O God! yonder is Charles! He stands for a moment as if struck by lightning, and gazes with fixed, wild stare on the funeral procession, which has suddenly come into view. He understands it all. His hair stands on end; he hastens on, and falls down beside the corpse, which the bearers have lowered to the ground. Violently he pushes the maidens aside, pulls off the pall, and lacerates his hands by tearing at the screws of the coffin-lid. He will open the coffin; he calls wildly and piteously upon his Lisa; he cries, he weeps, he laughs by turns! Some men advance and draw him forcibly away; but now another sight tears from him a cry of vengeance, so horrible, so desperate, that all tremble and recoil at the wild shriek. What, then, has his wildered eye beheld, that, sweeping all before him in his fury, he dashes headlong on some object with a cry like a scream of agony? Heavens! yonder, at the window of a tavern, stands the Baron!

Alas! alas! the youth, in his madness, draws a knife from his pocket; it glitters horribly in the sun. In a moment ne is in the tavern; he is about to commit a murder. But no. he stumbles on the threshold, and falls heavily like a stone with his head on the ground. The women raise their arms, and shriek, and tremble—but Charles does not rise again; he lies motionless, as if death had found a new victim in him. The Baron, his enemy, is the first at his side; he raises the young man sympathizingly from the ground. In his heart, too, penitence and remorse are at work; from within, a voice calls to him—" Thy wanton levity has had part in causing the misery which now rages so horribly on every side !"

Kobè runs to his assistance, and they place the youth upon a chair, and bathe his brow and breast with water; but he continues sitting death-pale and motionless.

Meanwhile the priest is uttering, in a low and tremulous tone, the last words of peace over a grave, and the dull heavy fall of clods upon a coffin-lid sounds sadly on the ear.

Charles has revived. The Baron tries to console him. Kobè speaks to him of his mother. But the young man knows no longer either friend or foe. There is a horrible look in his eyes; he laughs, too, and appears so happy.—He is a maniac!

Dear reader! if you should ever chance to go through the village which was the scene of this sad history, you will see sitting on a bench, in front of the brewery, two men playing together as if both were yet children. The younger has a lifeless face, though the wild-fire of insanity glows in his eyes; the other is an older man, who cares for his unfortunate with loving compassion, and endeavours to make him happy and cheerful.

Ask the attendant the cause of his master's misfortune; the good Kobè will tell you a melancholy tale, and point out the grave where Baas Gansendonck sleeps his last sleep by the side of his child; and you may be sure he will close his narrative with some proverb or maxim of world-wisdom.

BLIND ROSA.

On a beautiful day in 1846, the Diligence rolled as usual over the highway between Antwerp and Turnhout. The tramp of horses, the rattle of wheels, the creaking of the frame, and the loud voice of the driver, accompanied its onward progress. The dogs barked in the distance as it passed, the birds rose startled from the fields, and the shadow of the old coach danced grotesquely among the trees and hedges.

Suddenly the coachman pulled up not far from a lonely tavern. Springing from his seat, he opened the door of his vehicle, and without saying a word, proffered his hand to a traveller, who immediately leapt out upon the highway, carrying a leathern travelling-bag under his arm. With equal silence the coachman put up the steps, shut the door, and ascending the box, drew the whip gently across the horses' backs, as a sign to proceed ; and the clumsy machine rumbled on in its own spiritless and monotonous way.

Meanwhile the traveller had entered the tavern, and calling for a glass of beer, sat down at a table. He was a man of very high stature, and appeared to be about fifty years of age. One might have even supposed him to be sixty, had not his vigorous bearing, his lively eye, and the youthful smile upon his lips, shown that his heart and soul were much younger than his face would have indicated. His hair, indeed, was gray, his brow and cheeks furrowed, and his whole countenance expressed that waste of power which care and toil stamp on the face as the sign of premature old age. And yet one could see that his chest rose and fell with fulness and life, that his head sat erect and high, and his sparkling eyes expressed the energy of manhood.

From his dress one would have inferred that he was a wealthy citizen, although it perhaps would not have attracted attention at all, had not the coat been buttoned up to the chin—a peculiarity which, when taken in connexion with his great meerschaum, made one suspect that he was a soldier or a German.

The people of the house, after serving the traveller, resumed their work without paying any further attention to him. He saw the two daughters going and coming, the landlord fetch wood and peat for the fire, the mother fill the kitchen-pot; but no one said a word to him, although his eyes followed every one as if he desired to enter into conversation, and his sad and gentle smile seemed to say—" Ah ! do you not know me, then ?"

Suddenly a clock struck. This sound seemed to pain him, for an expression of melancholy surprise passed over his face, and chased the smile from his lips. He stood up, and with a disturbed look, gazed at the clock till nine strokes, one after the other, had died away in the room. The house-mother had observed the emotion of the stranger, and advancing to him, she also looked up at the clock with a wondering look, as if she expected to see something unusual about it, which she had never observed before.

"Yes, sir, it sounds prettily, doesn't it?" she said. "It has gone for twenty years so, and a watchmaker has never laid a finger on it."

"Twenty years," sighed the traveller; "and where then is the clock which used to hang here before? And where is the pretty image of the Virgin which stood there on the chimney-piece? Gone, destroyed, forgotten?"

The woman looked at the stranger with surprise, and answered—

"Our Zanna was playing with the image one day when a child, and broke it. It was so very badly made, at any rate, that the pastor himself had told us to buy a new one; and there it stands now. Is it not much prettier?"

The traveller shook his head.

"And the old clock you will hear immediately," she continued. "It is only a piece of lumber, and is always behind; it has hung for an age in our cellar. Listen, it is striking now!"

A peculiar noise might be heard proceeding from another part of the house. It was the voice of a bird, which cried "Cuckoo, cuckoo" for nine times in succession. A cheerful smile at once lighted up the stranger's face; and hastening, accompanied by the hostess, to a little cellar, he gazed with inexpressible joy at the old clock, as the cuckoo concluded its nine times repeated song.

Meanwhile, both the daughters of the family approached the traveller full of curiosity, and looked at him with wonder, turning their great blue questioning eyes alternately on him and on their mother. The looks of the two girls recalled the stranger to himself; and, apparently satisfied, he returned to the adjoining apartment, still followed by the mother and her daughters, all wondering at this mysterious conduct.

His heart was evidently gladdened by what he had seen; his countenance was lighted up with a sweet expression of love and genial feeling; and his eyes, moist with emotion, sparkled so joyously, that both the girls simultaneously approached him with visible interest. He took each by the hand, and said—

"What I do seems singular, children, does it not? You cannot understand, I daresay, why the voice of the old cuckoo moves me so deeply? Ah! I too was once a child; and in those days my father used to come every Sunday after church to drink his pint of beer in this very room. When I was good, I was allowed to come with him. And then I used to stand from hour to hour, waiting till the dear cuckoo should open its little door; I danced and skipt at its call, and in my childish soul I admired the poor little bird as an incomprehensible masterpiece of art. And the image of the Virgin, too, which one of you broke, I used to love, because it wore such a beautiful blue mantle, and because the little Jesus in her arms held out his little hands and smiled to me. The child of those days is now a man of threescore years; his hair is gray, and his face full of wrinkles. Four-and-thirty years have I lived in the wilds of eastern Russia; and yet I still remember the image and the cuckoo, as if only a single day had fled since my father last brought me here."

"Are you, then, from our village?" asked Zanna.

"Yes, yes," replied the traveller with joy. But the effect of his words was not what he expected. A smile played for a moment on the girls' features, but that was all: they seemed neither astonished nor overjoyed at his declaration.

"But where is the old landlord, Joostens?" he at last inquired of the mother.

"John the landlord, do you mean? He has been dead for more than five-and-twenty years."

"And his wife—the good, stout Peeternelle?"

"Dead too," was the reply.

"And the young shepherd, Andries, who could make such beautiful baskets?"

"Dead too," replied the hostess.

The traveller hung his head, and gave himself up for a time to melancholy reflections. Meanwhile, the woman betook herself to the barn, to tell her husband what had happened with this unknown visitor.

The farmer now entered the room heavily, and with the noise of his wooden shoes roused the traveller out of his painful reverie. The latter rose, and hastened to him with outstretched arms and a cheerful face, as if he would fain greet him as an old friend; but the farmer took his hand coldly, and looked at him with indifference.

"And you, too, Peer Joostens," he exclaimed sadly, "and you, too, do not recognise me?"

"No; I do not think I have ever seen you, sir," he replied.

"Then you do not know him who, at the risk of his life, dived under the ice at Torfmoor to rescue you from certain death."

The farmer shrugged his shoulders. The traveller seemed deeply pained, and said almost imploringly—

"Have you, then, forgotten the young man who used to take your part among your companions, and bring you so many bird's eggs to adorn your May-wreath?—him who taught you to make trumpets and whistles of the meadow-reeds, and took you with him when he drove Pauvel the brickmaker's son's fine cart to market?"

"I have forgotten," replied the farmer, doubtingly. "But I remember that my father, now in heaven, used to tell me that when I was six years old I was nearly drowned in the great Torfmoor. But it was Long John who pulled me out —and who, in the French time under Napoleon, was carried off, with many others, to be food for powder. Who knows in what unconsecrated ground his corpse is lying now? May God be gracious to his poor soul!"

"Ah! ah!" cried the stranger, with exultation, "now you know me: I am Long John—or rather, John Slaets, of High Dries."

As he got no immediate reply, he said with surprise—

"Do you not remember the rifle-shooter of the Muschen-guild?—him who for four leagues round was famed as the best rifleman? who had no equal in sureness of aim, and was envied by all the other young men because the young lasses looked so kindly on him? I am he, John Slaets, of High Dries!"

"It is possible," replied the farmer distrustfully; "but I do not know you, sir, and I hope you will not take it ill. There is no Muschen-guild in all our district; and what was formerly the shooting-ground is now the site of a country house, which has been for several years uninhabited, for Mevrouw is now dead."

Discouraged by the farmer's coldness, the traveller made no further attempt to recall himself to his recollection.

"In the village dwell many of my friends, who cannot have forgotten me," he said quietly, as he rose and prepared to go. "You, Peer Joostens, were very young indeed when all that happened; but Pauvel will fall on my neck the moment he sees me, I am quite sure of that. Does he still dwell on the moor?"

"The brickwork is long since burned down, and the clay-pits filled up. The finest hay in the whole parish grows there now; it is the rich Tist's pasture."

"And where is Pauvel?"

"The whole family were unfortunate, and left this quarter altogether. What has become of them I cannot tell: dead, without doubt. But I see, sir, you are talking of our grandfathers' times, and it will be a difficult matter to get an answer to all your questions unless you go to our grave-digger. He can tell over on his fingers everything that has happened these hundred years or more."

"I daresay, farmer; Peer John must now be ninety years old at least."

"Peer John? That is not our grave-digger's name: he is called Lauw Stevens."

A smile of pleasure overspread the traveller's countenance.

"God be thanked," he exclaimed, "that He has spared at least one of my old comrades!"

"Was Lauw, then, a friend of yours, sir?"

"My friend," said the traveller, shaking his head, "I can scarcely call him, for there was a perpetual rivalry, and sometimes strife between us. Love affairs were at the bottom of our differences. On one occasion, I well remember, when he and I were struggling, I threw him from the bridge at Kalvermoor into the stream beneath, and he was nearly drowned; but that is more than thirty years ago. Lauw will be glad to see me again. Well, Farmer Joostens, give me your hand; I hope to drink many a can of beer in your house!"

Taking his travelling-bag under his arm, he left the tavern, striking into a road behind it which ran through a plantation of young pines. Although the farmer's reception and information were not very cheering, they had notwithstanding poured some consolation and joy into his heart. The sweet odour of earlier years breathed round him; and with the flood of reminiscences which arose in his soul at every step, he felt as if born anew. The young pine-wood, it is true, which surrounded him on all sides, was strange to him; for on this spot a lofty fir-wood had stood, whose trees bore innumerable nests, and around whose borders grew the wild strawberry in abundance. The wood had disappeared like the people of the village: the old trees had died, and their children taken their place, to run their life-course in their turn. They were strangers to the traveller, and he consequently viewed them with indifference. But the song of the birds which resounded on every side was still the same; the wailing sough of the wind as it stirred the pine-tops, the chirping of the grass-hoppers, and the heath-breeze, with its delicious odours—all the eternal workings of nature were the same as in the days of his childhood and youth. Pleasing thoughts arose in the traveller's mind; and although he walked on with serene and happy feelings, he never raised his musing eyes from the ground till he had left the pine-wood behind him. Here fields and meadows were spread out before him, through which flowed a beautiful stream in pleasant windings; behind, at the distance of about a mile, the pointed church-steeple rose among the trees, with its gilded cock glittering in the sunshine like a day-star. Still farther off, the windmill lazily whirled its heavy red wings.

Overcome by the beauty of the scene, and the memories it suggested, the traveller paused. His eyes became moist, he let his travelling-bag fall on the ground, and spread out his arms, while the expression of a deep and fervent joy beamed upon his countenance.

At this moment the prayer-bell pealed forth the *Angelus*.

The traveller knelt down, and bending his head upon his breast, remained motionless in this attitude for a time, pro-longing his devotion, though visibly agitated and trembling. An earnest prayer streamed from his heart and lips, while he raised his eyes and folded hands to heaven, full of passionate gratitude. Then picking up his travelling-bag, he hastened impatiently on. Gazing at the church-steeple, he said in a low tone—

"You at least are not altered. humble little church. where

I was baptized—where, at my first communion, everything was so joyful, so wondrous, so beautiful, and holy! Ah! I shall see it once more, that image of the holy Mary, with its golden robe and its silver crown; St. Anthony, with his pretty little pig, and the black devil with his red tongue, of which I used to dream so often! And the organ, on which Sus the clerk used to play so beautifully, while we sang with loud and earnest voices—

'Ave Maria,
Gratia plena!'"

The traveller sang these last words with a loud voice. The associations which it suggested must have affected him deeply, for a glistening tear rolled down his cheek. Silently he moved on, sunk in self-forgetfulness, till he had reached a little bridge which led across the stream to a marshy meadow.

An indescribable smile now lighted up his countenance, as if his whole soul beamed there.

"Here," he said, with emotion, "I first took Rosa's hand in mine. Here our eyes first made that mutual confession which reveals heaven to the young and ardent, but yet trembling, heart. The yellow water-lilies sparkled in the sunshine then as now; the frogs croaked merrily, and the larks sang overhead."

Crossing the bridge, he stepped upon the heath.

"Ah," he said to himself, "even the little frogs which saw our love are dead—the flowers are dead, the larks are dead! Their children now greet the gray-haired man, who returns among them like a spectre from the past. And Rosa, my dear Rosa! does she still live? Perhaps! Married, it may be, and surrounded by her children. Those who are left behind forget, alas! the unhappy brother who roams far from his home!"

A serene and cheerful smile played round his lips.

"Poor pilgrim!" he sighed, "there boiled up in thy bosom

just then a feeling of jealousy, as if it were still spring-time for thy old heart! The season of love is long since past for thee. Well, it matters not, if only she recognises me, and has not quite forgotten our ardent attachment. O God! then I shall no longer lament my long journey of eight thousand miles; and shall go, half consoled, to join my parents and friends in the grave!"

Not far from the village, he entered a little tavern, of the sign of the "Plough," and asked the landlady to fetch him a glass of beer. On the hearth, by a great pot, sat a very aged man, who stared into the fire like an image of stone. Before the woman had returned with the beer, the traveller had recognised him, and, sitting down beside him, took his hand.

"God be praised, that He has granted you so long a life, Father Joris. You are one who belonged to the good old times! Do you not know me, then? No! The wild boy who used to creep through your hedge, and eat your apples before they were ripe?"

"Six-and-ninety years!" muttered the old man, without stirring.

"So it is," sighed the traveller. "But tell me, Father Joris, is Rosa, the wheelwright's daughter, still alive?"

"Six-and-ninety years!" hummed the old man, with a hollow voice.

The woman reappeared with the beer.

"He is blind and deaf, sir," she said. "Do not speak to him; he does not understand a word."

"Blind and deaf!" muttered the stranger despairingly; "what devastation inexorable time spreads in thirty years! Heavens! I wander here amid the ruins of a whole generation of men!"

"Did you ask after Rosa, the wheelwright's daughter?'

resumed the woman. "Our wheelwright had five daughters, but there was no Rosa among them; for the oldest is called Beth, and is married to the postman; the second is Gondè, who is a milliner; the third is called Nelé; and the girl, Anneken; and as for the little child, it is rather silly, poor thing!"

"But I do not refer to these people at all," said the traveller with impatience. "I speak of Kob Meulincz's family."

"Oh, they are all dead, long ago, sir," was the woman's reply.

This was a severe blow to the traveller; and, much agitated, he rose, and left the tavern with feverish haste. Before the door, he struck his hand upon his brow, and exclaimed, despairingly—

"O God! she too! My poor Rosa dead! Always, always that inexorable word 'dead!' 'dead!' Nobody on this earth knows me again. Not one looks on me with the eye of a friend!"

Tottering like a drunken man, he turned towards a pine-copse, and stood there quite unmanned by his grief, leaning his head on a tree. When his agitation was partially allayed, he went slowly towards the village. The path led by a solitary churchyard; pausing at the foot of the cross, he uncovered his head, and said, in a low and solemn voice—

"Here, before the image of the Saviour on the cross, Rosa plighted her troth to me; here she promised to remain ever true, and wait till I should return to my native village. We were overpowered by our sorrow; this bench was wet with our tears; and, quite mad with grief, she received from my hand the little golden cross—the love-pledge which I have so dearly redeemed. Poor friend! perhaps I am now standing on thy grave!"

With these melancholy thoughts, he sat down desponding

on the kneeling bench, and remained there for a long time, unconscious of everything around him. Slowly, at last, he turned his head, and gazed at the churchyard, where little hillocks indicated the most recent graves. It grieved him to see the many wooden crosses which had fallen through age; and which no child's hand had thought of raising up again over a father or a mother's resting-place. His parents, too, slept here; but who could help him to find their graves?

So mused he, long, sadly, and despondingly; mysterious, impenetrable eternity pressed upon his soul like a leaden tombstone, when suddenly a man's footsteps startled him out of his despairing thoughts.

Along by the side of the churchyard wall crept the old grave-digger, spade on shoulder. He bore the unmistakable marks of age and poverty; his back was bent by perpetual toil; his hair was white, and his face all covered with deep wrinkles; but strength and energy still lived in his eye. The traveller recognised his rival, Lauw, at first sight, and was about to hasten forward to greet him. But the bitter disappointments which he had already met with deterred him, and he resolved to say nothing, but wait to see whether Lauw recognised him.

The grave-digger paused a few paces off, and, after he had looked at him with apparent indifference, he began to mark off a long quadrangle, the limits of a new grave. Now and then, however, he cast a side look on the stranger, who sat before him on the bench, and a selfish and invidious kind of satisfaction seemed to sparkle in his eyes. The traveller, deceived by the expression which had suddenly passed over the grave-digger's countenance, felt his heart throb with the expectation that Lauw would approach and address him by his name.

The grave-digger looked at him again for a moment keenly,

then feeling in the pocket of his tattered waistcoat, pulled out an old book bound in dirty parchment, to which a pencil was attached by a leathern thong. Turning round, he seemed to note down something on one of the leaves. This act, taken in connexion with the exulting expression of his countenance, surprised the traveller so much that he went up to the grave-digger, and said with curiosity—

"What were you writing in the little book just now?"

"That is my affair," replied Lauw Stevens, gruffly. "You have stood a terribly long time on my list; I was making a cross at your name."

"You recognise me, then?" exclaimed the stranger joy-fully.

"Recognise!" said the grave-digger in a bitter and mocking tone; "I don't know that; but I remember well, just as if it had happened yesterday, that an envious villain once threw me into the river and nearly drowned me, because I was loved by Rosa the wheelwright's daughter. Since then, many an Easter candle has been burnt; but"—

"You were loved by Rosa!" interrupted the stranger. "It is not true, I tell you."

"Ah, you knew it well enough, spiteful fellow that you were! Had she not for a whole year worn the silver conse-crated ring which I had brought with me from Scherpenheu-vel? And did you not tear the ring forcibly from her, and throw it into the water?"

A sad smile passed over the traveller's countenance.

"Lauw! Lauw!" he exclaimed, "we do wrong; memory makes us children again. Believe me, Rosa did not love you, as you suppose; she took your ring only out of friendship, and because it was consecrated. In my youth, I was rough and rude, I fear, and did not always act nobly to my comrades. But shall four-and-thirty years have passed so destructively over men and things, and left nothing but our wretched passions unchanged? Ah, Lauw, shall the only man who recognises me be my enemy—and will he continue my enemy still? Come, give me your hand; let us be friends. I will make you happy for the remainder of your life."

The grave-digger withdrew his hand sharply, and said, in a gloomy and surly tone—

"Forget! I forget you? It is too late! You have poisoned my life. No day passes but I think of you; and do I think of you to bless your name, do you suppose? You yourself may determine that—you who have been the cause of my misery."

Folding his trembling hands, the traveller raised his eyes to heaven, and exclaimed in despair—

"God! God! hate alone knows me!—hate alone does not forget me!"

"You have done well," resumed the grave-digger, laughing, "in coming here to lie beside your blessed parents. I have kept a capital grave for you; I will lay the proud Long John under the roof-ledge, where the rain-water may get at him, and wash all the malice and villany out of his corpse."

A sudden trembling shook the traveller from head to foot, and a lightning-flash of indignation and wrath shot from his eyes. This violent excitement, however, quickly gave way to a feeling of dejection and pity.

"You deny your hand to a brother," he said, "who returns to the home of his youth, after an absence of four-and-thirty years! The first greeting which you address to your old comrade is bitter mockery! O Lauw, this is not right; still, be it so; let us say no more about it; only tell me where my blessed parents lie buried."

"I don't know," said the grave-digger surlily. "It is more than five-and-twenty years since they were brought here; and

I have dug fresh graves on the same spot three times since then."

There was something more than ordinarily painful to the traveller in these words; powerless, he let his head sink on his breast, while he stared intently on the ground, quite overwhelmed by his sorrow.

The grave-digger resumed his labour, but with an unsteady and hesitating hand, as if some deeper feeling were now at work within him. He looked and beheld the stranger's anguish, and seemed inwardly shocked at the secret and long-cherished revenge which had actuated his conduct, and impelled him to torture his fellow-man so mercilessly. This change of feeling was visible upon his countenance; the contemptuous smile had vanished, and he looked at his mourning comrade with rising sympathy. He then slowly approached him, and, taking his hand, said, in a low but impressive voice—

" John, friend, forgive what I have said and done! I have acted cruelly and maliciously. But, John, you do not know how much I have suffered through you."

" Lauw!" exclaimed the other, grasping his hand with emotion; " those were errors of our youth! And see how little I calculated on your hostility: your very naming me was itself an inexpressible joy to me. I am still grateful to you for that, though you have torn my heart by your bitter mockery. And now tell me where Rosa lies buried? In heaven she will rejoice to see us reconciled, and standing like brothers beside her last resting-place!"

" Buried!" exclaimed the grave-digger. " God grant that she were buried, poor thing!"

" What? what do you mean to say?" cried the traveller. " Is Rosa still alive?"

" Yes, she lives, if her heavy lot is worthy the name of life."

" You make me tremble.   For God's sake, speak! what
misfortune has befallen her?"

" She is blind."

" Blind? Rosa blind! She has no eyes with which to look
on me again! Alas, alas!"

Overcome by grief, he tottered back to the bench, and sank
down upon it.   The grave-digger approached him.

" For ten years she has been blind," he said, " and begs
her daily bread. I give her twopence every week ; and when
we bake, there is always a little loaf set apart for her besides."

The traveller sprang up, and warmly pressing the grave-
digger's hand, exclaimed—

" Thanks, thanks! God bless you for your kindness to her!
I will take it on myself to reward you in His holy name.   I
am rich, very rich.   To-day we shall meet again; but now,
without losing a moment, tell me where she lives; every
minute is another minute of misery to her."

With these words he drew the grave-digger by the hand
towards the gate of the churchyard.   From the wall Lauw
pointed with his finger to an object in the distance—

" Do you see the smoke rising from yonder little chimney
behind the copse?   There is the hut of the broom-maker,
Nelis Oems, and there Rosa lives!"

Without waiting for further directions, the traveller hastened in the direction pointed out, and passing through the
village, soon reached the solitary dwelling.

It was an humble hut, built of dry twigs and mud, but
clean outside and carefully white-washed.   Not far from the
door lay four little children sprawling on the ground in the
warm sun, or making wreaths of the blue corn-flowers and red
poppies.   They were barefoot and half-naked; the eldest, a
little boy of six, wore nothing but a linen shirt.   While the
three little sisters looked at the unknown visitor with shyness

and timidity, this little fellow, on the contrary, gazed at him
with a certain surprise and interest, mingled with an open-
hearted ingenuousness. The traveller laughed kindly to the
child, but, without stopping, entered the hut, where he found
the father busy with his brooms in a corner, and the mother
with her wheel by the hearth.

These people seemed to be about thirty years of age, and
appeared quite contented with their lot. For the rest, everything about them was as clean as rustic life would admit of in
a dwelling so confined. His entrance surprised them very little,
and they at once greeted him politely and put themselves at
his service, thinking that he wished to inquire the way;
and the husband, indeed, had already sprung from his seat to
accompany him to the door, and point it out. When he, however, said with manifest agitation and impatience, "Does Rosa
Meulincz dwell here?" the husband and wife exchanged a
strange look, and were so taken by surprise, that they
scarcely knew what to reply.

"Yes, sir," replied the man at last, "Rosa dwells here; but
she is gone on her begging rounds. Do you wish to speak
with her?"

"O God! where is she? Can she not be got at once?"

"It would be difficult, sir; she is gone on her weekly
rounds with our Trieny; but she will be home in an hour for
certain."

"May I wait here, then?" asked the traveller.

Scarcely had he uttered these words, when the man hastened
into a side-room and brought out a chair, which, though
roughly and coarsely made, was yet considerably cleaner than
the lame old chairs which stood in the room. Not content
with that, the woman drew a white cloth out of a chest, and
spreading it over the chair, requested the stranger to be seated.
He was delighted with this simple and honest kindness, and

returning the cloth with many thanks, he sat down. He then looked attentively about the room, hoping to find some tokens of Rosa's having been there. When looking to one side in search of some objects of this kind, he suddenly felt a little hand gently laid on his, and softly stroking his fingers. Surprised by this proof of affection, he turned round, and saw the blue eyes of the little boy gazing earnestly up at him with a beautiful smile of confidence and love, as if he had been his father or elder brother.

"Come here, little Peter!" exclaimed the mother. "You must not be so forward, child!"

Little Peter, meanwhile, seemed not to have heard this admonition, for he still continued to gaze at the unknown visitor, and to stroke his hands as before, so that the latter did not know what to make of it, so inexplicable was the interest which the child seemed to have in him.

"My dear little child," he sighed, "how beautiful your blue eyes are: you touch my heart deeply! Come, I will give you something, you are such a dear little fellow!"

He drew from his pocket a little gold purse, ornamented with silver and jewels of various colours—shook out some small coins, and gave them to the child, who stared at the present with astonishment, but did not, for all that, quit his hold of the traveller's hand. The mother now rose, and coming up to the child, said reprovingly—

"Peerken, Peerken, you must not be unpolite; thank the gentleman, and kiss his hand."

The little boy kissed his hand, nodded his little head, and with a clear voice said—

"Thank you, sir, Long John!"

A thunder-stroke could not have shook the traveller more powerfully than the simple utterance of his name by this innocent child. Tears rolled involuntarily over his cheeks; he took the child upon his knee, and looked deep into his eyes while he exclaimed—

"O you little angel! Do you then know me?—me, whom you have never seen? Who taught you my name?"

"Blind Rosa," was the reply.

"But how is it possible that you should have known me? or was it God himself who inspired your child's soul?"

"Oh! I knew you at once," said Peerken. "When I lead Rosa about, as she goes her begging rounds, she always talks of you; and she says that you are, oh so big! and that you have black eyes that sparkle; and she said that you would come home one day, and bring us all such beautiful things. And I was not afraid of you, sir, for Rosa told me that I was to be sure to love you, and that you would bring me a great bow and arrow."

The traveller listened earnestly to the sweet and simple revelations of the boy. Suddenly he took him in his arms and kissed him warmly; and then said in a cheerful tone—

"Father, mother, this child is from this time wealthy. I will train him, educate him, and endow him richly. His recognising me shall be the making of his fortune on earth."

The parents were quite overwhelmed with wonder and joy; and the man was scarcely able to stammer a reply—

"Ah! it is far too good of you. We knew you at once, but we could not be quite sure. Rosa has told us that you are a rich gentleman."

"And you, too, good people! you know me!" cried the traveller. "I am among friends here; I find a family and a relationship, where hitherto I have been met by nothing but death and forgetfulness."

The woman pointed to an image of the Virgin on the table, all blackened by smoke, and said—

" Every Sunday evening a candle is lighted there for the return, or . . . . the soul of John Slaets !"

The stranger raised his eyes devoutly to heaven, and fervently exclaimed—

" O God ! blessed be Thy name, that Thou hast made love mightier than hate ! My enemy has cherished my name in his heart, recalling it daily only to curse it ; but while my friend has lived in my memory, and breathed the love I felt for her on everything around me, she, too, has here preserved the memory of me, and made other hearts love me—while I was eight thousand miles away. I thank Thee, O God ! Thou art kind indeed !"

A long silence reigned till John Slaets had regained his calmness ; the people of the house observed his emotion, and the husband had considerately resumed his work, only looking up from time to time that he might be ready to run to serve the stranger, if any occasion arose.

The latter had now taken Peerken on his knee again, and said—

" Mother, has Rosa lived long with you ?"

The mother prepared herself to give him the beginning and the end, and the short and the long of the whole matter, and moving her spinning-wheel to his side, she sat down, and began—

" I will tell you, sir, how it has come about. You must know that when old Meulincx died, the children divided what he left among themselves ; and Rosa, who would not have married for all the money in the world—I need not tell you why—made over her share to her brother, on the condition that he should maintain her during her life. In addition to this, she was a dressmaker, and earned a considerable sum in this way, but did not give it to her brother. She devoted all her earnings to good works, visited the sick, and,

when the people were very poor, paid the doctor to attend
them. She had always a word of comfort for everybody, and
some reviving cordial in her pocket for those who were very
weak. It so happened that my husband—we had been only
half a year married then—came home one day with a dreadful cold ; listen—he has had that cough ever since. Next to
God, we have to thank the good Rosa that my dear Nelis
does not lie in his grave. Ah, sir, if you had but seen what
she did for us out of pure love and kindness ! She brought
warm coverings—for it was cold, and we were very poor. She
fetched two doctors from other parishes to consult together
about our Nelis ; she watched by my husband's bedside, she
lightened his sufferings and my grief with her kind, loving
words, and gave us all the money we required to pay for
medicine and food—for Rosa was beloved everywhere ; and
when she went to Mevrouw Hall, or to the wealthy farmers
about, a small gift for the poor was never refused her. And,
sir, our Nelis lay sick in bed for six long weeks, and all that
time Rosa took care of us, and helped us through, till my
husband, by degrees, picked up his strength again, and was
able to work."

" How you must have loved the poor blind Rosa !" sighed
the traveller.

The man raised his head for a moment from his work, and
with tears in his eyes, exclaimed with ardour—

" Could my blood restore her sight, I would let it be drained
to the last drop."

This fervent utterance of gratitude made a deep impression
on John Slaets. The woman perceived this, and giving her
husband an admonitory nod to be silent, she continued—

" Three months after, God sent us a child—it sits on your
knee. Rosa, who knew long before of its coming, wished
to be its godmother, and Peer, my husband's brother, was to

be godfather. On the christening-day, there was some conversation about the name which should be given to the child.
Rosa begged us to call the child John, but the godfather—a
good man, but rather obstinate, wished, and there was nothing
to object to it, that it should be called Peter after him. And
so, after a long discussion, it was baptized John-Peter; and
we call him Peerken, because his godfather—to whom he
belongs more than to Rosa, being a boy—will have it so, and
would be offended if we did not do it. But Rosa will not
hear of Peerken—she will call the child nothing but Johnny;
and the little fellow is accustomed to it already, and knows
that he is called Johnny, because it is your name, sir."

The traveller pressed the child passionately to his breast,
and kissed him warmly. Silently musing, he gazed intently
at the boy's laughing countenance, while his heart melted
with a sweet sadness. The woman continued—

"Rosa's brother had made an arrangement with some
people in Antwerp, to buy up victuals of every kind, in all
the places about, to send to England. He would soon grow
rich with this trade, people said, for every week he took ten
carts full of provisions to Antwerp. At first, all went well;
but suddenly some one failed in Antwerp, and the unfortunate
Tist Meulincz, who had been security, was ruined, and was
made so very poor by it, that all his goods were not enough
by half to pay his debts. He was not able to bear up under
it all, and died, poor fellow! may our Lord receive his soul!
—Rosa then went to live in a little room at Nand Flinck's,
in the corner yonder; but in the same year, Karel, Nand's
son, who had been taken for a soldier, came home with inflamed eyes. He had not been a fortnight at home, when he
lost his sight altogether. Rosa, who had felt great pity for
him, and always did what her kind heart bade her, had nursed
him during his illness, and now used to lead him about to

keep up his spirits, and refresh him a little. But Rosa soon caught the same disease, and has never since beheld the light of day! Nand Flinck is dead, and the children are scattered; the blind Karel is provided for by a farmer not far from Lier. We then begged Rosa to come and live here, and told her that we should be very much pleased to see her beside us, and would willingly work for her all our lives; and she came with pleasure.—And before God we can declare, that she has now been nearly six years here, and has never heard from us anything but words of kindness; but, then, she is all goodness and love; and if anything were to happen, which was to be pleasant to Rosa, I do believe our children would fight and tear each other's hair to be the first to "—

"And she begs!" sighed the traveller.

"Yes, sir, but that is not our fault," replied the woman with offended pride. " Do not think that we have forgotten what Rosa once did for us. Had it been necessary to yoke ourselves to the plough, and endure hunger for her sake, she would not have required to beg. What do you think of us, sir? No! we prevented it for more than six months; and that is the only wrong we have done to Rosa. As our family increased rapidly, Rosa feared in her angel heart that she would be a burden to us, and wished to assist a little. It was all in vain to oppose; she became quite ill with vexation; we saw this, and after half a year's entreaties, we were at last compelled to allow her to take her own way. But it is no disgrace to a blind woman. Though we are very poor, we are, thank God, not so needy as to require it; but she compels us for all that to take now and then a share of her gains, for we cannot be at variance with poor blind Rosa; but we give it back again in another way. For although she does not know it, she is better clothed than we, and the food which we prepare for her is much better than our own. A little pot is always devoted to her. See, there it is, two eggs with butter-sauce, in addition to potatoes! The remaining money she lays aside, if I understand her rightly, as a little portion to our children when they are grown up. We thank her from our hearts for her love; but, sir, we can do little else"

The traveller had listened with the deepest silence to this explanation; a quiet smile which beamed upon his countenance, and a slight occasional movement of tne eyes, were the only indications of the feelings of intense joy which filled his heart.

The woman had ceased speaking, and had set her wheel in motion again; while the traveller remained for a time occupied with his own reflections. Suddenly he put the child on the floor, and turning to the man, who was busy with his brooms, said in a tone very like a command—

"Cease working!"

The broom-maker did not understand at first what he was after, and rose from his seat, astonished at the tone of the stranger's voice.

"Cease, I say—and give me your hand, farmer Nelis."

"Farmer!" muttered the broom-maker with surprise.

"Come, come," cried the traveller. "To the door with your brooms! I will give you a hide of land, four milch-cows, a heifer, two horses, and everything else which goes to make up a comfortable farm-steading.—You do not believe me?" he continued, showing the broom-maker a handful of gold pieces. "What I say is true. I might give you this gold, but I love and respect you too much to put money in your hand. I will make you the possessor of a good hide of land, and even after my death, I will benefit you and your children."

The good people gazed at him with moist eyes, and appeared not yet quite to comprehend all he said. When the traveller was about to renew his promise, Peerken eagerly seized him by the hand, as if he would say something to him.

"What is it, my dear child?" he asked.

"Mr. John," replied the boy, "see!—the workers are coming from the fields. I know where Rosa is. Shall I run to meet her, and tell her that you have come?"

The traveller took Peerken's hand, and drew him towards the door—

"Come along; we shall go together!" he said; and taking leave of the family with a slight and hasty gesture, he accompanied the child, who led him towards the middle of the village. As soon as they had reached the first houses, the rustics came out of their barns and stables, and looked gaping after the traveller, as if they had seen a miracle. In truth, it was a wonderful spectacle to see the child in his shirt, and with his bare feet, laughing and talking merrily, as he skipt along by the side of this unknown stranger. The astonished villagers could not understand what the rich gentleman, who seemed to be a baron at least, meant to do with the broom-maker's little Peter. Still greater was their astonishment, when they saw him stoop and kiss the child. The only explanation of the matter which occurred to the wisest heads among them, and was soon pronounced before every house-door to be the true account of the matter, was, that the rich gentleman had bought the boy from his parents, and meant to adopt him as a son. This had often been done by city people who had no children of their own; and little Peter, with his great blue eyes and fair curly head, was certainly the prettiest boy in the village. But for all that, it was both strange and pretty to see the rich gentleman carry off the child in nothing but his shirt.

Meanwhile the traveller stept on. The whole village seemed to him irradiated with a heavenly light; the foliage coloured with a fresher green; the humble little cottages smiled to him, and it was for him the birds were singing their enchanting song; the air seemed filled with glowing life and balmy odours.

Revelling in this new feeling of happiness, he had turned his attention from the child. His eyes were fixed upon the distance, and his glance tried to penetrate the trees which limited the prospect at the other end of the village. Suddenly the child pulled his hand, and cried with a loud voice—

"There! down there, comes blind Rosa with our Trieny!"

An old blind woman might be seen, led by a little girl of five, entering the broad street of the village from behind a little house.

Instead of responding to the child's eagerness and haste, the traveller stood still, and looked earnestly and sadly at the poor blind woman as she slowly approached. And was this, then, his Rosa?—the beautiful, the lovely maiden, whose image, so fresh and young, was yet deeply engraven on his heart?

In a moment these thoughts vanished, and he hastened on to meet his friend. When he had approached to within fifty paces of her, he could restrain his emotion no longer, but, "Rosa, Rosa!" burst involuntarily from his heart. When the voice fell upon the blind woman's ear, she withdrew her hand from her guide, and trembled as if she had been struck by paralysis. She stretched out her arms gropingly before her, and, exclaiming, "John, John!" hastened towards her long-lost lover. At the same moment, she put one hand in her bosom, and tearing a string which hung round her neck, she held out a golden cross with an unsteady and trembling hand : and so she fell into her friend's arms. Then gently withdrawing from his embrace, she took his hand, and exclaimed—

"O John, I die of joy—but I have vowed a **vow to God** Come, come, lead me to the churchyard."

John Slaets did not understand what Rosa's purpose was; but feeling, from the tone of her voice, that an earnest, perhaps a sacred work was about to be done, he at once complied with her wish; and, without paying any attention to the villagers, who by this time surrounded them in great numbers, he led his blind friend to the churchyard. Here she turned towards the kneeling-bench, and with the words—

"Pray, pray; I vowed it to God," she forced him to kneel by her side.

She raised her hands, and for a long time prayed in a low murmuring voice. She then threw her arms round her friend's neck, and kissed him; but her strength had now failed her, and speechless, but smiling, she laid her head upon his throbbing breast.

Peerken, meanwhile, danced among the villagers, and as he clapped his hands, kept shouting as loud as he could—

"It is Long John! it is Long John!"

On a beautiful day in the autumn of 1846, the Diligence rolled as usual over the highway between Antwerp and Turnhout. Suddenly the driver pulled up, not far from a lonely tavern, and descending from his box, opened the carriage-door. Two young travellers sprang out upon the road, laughing, rejoicing, and swinging about their arms like two birds just escaped from a long imprisonment. They looked at the trees and the beautiful blue autumnal air with the cheerful, bright expression of people who have left the crowded city, and would now fain inhale with their breath the whole of broad, laughing nature. Suddenly the younger of the two turned his face towards the fields, while his face shone with poetic enthusiasm.

"Listen, listen!" he said.

From behind the fir-clumps there came the sound of distant

music. The measure was so light and gay, that one was compelled to associate it with the quick beating of dancers' feet.

The younger companion pointed with silent delight towards the pine-copse, and then exclaimed in a jocular way—

> "Oh! hark to the sound of the fiddle and horn,
> The dance and the song—'tis a festal morn.
> Oh! little they reck of dull care or of sorrow:
> They will laugh for the day—tho' they weep on the morrow."

"Come, come, friend John, your inspiration is premature. It is probably only the new burgomaster whom they are inaugurating."

"No, no, that is no official merriment. Let us go and see the peasant girls dancing—it is so wonderfully pretty."

"We shall first drink a glass of beer with mine host Joostens, and ask him what is going on in the village."

"And defraud ourselves of the pleasure of surprise? Prose!"

The travellers entered the tavern, and both burst into a loud laugh the moment they had put their heads into the room.

Mine host Joostens stood in front of the fireplace, as straight as an arrow, and as stiff as a log. His long, brown, copious Sunday-coat hung round him, reaching to his feet. He greeted the guests with a constrained smile, in which appeared a certain perplexity, for he dared not move his head in the least, as his high stiff shirt-collar took every opportunity of pinching him behind the ears. When the travellers entered, he called out with impatience, but without the slightest movement of his head—

"Zanna, Zanna, I hear the music. Did I not tell you that you would be too late?"

Zanna came running into the room with a great basketful of flowers. Oh! she was so beautiful with her folded lace-cap, her gown of pilot-cloth, the great golden heart upon her breast, and the dear little ear-rings! Her face was red with joy and delighted anticipation; it looked like a gigantic flower which is just on the point of unfolding its petals.

"A majestic peony opening its cup on a beautiful May-day!" whispered the younger.

Meanwhile she had fetched two glasses of beer, and then hastened out of the house with her flowers, singing and laughing as she went. With the greatest impatience mine host now shouted—

"Beth, Beth, if you do not come down at once, I shall go alone, as true as I stand here!"

Just at this moment the old clock, which hung on the wall, pointed to nine, and a bird's voice called in a plaintive tone—"Cuckoo! cuckoo! cuckoo!"

"What is the meaning of that?" asked one of the travellers. "You have sold the clock, I suppose, which used to hang here, to be tormented all the year round with that detestable song?"

"Yes, yes," said mine host with a cunning smile, "laugh at the bird as you please; it brings me fifty Dutch florins a year, and a bunder* of good land into the bargain."

In the distance, four gun-shots resounded at equal intervals.

"O Heavens!" cried mine host, "the fest has begun. The wife wears my very life away with her off-putting and dawdling!"

"But, mine host Joostens," asked the other traveller, "what is afoot here? Is it the church-fest to-day? That would be singular on a Thursday. Or is the king coming?"

"Things of far greater importance, sir, are going on here to-day: the like was never heard before! If you only knew it, you would not require—this time at least—to draw long

* Two hundred and forty feet long by one hundred and twenty broad.

bows and invent lies in order to fill your books. And this old cuckoo, too, has something to do with the tale of Blind Rosa."

"Blind Rosa!" cried the younger companion with joyful surprise. "What a beautiful title! It would be a good *pendant* to the *Zieke Jongeling*."*

"Hallo! that won't do," replied the other. "We have come out together to hunt after tales, and the spoil must be honourably shared."

"Well, well, we shall draw lots for it at once," muttered the younger, half sorrowfully.

"But," said the other, "it is all a mystery to us yet. Come, mine host Joris, off with that detestable collar, and let us have the story in a friendly way. You will get the book for nothing when it is printed."

"Yes, but I cannot tell you all the outs and ins of it at present," replied mine host. "There, I hear my wife on the stair; but come along with us to the village, and by the way I will let you know how it comes about that guns are firing and music playing so merrily to-day."

The wife entered with a dress which immediately fixed the attention of the younger traveller, by its flaming red, blue, yellow, and white colours. She ran up to her husband and affectionately tugged his shirt-collar up a little higher, and then taking his arm, ℓed him hastily out of the house. Both travellers followed.

Mine host Joostens now told the whole history of Blind Rosa and Long John to his attentive companions as they walked towards the village; and although he had spoken himself quite out of breath, the travellers did not cease to ply him with all sorts of questions. He told, likewise, how Herr

---

* These two travellers were Hendrik Conscience, the author of these tales, and Jan van Beers, unquestionably the greatest Flemish lyric poet of the day, and the author of the poem *De Zieke Jongeling*.

Slaets had purchased the old cuckoo clock, and promised him fifty florins a year if he would let it hang in his tavern-room as of old; how Long John had lived four-and-thirty years in Russia in Asia, and had amassed considerable wealth by the fur-trade; how he had purchased the estate of old Mevrouw, and meant to live on it with Rosa and Nelis's family, all of whom he had adopted; how he had given the grave-digger a large sum; and finally, how this very evening a grand peasants' banquet was to be given at the Hall, and for which a whole heifer was to be roasted, and two huge pots of rice-soup were to be boiled. Mine host was still in the full flow of his description, when they reached the broad central street of the village.

The travellers listened no longer to his talk, for they were now staring their eyes out of their heads, gazing at all the striking and beautiful things which presented themselves on every side. The whole village was adorned with pine-branches along the front of the houses in an uninterrupted line, bound together by snow-white kerchiefs or flower-wreaths. Interspersed, and above the spectators' heads, swung inscriptions in great red letters. Here and there a fine May-tree was planted, with its hundred tiny flags of gold leaf flittering against one another, with chains of birds' eggs, and ringing little glass rods. On the ground the boys and girls had scattered heath-flowers profusely, and formed out of them as usual the initials of Jesus and Mary. Alongside might be seen J. R., prettily woven with flowers. This was meant to stand for *John—Rosa*, and was the invention of the school-master. Amid all these beauties moved a living mass of people, who had flocked from the neighbouring villages to be present at this singular marriage-festival.

The young travellers amused themselves by moving from one group to another, and listening to the people's remarks. But when the procession was seen approaching the village through the fields, they hastened to the churchyard gate, and took up their position on an eminence whence they could see all that was going on. They looked upon the procession with a kind of reverence; and indeed, it was so beautiful and impressive, that the hearts of the travellers throbbed with emotion—for their hearts were young, and full of poetic enthusiasm. More than sixty little girls, between the ages of five and ten, all clothed in white, with a bright, child-like smile on their faces, advanced through the blue air like a little flock of lambs. Above their fresh little faces, and on their loose and flowing hair, lay a wreath of monthly roses, which seemed as if they would fain contest the prize of beauty with the laughing lips of the little maidens.

"It is one of Andersen's fairy tales," said the younger in a low voice. "The sylphs have left their flower-cups—Innocence, Purity, Youth, Joy! How beautiful it is!"

"Ha!" said the other, "there come the peonies all in a row, and Zanna Joostens at the head of them!"

The younger was, however, too much enchanted to condescend to notice this unpoetical remark. With a kind of rapture he was gazing at the great number of marriageable young maidens who followed the little children, all in their best ornaments, and beaming with life and health. How finely the features of those blooming girls came out under their snow-white lace caps! how charmingly their quiet virgin bashfulness was painted on their blushing cheeks! how bewitching was the shy smile which hovered round their lips!—like the gentle ripple which the summer-breeze stirs upon the lake, when it plays with the water and makes it laugh.

Ha! there comes Blind Rosa, leaning on her bridegroom's arm. How happy must the poor woman feel!—she has en-

dured so much; she was reduced to bear the beggar's wallet.
For four-and-thirty years she mourned her absent lover, and
cradled her soul in a hope which she herself half-suspected to
be a delusion. And there he is now, the friend of her childhood and youth! Leaning on his arm, she walks to the altar
of the God who has heard her prayers. The vows which they
interchanged under the cross near the churchyard are about
to be fulfilled. She is his bride! On her breast glitters
the plain golden cross which Long John gave her so many
years ago. She hears now the joy, the welcomings, the song,
and the music which celebrate his return. She trembles in
her agitation, and nervously presses her bridegroom's arm, as
if she almost doubted the reality of her happiness.

Behind comes Nelis, with his wife and children; they are
clothed now like country people well-to-do. The parents hang
their heads as they walk, and dry a tear of admiration and
gratitude from their eyes every time they look at their blind
benefactress. Peerken holds his head erect with a simple and
natural independence, and shakes his waving blond hair,
which falls in curls upon his neck. He leads his little sister
by the hand.

But what group is that? The ruins of an army, which
has been devastated by the sword of Time! Behind Nelis's
children totter twenty aged men: a singular spectacle indeed!
All are gray or bald; the backs of many are much bent; the
greater number support themselves on staves; two walk with
crutches; one is blind and deaf;—all suffer from age in one
form or another, broken down by the weight of labour and of
years, so that one might have supposed that Death with his
scourge was driving them before him, like a herd of cattle,
to the grave.

Lauw Stevens, with his hands almost touching the ground,
goes foremost; and the blind and deaf landlord of " The

Plough " is led by the miller's grandfather. These old people had lived when Long John was the cock of the parish, when every one had to yield to the courage and haughtiness of his lusty youth.

Behind these followed the villagers, men and women, who had been invited in a body to partake of the marriage-feast in the Hall.

The procession entered the church. Outside, the solemn pealing of the organ was heard.

———

The younger traveller took his comrade aside into the churchyard, and stooping and turning round, held out two blades of grass, whose points were just visible beyond his closed hand.

" Already ?" said the other; " you are in very great haste."

" Choose, choose at once !   I am eager for this subject, and I am impatient to know whether I may write upon it to-morrow or not.'

The elder drew one of the blades of grass out of his companion's hand : the younger let the remaining one fall to the ground, and sighed sorrowfully—

" I have lost !"

———

And so it happens, dear reader, that the elder of those two friends now narrates to you the tale of Blind Rosa. It is vexing, certainly; for, as it is, you have the story in prose, whereas you might have been reading it in inspired rhythmical verses. Another time may fate be more propitious to you !

THE POOR NOBLEMAN.

CHAPTER I.

TOWARDS the latter end of July 1842, an open carriage might be seen proceeding on its way to Antwerp, along one of the three great roads which lead from the confines of the Dutch territory.

This vehicle, though made to look its best, by careful and elaborate polishing, yet betrayed too clearly the poverty of its owner. It bore the marks of old age, swayed to and fro on its framework, and clattered in its wheel-boxes like a loose window-pane. The leathern covering, which was partly thrown back, glanced in the sun with the grease with which it had been besmeared, but the oily polish failed to conceal the scratches and rents in the leather. The door-handles, it is true, as well as the rest of the brasswork, were very carefully furbished, but the last remnants of what had once been silvering, and which might just be discovered by a minute examination of the ornaments, spoke of former wealth, now sadly diminished, if not entirely dissipated. The single horse which drew the carriage, was a strong but coarse animal; and it was easy to see, from its short and clumsy steps, that it had been intended for heavier work, and was more accustomed to the cart and the plough than to the light labour in which it was now engaged.

On the box, sat a peasant lad of seventeen or eighteen years, dressed in a faded livery, with gold lace round his hat, and white metal buttons on his coat; but the hat fell over his ears, and the coat was so long and wide that it hung round him like a great sack. This dress, the property of the master, had apparently been worn by many a servant, and was evidently still destined to adorn the person of many a successor.

The sole occupant of the carriage was a gentleman about fifty years of age. No one would have suspected that he was the master of such a servant, and the owner of such a crazy vehicle, for his appearance immediately inspired the spectator with respect and esteem.

With downcast eyes, and apparently sunk in deep reflection, he sat there motionless, till a rumbling of wheels announced the approach of another carriage. He then raised his head; his expression suddenly became more open, and assumed the clear lustre of contentment and complacency; and a gentle pride, which perhaps might rather be called self-respect, lighted up his features. Scarcely, however, had he exchanged a polite greeting with the passer-by, when his head slowly sank again upon his breast, and a quiet melancholy again took possession of his countenance. Spite of that, it needed only the glance of a moment to be attracted powerfully to this man by some secret sympathy. Although very thin, and covered with innumerable wrinkles, his face was yet so regular and noble; his expression so gentle, and yet so deep; his high-vaulted brow, so clear and strong, that one instinctively felt persuaded that this man was richly endowed with intellect and feeling.

Apparently he had suffered much. If his countenance had

not given this impression, it might have been inferred from the silver-gray hairs which already covered his head, and with which a peculiar flash of his dark black eyes, when he he was visited by some overwhelming thought, finely contrasted.

His dress was in perfect keeping with these outward characteristics; it bore the stamp of that rich, one might almost say, splendid simplicity, which considerable experience of the world, and a fine sense of the becoming, usually give. His linen was fine, and strictly clean; his clothes of excellent material; and his hat carefully brushed. At times too, and especially when any one passed, he drew from his pocket a beautiful golden snuff-box, and took a pinch with such neatness, and even elegance, that one might have inferred from this insignificant circumstance alone, that he was accustomed to move in the most refined society.

A critical or ill-natured eye, to be sure, might easily have discovered, on closer examination, that this gentleman's clothing was brushed thread-bare, that the nap of his hat had been elaborately smoothed over the worn-out rim, and that his gloves were sewed in more places than one. Nay, had one been able to peep into the carriage, one might have seen that there was a rent in his left boot, and that the stocking under it was blackened with ink. But all these marks of poverty were so skilfully concealed, and the dress was worn with such an air of wealth, and such a noble dignity of bearing, that most men would have at once concluded that if this gentleman did not wear finer clothes, it was only because he did not choose to do so.

The carriage had already rolled over the highway with considerable rapidity for about two hours, when the servant drew up in the causewayed court of a small inn outside Antwerp. The landlady and the hostler came out, and overwhelmed the gentleman with tokens of respect, while **helping** to unyoke the horse. The owner of the carriage must have been in the habit of putting up here, for every one addressed him by his name.

"Beautiful weather, Herr von Vlierbeke? But it grows rather warm; a little rain would do no harm to the high country, Herr von Vlierbeke. Shall we give the horse a feed of our oats? Ah! the servant has brought oats with him, I see. Have you any commands, Herr von Vlierbeke?"

While the hostess was uttering in rapid succession these and similar questions, Herr von Vlierbeke stepped out of his carriage, said some friendly words to the woman, hoped she was well, inquired after her family, and ended by saying that he must go immediately into the city. He shook hands with her heartily, yet with just so much of the manner of a kind patron, that the difference of rank between them was not thereby compromised. Then, after giving some directions to his servant, he turned quickly, but with a polite greeting, towards the bridge which led to the city.

At a solitary part of the outworks, Herr von Vlierbeke stood still to brush the dust from his clothes, and smooth his hat with his pocket-handkerchief; and then passed through the Red Gate. Now that he found himself in the city, where he had to pass men of all kinds, and where he could not be for a moment unobserved, he held his head and body erect, and gave to his mien that serene expression of self-satisfaction which impresses others with the belief that one is happy.— Such was the outward seeming, but, in secret, deep sorrow and anxiety oppressed his heart.

A humiliation awaited him, the very probability of which made his heart bleed. But there was a being on earth whom he loved more than his life or his pride of rank. For her he had already offered up that pride as a sacrifice—for her like a martyr suffered; and yet so powerful was that feeling of love in him, that every pain, every humiliation which he endured, exalted him in his own eyes, and made him regard sorrow as something which ennobles and sanctifies.

None the less, however, did his soul tremble and recoil under the effort; and the further he plunged into the city, and the nearer he approached the house where a sore trial of moral strength awaited him, the more impetuously did his blood course through his veins. He soon stood before a door: and as he pulled the bell, his hand trembled spite of the surprising self-command which he possessed; but the moment the servant appeared, he was again master of his feelings—

"Is the Herr Notary at home?" he asked.

After replying in the affirmative, the attendant conducted him into a small room, and then went to inform his master. So soon as he found himself alone, Herr von Vlierbeke threw his right foot over his left in such a position that the rent in his boot could not be perceived, and then drawing forth his golden snuff-box, took a graceful pinch.

The Notary entered with a business face, seemingly quite prepared to give a polite greeting; but scarcely had he perceived who his visitor was, when he assumed that expression of cold reserve which serves as a kind of armour of defence, when one foresees a troublesome business, and would fain get rid of it. Far from showing his usual loquacity and cordiality, he sat down, after a few words of ordinary politeness, opposite Herr von Vlierbeke, silently and with an inquiring look. The latter, hurt and humbled by this ungracious reception, felt a cold shudder pass over him; but making a great effort, he picked up courage, and said in a tone of expostulation—"Pardon me, Herr Notary; compelled by an unavoidable necessity, I once more throw myself on your goodness for a small service."

" And what do you wish from me?" asked the Notary.

" My object in coming to you is to obtain another and a final advance of a thousand francs, or even less, on mortgage of my estate. But I have a smaller and more urgent request. This very day I need money, and would fain borrow two or three hundred francs from you. You will not, I hope, refuse me this trifling assistance, which will rescue me from a great embarrassment."

" A thousand francs! on mortgage!" muttered the Notary. " Who would pay the interest? Your property is already burdened beyond its value."

" Oh! it cannot be, Herr Notary; you must certainly deceive yourself," replied the nobleman with great anxiety.

" Not at all, I assure you. At the request of those who have advanced money on your property, I have taken a valuation of all you possess, and put as high an estimate on it as it will bear. The result has been, that it is only in the event of a peculiarly favourable sale that it can meet the demands which will be made on it. You committed an irremediable folly, sir! Had I been in your place, I should not have sacrificed all my possessions, and my wife to boot, to an ungrateful, and I might almost venture to say, a dishonourable man, whether he were my brother or not."

Herr von Vlierbeke, seemingly overpowered by painful recollections, bent his head sadly, but gave no answer to the imputation thrown on his brother's character. He seemed to struggle with his feelings, and his finger pressed the gold snuff-box convulsively as the Notary proceeded—

" Through this one imprudent act you have brought yourself and your child to poverty: this can be concealed no longer. For ten long years have you, with God knows how much suffering, preserved the secret of your ruin; but now the moment approaches when you must sell all you have."

The nobleman looked at the Notary with an expression of agony and despair.

"It is as I have said," the latter continued. "Herr von Hoogebaen has died while travelling in Germany, and the heirs have got possession of the bond for four thousand francs, and have instructed me not to renew it on any terms. Herr von Hoogebaen was your friend, but the heirs know nothing about you. For ten years you have postponed taking up this bill, and during that period have paid two thousand francs as interest.—For your own good the thing must come to an end. The date of the bond gives you still four months' respite, Herr von Vlierbeke."

"Four months more," sighed the nobleman in a melancholy tone, "and then—O God!"

"Then, your goods will be sold by order of a court of law. Such a prospect, I easily conceive, must be very painful to you; but as an unavoidable misfortune threatens you, do your best to meet it with courage, and prepare yourself for the stroke. Permit me to dispose of your property at once, under some pretext or other, and so escape the disgrace of a compulsory sale."

Herr von Vlierbeke had been sitting for some minutes with his hands over his eyes, as if the sad intelligence which he had just received, had quite overwhelmed him. When the Notary suggested the voluntary sale of his property, he raised his head, and said with a constrained but painful composure—

"Your advice, Herr Notary, is both good and generous; but I cannot follow it. You know that all my sacrifices—my submitting to this life of misery, my never-ceasing anxiety— have but one object, the happiness of my only child. You are aware, and you alone, that everything which I do has a single, and, as I believe, a sacred purpose. Now, it almost seems at present as if God was about to answer my ten years' prayer. A tender affection has sprung up between my child and a wealthy man whose goodness and excellence I admire. His guardian seems favourable to the attachment. Four months! the period is a short one; but am I, by this proposed sale, at once to destroy all my hopes, and expose my child and myself to starvation, just at the very time when I may bring all my anxieties and sufferings to a happy termination?"

"So you mean to deceive these people, and perhaps expose your child to a still greater misfortune than poverty?"

The word "deceive" made the nobleman tremble; a cold shudder ran through his limbs, and a blush of shame overspread his fine brow.

"'Deceive!'" he sighed bitterly; "oh, never! But I do not wish to crush the feeling of love which has grown up so gently and insensibly between these two young hearts, by an unseasonable proclamation of the wretched state of my own fortunes. If any decided step were about to be taken, I should explain honestly how I stood. If my doing so shall blight my hopes, I shall then follow your counsel, sell my property, and leave my fatherland for some country where I can procure, by teaching, a maintenance, however miserable, for my daughter and myself."

For a time he was silent, and then added, as if struggling with his own feelings—

"By the deathbed of my wife, and by the altar of God, I vowed that my child should not participate in my calamity—that she should not feel the pressure of poverty, but lead a peaceful, a happy, and a free life. Hitherto I have fulfilled my vow; but these ten years' sufferings and ten years' humiliation have not enabled me to place her fortunes on a sure basis; but now, one ray of hope irradiates our dark future."

Then, trembling, he seized the Notary by the hand, looked

Into his face with a wild and anxious expression, and said imploringly—" Help me, my friend, at this critical time; do not torture me any longer, but give me what I ask. I will bless the name of my benefactor, the deliverer of my child, while I live!"

The Notary withdrew his hand, and replied with visible annoyance—

" But I do not understand what bearing all this has on the sums you wish to borrow?"

Herr von Vlierbeke put his hand in his pocket, and said, in a peculiar tone—

" Ah, it is amusing, is it not, to sink so low as to see life-long happiness or misery dependent on things which other men would laugh at? Well, to-morrow the young man and his uncle dine with us. The uncle invited himself. We have nothing to set before them; and my daughter requires a few articles of dress to make her presentable, especially as we shall also be invited by them in turn. Our solitude, therefore, can no longer conceal our poverty. Sacrifices of every kind must be made to save us from shame."

At these words, he drew his hand out of his pocket, and showed two francs in a little purse.

" See!" he said with a bitter smile, " that is all I possess in the world; and to-morrow I have to entertain wealthy visitors. If my poverty is in the smallest degree betrayed, then all hope for my child is at an end. For God's sake, Herr Notary, do not deny me your generous aid."

" A thousand francs!" muttered the Notary; " I cannot deceive my clients. What security will you give me? You possess nothing which is not overburdened already."

" A thousand, or five hundred, or two hundred—let me have something, whatever it may be, which will deliver me from the present difficulty."

"I have no money at my disposal at present," was the cold reply. "Perhaps in a fortnight; but I cannot say for certain."

"Then, for our friendship's sake, lend me out of your own purse."

"I cannot hope that you will ever be in a position to repay the loan," interrupted the Notary impatiently. "It is, therefore, alms which you are asking."

The nobleman wrung his hands painfully; he grew pale; his eyes flashed, and his brow grew dark with passion; but he controlled this violent emotion, and, looking up, he muttered with a kind of melancholy indifference—

"Alms, do you say? Be it so. Even this last drop of the cup of suffering will I drink—it is for my child!"

The Notary took some five-franc pieces out of a drawer and offered them to him. Whether it was that he now felt more keenly the degradation of taking alms, or that the sum offered was so entirely inadequate, he looked at the money for a time with a wild stare, and then, throwing himself back in his chair, he covered his face with his hands.

At this moment a servant entered and announced a stranger; the nobleman sprang up the moment the servant left the room, and wiped a few tears from his eyes. The Notary pointed to the money on the table; but Herr von Vlierbeke, shuddering, turned aside his head, and said hastily—

"Herr Notary, pardon my boldness; I have still one favour to beg of you."

"What is it?"

"In the name of my child, secrecy!"

"On that point, you have already had long experience of me. Have entire confidence. Will you, then, not accept this small help?"

"Thanks! thanks!" cried the nobleman, as he pushed

aside the Notary's hand, trembling as if an ague were on him, and hastened from the room and the house, without waiting to be shown out by the servant.

Overwhelmed by the humiliating blow which he had received, almost unconscious, and tortured by a deep sense of shame, his head on his breast, and his eyes fixed on the ground, the wretched nobleman hastened, apparently without a purpose, from street to street, and seemed not to know where he was, or whither he was going. At last, the feeling of necessity roused him from his feverish dream, and, turning his steps towards the Burgerhout gate, he wandered along the fortifications, till he found himself alone in a solitary spot.

There, pausing, a severe internal struggle seemed to commence. His lips moved rapidly, while his countenance expressed pain, despair, and shame, by turns. Meanwhile he drew the gold snuff-box from his pocket, and, with an expression of intense grief, gazed for a long time on the arms engraven on its lid, and then relapsed into a melancholy reverie. Soon after, he shook off his sad thoughts, as if he had come to some important conclusion, and said, with a low but faltering voice, full of deep emotion—

"Last token of a mother's love! Guardian angel, who hast so long concealed my misery!—sacred shield, which I have thrown over a penury which all else, alas! too clearly indicated; thou time-honoured heirloom of my father! to thee, too, must I say farewell—thee must I with my own hand dishonour! May this last resource in our necessity rescue us from a still deeper humiliation!"

A tear rolled over his face as he proceeded with his singular business, and with a knife scraped the snuff-box till the arms were quite indistinguishable. He then returned to the city, where he threaded his way through narrow and solitary streets, examining the signboards as he passed along with a timid and shy look. After he had crept about in this way for more than an hour, he came to a small lane in the St. Andrew's quarter, where, as his face at once indicated, he found the object of his search. His eye was fixed upon a signboard on which were inscribed the two words, "Sworn Hill-carrier." This signified that some one lived in the house who lent money for pledges, as the representative of the establishment called *Mont de Piété*. The nobleman passed the house, and walked to the end of the street; then turned, and walked, now slowly and now quickly, up and down, always quickening his step when he saw any one approaching. At last he found a favourable moment, and trembling as he crept along the wall, he slipped into the house on which he had perceived the signboard. He reappeared after a considerable time, and fled round the corner of another street. A certain satisfaction was perceptible in his eyes; but the dark red which still suffused his face clearly indicated that he had obtained the desired relief only at the cost of a new humiliation.

He proceeded into the middle of the town, and entering an eating-house, purchased a fowl, a meat-pie, some preserved fruits, and other little dishes, and having got them packed in a basket, said that he would send his servant to fetch them. He then purchased at a silversmith's a pair of silver spoons, and a pair of ear-rings, and then left this quarter apparently with the intention of providing himself with various other articles.

CHAPTER II.

On many of the waste heaths of our country, man has begun a victorious contest with nature, in his efforts to awaken the soil out of its sleep of ages. He has stirred up the arid entrails of the earth, and dropt the sweat of his brow into its lap; has called science and industry to his aid; has drained marsh and moor; has led the rich mountain-water from the bed of the Meuse into diverse channels, and so caused its fertilizing life-veins to permeate the soil which for more than a thousand years has lain in a sleep of death.

Glorious struggle of man with matter! ever-to-be-lauded victory, which one day will convert the barren Kempenland into a fertile garden! Truly, our posterity will scarcely believe that where a waving sea of corn or a green meadow is spread out before their enchanted gaze, the sun's rays were once reflected by the bright and barren sand.

To the north of the city of Antwerp, towards the borders of Holland, one can perceive scarcely any traces of these beginnings; here and there only, close by the highway, a part of the heath is enclosed; but more inland, in the heart of the district, everything is waste and sterile. Yonder, as far as the eye can reach, nothing is visible but a scorched plain, whose only ornament is the never-failing heath-flower. Yonder are wide-extended lands where nothing bounds the horizon save that bluish mist—always a sure sign that the waste extends much farther than the eye can reach. If one has wandered far over these plains, he will know that here and there he comes unexpectedly upon some winding little brook, whose banks are adorned with wild-flowers and low willow clumps. By the side of this murmuring heath-stream, farm-houses, villas, and whole villages may be met with, as if man, like the soil beneath him, needed only running water to enable him to find nourishment and to live. In one of those spots where willows and bushes of various kinds abounded, stood a Hall of considerable size, to which a retired path led. The lofty trees which threw their shadow so majestically round, showed that man had been here for centuries; and the moat which surrounded the hall and its immediate environs, as well as the stone bridge before the gate, justified the inference that a lordly estate must be attached to it. This property went by the name of Grinselhof.

The farm-house, with its stables, barns, and out-houses, occupied the whole front of the domain, and almost prevented the passer-by from seeing what was going on behind the thick wood, and within the moat. That, indeed, was to a great extent a secret to the farmer himself. Behind his house and farm-yard there rose a thick plantation, which, like a curtain, concealed the interior of the domain from his curious eyes. Neither he nor any one of his family were allowed to pass this limit uninvited. In the depths of this seclusion, among the highest trees, stood a large house, called by the peasantry the Castle. Here dwelt a nobleman and his daughter, as lonely and retired as hermits, without attendants either male or female, and carefully avoiding all society. The rumour was that this nobleman, notwithstanding his extensive possessions, avoided the intercourse of his fellow-men through avarice and parsimony.

So far as the farmer was concerned, the secret was impenetrable; for he honoured his master's privacy too much to throw any light upon his circumstances and mode of life. It was to him a profitable farm. The soil was fruitful there, and the rent moderate. He showed himself grateful to his master for this, and willingly lent him a horse to convey him every Sunday morning to the village, where the nobleman and his daughter regularly attended Divine service. On urgent occasions, too, his younger son acted as servant to the proprietor

It is late in a July afternoon, and the sun has nearly completed its daily course in the heavens, and dips towards the western horizon; but its rays, though they have lost their mid-day heat, are still warm, and pour over nature a rich and varied glow. On Grinselhof, too, the declining sun beams brightly and serenely down between the over-arching foliage. While its rays paint the tops of the trees with softer tints, the green on the farther side grows darker, and the interior of the wood more mysterious and gloomy. Giant shadows now stretch over the ground; and after the sultry heat of the day, a fresh evening coolness slowly rises from blade and leaf, and fills the air with its reviving odour. Spite of all this, however, everything is gloomy round Grinselhof. A deathlike stillness lies like a funeral pall over the lonely dwelling; the birds are silent, the wind is hushed, and not a leaf stirs. Nothing but light; it alone seems to live here.

One might have supposed, from the absence of all motion and of all sound, that amid these melancholy shades nature lay sunk for ever in a magic sleep. If one let his eye wander round in the impenetrable gloom, in the vain endeavour to pierce through the wild entangled foliage, it was only to recoil with a shudder, as if the quiet mystery of this spot held some yet undivulged horror in its breast.

Suddenly a rustle is heard among the bushes, and the little branches bend and quiver; some one swiftly springs through them; many birds leave the copse in alarm, and fly terrified hither and thither, as if endeavouring to escape some approaching danger. Perchance there comes some human being, to bring life and sound where death and silence seemed to have an eternal empire.

Yonder the copse opens, and a young maiden, all clothed in white, springs forward from among the hazel bushes, chasing a butterfly with a silken net in her hand. She leaps and runs more swiftly than a roe; stretching her slender body, with her arms above her head, and scarcely touching the ground with her tiptoes, she seems winged, and more agile than the birds which she had just startled from their hiding-places. Her long hair falling in thick clusters on her beautiful neck —see with what a bound she rises from the earth!

How beautiful! how magnificent is that butterfly, which flutters and dances overhead as if it had pleasure in sporting with the young girl—its indented wings all over-sown with eyes of azure, purple, and gold!

A cry of joy, like a clear musical tone, burst from the maiden's lips. She thought she had caught the object of her chase, but she had only touched it with the edge of the net and ruffled its wings. The butterfly rises high into the air, and is soon far beyond reach; while she looks sadly after it, till its colours melt into the blue of the sky.

The girl stands panting for a moment till she has regained her breath, and then with slow steps strikes into a broad footpath. How beautiful she is! The sun has somewhat embrowned the soft colouring of her face, but only to deepen the glow upon her cheeks, and to give to it the full expression of mental energy and bodily health. Under her high brow her black eyes gleam like stars through her long eyelashes;

her finely-cut mouth encloses two rows of glancing pearls, which peep out between lips which might shame the bloom of the fairest rose. All the charms of this bright virgin face are surrounded by a crown of wavy and flowing hair, which lies cradled on her shoulders, here and there revealing a white and swan-like neck. Her form is slender, and scarcely concealed by the simple white garment which she wears. When she raises her head, and bending back, gazes into the blue heavens above her, one might almost believe that he saw the dream-form of some spirit of the air, and imagine that this maiden was the elf of Grinselhof.

Wandering over the winding paths—now visited by some pleasing memory which lighted up her face with a smile, at another time repressing some deeper emotion of the heart, and standing with earnest face, and eyes fixed upon the ground—she approached a flower-bed, in which some favourite pinks were fast withering under the heat. These flowers were evidently objects of more than ordinary affection, for they were all bound carefully to white stakes, and not a weed was permitted to show its head among them. The selection of the flowers, the childlike precautions by which they were surrounded, a tone of motherly care which could be felt better than expressed—all betokened that they were reared and tended by a female, or rather a loving virgin hand. The maiden had already perceived from a distance that the flowers were drooping; she approached them with an anxious face, stooped down, and taking a faded blossom in her hand, said—

"Alas, my poor flowers! I forgot to water you yesterday. You are thirsty, are you not? And now you stand patiently there, pining away waiting for me, and hanging your little heads as if you would die!"

Musing a little, she added: "But since yesterday I have been so distracted, so joyful, so very happy!"

Then looking to the ground modestly and bashfully, she whispered, with a scarcely articulate voice—" Gustav !"

For a time she stood motionless in this attitude, and forgot her flowers, and the whole world besides—seemingly all alone with some charming creation of her fancy. Again her lips moved, and she whispered—

" Ever, ever, his image before my eyes—ever his voice haunting me ! It is impossible to free myself from this magic spell; how my heart beats ! Heavens ! what is this I feel ? Now my blood boils in my veins, now flows cold and slow, and again hastens in wild pulsations through my heaving bosom. My heart is heavy ; a vague anxiety, which I cannot name, possesses me ; and yet my soul exults, and is filled with a deep and mysterious rapture !"

She stood silent and motionless for some time ; then, seeming suddenly to awake, she raised her head, and with a characteristic movement shook the thick curls hastily from her face, as if she would thus free herself from some overpowering thought.

" Wait a minute," she said to the pinks with a smile ; " I will bring you help and refreshment." And springing aside, she broke a few twigs and constructed a screen for the flower-bed ; then, picking up a watering-pot which lay near, ran through the grass to a little fish-pond overhung by weeping willows. When she approached, the surface of the water was smooth and calm ; but scarcely had her form been reflected in it, when the whole pond seemed to swarm with living beings : hundreds of little fishes, of every size and colour—red, white, and black, came shooting from every side, and pushed their little heads out of the water, snapping their mouths as if they would fain talk with their young mistress. Holding fast with one hand by the stem of the nearest willow, she bent gracefully over the water, and endeavoured to fill the can without touching her little friends.

"Come, come, let me alone," she said, as she gently pushed the fishes aside to make room for the pot; "I have no time to play with you at present. I shall fetch your dinner very soon."

But the fish insisted on playing round the watering-pot while it remained; and even after the young girl was gone, they seemed attracted to the spot on the edge of the pond which had been pressed by her feet, and passed and repassed it with swift and shooting motions.

The maiden had watered the flowers, and the watering-can had slowly dropt from her hands. With thoughtful and downcast eyes she directed her steps towards her lonely dwelling, then returning with some bread for the fishes, wandered round the garden-paths sunk in a deep reverie.

At last she approached a spot where an old Indian jessamine stretched its hanging branches over the path. Under its broad shadow were a table and two chairs. A book, inkstand, and some ladies'-work, indicated that she had already spent part of the day here. She sat down, and taking up the book and the work by turns, let both fall heedlessly from her hands; and then giving herself entirely up to her musing, she rested her graceful head upon her hand, as if weary, and needing repose.

For some time her eyes wandered unsteadily from object to object : a sweet smile played at intervals round her mouth, as if she were conversing with some beloved friend. But ere long her wearied eyelids slowly sank—rose again only to sink more heavily, till at last a deep sleep fell upon her.

"Did she sleep?" Her soul, at least, was awake and happy; for that charming smile was still visible on her countenance, vanishing at times to give place to a calmer expression, and then coming again, as a token of the perfect peace and joy which existed in the mirror-like purity of the maiden's soul. Surely the creations of her dreaming fancy took shape and hovered before her eyes in the evening red, pouring a flood of happiness over her heart!

Long she lay there, in entire self-oblivion, and cradled in delicious dreams.—

There was a noise at the front gate near the farm-house, and the loud neighing of a horse broke the stillness of Grinselhof; but the maiden did not awake. The old vehicle had returned from the town and had stopped at the farm-yard, and the farmer and his wife hastened up to welcome their master and unyoke the horse.

While they were busying themselves in this way, Herr von Vlierbeke stepped out of the carriage and addressed some friendly remarks to them, but in a tone so melancholy, that both simultaneously looked at him with surprise. At other times, and even in his most kindly and cheerful moods, a quiet earnestness and gloom never left him; but on this occasion a more than ordinary dejection was imprinted on his face. He seemed very much exhausted; and his eyes, usually so full of vivacity, had now a dull and heavy motion under his hanging eyelids.

The horse had been put in the stable; and the young man, who had already laid aside his livery, took some baskets and packets out of the carriage, and carried them into the house Meanwhile, von Vlierbeke went up to the farmer and said—

"Hans, I shall need you to-morrow; there are to be visitors at Grinselhof. Herr Denecker and his nephew dine with us."

The farmer looked at his master with astonishment; he could scarcely believe that he heard rightly. After a short pause, he said, with a doubting look—"The stout, rich gentleman, who sits beside you in church on Sundays?"

"Well, Hans, what is so surprising in his paying me a visit?"

"And the high-spirited young Herr Gustav, who after service yesterday spoke with our young lady?"

"The same."

"Ah, sir, those are very wealthy people; they have purchased all the property round Echelpoel. At their country seat ten horses stand in their stables, in addition to those which they have in town. Their carriage is all adorned with gold and silver from top to bottom."

"So I believe, and it is just for that reason that I am particularly desirous to receive them as becomes their position. Hold yourself and your wife and son in readiness; I will call you early to-morrow morning, and you will not object to lend me a hand, I hope?"

"Not at all, sir, not at all. We shall do what you wish with the greatest pleasure; a word from you is enough. We are too happy to be of any service to you."

"I thank you for your kindness. It is arranged, then: to-morrow morning early." And so saying, Herr von Vlierbeke entered the farm-house; and after giving some orders with respect to the baskets which had been taken out of the carriage, he struck into the wood which stretched from the farm to Grinselhof.

So soon as he was out of sight of the farmer, his countenance assumed a freer expression, and a cheerful smile lighted up his face as he looked about apparently in search of some one in this solitude. Suddenly his eyes fell on the sleeping girl. As if under the influence of some magic power, his steps became slow and cautious, and he finally stood still, gazing with rapture at his child.

How beautiful was the sleeping girl! Her wavy locks lay in graceful disorder on her cheeks; the setting sun cast a

mellow radiance around her, and bathed her in its rich warm
glow. The Indian jessamine had dropt some of its blossoms upon her head, and strewed the ground with its white
cups. She still dreamed, and a smile of calm happiness
dimpled her features, while her lips moved and whispered
some scarcely articulate words—as if her soul, too full of joy,
had wished to unburden itself by utterance. Herr von Vlierbeke stood long, scarcely daring to breathe, and caressing
with loving eyes that sweet and maidenly creature. With
deep feeling he raised his eyes to heaven, and said—

"Thanks be to Thee, O Almighty God! she is happy. Let
me be for ever miserable; but, oh, may my suffering make
Thee merciful to her! Thy favour and protection for my child
is all I ask. May this her sweet dream be true, O God!"

After this short but fervent supplication, he sat down on the
chair which stood near her, and cautiously leaning his arm upon
the table to support his head, he gazed on his daughter with a
smile of joy and admiration. Her virgin beauty must have
been to him a source of intense happiness, for its miraculous
power seemed in a moment to dispel his sufferings and anxiety.
He kept his eye fixed intently upon her, with an indescribable
rapture; and the changing emotions which played over the
girl's features were repeated in his, as in a faithful mirror.
Suddenly a deep blush suffused her brow; her lips moved
again with more distinctness; her father watched them with
eager attention; and though she had said nothing audibly,
he was yet able to distinguish one of those empty soundless
words which had vanished into the air with her breath.

With a pleasure equal to hers, he added—

"Gustav!—she dreams of Gustav! Her heart is one with
mine; may all go well—may God look on us propitiously!
Yes, my child, open thy heart to the delicious feeling of hope
alone—dream on! But who knows? Yet I will not imbit-

ter these sweet moments by the cold image of reality. Sleep on, sleep on, and let thy soul bathe itself in the magic stream of a budding love!"

Herr von Vlierbeke sat for some time in still contemplation of the young girl; then, rising, went behind her, and imprinted a long kiss upon her brow. Still half dreaming, she opened her eyes slowly; but scarcely had she perceived who had roused her, than she sprang up, and throwing her arms round her father, hung on him affectionately, and asked him all sorts of questions in the midst of her tender caresses. The nobleman turned from his daughter, and said, with a sly jest—

"I suppose, Lenora, I need scarcely ask to-day what beauties you have discovered in Vondel's *Lucifer?* You cannot have had time, I fear, to begin a comparison of this masterpiece of our language with Milton's *Paradise Lost?*"

"Ah, father, I do not know what is wrong with me to-day; but I have such singular feelings—feelings which I cannot describe. I have not been able to read with attention."

"Well, Lenora, do not trouble yourself about it. Sit down, my child, I have something important to say to you. You do not know why I went to town to-day?—we have guests to-morrow."

She was astonished at this news, and looked at her father with surprise.

"It is Herr Denecker who is to be our visitor to-morrow; the wealthy merchant who sits near us at church, and lives in Echelpoel Castle."

"Yes; I know him very well. He has always a kind greeting for me, and hands me out of the carriage when we stop at the church-door. But"—

"Your eyes ask whether he comes alone. No, Lenora, some one accompanies him."

"Gustav?" she exclaimed, while a blush of modesty over spread her brow.

"Yes," replied her father, "it is Gustav. Do not tremble or be alarmed, my child, because your soul is now for the first time opening itself to a new sentiment. Between you and me, there can be no secret which my deep love cannot penetrate."

The maiden looked into her father's eyes, and seemed to seek the solution of this mysterious language in his mild and amiable expression. Suddenly, as if her heart had been enlightened all in a moment, she threw her arms round his neck, and said, with fervent gratitude—

"Father, dear father, your goodness is infinite!"

For a time the nobleman, with joy depicted on his countenance, held his daughter in his embrace; but gradually an expression of deep sadness overspread his features, and a tear glistened in his eye, as he said with emotion—

"Lenora, whatever occurs in life, and whatever misfortunes await us, you will ever love your father as you do now, will you not?"

"Always! always!"

"Lenora, my child," sighed the father, "your sweet affection is my only joy on earth—my very life. Do not rob my soul of this consolation."

The melancholy tones of his voice so alarmed the maiden that she took his hand affectionately in hers, and, laying her head on his breast, began to weep in silence.

For some minutes they remained in this position without stirring a limb, and overpowered by something which could be called neither joy nor sorrow, but mysteriously partook of both these feelings. The father's countenance was the first to alter its expression; he looked serious, and shook his head, as if reproaching himself. In truth, the singular words which had drawn tears from his daughter's eyes, had been prompted by the thought that another would one day share his child's affection, perhaps estrange it entirely from him. Ready for any sacrifice, even if it were disproportionately great, which could in the least contribute to his child's happiness, still, the idea of such a separation painfully affected him.

"Come, come, Lenora," he said caressingly, "be cheerful and happy again. There is a happiness sometimes in unburdening our souls when an excess of feeling oppresses them. Let us go in; I have still much to tell you to prepare you for receiving our guests in a proper way."

Both approached the house with slow steps, but a few tears still lingered in Lenora's beautiful eyes.

Some hours later, Herr von Vlierbeke sat in the largest room in the house, leaning his elbow on the table, on which stood a little lamp. The apartment, which was only lighted in one place, while all the corners were lost in a deep gloom, had something dismal and deathlike about it. The flickering flame of the lamp threw its light in long streaks upon the walls, conjuring up spectre-like forms out of the darkness, while the old portraits kept their eyes fixed on the table with an obstinate stare. The fine and calm countenance of the nobleman was the only object which stood out from the appalling gloom. His bright eye appeared to be gazing intently into the darkness, and he sat like an immovable statue, apparently listening attentively to catch some expected sound. At last he rose quietly, and, noiselessly approaching the other end of the room, he applied his ear to the lock of a door.

"She sleeps," he whispered to himself, and then, as he raised his head, looked upward, and said—

"May God guard her repose!"

Approaching the table, he took the lamp in his hand, and

opened a press which was fitted into the wall. Kneeling down, he took from a drawer some napkins and a table-cloth, unfolded them, and looked at them with a scrutinizing glance to see that they were free from any stain. A smile of satisfaction showed that he was pleased with the result of his examination.

He then took out a little basket, and placing it on the table, brought a rag and a piece of chalk from a drawer, and breaking the latter with the handle of the knife, he began to rub and furbish the silver knives and forks which lay in the basket. He did the same with the salt-cellar and other little dishes, which were chiefly of silver, and which, with their thin embossed ornaments, gave the appearance of considerable wealth.

While he was engaged in this humble occupation, his mind was given up entirely to the past. The fixedness of his face and eyes, although now and then he looked round timidly and anxiously, showed that he was sunk in deep reflection. From time to time his lips moved, and half audibly uttered some words in impressive and affectionate tones; words evidently associated with beloved memories, for they were always accompanied by a smile. He had named all the names which had been dearest to him on earth, and perhaps enjoyed again the pure happiness of his youth. His voice became clearer as he sighed—

"Poor brother! one man alone knows what I did for you, and he dares to call you an ingrate and a deceiver; while you, sick and sorrowing, wander forlorn the wide plains of North America. For small recompence, you roam over the wastes and prairies, where for months you are never cheered by the sight of a human face. You, a nobleman like myself, are the servant of the Saxon; and for a scanty subsistence procure the furs which serve to adorn the persons of the wealthy. Ah, bitter are the sufferings I have endured, and still endure, for your sake; but God is my witness, that love of you still lives undiminished in my heart. May your soul, O my brother! while you sit and mourn amid these solitary plains, feel this sigh of mine, and may its sympathy console thee in thy misery!"

The nobleman sat for a time sunk in contemplation of his brother's fate; at last, by an effort he dispelled these thoughts, and fixed his attention exclusively on his work. He laid the silver-plate on the table, and said musingly—

"Six forks and eight spoons, and four of us sit down to table; things must be well managed, otherwise there will be a deficiency somewhere. Still, it will suffice; I shall give the farmer's wife particular instructions; and she is a clever woman."

During the latter part of this soliloquy, he had shut up everything again in the cupboard. Then taking the lamp in his hand, he left the room slowly and cautiously, and descending a few steps into a large vault, he opened a little door which led into a low cellar, which he had to stoop to enter. Aided by the light, he groped among a great many empty bottles, till he found the object of his search; and taking three bottles out of the sand, he said, with a pale and anxious face—

"Heavens! only three bottles of table wine! No more; and they say that Herr Denecker has a pride in drinking freely! What am I to do when these three bottles are emptied, and more are needed? I drink none, and Lenora little, so two bottles for Herr Denecker and one for his nephew may perhaps be enough. Complaining cannot mend the matter, however; I must hope the best."

Without saying anything further, the poor nobleman went to the opposite corner of the cellar, and collecting there a few cobwebs, he hung them artfully over the three bottles, sprinkling a little sand over them at the same time. Returning to the room, he pasted the paper on the wall wherever it happened to be a little loose. Then, after he had brushed his clothes for half an hour, and had done his best to conceal the shabby parts, especially about the knees and elbows, with ink and water, he again sat down by the table, and applied himself to a still more singular occupation. He took a strong thread, a cobbler's awl, and a bit of rosin, out of a drawer, laid his boot on his lap, and began like an experienced shoemaker to sew the rent.

This work must have awakened sad thoughts in him, for he smiled contemptuously at times, as if he took a bitter pleasure in self-mockery. A violent internal struggle, however, soon made itself visible on his countenance; the blush of shame alternated with the paleness of mental agony, till he at last hastily cut the thread, threw the boot on the table, rose, and stretching out his hands towards the portraits on the wall, exclaimed, with a suppressed but feeling and earnest voice—

"Yes, look on me, ye whose noble blood runs in my veins! Thou, Field-Marshal, who for thy fatherland offered up thy life by Egmont's side, on the field of St. Quentin! thou, Statesman, who, after the battle of Pavia, didst render such distinguished service to the Emperor Charles! thou, Benefactor of mankind, who didst endow so many churches! thou, Prelate, who, as Priest and Scholar, didst so manfully defend the church of thy God! look on me, not alone out of that dead canvas, but from heaven, where now you are! He who sits here patching his boots, concealing his wretchedness in the stillness and solitude of the night, *he* is your son—the last representative of your illustrious line! If he quails before the eye of man, before you at least he is not ashamed of his humiliation. O my ancestors! with sword and pen you have striven against the enemies of your fatherland, while I struggle here against

mockery and unmerited contempt, without hope either of victory
or of fame. I suffer, and my soul wears away with my sufferings; and the world awards me nothing but mockery and contempt. And yet I have not cast a stain upon your arms; what
I have done is good and virtuous in the sight of God. Love,
compassion, and generosity, are the sole causes of my misfortune. Yes, yes, direct your eyes on me; behold how sunk
I am in poverty! And yet out of the depths of my humiliation, even before you, I will proudly raise my head, and my
eyes shall not sink before your glance. Here, in your presence, I am alone with my soul—with my conscience; and
here I feel that no shame can touch him who is a martyr to
his duty as Noble, brother, Christian, and father!"

Herr von Vlierbeke was quite carried away by his excitement; walked up and down the room with long strides,
pointing in quick succession with his hand to the portraits of
his fathers. There was something majestic in his mien;
with head erect, he looked a prince; his dark eyes sparkled
in the gloom, his fine countenance was full of dignity, and
his expression and whole bearing was manly, even grand.
Suddenly he stood still, laid his hand upon his brow, and
muttered, with a sad smile—

"Poor fool! thy soul seeks more room; it would fain
burst the narrow limits which its degradation imposes; and
dreams"—

Clasping his hands and looking towards heaven, he said—

"Yes, it is a delusion; but still, I thank Thee, good God,
that Thou hast caused courage and patience to spring up in
my soul! Enough; reality again stands before me, like a
grim skeleton grinning at me from out the darkness; but
now I am strong, and can laugh at the stern spectre of despair."

As the recollection of his actual circumstances recurred

to him, dejection was again depicted on his features, and letting his head sink upon his breast, he uttered a sigh of painful anxiety.

"And to-morrow—to-morrow will the eye of man again look distrustfully upon thee; thou wilt tremble before the wondering and curious looks of those who seek to solve the problem of thy acts; thou wilt drain once more with full draughts the cup of shame. Still, learn well thy part; calculate every expression of thy face—play on, to the last scene, the coward farce. And be mindful of thy noble race, that thou mayest be ready to bleed in every vein of thy heart, and die a hundred deaths! Go, thy night's work is done—go, and seek repose, and forget in sleep what thou art, and what awaits thee.— Mockery! yonder is the stage of thy final abasement; yonder thou mayest see a stranger take possession of the estate of thy forefathers; the cold and heartless laugh over thy ruin—over thy flight from thy fatherland with thy only child, to seek the bread of wretchedness in a distant country.—Sleep! it makes me tremble—the bond!—the bond!"

Repeating this word with increasing agony, he put aside everything that was on the table, and taking the lamp in his hand, disappeared through a door which apparently led to his chamber.

CHAPTER III.

On the following day, so soon as the morning dawn coloured the sky, every one about Grinselhof was in activity; the farmer's wife and her maid scoured the steps and passages; the farmer cleaned the stable, and his son hoed and weeded the approach. Lenora was early in the dining-room busy cleaning it, and arranging tastefully the furniture and various little ornaments.

There was more life and movement than had been seen in Grinselhof for ten years; it seemed as if the people of the farm-house enjoyed the novelty of the work in an especial manner—for there was visible on their faces a kind of triumphant expression, as if they imagined that they were waging a successful war with the deathlike solitude which had reigned here so long undisturbed.

Herr von Vlierbeke, although in his heart more excited than any of the others, walked up and down with an assumed indifference, going from one to another, directing their operations, and encouraging them now and then with a kind and amiable word, without confessing even to himself that he was nervously anxious about the preparations for this eventful day. With a smiling countenance, he flattered the self-love of these simple people, by telling them, in a jocular way, that it was an honour to them if his guests showed themselves satisfied with their reception. The farmer and his wife had never

seen Herr von Vlierbeke so cheerful and communicative; and
as they really loved and honoured him from their hearts, they
were in as high spirits as if they had been at a Grinselhof
festival. They did not perceive that this more than ordinary
kindness and good-will on the part of the poor nobleman was
an effort to repay them for their willing labour, since he could
not afford to remunerate them in any other way.

When the heaviest work was done, and the sun was now
pretty high in the heavens, Herr von Vlierbeke called his
daughter down, and gave her very minute directions about
cooking the food; telling her at the same time to look after it
now and then, and explain to the farmer's wife how she should
prepare certain dishes, which she had never seen before.

The fire was lighted in the old stove; the wood blazed and
crackled in the fireplace; the coals glowed in the grate, and
the smoke rolled in playful volumes over the roof.

The basket was unpacked, the stuffed fowl, the meat-pie,
and other exquisite dishes taken out; then whole baskets of
pease and beans, and other vegetables were brought in; and
the women began to clean and prepare them. Lenora herself
took part in this work, and chatted pleasantly the while with
the farmer's wife and the maid. The latter, who had very
rarely, indeed, had a close view of the young girl, and had not
at any time been more than a few moments in her presence,
was never tired gazing, with a species of wonder and profound
veneration, at her beautiful maiden features, her slender form,
and her bright, sparkling eyes; and these emotions were still
more vividly depicted on her face, when Lenora dreamily sung
a few verses of a well-known popular ballad. The maid rose
from her chair, approached her mistress shyly, and said in a
low and beseeching tone, but loud enough for Lenora to over-
hear her—

" Ah, mistress, beg the young lady to sing a bit of that

ballad; I heard it yesterday, and oh! it was so beautiful that I could not help weeping for a quarter of an hour after, behind the hazel-bushes."

"O do!" begged the farmer's wife of Lenora; "if it is not too much trouble to you, Miss, you would give us so much pleasure; you have a voice like a nightingale, and I remember well that my dear mother—she is long since with God—used always to hush me asleep with that very song."

"It is so long," replied Lenora, smiling.

"If it were only a few verses," she replied; "this is such a happy day with us all."

"Well, then," said Lenora, "if it will give you pleasure, why should I refuse? Listen, then."

THE ORPHAN GIRL

Swiftly but gently flowed the stream,
  So flowed a maiden's tears,
Who by the river wailing sat,
  Few were that maiden's years.

Idly into the stream she flung
  The blossoms by her side;
And "Father dear! ah, brother, come!
  Most piteously she cried.

A youthful knight by chance o'erheard
  The moan which she did make;
He wept and paused to learn her grief,
  And vowed her part to take.

"What ails thee, dearest child," he said,
  "Come, tell thy grief to me;
If this stout arm can lend thee aid,
  It shall not lacking be."

She raised her sad and heavy eye,
  And sighed, "O brave young man!
My grief is great, no mortal hand
  Can aid—God only can.

"See'st thou the grassy mound hard by!—
  It is my mother's grave!
Look on this stream—my father dear
  Lies deep beneath its wave!

"The wild stream swept him with its tide,
My brother plunged to save—
In vain, in vain !—he also sank,
And found a watery grave !

"Now have I left my lonely cot,
Where naught but sorrow dwells "—
So sad and simple is the tale
The maid despairing tells.

"No longer weep," then spake the knight,
"Let all thy care have end,
And find in me, O maiden fair !
Thy father, brother, friend."

Then gently grasp'd her hand, and call'd
The Orphan Girl his bride ;
And cloth'd her gay in wedding robes
There by the river side.

Of food, and drink, and raiment now,
And joy she hath full store—
Praise to the gallant youth who did
So brave a deed of yore !*

At the beginning of the last verse, Herr von **Vlierbeke had made** his appearance at the kitchen door, and the farmer's wife had risen respectfully, and seemingly afraid that he might be angry at what had happened ; on the contrary, he had given his daughter a sign to finish the song. When she had stopped, he said in a kindly tone—

" Ah, I am delighted to find you all so happy here. I should like your assistance for a few minutes up stairs, my good woman."

Both now went up stairs to the room above, where the cloth was laid for dinner, and found that the young peasant had already taken his place there, dressed in his old livery, and with a napkin thrown over his arm. After the nobleman had, by a short address, convinced the mother and son, that what he was going to do had this special object—namely,

* This popular ballad, known by the name of *Die Waise*, is much sung in the Kempen. The melody is sad but sweet and pleasing, and as Willens has remarked (*Oude Vlaemsche Liederen*, p. 223), has a great resemblance to Catalani's favourite song, " *Nel cor più, non mi sento.*" It is pre-eminently an indigenous German ballad.

their gaining credit for their able service at table, be began to play a real comedy, and made each go through their parts several times. He especially drilled them in changing the plates and spoons with great rapidity, and was so skilful in letting all the casualties and emergencies, which he feared, happen, as if naturally, during this lesson, that he at last could stop the rehearsal with a pretty confident anticipation that all would go well.

At last the hour of dinner approached; everything was ready in the kitchen, and every one in his place. Lenora was dressed, and waited with throbbing heart behind the curtain of a side window. Her father sat with a book under a chestnut-tree, and feigned to read, and thus concealed his rising anxiety from the farm-people.

About two o'clock in the afternoon, a splendid carriage, drawn by beautiful English horses, entered the grounds of Grinselhof, and drew up before the house-door. The nobleman greeted his guests with that bland dignity which was peculiar to him, and made some cheerful remarks; while the merchant gave orders to his coachman to call for him precisely at five o'clock, as he had still to go to the city on business which could not be postponed.

Herr Denecker was a stout man, whose dress, though very rich, seemed to be arranged with a careful neglect, in order to give him an independent exterior; his face was not very significant; it bore the marks of a certain shrewdness, and also of considerable goodness of heart, which, however, had perhaps never been allowed a fair field of action on account of the indifference which was a leading feature in his character.

The whole appearance of his nephew, Gustav, on the contrary, was noble; to a fine form, and an independent, manly countenance, he added an education of the highest order, and in refinement of manners and expression was scarcely excelled even by the nobleman himself. His fair hair and dark-blue eyes gave something poetic to his countenance, while his firm collected look, and a few slight wrinkles on his brow indicated that he was richly endowed with intellect and feeling.

With the customary phrases of politeness, Herr von Vlierbeke conducted his guests into the room on the ground-floor, where his daughter awaited their arrival. The merchant greeted her with a friendly laugh, and exclaimed with genuine admiration—

"So beautiful and charming, and to be shut up in Grinselhof! Ah, Herr von Vlierbeke, this is not right!"

Meanwhile Gustav approached the beautiful girl, and uttered a half-inarticulate greeting. The brows of both were suffused with blushes, and their eyes fell; but the young man quickly regained his presence of mind, and began to converse with Lenora intelligently.

The merchant directed Herr von Vlierbeke's attention to their mutual embarrassment, and whispered in his ear—

"Do you see what is going on there? My nephew does not know whether his head is off or on; the young lady puts out his eyes. I do not know how far the affections of these two young people have been already engaged. If, however, you do not look favourably upon its growth, and a pretty early maturity too, it would be well to pay attention to it betimes, otherwise it will soon be too late. For, I assure you, that my nephew, with his quiet countenance, is not a youth to see an obstacle. See, they talk together now easily; their mutual fear is gone."

Herr von Vlierbeke felt deeply moved by the merchant's words, because they strengthened his last hopes of deliverance; but concealing his feelings, he replied—

"You are jesting, Herr Denecker; there is no harm in

their intercourse; they are both young, and it is not surprising that a slight affection should spring up between them. It is of no importance."

"Come," he then said with a loud voice, "the dinner is on the table; let us go."

Gustav shyly offered Lenora his arm, and blushing, and with a slight trepidation, she took it. Both seemed perplexed, and yet there beamed from the eyes of both an inexpressible joy, and their hearts beat fast with a feeling of rapture. The uncle held his finger up to his nephew, shaking it with feigned displeasure, as if he would say, "I see already what is going on there." This made the young man redden still more, although the manifest approbation of his uncle at the same time filled his heart with sweet hopes; besides, Lenora had fortunately not observed the movement.

They took their seats—the nobleman opposite Herr Denecker, and beside Gustav, who again sat opposite Lenora.

The farmer's wife carried up the dinner, and her son in livery waited the table. The dishes were pretty well prepared, and the merchant more than once testified his satisfaction with them. The good food, and especially its abundance, took him by surprise, for he had expected a very meagre dinner, as Herr von Vlierbeke was decried in the whole neighbourhood as an avaricious and niggardly miser.

The conversation was now general, and consequently Lenora felt more at ease in replying to the merchant's remarks, and astonished both the guests by the signs she gave of a well-cultivated and refined intellect. It was quite otherwise, however, when she had to reply directly to Gustav; then her self-possession seemed all at once to desert her; and with downcast eyes she had not courage to give him anything but an abrupt and unmeaning reply. The young man himself did not fare much better: both felt deeply happy in their hearts; and yet one would have thought that they did not enjoy themselves very much.

Herr von Vlierbeke, meanwhile, led the conversation to subjects of a kind which he thought would be agreeable to his guests. With the greatest complaisance he listened to the merchant, and gave him opportunity to speak of things with which, as a merchant, he was likely to be well acquainted. His guest perceived this kindness, and thanked him for it in his heart. The merchant felt himself attracted to Herr von Vlierbeke with a genuine feeling of friendship, and endeavoured to vie with him in politeness.

Thus everything went well: everybody was pleased with himself and his company; above all, it was gratifying to the nobleman to see the mother and son understand their duties so well: they took away the plates and spoons which had been used, and brought them back clean with such expedition, that it would have been impossible to perceive that there was a deficiency. One thing alone was the source of some uneasiness to the nobleman. He looked with anxiety as Herr Denecker emptied one glass of wine after another, during the conversation. The young gentleman, too, frequently asked Lenora to drink more wine, either out of mere kindness, or that he might have occasion to address her; and so it happened, that the first bottle was nearly drained before the dinner was well begun. Herr von Vlierbeke, meanwhile, took stolen glances at the liquor which still remained, and trembled secretly every time he saw the merchant empty his glass. The attendant had now to produce the second bottle at the nobleman's order, and the latter gradually let the conversation flag, that he might not increase the merchant's thirst, for he perceived that his guest could not speak without perpetually carrying the wine to his lips. He saw himself sadly mistaken, however, for Herr Denecker turned the con-

versation to the subject of wine itself—began to praise the
noble juice, and to express his surprise at the nobleman's extraordinary abstemiousness. Meanwhile he drank more than
ever, and was supported in his potations by Gustav also, who,
however, drank much more moderately.

The anxiety of the nobleman increased with every draught
which the merchant took, and he restrained from pledging
him, although it was most painful to him to do so, and showed
himself in this one point at least inhospitable, through fear of
a greater shame. When the second bottle was finished, the
merchant said in a light easy tone to Herr von Vlierbeke,
who, with a weight at his heart, though to appearance merry
and gay, was narrowly watching his guest's progress—

" Yes, Herr von Vlierbeke; the wine is old and tempting:
I confess that; but one must change when drinking, otherwise it is impossible to enjoy the flavour. I cannot help
thinking that you have a capital cellar, if I may judge from
this specimen. Let us have a bottle of *Château-Margaux*;
and if we have time after that, we shall close our meeting
with a draught of *Hochheimer*. I never drink champagne;
it is a poor wine to connoisseurs."

While the merchant was speaking, a sudden pallor overspread the nobleman's face; but in order to conceal his alarm,
he rubbed his brow and eyes for a minute, exerting his mind
at the same time to discover some way out of this difficulty.
When his guest concluded, the nobleman took his hand from his
face, and a quiet smile was all that could be perceived on it.

" *Château-Margaux?*" said he. "As you please, Herr
Denecker." Then turning to the servant, he said, "John, a
bottle of *Château-Margaux*. Left hand, third row."

The peasant youth stared at his master as if he were addressing him in an unknown tongue, and muttered some unintelligible words.

" Excuse me," said the nobleman rising. " He does not know where to find it—a moment!"

He descended the stairs, and entering the kitchen, took up the remaining bottle, and carried it with him to the cellar. Here finding himself alone, he stood still and drew a deep breath, while he said to himself—

" *Château-Margaux, Hochheimer, Champagne!* Nothing in the house except this last bottle of Bordeaux. What shall I do? There is no time to reflect! The die is cast—may God help me!"

He now ascended the stairs, and re-entered the dining-room smiling, and with the screw in the cork of the only remaining bottle. Meanwhile, Lenora had ordered other glasses to be brought.

" This wine is fully twenty years old; I hope it will please you," said the nobleman, while he filled the glasses. Trembling, he watched the merchant's face as he tasted it. The latter had scarcely put the glass to his lips, when he withdrew it again, with an air of discontent, and exclaimed—

" There is some mistake here: it is the same wine."

Herr von Vlierbeke likewise tasted the wine, with an assumed expression of doubt on his face, and then exclaimed, as if taken by surprise—

" It is as you say—I have made a mistake. However, as we have begun this bottle, we shall empty it first. We have plenty of time."

" As you please," replied the merchant; " but on condition that you drink more freely, and help me. We can stay a little later than we intended."

In this way the wine gradually disappeared in the third bottle likewise, so that only a glass or two remained.

The nobleman could no longer conceal his agitation; he

turned away from the bottle, but, spite of himself, his looks always returned to it. Already there rang in his ears the dreadful word, *Château-Margaux*—the word which was to cover him with shame. The cold perspiration broke from every pore; the colour of his face changed several times in the same instant; yet his shifts were not yet exhausted, and he struggled bravely against the approaching exposure of his poverty. By rubbing his face and brow with his hands and pocket-handkerchief, by coughing and turning round at times, as if he would sneeze, and by other devices of a similar kind, he succeeded in concealing his agitation, and escaping the notice of his guests, till Herr Denecker put his hand on the bottle to drain it of its last glass of wine. When the nobleman saw this, he shuddered; and growing deathly pale, covered his face, and with a long sigh, let his head sink slowly on the arm of the chair.

Was it a feigned swoon, or was the nobleman only making use of his real agitation and alarm to help himself out of his painful difficulty?

All rose. Lenora uttered a shriek, and hastened to her father's side with an anxious countenance; while he, raising himself slowly up, endeavoured to smile, and said—

"It is nothing; I feel the atmosphere here suffocating; let me go into the open air for a minute, and I shall soon be better."

So saying, he left the room, and descended the front steps into the garden. Lenora had taken his arm to help him down, although he had no particular need of her assistance; and Denecker and his nephew followed with faces expressive of deep concern.

After the nobleman had sat for a few minutes under the shade of the old jessamine, the paleness disappeared from his face, and with a steady and lively voice he said to his

guests, that he felt quite better, but would ask their permission to remain for a time in the open air, lest the faint
should return; and soon after, standing up, he expressed a
desire to walk.

" With the greatest pleasure," said the merchant, " for at
five o'clock my carriage comes, and I must drive with my
nephew into the city; and I should not like to leave without
first seeing your grounds. Let us walk about a little, and
then, before going, we shall drink in front of the castle, a good
bottle of wine to our lasting friendship." At these words he
offered his arm to Lenora, who took it frankly. Although
Herr Denecker had a wish by doing so to tease his nephew a
little, the young man was, in truth, not at all displeased to
see his uncle show such a liking for the object of his own
attachment.

The walk commenced, agriculture, the enclosure of the
heath, the chase, and various other topics, formed in succession
the subjects of conversation. Lenora, who, now that she was
in the open air, felt all her freedom and vivacity return to her,
put no longer any restraint upon herself. The cheerful serenity
and virgin purity of her nature were now revealed in all their
charm. Like a playful young roe, she wished to make the
merchant run; and skipping gaily by his side, she was lavish
of every demonstration of genial and hearty enjoyment of life.
Herr Denecker was excessively charmed with the high spirits
of the girl, and almost allowed himself to be persuaded to
dance and play: he could not gaze sufficiently at Lenora's
fascinating countenance, which indeed had already given birth
in his breast to a very pleasing sensation; and he remarked to
himself, while a smile played upon his lips, that his nephew
had a pretty good taste.

While the nobleman, however, was busy explaining something to his guest, and drawing a sketch on the ground, Lenora

and Gustav had walked off a little way, and seemed engaged in a very earnest conversation. When the father and his guest again renewed their walk, the young people were fully fifty yards in advance, and, either by intention or accident, this distance between the two parties was henceforth maintained.

Lenora showed Gustav her flowers, her gold fishes, and everything which she loved and tended in her solitude. He scarcely distinguished her sweet and childlike words, for what she said seemed to vanish at the very moment it reached his ears, and melt away into a kind of heavenly music, which filled him with enchanting dreams, and transported his soul into a region of unutterable bliss.

Herr von Vlierbeke, again, on his part, gave himself inconceivable trouble to entertain his guest, and keep him in a cheerful humour, that he might drive from his recollection any intention which might still linger there of returning to the table; he called into requisition all his extensive knowledge, —told him remarkable stories, and endeavoured to penetrate the innermost folds of the merchant's breast, that he might know how to please him—nay, even when the conversation showed symptoms of flagging, he began to make jests, and said and did things, which, it is true, were perfectly becoming, but far removed from his usually dignified and earnest manner.

The time was now approaching which Herr Denecker had fixed for his departure. The nobleman was thanking God, from the bottom of his heart, that He had enabled him to get through his difficulties thus far so successfully, when the merchant suddenly turned to his nephew, and said—

"Now, Gustav, we are going in to drink a parting cup; do not lose time, it is already five o'clock."

Again Herr von Vlierbeke grew pale, and looked with a

visible expression of alarm at the merchant, who could not understand the effect which his words seemed to have on his host, and did not conceal his surprise—

"Do you feel unwell?" he asked.

"I take a pain in the stomach sometimes at the mere mention of the word *wine*," stammered Herr von Vlierbeke; "it is a peculiar, nervous pain."

Suddenly his countenance assumed a livelier expression, and pointing with his finger towards the gate, he said—

"There, I hear your carriage, Herr Denecker."

The carriage drove up to the door of Grinselhof.

The merchant said no more about the wine, but he thought it singular that his departure should give such manifest pleasure; and doubtless this suspicion would have seriously offended him, had not the extremely friendly manner and hospitable reception of the nobleman convinced him of the contrary. He could not ascribe his unpoliteness to any other cause but his indisposition, which he, perhaps out of consideration for his guests, had been making great efforts to conceal. Accordingly Herr Denecker said affectionately, as he pressed the nobleman's hand—

"Herr von Vlierbeke, I have spent a particularly agreeable afternoon with you : in your society, and that of your amiable daughter, one feels truly happy. I am overjoyed to have made your acquaintance, and I hope that a nearer connexion may one day secure me your friendship. Meanwhile, let me thank you for your very kind and friendly reception."

Gustav and Lenora meanwhile approached, while the nobleman was uttering a few words in polite disavowal of his guest's complimentary language.

"And my nephew," continued the merchant, "is, I am sure, of my opinion, that few hours of his life have been so pleasant as those which we have spent to-day at Grinselhof.

You will likewise do me the honour, Herr von Vlierbeke, to dine with me, in company with your amiable daughter, though I am forced to postpone this pleasure for a little. I go to Frankfurt to-morrow on business, and shall be absent probably for some months. In the meantime, my nephew will do himself the honour of visiting you frequently, and I hope he will continue to be welcome."

The nobleman repeated his friendly expressions. Lenora was silent, although Gustav looked into her eyes, and seemed to ask some encouragement. The uncle moved towards the carriage.

" And the parting cup?" said Gustav with surprise. "Pray let us go in for a little yet."

" No, no !" said Herr Denecker; " were I to wait till you were willing to leave, I suppose we should not be gone to-day. But it is high time to be off; so, say nothing more about it; a merchant must keep his appointments, and you know yourself what we have promised."

Gustav and Lenora exchanged a long look, in which could easily be read sorrow that they should part so soon, and the mutual hope of meeting again ere long. The nobleman and Herr Denecker shook hands heartily and affectionately, and then both guests stepped into the carriage.

Laughing in a friendly way, and kissing their hands as long as they were within sight, the strangers left Grinselhof.

CHAPTER IV.

On the second day after his uncle's departure, Gustav presented himself at Grinselhof. Father and daughter received him as kindly as on the former visit; and having spent the greater part of the afternoon in their society, he returned to Echelpoel Castle at the approach of evening, with his heart full of warm recollections.

At first he did not venture to show himself often at Grinselhof; either from a feeling of propriety, or because he was afraid of being troublesome to the nobleman. Before two weeks had elapsed, however, the hearty way in which the nobleman always received him, dispelled the feeling, whatever it was; and the young man no longer resisted the longing which drew him so powerfully to Lenora's side. No day passed without a visit to Grinselhof; and there, the too swift hours glided away in a calm and dreamy happiness. He took pleasure walks with Lenora and her father, through the shady paths round Grinselhof; was present at the instructions which the father gave his daughter in many arts and sciences; listened with rapture to the maiden's beautiful voice as she sang her favourite songs; entered into instructive conversation with both, or sat under the jessamine dreaming of a happy future; while he gazed with loving eyes at the young maiden, who, he earnestly hoped—in fulfilment of the ardent prayers which he continually offered to God—should one day be his wife.

Lenora's noble and charming countenance had first attracted him; but now, when he perceived the beauty of her soul, his feeling for her became so fervent, so unbounded, that the whole universe seemed to him colourless and dead, when the loved object was not present to throw a light and a glory over everything. To him no angel, depicted in the finest sacred poetry, could be half so beautiful as his virgin friend. And, indeed, while she was adorned with all the personal beauty with which the Creator must have clothed the first woman, there beat in her bosom a heart whose mirror-like purity had never been dimmed by the smallest breath of the world, and out of which, at the slightest touch, feeling, fresh and ardent, sprang like a clear fountain.

Gustav had never been quite alone with Lenora, as she never, in his presence, left the room in which she usually sat with her father, unless the latter expressed a wish to walk in the open air; yet the young man felt no desire to conceal his affection from Herr von Vlierbeke, or to tell the maiden how entirely her image filled his soul. It would indeed have been superfluous to express in words what was passing in the hearts of each. Love, friendship, respect, beamed from the eyes of all; three souls lived here, in one sentiment, united by one bond, blended in the same feeling of affection and hope.

Although Gustav felt a deep reverence for Lenora's father, and loved him truly like an affectionate son, there was yet one thing which threatened to disturb his high estimation of him. What he had heard in the neighbourhood, of the excessive niggardliness of Herr von Vlierbeke, had now become to him a certainty. On no occasion had the nobleman offered him a glass of wine, or invited him to eat the evening meal with himself and his daughter; on the contrary, Gustav had often observed with grief the great efforts which were made to conceal from him this unexampled stinginess.

Avarice is a passion which is universally visited with abhorrence and contempt, because one almost instinctively perceives that the moment this vice begins to show itself, it renders all nobility in the human heart impossible, and fills it instead with a cold and coarse selfishness. Gustav accordingly had to struggle long with his feelings, before he could bring himself to overlook this failing of Herr von Vlierbeke, and to convince himself that it was only a caprice in him—a mere aberration of judgment, which had left unharmed the native nobility of his character. Had the young man only known the truth! Had he only been able to look further into the nobleman's heart, then would he have seen that, behind that smile, a sorrow lay concealed; and that every tremor which shook those nervous features, was the expression of the agony of a soul which was afraid of exposing its secret. He knew not, happy youth, that while he sunned himself in Lenora's eyes, and sipped so sweetly from the golden cup of love, the nobleman's life was a perpetual suffering, that he dreamt day and night of a horrible future, and with the sweat of agony on his brow counted the hastening hours, as if every minute brought him nearer to some fearful and unavoidable calamity. And, indeed, had not the Notary said to him—" Only four months! only four months, and the bond falls due! then will your property be sold by auction by order of a court of law ?"

Of these four momentous months two had already passed.

If the nobleman appeared to encourage the young man's love, it must be confessed that it was not entirely from affection towards him. No, no; the drama of his sufferings must be played out within a limited time. If it did not, then the fate which awaited himself and his child was open shame— moral death. Within that period, destiny would irrevocably determine whether he was to emerge victoriously out of this ten years' struggle with misery, or sink overwhelmed under the public obloquy.

On this account he all the more carefully concealed his poverty; and although he watched like a guardian angel over both young people, he yet did nothing to check the speedy development of their mutual love.

When the time fixed for Herr Denecker's return arrived, the two months of his absence seemed to Gustav to have fled like a dream. Although he was quite convinced that his uncle would have no objections to the prosecution of his love, he yet foresaw that he would not permit him to devote so much time to it: and the thought of being separated from Lenora, perhaps for weeks, made him look forward to his uncle's return with no little anxiety and vexation. He, on one occasion, communicated his fears to Lenora with much sadness, and painted vividly the sorrow with which even a temporary separation from her would fill him. For the first time he saw tears in her eyes. This token of affection moved him so deeply, that he silently took her hand, and sat for a long time by her side without uttering a word. Meanwhile, Herr von Vlierbeke endeavoured to console him, but his words seemed ineffectual. After a long silence, Gustav rose to take leave, although the usual hour of departure had not arrived. The maiden read in his countenance that a change had taken place in his mind, and that his features were lighted up with an unaccountable vivacity and joy. She sought to detain him in order to discover the ground of his apparent cheerfulness. But he escaped with a few friendly remarks, simply telling her that she would probably learn his secret on the following day. He then left Grinselhof with hasty steps, as if some overwhelming purpose was driving him on.

Herr von Vlierbeke believed that he had read in the young

man's eyes what was passing in his heart; and beautiful dreams made the nobleman's sleep calm and sweet that night. On the following day when the usual hour of Gustav's visit arrived, the father's heart beat high with expectation. He saw Gustav pass through the gate and approach the house.

The young man's dress was not on this occasion composed of light materials, as was usual. He was clothed entirely in black, as on the day on which he first visited Grinselhof. A cheerful smile played round the nobleman's features as he went to meet his visitor, for the choice of the dress had confirmed his hopes, and convinced him that Gustav had come on a solemn errand—indeed, formally to solicit his daughter's hand.

Gustav expressed a wish to see him for a few minutes alone. Herr von Vlierbeke led him into a side-room—offered him a chair—sat down opposite him, and said—

"I am prepared to listen, my young friend."

Gustav kept silence for a time, as if he would collect his thoughts, and then began with visible anxiety, but at the same time with firmness—

"Herr von Vlierbeke, I venture to take a very important step with you, and it is your extreme kindness alone which gives me the necessary courage; and I hope that, let the answer be what it may, you will at all events excuse my boldness. It cannot have escaped your notice, sir, that from the first day on which I had the good fortune to see Lenora, my heart has been filled with an irresistible love for her—for she appeared to me then, and appears now, an angel. Perhaps, before permitting this feeling to gain such entire possession of me, I ought to have asked your consent; but I could not but suppose, from the polite and friendly way in which you always received me, that you had read my heart!"

The young man paused, in the hope of receiving some encouragement from the nobleman. The latter, however, only looked at him with a quiet smile, in which it was impossible to read how he received the young man's declaration. A wave of his hand, as if he would say, "Go on," was the only reply. Gustav felt his confidence entirely forsake him for a moment, but immediately mastering his fears, he took courage, and said with fervour—

"Yes, I have loved Lenora since the moment in which her eyes first met mine; she lighted then a spark of love in my bosom, which has since become a flame, and which would consume me entirely if any one should try to smother it. It may be, sir, that you imagine that her beauty alone is the ground of my love? Certainly this ground is sufficient to make even the most unimpressible love her: but I have discovered, in the heart of this angel, a treasure far transcending that—her virtue, the unspotted purity of her soul, her gentle and high-toned sensibility—the gifts with which God has so lavishly endowed her—these are the things which have led me from admiration to love, and from love to worship. Ah! why then conceal it longer? Without Lenora, life is impossible—the very thought of separation from her fills me with sadness, and makes me tremble: I must see her daily, hourly —hear her voice, and drink in happiness from her looks. I do not know, Herr von Vlierbeke, what your decision may be; but if it is not favourable, believe me, my heart will be broken for ever. Were you to separate me from my beloved—my sweet Lenora, it would be a fatal blow—life would be for ever hateful to me."

With deep emotion and great emphasis Gustav had uttered these words. Herr von Vlierbeke took his hand sympathizingly, and said—"Do not be alarmed, my young friend; I know that you love Lenora, and that your love is requited; but what do you wish from me?"

With downcast eyes the young man answered—"If, after

all the tokens of your affection which I have received, I still have some doubts of receiving your final consent, it is because I am conscious of one fact which may, I fear, make you think me unworthy of enjoying the happiness which I now desire. I have no family tree which strikes its roots deep into the past; the deeds of my ancestors are not blazoned in the history of our country; the blood which flows through my veins is plebeian blood.

"Do you think, then, Gustav," said Herr von Vlierbeke, "that I did not know that before you began to visit here? Your heart is great and noble, otherwise I would not have loved you as my son."

"Then," exclaimed Gustav with joy, "you will not deny me Lenora's hand, if my uncle also gives his consent to our union?"

"No, I would not in that case deny it. I would, on the contrary, confide my child's happiness to you with the greatest pleasure; but there is an obstacle yet unknown to you."

"An obstacle!" sighed the young man, growing pale. "An obstacle between me and Lenora!"

"Moderate your ardour for a minute," rejoined von Vlierbeke, "and listen without prejudice to what I shall now tell you. You believe, Gustav, that Grinselhof and the adjoining possessions are mine; you deceive yourself; we possess nothing; we are poorer than the farmer who lives at the lodge."

The young man looked for a short time with an expression of surprise and doubt; and then an incredulous smile passed over his face, which made the nobleman redden and tremble. He resumed with anxious emphasis—

"Ah, I read in your eyes that you have no faith in my words. You believe me to be a miser, a man who conceals his gold, who exposes himself and his child to want, that he may heap paltry treasure together, and who sacrifices everything to his insatiable avarice—a selfish being who is either feared or despised."

"Oh, pardon me!" exclaimed Gustav anxiously, "my esteem for you is unbounded."

"Do not be alarmed at my words," said the nobleman, more calmly. "I do not blame you; your smile convinced me that you also believe, with others, that I use poverty as a cloak for the most detestable avarice. For the present it is unnecessary to enter into more minute details—what I have said is true: I possess nothing—literally nothing! Return home without seeing Lenora: consider maturely, with coolness and composure, whether no grounds exist for altering your resolution; let a night pass over your head, and if to-morrow morning you can still love the *poor* Lenora, and if you believe that you can still make each other happy, then ask your uncle's consent. Here is my hand; you may press it then as the hand of a father, and my most fervent wishes will be at that moment fulfilled."

The solemn and calm tone in which these words were uttered, convinced Gustav of their truth, however much the information they conveyed took him by surprise; and his countenance at once expressed a joyful animation—

"If I can love the *poor* Lenora!" he exclaimed. "To call her my wife, to become united with her by the bond of everlasting love, for ever to draw happiness from her sweet looks! To know that I am her protector, that my labour contributes to her happiness! Palace or hut, riches or poverty—everything is to me indifferent, if only she is present to breathe a soul into the spot where I am. Night can bring me no counsel, Herr von Vlierbeke; if I may now possess Lenora's hand through your generosity, I will thank you on my knees for the priceless gift!"

"I believe it," replied the nobleman. "This fervent passion, this steady devotedness, are natural to your youth and ardent disposition—but your uncle?"

"My uncle?" muttered Gustav, visibly annoyed. "It is true, I must have his consent; what I possess in the world, or may henceforth possess, depends on his favour. I am an orphan—his brother's son; he took me when a child, and has loaded me with benefits. He has, therefore, a right to control my acts—I must obey him."

"And will he, who is a merchant, and probably sets a high value on money, because he has learnt what one can accomplish with it—will he likewise say, 'Poor or rich, palace or hut, it is the same'?"

"Ah, I cannot tell, Herr von Vlierbeke," replied Gustav, troubled; "but he is so kind to me, so extremely kind, that I have cause to hope for his consent. To-morrow is the day of his return; at our very first meeting I shall tell him of my intentions, and say that my peace, my happiness, and my life depend on his consent. He has a more than ordinary regard and affection for Lenora, and seemed to encourage me to sue for her hand: your explanation, it is true, will surprise him very much, but my entreaties, believe me, will move him."

The nobleman rose to bring the conversation to a close, and said—"Well then, ask your uncle for his consent, and realize your expectations; and then request him to come to me to enter into more details. Whatever may be the consequence, Gustav, you have acted towards us as a brave and honest youth ought. My esteem and friendship shall certainly always remain with you.—Go, leave Grinselhof for once without seeing Lenora; she cannot again be in your presence till this matter is settled. I will tell her what she ought to know of it."

Half pleased and half sad, joy and anxiety in his heart, Gustav took leave of Lenora's father.

CHAPTER V.

On the following morning Herr von Vlierbeke sat by a table in an upper room of the Castle, his head resting on his hand. He must have been in deep reflection, for his eye wandered unsteadily and unconsciously from object to object; and hope and pleasure, sorrow and anxiety, by turns revealed themselves on his countenance.

Lenora made her appearance in the room, remained for a minute in a wavering and uncertain way, went from one side to another, looked through the window into the garden, and then hastened down stairs again. There could be no doubt that she was waiting with great impatience for some expected visit; her countenance, however, expressed an undisguised cheerfulness, from which one could infer that her heart was full of the sweetest hopes. Had she been able to see the anxiety which at times overspread her father's face in the midst of his musings, she would not perhaps have dreamt so confidingly and cheerfully of a happy future; but Herr von Vlierbeke carefully concealed his sadness when she was present, and laughed gaily and affectionately at her impatience, as if he also looked forward with confidence to the events of this critical day.

At last, quite tired of going and coming, Lenora sat down beside her father, and gazed into his face with a clear and inquiring look.

"My dear Lenora," he said, "do not oe so impatient. To-day we can hope for nothing; to-morrow, perhaps. Moderate your joy, my child, and then your sorrow will be less difficult to overcome, if God should decide in this matter contrary to your hopes."

"Ah, father," stammered Lenora, "God will be gracious to me. I feel in my heart that I am happy; do not wonder at it, father. I see Gustav speaking with his uncle—I hear what he says, and Herr Denecker's reply. I see him embrace Gustav, and give his consent. Surely I may hope the best; for you remember Herr Denecker also liked me, and was always so very friendly at church."

"Would you be very happy indeed if Gustav were to be your bridegroom?" asked Herr von Vlierbeke, smiling.

"Never to leave him," exclaimed Lenora; "to help to make him cheerful and happy! To infuse life into the solitude of Grinselhof with our love! And then to sweeten your days, father! for Gustav understands so much better than I do how to chase away from your heart the melancholy which at times darkens your countenance. You will go walking and hunting with him, talk, and be merry; he will love and honour you as a son, and tenderly care for you. His great object on earth will be to make you happy, because he knows that your happiness is mine; and I will reward his generous nobleness, strewing his path with the beautiful flowers of a grateful heart. O yes, we shall live together in a paradise of peace and love!"

"Poor, innocent Lenora!" sighed Herr von Vlierbeke; "may God grant your beautiful wish! but there are laws and usages which regulate the world, of which you are ignorant —a woman must follow her husband wherever he goes. If Gustav selects you to be his wife, you must obey him without resistance, and console yourself gradually for absence from me. Such a separation would in other circumstances be inconceivably bitter to me; but if I knew you to be happy, I could learn to bear the loneliness."

Lenora had listened to her father with surprise and alarm; and now when he had ceased speaking, she let her head sink slowly on her breast, and shed a few quiet tears. Herr von Vlierbeke took her hand, and said with a gentle voice—

"I knew, Lenora, that I was saying what would grieve you; but you must accustom yourself gradually to the thought of this separation."

She raised her head, and said, in a firm and animated tone—

"What—will Gustav wish me to leave you? Shall you remain by yourself at Grinselhof, and spend your days in sadness and solitude, while I and my husband enter the world, and dwell in the midst of gaiety and pleasure? Then would there be no longer one peaceful or happy moment for me; everywhere the voice of conscience would call out to me, ' Ungrateful, unfeeling creature, your father suffers !' Yes, I love Gustav; he is dearer to me than my life, and I would receive his hand as a blessed gift from God; and yet, if he said to me that I must leave my father—choose between my father and him—I would reject *him ;* weep, mourn, perhaps die. But in your eyes, my father "....

She hung her head for some moments, as if overwhelmed by sad and desponding thoughts; but almost immediately she looked up at her father with spirit and energy in her glance, and said—

"You doubt Gustav's affection for you; you consider him capable of filling your life with sorrow, of separating me from you? O father, you do not know him; you do not know how much he loves you, and what a treasure of love and goodness his heart is."

Herr von Vlierbeke drew his somewhat excited daughter to

his side, and imprinted a kiss on her brow. He was about to soothe her with some consolatory words; but suddenly she tore herself from his arms, and sprang up smiling and trembling. Pointing with her finger to the window, she seemed to listen to an approaching sound.

The tramp of horses and the roll of wheels informed Herr von Vlierbeke what had so suddenly disturbed his daughter; and with a joyful countenance he hastened down, and reached the front door as Herr Denecker stepped out of his carriage.

The merchant seemed to be in very good humour, and pressed Herr von Vlierbeke's hand cordially, as he said to him—

"Ah, Herr von Vlierbeke, I am delighted to see you again. How goes it with you? My nephew seems to have known how to make good use of his time during my absence."

While he was being conducted by the nobleman with his usual courtesy to a room, he put his hand on the shoulder of the latter in a friendly way, and said, laughing—

"Ha! ha! we were good friends before, and now we shall be relations; I hope so, at least. My rascal of a nephew has no bad taste, I confess. He might search far before he found such a beautiful and charming young girl as Lenora. Why, you see, Herr von Vlierbeke, we must have such a wedding as will be spoken of for twenty years to come."

Meanwhile they had entered a side-room, and had sat down. Although the nobleman's heart beat with a kind of timid joy, he did not venture quite to believe all that Herr Denecker's manner appeared to convey, and looked at him doubtingly. The merchant continued—

"It would appear now as if Gustav was longing with a burning impatience to complete his happiness, for he has begged me on his knees to hasten matters. I have had pity for the young fool, and have left business for a day, and come running here to make the necessary arrangements at once. He has told me that you have given your consent; that is well done on your part, sir. I likewise have thought over this marriage during my journey, for I had perceived that love's arrow had quite pierced my nephew's heart; but I was not without fear regarding your intentions; the inequality of rank—a notion of older times—might have been an objection."

"Gustav, then, has informed you that I consent to his marriage with Lenora?" asked the nobleman.

"He has not surely deceived me?" replied Herr Denecker with surprise.

"No; but did he say nothing else which in your eyes must be of no small importance?"

The merchant shook his head laughing, and said, in a jocular tone—

"Oh, you refer to that good joke which you played off upon him so successfully; but we shall very soon arrange all that. He has told me that Grinselhof does not belong to you, and that you are poor. You have, however, a better opinion of my understanding than to think that such jests will pass for truth with me, ha, ha!"

The nobleman trembled; his hopes had risen for a moment with Herr Denecker's merry and confident tone; he had imagined that he knew all, and was, notwithstanding, prepared to fulfil his nephew's wishes; but what he had said showed him that he must enter once more into melancholy explanations of his poverty; and he accordingly braced himself for this new victory over his pride.

"Herr Denecker," he said, "be so good as not to have the slightest doubt of what I am about tell to you. I am quite willing that my Lenora should be married to your nephew, but I declare to you here that I am poor—extremely poor!"

"What!" exclaimed the merchant: "I am well aware

that you are desperately attached to your gold—that has been long known; but at a time like this, surely—the marriage of your only child—you ought to open your heart and purse for once, in order to give your daughter a dowry befitting her position. People have long said—pardon me for repeating it—that you are a miser as it is. But what would be said were you to let your only daughter be married dowerless?"

The nobleman seemed to be sitting on needles, and struggled painfully with the jesting incredulity which Herr Denecker displayed, and which did not permit him to bring this unhappy subject to a speedy close by short and clear statements. Almost imploringly, he exclaimed—

"For Heaven's sake, sir, spare me this bitter mockery; I declare to you, on my word as a gentleman, that I do not possess a penny."

"Well, then," replied the merchant with a cunning smile, "we shall bring the thing to figures, and soon see whether the proof and the reckoning agree. You imagine, perhaps, that I have come hither to talk you over to make a great sacrifice; not so, Herr von Vlierbeke. God be thanked, I do not require to drive so close a bargain; but a marriage is a transaction which two enter into with one another, and in which it is proper that both parties should pay a little into the common purse, even if the portions be unequal."

"O God!" sighed the nobleman.

"Listen," said the merchant; "I will give my nephew a hundred thousand francs, and he will remain in the business, where my credit will be of great value to him. I do not wish, indeed I could not permit, that you should endow Lenora with an equal sum. Her distinguished birth, and her own worth more than overbalance any deficiency in her marriage portion. But the half of that—say about fifty thousand francs—you can manage to give, or I am very much deceived. Let us shake hands on this."

The nobleman sat on his chair pale and trembling, as if he had unexpectedly received some dreadful blow; in a troubled and desponding tone, he replied—

"Herr Denecker, this conversation is more than I can bear : cease to pain me so much. I repeat it, I possess nothing; and since you compel me to speak before I know your determination, then know that Grinselhof, and all the lands appertaining, are mortgaged beyond their true value. It is unnecessary to explain to you how these debts have been incurred, it is sufficient to assure you that I speak the truth; and I request you, before we proceed further, to state explicitly to me what your intentions with reference to your nephew's marriage may be, now that you know my circumstances ?"

This communication, which had been uttered by the nobleman with all solemnity and emphasis, still failed to convince the merchant. A little astonishment was all that was visible in his countenance, and then, with an incredulous laugh, he rejoined—

"Pardon me, Herr von Vlierbeke, but I could not have believed that you would have been so pertinacious. But be it so, every one has his failings: one man is too niggardly, another too lavish. Well, then, I am ready to stretch a point to make Gustav happy. Give your daughter twenty-five thousand francs, on the condition that the amount of her portion remain a secret, so that I be not a laughing-stock to my friends. Twenty-five thousand francs, you must confess, is not too much; such a trifle will do little more than meet her necessary preparations. Come now, act candidly and honestly—here is my hand!"

Trembling, as if seized by an ague-fit, the nobleman sprang up suddenly and unlocked a little press in the wall, and then taking out a packet of papers, threw them on the table, saying—

"Read, and convince yourself."

As the merchant looked through the papers, his countenance altered gradually, and he shook his head musingly at times. Meanwhile, the nobleman said, with a mixture of jest and anger—

"Ah, you would not believe me; but guard yourself against coming to a conclusion even from these papers alone. You must know all at once, and then I will not again have to expose myself to the torture of these humiliating disclosures. Here is a bill for four thousand francs, which I cannot pay. You perceive I am more than poor—I have debts."

"It is, then, true," said Herr Denecker, astonished: "you possess nothing. I see from these papers that my Notary is also yours. I spoke with him about your wealth, and he left me in my wisdom, or rather in my error."

The nobleman now breathed freely, as if a load had fallen from his heart; and his countenance again assumed that air and dignity which was peculiar to him. He sat down, and said with a constrained coldness—

"Now that you have no longer any doubts of my poverty, I ask you, Herr Denecker, what is your decision?"

"My decision?" replied the merchant; "my decision is, that we continue good friends as formerly. But the marriage? —That must no longer be thought of; we shall speak no more of that. So, then, Herr von Vlierbeke, you had made your calculations, as I now begin to see, and would fain have struck a good bargain, and sold your wares as dear as possible?'

"Sir," cried the nobleman, with an angry glance, "speak of my daughter with respect, be she poor or rich. Do not forget who she is."

"Do not be angry, Herr von Vlierbeke," replied the merchant. "I do not mean to offend you : I am very far from meaning to do that. Had you been successful, I would perhaps have rather admired your tactics; but he who would overreach me, must rise early in the morning. And since you are so nice on the point of honour, permit me to ask you if you acted honourably in inviting—I may say, enticing—my nephew to frequent this house, till this unhappy love struck so deep a root in his heart ?"

Herr von Vlierbeke let his head sink to conceal the blush of shame which, like a cloud, overspread his brow, and sat quite overwhelmed for a time, till the merchant roused his attention by the word—"Well ?"

"Ah," sighed Herr von Vlierbeke, "have pity on me ! Perhaps love of my child led me into this error. God has endowed my Lenora with all the gifts which can adorn a woman on earth; I had hoped that her beauty, the purity of her soul, and the nobility of her race, might be treasures at least as valuable as gold."

"Yes, to a nobleman, perhaps; but not to a merchant," muttered Herr Denecker.

"Do not reproach me with having enticed your nephew to visit here; the word pains me deeply, and is unjust. But when I saw a mutual attachment spring up at the same time between Gustav and Lenora, I did not, I confess, do anything to check this feeling. On the contrary, I daily thanked God in my prayers that he had sent me one who was to be my child's deliverer. Yes, for Gustav is no ordinary man, and one who would have made her happy—not by his wealth, but by his noble character and good heart. Is it then so great a misdeed if a father, whom unavoidable misfortune has beggared, should cherish the hope of seeing his child rescued from the miseries of poverty ?"

"Certainly not," replied the merchant. "Everything depended on its success; but you made a bad choice, Herr von Vlierbeke. I am a man who examines goods twice before he concludes a bargain, and it is excessively difficult, I can assure you, to pass apples for citrons with me."

This style of talk, borrowed from trade, seemed to pain the nobleman deeply, for he sprang up quickly and said, with rising anger—

"You have, then, no pity for my misfortunes? You would give me to understand that it has been my purpose to deceive you? Was it you who discovered my poverty? Were you not at liberty to do what you pleased after my voluntary explanation? Do you think that, because I listen humbly to your reproaches, and confess my mistake—my fault, that every feeling of self-respect is dead in my heart? You speak of wares as if you had come here to buy something! Do you mean my Lenora? All your wealth cannot reach that, sir. If love for her is not powerful enough to cause inequalities of another kind to disappear, know that my name is Von Vlierbeke, and that this name, even in poverty, weighs heavier than all your gold!"

A deep indignation was visible on the nobleman's features while he uttered these words; his eyes shot fire at the merchant, who, terrified by his rapid movements, drew back and looked at him with some alarm.

"Well," said Denecker, "we will not waste so many words about it; every one remains what he is, every one keeps what he has, and so the matter is settled. I have only one request to make—namely, that you no longer permit my nephew to visit you, otherwise "—

"*Otherwise!*" cried the nobleman with passion; "do you threaten me?" And then controlling himself, he said, with subdued passion—

" Enough of this: shall I order Herr Denecker's carriage?"

"As you please," replied the merchant; "we can transact no business with one another, but that is no reason why we should be enemies."

"Good, good; let us stop, sir. This conversation pains me; it must have an end."

With these words, he conducted the merchant to the door, and took leave of him curtly.

Herr von Vlierbeke returned to his room, sank into a chair, and covering his face with his hands, sighed deeply, while his breast heaved violently with a mingled excitement, indignation, and grief. He remained in this attitude for a time, silent and motionless; his hands then sank powerless on his knees, and a deathlike pallor overspread his face. He appeared overpowered by the most painful reflections; but no movement, no feature of his countenance, indicated the silent agonies of his soul.

Suddenly he heard a noise in the room overhead, which roused him out of his unconsciousness, and made him tremble with fear and anxiety.

"O God! my poor Lenora!" he exclaimed. "She comes. I have not yet suffered enough; I must break my poor child's heart too!—with cruel coldness rob her of all her bright hopes, destroy her sweetest dreams, and behold her despair! Would to God I could escape this fearful interview! What shall I say? how tell her all?"

He laughed bitterly, and said, muttering to himself in a tone of despair—

"Ah, conceal thine own suffering—take courage! Even if thy heart is broken, if despair overmasters thee, still smile, smile! What is thy fate after all, but a perpetual self-mockery? What else canst thou do, miserable slave?—Keep down this rebellious feeling! Be calm, be calm, there is thy child!"

Lenora entered, and turned toward her father with an inquiring but hopeful glance. Whatever exertion Herr von Vlierbeke might have made to conceal his agony, he was not successful on this occasion. Lenora at once perceived that he was suffering from some great sorrow; and when he continued silent, spite of her anxious and questioning looks, she began to tremble, and said with alarm—

"Well, father, well?"

"Ah, my child," said the father, "we are unhappy! God tries us severely; we must bow to His almighty will."

"What must I fear?" cried Lenora in perplexity. "Speak, father; has he refused his consent?"

"He has refused it, Lenora."

"No, no!" cried the maiden, "it cannot be!"

"Refused—because he has millions, and we are poor."

"Is it true? Is Gustav lost—hopelessly lost?"

"Hopelessly," repeated the nobleman with a hollow voice.

The young girl uttered a loud cry of anguish, and hastening forward, sank down with her head upon the table. She sobbed audibly, muttering at times the name of her beloved in a tone of utter despair. The nobleman rose, and for a long time gazed at his suffering child. An unutterable sadness was imprinted on his features; his eyes, at other times so clear and sparkling, were restless and troubled; he closed his hands convulsively, and at last folding them, he approached his daughter, and said imploringly—

"Lenora, have pity on me; moderate your grief for my sake, my child! In this unhappy interview with Herr Denecker, I have endured all the agonies which can torture a nobleman's and a father's heart. I have drunk, in full draughts, the bitter gall of shame, and emptied to the dregs the cup of humiliation. But all this is nothing when I behold your sorrow. Oh, try to control yourself; show me your face; let me find consolation in your tranquillity! My brain whirls—I die of despair!"

When he said this, he sank into a chair, quite exhausted by his prolonged sufferings. The maiden approached her father, and rested her head on his shoulder, saying with difficulty, as tears and sobs would allow her—

"Never to see him again! to renounce his love, and all the happiness which I dreamt of! Ah, he will die of sorrow!"

"Lenora, Lenora!" sighed the nobleman.

"O dear father!—Gustav for ever, for ever lost! I could die at the dreadful thought : still, so long as I possess you, I will bless and praise God; but I can do nothing but shed tears *now!* O let me weep!"

Herr von Vlierbeke pressed his child to his breast, and in silence respected her grief. A profound stillness reigned round father and daughter. Both sat there for a long time, till the very excess of their sorrow had brought fatigue, and mere exhaustion made their hearts accessible to **mutual consolation.**

CHAPTER VI.

FOUR days after Herr Denecker had refused his consent to Gustav's marriage with Lenora, a hired carriage drove over the heath, and drew up at a lonely part of the road, about a mile from Grinselhof. A young man sprang out of the vehicle, and pointing out a distant inn, at which the carriage was to wait, hastened with rapid strides in the opposite direction. He appeared driven on by an uncontrollable impatience, and trembled at times as if his own thoughts terrified him. So soon as he saw Grinselhof glimmering through the trees, he advanced cautiously, keeping close by the wood, and going from one side to another, wherever the foliage was thickest. When he reached the Castle, he uttered a cry of joy—for the gate fortunately stood open. Cautiously he crept through the bushes till he gained the bridge, and then, passing the farm-house on tip-toe, disappeared among the lofty trees, which, like a wall, enclosed Grinselhof, separating it from the rest of the world.

He had advanced only a few paces within the grounds, when he suddenly paused with visible agitation. Under the Indian jessamine sat Lenora, resting her head on the table ; her breast heaved convulsively, and a few glistening tears forced their way through her fingers, and fell on the ground.

The youth approached lightly ; but slow and quiet as his motions were, the maiden suddenly raised her head, and sprang up trembling, while the word "Gustav" escaped from her breast, like a cry of pain, and resounded among the trees. She would have fled, but before she could advance a step, the young man was on his knees before her, and addressing her with ardour, while he held her hand firmly in his own—

"Lenora, Lenora, hear me! If you flee from me, if you deny me the consolation to tell you, with my last farewell, what I suffer and what I hope, I shall either die at your feet, or, carrying a serpent of torture in my heart, perish far from my fatherland, far from you, my sister, my beloved, my bride! O Lenora, by your earnest, pure love. I conjure you, do not drive me from you at this time!"

Although Lenora trembled in every limb, her countenance yet expressed dignity and self-command, and she replied, calmly and coldly—

"Your boldness surprises me, sir; it required much to appear at Grinselhof again, after the insult which has been offered to my father. He is now in bed ill; his high soul sank under his sufferings, and a violent fever has seized him. This is the reward of my love for you."

"Ah, Lenora, you blame me! what have I, then, done wrong?" exclaimed the young man despairingly.

"There can be no longer any intercourse between us," replied the maiden. "We are not so rich as you, sir, it is true; but the blood which flows in our veins brooks not contempt. Stand up, go, I must never see you more."

"Pity, favour," implored Gustav, raising his hands imploringly; "I am innocent, Lenora!"

The maiden endeavoured to conceal the tears which she could not restrain, and turned to go.

"Oh how cruel!" he exclaimed. "You leave me for ever, without even saying farewell, without one word of comfort;

you are deaf to my entreaties, insensible to my sorrow. Well
then, I must endure my fate, for you have willed it so."

Then springing up, he exclaimed with a flood of tears—

"Lenora, my friend, you pronounce my death-sentence.
I forgive you; may you be happy on earth without me.
Farewell—farewell for ever!"

When he had said this, strength seemed to fail him, and
sinking on a chair, his arms fell powerless and outstretched
upon the table.

Lenora had already moved a few paces from the arbour,
but the evident despair of her lover drew her back irresistibly;
one could easily read in her face a violent struggle between
duty and love. At last her heart seemed to yield, tears gushed
from her eyes, and slowly approaching the young man, she
took his hand and sighed tenderly—

"Gustav, my poor friend, we are unhappy, very unhappy,
are we not?"

The affectionate grasp of her hand, and the sweet tones of
her voice, restored the young man to himself; and with a
happy smile, looking in the maiden's eyes, he said with rapture—

"Lenora, dear Lenora, you have returned to me; you have
pity for my sufferings; you do not, then, hate me?"

"Can a love like ours die, Gustav?"

"O no, no!" cried the youth with ardour, "it is eternal,
eternal! too mighty for misfortune or misery, indestructible
while our hearts beat in our bosoms!"

The maiden hung her head and looked down, as she replied
solemnly—

"Do not think, Gustav, that our separation gives me less
pain than it gives you. If the assurance of my love can
console you in your absence, then be strong and brave, for I
will ever cherish your memory in my mourning heart; I will

follow you in spirit, and love you, till the grave fills up the
gulf which yawns between us: yonder with God we shall
meet again—on earth, never."

"Oh! you deceive yourself, Lenora," exclaimed Gustav,
with animation. "My uncle is not inexorable—he will yield
out of compassion for my despair."

"That may be, but my father's feeling of honour is un-
bending," said the maiden with a sorrowful pride. "You
must go, Gustav; already too long have I transgressed his
command, too long forgotten my duty in remaining alone
with a man who cannot be my husband. Leave me! Were
any one to surprise us, my unhappy father would die of grief
and shame."

"Good, dear Lenora! only one moment more; hear what I
have to say to you. My uncle has refused his consent to
our union; I have wept, entreated—nothing availed to shake
his resolution. Despair, then, obscured my intellect; I re-
belled against him, threatened him like an ingrate, and said
things which have made me abhor myself since I recovered
my senses. On my knees I begged forgiveness; my uncle is
good-hearted, and he pardoned me on condition that I immediately, and without offering any objection, should accompany
him on a long-purposed journey to Italy—he hopes in this
way that I shall forget you. Forget you, Lenora!—I have,
however, embraced this plan with secret joy. I shall be alone
with him for months, show him all the love which I really
entertain for him, soften his heart by my great respect, unceasingly entreat him for his consent, persuade him, and
return victoriously, Lenora, to offer you my life and my hand,
to deck your brow with the happy bridal wreath, and kneeling before God's altar, to receive you as my beloved wife."

A bright smile beamed for a moment on the maiden's countenance, and her eyes sparkled with pleasure at this charm-

ing picture of a still possible happiness; but soon the delusion vanished, and she replied calmly, though sadly—

" My poor friend, it is cruel to be compelled to tear rudely even this feeble hope out of your heart. Your uncle may consent, but my father ?"

" Your father ! he will pardon all, and receive me into his arms again like a son that was lost and is found."

" No, no, do not believe it, Gustav ; his honour has been hurt—as Christian he will forgive, but, as nobleman, never forget the insult."

" O Lenora, you do your father injustice ! If I, with the full consent of my uncle, return and say to him, ' Here I am, the man who can make your child happy ; I will adorn her life with all the love and joy which a husband ever lavished on a wife ; her destiny on earth shall be enviable : give me Lenora !'—what do you think he would reply ?"

With downcast eyes, Lenora answered—

" You know his boundless goodness of heart, Gustav ; my happiness is the one wish of his soul ; he would bless you, and thank God."

" Is it not so, Lenora ? he would consent. You see all is not lost—a bright ray still lights up our future. Lay this sweet hope to your heart ; do not mourn ; let me carry with me on this weary journey the consolation that you, confiding in God's goodness, will wait for me. Think of me in your prayers ; utter my name at times in these shady walks where love so sweetly filled our hearts—where I, during two happy months, drank from your countenance a century of infinite bliss. Smile to me in your solitude ; my spirit will be conscious of your distant greeting, and I will rejoice and find courage to bear patiently our temporary separation."

Lenora wept in silence ; the sweet and touching words of her lover had quite conquered her pride ; in her heart nothing remained but love and sorrow. The young man perceived it, and continued—

"I go, Lenora; but I leave my fatherland and my beloved with a fully assured hope. Come what will, I will bear it cheerfully. Lenora, you will think on me—daily think on me, will you not?"

"O God! I have promised my father to forget you!"

"Forget me! Would you do your heart violence to forget me?"

"O no, Gustav!" was the low reply. "I will, for the first time, disobey my father; for I feel—I feel that I have not strength. My promise was a lie. To forget you is impossible for me; I must love you while I live; it is my earthly destiny."

"Oh, thanks, thanks, Lenora!" exclaimed Gustav with rapture. "Your loving words give me strength and courage. May God Almighty keep you! Your image will be ever present to me, and be my guardian angel, in joy as in sorrow, by day as by night; it will continually hover around me. It breaks my heart to leave you; but duty commands, and I must go: farewell! farewell!"

With feverish ardour, he then pressed both her hands, and quickly disappeared among the trees.

"Gustav, Gustav, farewell!" cried Lenora, half unconsciously, and overpowered by her emotion. With tremulous hand she sought a chair; then sinking powerless upon it, laid her head upon the table, and yielded to the anguish of her heart, while the hot tears streamed over her hands.

CHAPTER VII.

LENORA had told her father of Gustav's last visit, and had laboured to impart to his heart those sweet hopes of a better future which now lived in her own; but Herr von Vlierbeke was quite unimpressed by her account of what had taken place, and had even received it with a kind of satirical laugh, and without giving her any definite reply.

From that day Grinselhof had become still more lonely and melancholy than ever. Visibly tortured by a secret suffering, the nobleman generally sat with his head resting on his hands, and his eyes fixed on the ground; he saw continually before him the unhappy day on which the bond fell due, and which was rapidly and inevitably approaching, to drive the father and his child for ever into misery and destitution. Lenora concealed her own sorrow, that she might not aggravate her father's inexplicable grief by allowing her own melancholy to appear. Although her heart was full of anxious thoughts, she assumed cheerfulness and serenity. She did and said to him all that her loving heart could suggest, to draw him out of his painful reflections. Her exertions, however, had been quite fruitless; her father rewarded her with a smile, or with a tender caress; but the smile was sad and bitter—the caress was feeble and lifeless. On several occasions she had inquired with weeping eyes into the cause of her father's sadness, but he avoided every explanation. For whole days he would

wander about in solitude, and sunk in gloomy thoughts, through
the most shady and secluded paths in the garden, and appeared
to flee even his daughter's presence. When Lenora saw him
from a distance, she could perceive his look of anguish and
despair, and the violent gesticulations which he occasionally
made; but when she approached to soothe his excitement and
alleviate his sorrow by marks of deep affection, he scarcely
replied to her loving inquiries, and abruptly left her, to seek
some retired corner of the house in which he might indulge
his feelings unseen.

So passed a whole month—a month of silent suffering and
deep melancholy. Lenora, meanwhile, perceived with despair
how rapidly her father's countenance was growing pale and haggard, and how his eyes were losing their wonted brilliancy, as
if some consuming malady was wasting his life away. About
this time, however, an alteration in his conduct convinced her
that some sad and fearful secret lay heavy on his heart. For
a week past his eyes had beamed again with more than their
accustomed fire. He now seemed to be continually the victim
of a feverish agitation; his words, his thoughts, his gestures,
his acts, all showed impatience and excitement. About this
time, too, he went twice or thrice every week to the city without letting any one know what he did there. Late in the evening, he returned to Grinselhof, and then seated himself quietly
and thoughtfully by the table; soon after, he generally asked
Lenora to go to her room, and then disappeared with the lamp
into his own. But not to rest, as his sorrowing daughter knew
too well; for as she lay awake through anxiety, she often heard
during the night her father's footsteps, as he restlessly paced
the floor overhead; and she trembled, as she lay, with grief and
alarm. Lenora possessed great courage, and had acquired, from
her unusual training and education, an almost masculine energy
of soul; and so there gradually arose in her heart the resolu-

tion to force her father to impart his secret to her. However much her exceeding respect for her father withheld her from taking this step, her love and concern, on the other hand, daily and irresistibly urged her to make a bold effort. She had frequently sought her father with the intention of executing her plan, but the piercing glance with which he met her approach, and the whole expression of his face, had always deterred her. She saw that her father suspected her intention, and seemed to tremble in her presence, as if he feared her questions.

One day Herr von Vlierbeke had gone to the city as usual, early in the morning. It was now past noon, and Lenora wandered slowly, lost in sad reveries, through the rooms of the Castle, which were pervaded by a deathlike stillness. At times, she gave expression to her troubled thoughts in words, then paused for a time, and raised her hand to wipe a tear from her eye. In her abstraction, and scarcely knowing what she did, she drew out the drawer of the table on which her father was accustomed to write. Perhaps the desire she felt to discover his secret urged her unconsciously to do this. She found a document lying open, and scarcely had her eyes fallen on it, when a mortal paleness overspread her face, and she read with trembling what this paper revealed to her.

She shuddered as she shut the drawer; and left the room with downcast eyes, and a slow motion, like a person absorbed in the most painful and distressing thoughts. She sat down in the front room, gazed fixedly on the ground for a time, and then sighed—

"Sell Grinselhof! and wherefore? Herr Denecker mocked my father's poverty. What a secret this is! Are we then really so very, very poor? What a light is here! This accounts for my father's grief."

* * * * * * * *

CHAPTER VIII.

As Lenora now suspected, it was but two days after this that the announcement of the sale of her father's possessions appeared in the newspapers, and was posted throughout the city and the surrounding villages. It attracted considerable attention, and the poverty of a nobleman, whom everybody had considered so wealthy and avaricious, was a great subject of wonder. The sale had been announced as taking place " on account of his leaving the country;" and no one would have suspected the real grounds, had not the news spread from the city that Herr von Vlierbeke had been forced to this, in order to pay his debts; and that he consequently was excessively poor. Even the true cause of his misfortune—the assistance which he had lent his brother—became currently reported, although the details, of course, were not accurately known. Since the announcement, the nobleman had kept himself more secluded than ever, that he might escape all explanations. He awaited with patience the approach of the appointed day; and although a feeling of sadness often threatened to overpower him, he found in the never-flagging cheerfulness of his daughter, strength to look forward, with a certain courage and spirit, to the day of trial.

In the meantime, he received a letter from Gustav, who was then in Rome, containing also a few lines to his daughter. The young man declared that his attachment to Lenora had been only strengthened and deepened by absence ; and that he found his only consolation in the hope of being one day united with her in the bond of marriage. In other respects, however, his letter was not so encouraging ; for he informed them sadly and complainingly, that his attempts to gain over his uncle had been hitherto quite unsuccessful.—The father had thrown aside the letter with indifference, and did not conceal from Lenora that he no longer cherished the faintest hope of their possible union ; and counselled her entirely to blot out the memory of this unhappy attachment, that she might not prepare for herself still greater sorrow. Lenora herself was convinced that now that her father's poverty had become generally known, she must give up all hope ; and yet it was such a blessed and cheering feeling to be assured that Gustav still loved her—that he whose image filled her heart and inspired her dreams, continually thought on her, and lamented their separation ! True to her vows, she often uttered his name in her solitude ; many a sigh was breathed for him under the old jessamine, as if she were confiding to the winds the longing of her soul to bear to a milder sky. In her solitary hours, too, she sometimes repeated Gustav's tenderest confessions of his love ; and in her meditative walks, through the shady paths of Grinselhof, she paused at every spot where a word, a pressure of the hand, or a glance from him, had made her heart glow with rapture.

As if every misfortune which could afflict the nobleman's heart were to be poured upon him at once, to overwhelm him by one concentrated stroke, he at this time received news of his brother's death in America. The unfortunate man had died of a fever in the wilds, lying to the west of Hudson's Bay. Herr von Vlierbeke mourned for several days the death of his beloved brother ; but the approaching crisis of his own fate did not permit him to dwell long on this subject.

At last the day of sale arrived.

By early morning, people of all kinds had made their appearance at Grinselhof, partly from curiosity, partly with the intention of purchasing; and wandered about, looking at the furniture, and calculating beforehand the value of every article. The poor nobleman had collected into the large hall, everything in the house which was saleable. Assisted by his daughter, he had laboured, during the whole preceding night, to freshen and furbish things up a little, in order that their clean and polished exterior might induce the fancier to offer a good price. They did this from no selfish motive—for as the estate had been sold some days before very disadvantageously, they knew that even in the event of the most favourable sale, the proceeds would fall considerably short of the amount of their remaining debts. His honesty alone had induced him to sacrifice his night's rest to the interests of his creditors, in the hope of lessening their loss as much as possible. Apparently Herr von Vlierbeke had determined not to sleep another night at Grinselhof; for among the furniture exposed for sale were two beds, in addition to many clothes belonging to him and his daughter. Lenora had betaken herself early in the morning to the farm, to remain there till all was over.

At ten o'clock, the hall where the sale was to be carried on, was filled with people. Nobles, and distinguished ladies, were mingled there with old clothesmen and wrangling pawnbrokers, who had come out of the city in the hope of making a good bargain. Here and there, too, stood groups of peasants, and talked with an air of secrecy and wonder about the misfortune which had befallen Herr von Vlierbeke. Not a few of those present laughed loudly, and entertained themselves with all sort of jests, till the clerk began to read a list of the articles to be sold. Half an hour after, the sale began.

The clerk was just engaged commending a beautiful inlaid wardrobe, when Herr von Vlierbeke himself entered the hall, and took up his position beside the auctioneer. His appearance caused a general movement among the bystanders: heads were put together, and they whispered to each other, looking at the nobleman at the same time with a sort of impudent curiosity, with which in some cases a feeling of sympathy was mingled; but on the countenances of the majority, nothing could be read but indifference or cheerfulness. This, however, lasted only for a minute; for the calm and dignified look of the nobleman soon inspired them with respect and admiration. He was certainly poor, and misfortune had done what it could to prostrate him so far as wealth was concerned; but out of his eyes, and his clear, calm features, there beamed a free, courageous soul, whose greatness and gentle dignity were unimpaired by adversity.

The clerk, meanwhile, proceeded with the auction, and was instructed in the recommendation of certain articles by Herr von Vlierbeke, who gave him information regarding their origin, their age, and real value.

Some noblemen from the vicinity, who in earlier times had been on friendly terms with Lenora's father, now advanced to speak with him about his misfortune; but he successfully evaded both their curiosity and their compassion. He spoke so unconstrainedly, and remained so entirely master of himself, that they found no opportunity of displaying their useless sympathy. In his conduct, his bearing, his smile, there was something so dignified and commanding, that every one left him with the deepest respect.

But calm and collected as the countenance of Herr von Vlierbeke was, strong and undiminished as was the energy of soul, and high sense of personal dignity, which sparkled in his eye, the most painful sufferings secretly oppressed his heart.

Everything which had belonged to his ancestors, objects which bore the arms of his family, and had been piously cherished in his house for centuries, he now saw sold for a trifle, and pass into the hands of pawnbrokers and second-hand dealers. As these precious memorials of the past were one after the other placed upon the table, the famous history of his forefathers was unrolled before him, and he endured a pang as painful, as if in the parting from every little treasure a fond memory had been torn from his bleeding heart.

The sale was nearly at an end, when the portraits of the distinguished men who had borne the name of Vlierbeke were taken from the wall and put up to auction. The first, that of the hero of St. Quentin, fell to an old broker for the wretched sum of three francs! There was such a bitter mockery in the sale of the portraits, and the ridiculously low prices which they brought, that the anguish of the nobleman's heart now first began to reveal itself in his face, spite of his utmost efforts at self-control. With downcast eyes, he sank for a time into sad and desponding thoughts; then raised his head, and, evidently deeply affected, left the room, that he might avoid witnessing the sale of the remaining portraits.

The sun had still a fourth of its daily journey to perform before reaching the western horizon. At Grinselhof, a profound quiet has succeeded the tumultuous noise of tradesmen: no human being is any longer visible in the lonely garden walks. The gate is shut, and everything has returned to its accustomed calm: one might suppose that its stillness had never been broken.

The door of Herr von Vlierbeke's dwelling opens, and on the threshold appear two people, an aged man and a young maiden, each with a bundle in their hands, and seemingly prepared for a journey. It is difficult at first to recognise in these

poorly-clad people Herr von Vlierbeke and his daughter; but
such they are, though one would scarcely suspect it. They
have evidently endeavoured to dress in a manner suitable to
their altered circumstances, and to appear as modest and un-
pretending as possible.

Lenora wears a gown of dark calico, a hood, and a little
square neckerchief; her beautiful curls are invisible—either
concealed by her hood, or more probably fallen under the
scissors. The poor nobleman wears a coat of coarse cloth,
buttoned to the chin, and a cap with a broad shade, which
almost entirely conceals his countenance.

Spite of what they have done to conceal their former rank
and descent, there yet reigns, even in their dress, a certain
grace, and something undefinable in their gait and air which
indicate a high breeding. The countenance of the father
was calm; and it was impossible to say whether sorrow, joy,
or indifference was most conspicuous in it. Lenora looks
firm and courageous, although the departure from her birth-
place, and the home which she had loved from her childhood
—from those richly-foliaged trees, under whose shade her
heart had experienced the first rapturous feeling of love—from
the graceful jessamine, at whose foot the timid confession first
fell upon her ear from the lips of Gustav!—yes, she is firm
and courageous, although this solemn farewell fills her heart
with sadness. But she must support her suffering parent;
watch the fluctuating emotions of his soul as they appear and
disappear on his countenance; like a sentinel keep guard over
his heart, that by proofs of her infinite affection, she may chase
away the grief which would overpower it. And therefore it
is that her look is so clear and sweet when it meets her
father's. With slow steps, father and daughter approach the
farm, and enter to take leave of the farmer and his wife.

The latter was alone with her maid, on the ground-floor.

"Mother Beth," said the nobleman, in a gentle and feeble tone, "we come to bid you farewell."

The woman looked at them for a moment, arranged her dress hurriedly, and then putting her apron before her eyes, ran out by the back-door lamenting loudly as she went. The maid laid her head on the window-sill and began to sob, and refused all consolation. The woman returned in less than a minute, accompanied by her husband.

"Alas, it is true then, sir!" said the farmer's wife, with choking voice. "You leave Grinselhof, and we are never to see you again!"

"Come, come, good Mother Beth," said the nobleman, taking her hand, "do not weep on that account; you see that we endure our fate patiently."

The woman raised her head, again looked at her former master and mistress, and began to weep more uncontrollably than ever. The farmer stood for a moment with his eyes fixed on the ground, and then suddenly said to the nobleman with a firm voice, in which considerable effort was apparent—

"I beg, sir, that you will let me have a few words with you alone."

Herr von Vlierbeke followed him into another apartment. The farmer shut the door, and said timidly—

"Gracious sir, I scarcely venture to tell you what my prayer is. Will you forgive me if it displeases you?"

"Speak out freely, friend," replied the nobleman, with a kind smile.

"You see, sir," stammered the farmer, much affected, "it is to you that I owe all that I have ever earned. When I married my Beth I had nothing, and you gave us this farm at a low rent. We have prospered by God's favour, and under your protection; while you, on the contrary, our bene-factor, have met with misfortune, and now are forced to leave

your home. God alone knows whither you are bound, or what
fate awaits you. Perhaps to endure poverty and want—but
no, that must not happen. I would reproach myself all my
life long, and it would be to me a continual grief; everything, sir, which I possess, is at your service."

Herr von Vlierbeke tremulously pressed the farmer's hand,
and said, deeply moved—

"You are a good man. I should be happy to be obliged
to you; but give up your kind intentions, my friend, and
retain what you have earned by the sweat of your brow. Do
not be anxious about us; with God's help, we shall be able
to find some tolerable way of life."

"Ah, sir," implored the farmer, "do not refuse the little
assistance which I can give." He opened a drawer, and pro-
duced a heap of silver coins. "See," he continued, "this
could not compensate for the hundredth part of the kindness
which you have always shown to us. Grant me this one favour, which I beg from your magnanimity. Take this money:
if it were to spare you a single hour's misery, I would be
grateful to God for it during my life."

Tears of emotion gushed from the nobleman's eyes, and
with difficulty controlling his feelings, he said—

"Thanks, thanks, my good friend; but I must refuse it.
Every further attempt is useless. Let us go into the other
room."

"But, sir," cried the farmer despairingly, "whither do you
go? For God's sake, tell me!"

"It is impossible," replied Herr von Vlierbeke, "for I do
not myself know. And did I know it, prudence would prevent my informing any one."

He entered the other room as he uttered these words, and
found all, even Lenora, in tears. The maiden hung on the
woman's neck, while the servant girl kissed her young mis-

tress's hand. The nobleman at once perceived that it was necessary to bring this painful scene to a close; and addressing a few earnest words to his daughter, she controlled her emotions, and made an effort to appear calm. They now warmly pressed each other's hands, and gave the parting kiss; and then father and daughter took up their little bundles, and went across the bridge of Grinselhof, on their way towards the open heath. For long, the people of the farm followed them with their eyes, till they disappeared behind the trees.

Silently Herr von Vlierbeke walked along the heath road, till he gained an eminence behind which rose a thick fir·wood, limiting the prospect on one side. He knew that when he struck into the path through this wood, Grinselhof would be lost to view. On this spot, then, he paused, and turned slowly round. Once more he threw a parting look on the estate and the house which his forefathers had possessed, and where his own cradle had stood. Agonizing thoughts must now have been passing through his soul, for Lenora trembled as she looked at him; still, she had not the courage to interrupt his sad and solemn contemplation. At last two glistening tears trickled slowly down the broken-hearted nobleman's face. Lenora, throwing her arms around him, kissed them away, and then, with consoling and affectionate words, drew him gently into the forest path.

They were soon lost in the gloomy depths of the wood.

CHAPTER IX.

SCARCELY eight days after Herr von Vlierbeke's departure, a second letter arrived from Italy. The postman asked the farmer whither the former owners of Grinselhof had removed; but neither he nor any other could give him information, for all were alike ignorant of the country in which they had taken refuge. The Notary was equally unable to throw any light upon the matter. The letters were then laid aside in the post-office, along with several others which afterwards came from the same quarter; and nobody concerned himself further about the fate of the poor nobleman, except the farmer of Grinselhof, who never failed, every Friday when he went to market, to make diligent inquiry of the country people whether they had seen his old master; but no one had anything to communicate.

Almost four months had now elapsed, when one day a handsome travelling-carriage drew up before the Notary's house. The door was opened, and a young man in travelling clothes hurriedly entered the hall.

"The Herr Notary," he said impatiently to the servant. The latter replied that his master was engaged, and could not see him for a few minutes; and then, conducting the young gentleman to a room, requested him to wait; and there left him. The youth seemed very much annoyed at the delay, and, throwing himself into a chair, muttered a few words of impatience.

The impatience, however, soon gave way to melancholy, and, looking to the ground, he became absorbed in deep and apparently sad thoughts.

Gradually his features brightened, and a cheerful smile played round his mouth as he raised his head, and said with joy and ardour—

"Ah, how my heart throbs with desire! How sweet is the hope—the certainty—of seeing her again on this very day; of rewarding her for her fidelity; of compensating her for a six months' sorrow; of kneeling before her, and exclaiming— 'Lenora, Lenora, my sweet bride! he has consented to our union. I bring you wealth, love, happiness! I return with the will and the power to gladden your father's heart, and make his old age happy; and to live with you both in the paradise which we dreamt of. O my beloved! freely receive me into your arms; accept my bridal kiss; I am your bride-groom, and nothing in life will ever again separate us. Oh, come—one embrace, one eternal bond unites the father and his child with me. Ah, yes, I feel that our souls are one— one in their desires and one in their love. Thanks, thanks, O God!'"

While he uttered these words, indulging in the bright pic-tures which his fancy painted, he had quite forgotten the pre-sent, and, rising from his chair, walked up and down in his excitement. A noise outside the room-door brought him back to reality, and restraining his feelings, he assumed an expres-sion of tranquillity, although the cheerful smile still lingered on his face. In a short time, he again relapsed into musing : a different feeling seemed now to arise in his heart, for a gentle tremor came upon him, and he now seemed as anxious and desponding, as he was formerly hopeful and glad.

"But what if I am the victim of a self-delusion ! My letters have been unanswered, my entreaties unheeded ; even my tears have been vain. And if Lenora"—

He stood for a time motionless, his hand upon his brow ; but suddenly he cast these gloomy thoughts from him, and with conviction and fervour exclaimed—

"Away, away with these suspicions, which would creep like a poisonous snake into my bosom ! Lenora forget me—reject me ? No, no ; it is impossible ! Has she not said that our love is eternal and indestructible ? Can Lenora's lips lie ? Can a heart like hers be unfaithful ? Oh, peace, peace—you slander her !"

Scarcely had he uttered these last words, when the door of the apartment was opened ; and the young man, concealing his emotion, approached the Notary with a composed countenance. The latter entered the room with an official look, ready to adapt his words and bearing to the rank of his visitor. Scarcely however had he recognised the young man, when a friendly smile lighted up his countenance, and he approached him with open arms, saying—

"Welcome, welcome, Herr Gustav ! I have expected you for some days, and am overjoyed to see you again. No doubt we have some weighty matters to arrange together ; I thank you for the confidence you place in me. And how stands it with the legacy, to talk more particularly ? Is there a will ?"

Some melancholy recollection seemed to occur to Gustav ; and as he drew out his pocket-book, an expression of heartfelt grief overspread his face. The Notary perceived it, and remarked—

"It grieved me deeply to hear of your loss. Your good uncle was my friend, and I was in a special manner sorry to hear of his death. When far from his fatherland, the call of God reached him. It is a great misfortune; but such is man's destiny; and we must console ourselves with the thought that we are all mortal! Your uncle had no ordinary affection for you, sir; and no doubt he has remembered you in the final arrangement of his property."

"Have the goodness to convince yourself how dearly he loved me," said Gustav, laying a document on the table.

The Notary glanced through the paper. What he read seemed to be as agreeable as it was unexpected.

Gustav meanwhile sat with downcast eyes; but moving about restlessly on his seat, as if the victim of an irresistible impatience.

After some minutes, the Notary rose from his chair, and said, in a very respectful tone—

"Permit me, Herr Denecker, to wish you much happiness. These papers are unassailable, and in complete and legal form. Sole heir! Are you aware of all, sir? You possess more than a million!"

"We shall speak of this at greater length at another time," interrupted Gustav impatiently. "I drove here immediately on my arrival to beg a favour of you."

"I wait your commands, sir."

"You are, I believe, Herr von Vlierbeke's man of business?"

"At your service."

"I learned from my departed uncle that Herr von Vlierbeke was reduced to extreme poverty. I have reasons which make me most anxious to free him from his difficulties."

"I imagine, sir," replied the Notary, "that you wish to perform a deed of benevolence; you cannot apply your wealth better than in this instance. I know how Herr von Vlierbeke fell into difficulties, and what he has suffered; he was a sacrifice to his own generosity and honour. Perhaps he pushed those virtues to the verge of folly; however that may be, he certainly deserved a better fate."

"Well then, Herr Notary, I entreat you to be so good as to inform me what must be done in order to assist Herr von Vlierbeke without hurting his sense of honour. Among other things, I am aware there exists a bond for four thousand francs in favour of the von Hoogebaen family. This bond I must get possession of at once, were it to cost me ten times its value."

With visible astonishment, and without replying, the Notary looked at Herr Denecker with such a peculiar expression, that the latter asked anxiously—

"What is there in my purpose to alarm you? You make me tremble."

"I cannot know the precise extent of your anxiety; but I fear that the information which I have to give you will grieve you deeply. I have scarcely courage to speak it. If my conjecture is well grounded, I am sorry for you, sir."

"Heavens! what do you say?" cried Gustav with alarm. "Explain yourself, quickly. Has death visited Grinselhof? Is the only hope of my life annihilated?"

"No, no," exclaimed the Notary quickly. "Do not be alarmed; both still live; but a great misfortune has befallen them."

"What is it?" said the young man with feverish anxiety.

"Compose yourself," replied the Notary. "Pray sit down, and listen. It is not so bad as you suppose; your wealth is able materially to alleviate their misery."

"Oh, God be thanked!" exclaimed Gustav with joy. "But I conjure you, sir, to make haste to put my mind at ease. Delay is torture."

"You must know, then, that the bond fell due during your absence. Herr von Vlierbeke spent months in the vain endeavour to procure money to meet it. In addition to this, his property was burdened with the heaviest mortgages. In the end, in order to avoid the disgrace of a sale by order of a court of law, he had his entire real and personal estate sold by public auction. The proceeds very nearly cleared his debts; every creditor has been satisfied; and all have expressed their admiration of the noble and upright conduct of Herr von Vlierbeke, who preferred to expose himself to extreme misery rather than permit the slightest reproach to be attached to his name."

"Does Herr von Vlierbeke, then, now occupy his paternal property as a tenant?"

"No; he has left the place."

"And where is he to be found? I must see him and speak with him before this day is over."

"I cannot tell where he is to be found."

"How—you do not know?"

"Nobody knows; they disappeared without informing any one of their intentions."

"Heavens! is it possible?" exclaimed Gustav with anxiety. "What! am I to be still longer separated from her, and without knowing even what has befallen her? I tremble when I think of her possible fate. Do you not possess the slightest clue to their place of residence? Does no one, no one know where they are?"

"No one," repeated the Notary. "On the very evening after the sale, Herr von Vlierbeke left Grinselhof on foot, and crossed the heath, in what direction is unknown. Since then I have often endeavoured to discover his place of retreat, but always in vain."

This melancholy intelligence affected the young man deeply. He grew pale, and covered his face with his hands, to conceal the emotion by which he was agitated. Though it pained him deeply to learn from the Notary the full **extent** of the father's poverty, he partially knew it before; but the certainty of not soon meeting his beloved, and rescuing her out of her misery, filled his heart with intense grief; while the uncertainty which hung over her fate made him fear the worst.

The Notary contemplated the young man in silence, shrugging his shoulders at times, and with an expression of sympathy on his countenance. At last he said, with an attempt at consolation—

"You are young, sir; and, after the manner of youth, you carry both joy and sorrow too far. Your despair has no sufficient ground. In the time in which we live, it is an easy matter to find out people if we will only seek for them. With money and activity, one is almost certain of discovering Herr von Vlierbeke's retreat within a few days—even if it is in a foreign land. If you will commission me to make the search, I will spare neither time nor labour to procure you satisfactory intelligence as soon as possible."

"And I, on my side, will put into requisition the extensive correspondence of my house, and never cease to search till I discover their hiding-place."

"Take courage, then, Herr Denecker; I have no doubt that our efforts will quickly be crowned with success. And now that you are convinced of my readiness to serve you, I should like, with your permission, to take the liberty to address to you a few calm and earnest words; though, perhaps, I have no right to question you about your plans, and still less to allow myself to imagine for a moment that they are not in the highest degree praiseworthy. Your intention is, then, to marry Miss Lenora?"

"My unalterable intention," replied the young man.

"Unalterable!" rejoined the Notary; "so be it, then. But

the confidence which your honoured uncle continually placed
in me, and my office as notary and adviser of the family, make
it my duty to open your eyes calmly to what you are about to
do. You are a *millionnaire*, and bear a name which is itself
worth a handsome capital on the Exchange. Herr von Vlierbeke possesses nothing—his poverty is universally known;
and whether the world acts justly or unjustly, certain it is,
that it condemns the fallen nobleman to disgrace and contempt. With wealth, youth, and a person like yours, you
may aspire to the hand of a very rich heiress, and double
your possessions.

Gustav had at first listened with undisguised impatience to
these words; and then, turning his eyes from the Notary, had
begun to think of other things. At this point, he turned
round hastily, and said—

"It is well; you do your duty, and I thank you. Enough.
Now tell me to whom Grinselhof belongs at present?"

The Notary seemed somewhat offended at this sudden interruption, and at the small impression which his words seemed
to make; but concealing his vexation under a polite smile, he
replied—"I see that you have resolved on your course; act,
then, according to your inclination. The holders of the mortgages still keep possession of Grinselhof, because it sold for
less than its value, and their claims."

"And who dwells in the Castle?"

"It is at present uninhabited. No one leaves town during
the winter."

"It is possible, then, to purchase it from the present
owners?"

"Certainly; I myself have orders to dispose of it for the
value of the mortgages."

"Grinselhof, then, belongs to me, Herr Notary. Have the
goodness to inform the owners of this immediately."

"Very good, sir; you may consider Grinselhof henceforth as your property. If you have any desire to see the place, you will find the keys with the farmer."

Gustav took up his hat to go; and bidding the Notary adieu, he said—

"I am worn out, and require rest: I feel deeply the melancholy intelligence which you have given me. Farewell for the present, sir, and have the goodness to fulfil your promise with as little delay as possible. My gratitude will be greater than you suppose. Adieu till morning."

Sorrowfully and anxiously Gustav left the lawyer's house, to mourn in solitude over the sad news which he had so unexpectedly heard.

CHAPTER X.

THE charming spring had now divested the earth of its gloomy winter garment, and breathed new life and energy into every created thing. Grinselhof, too, shone again with that wild and free beauty which was peculiar to it: the stately oaks unfolded their leaves; the Alpine roses were already in full blossom; the insects swarmed and hummed among the bushes; and the reviving sunlight shed its gentle warmth on the tender opening leaves.

Grinselhof is still the same: its walks are as solitary as ever, and a deathlike stillness reigns among its groves and copses; but around the house there are signs of motion and life. Two servants may be seen engaged in cleaning a costly chariot, and the neighing and stamping of horses may be heard proceeding from the once untenanted stables. A young girl stands at the door, and talks and laughs with the servants. Suddenly the sound of a silver table-bell is heard, and the maid runs into the house, exclaiming—

"Heavens! there is the master's bell. He rings for breakfast, and there is nothing ready!"

After the lapse of a short time, she ascends the stairs, carrying the handsome breakfast-service into the upper room, and places it before a young man, who sits there silent and musing, with his head resting on his hands.

Awaking from a reverie, he takes his breakfast with the air of one who is unconscious of what he is doing.

The room is singularly furnished. While some pieces of furniture are remarkable for beauty and costliness, and as products of the most recent taste, various chairs and cabinets are as conspicuous for the high antiquity indicated by their dark-brown hue and their elaborate carving. One sees clearly that some things have stood the tear and wear of two or three centuries. On the walls hang many pictures somewhat smoked, and of very ancient date, whose gilded frames, all covered with dust, have long since lost their brightness; they are portraits of statesmen, abbots, and prelates. These pictures, and many other objects in the room, bear the arms of Herr von Vlierbeke's family. It was universally known that a public auction had been held at Grinselhof, where everything which had belonged to Herr von Vlierbeke had been distributed among many purchasers, and found its way into the most diverse places; and how was it possible that those objects could have returned to the spot which they seemed to have left for ever?

The gentleman rises from his chair, but still with the same air of abstraction, and walks slowly up and down the room, pausing at times to gaze sadly at the portraits; then resuming his walk, he holds his hand before his eyes, as if he would prevent any interruption of his reverie. Approaching an old-fashioned cabinet which stands on a corner table, and opening it, he takes out a few trifling articles, and among the rest a pair of golden earrings and a necklace of red coral beads. He gazes at these objects for a long time with a sweet and melancholy smile; a deep sigh escapes his lips; he raises his mournful eyes to heaven; and then replacing the ornaments in the cabinet, he descends the stairs into the court. Replying silently to the respectful greetings of his servants, as he passes, he is soon lost among the gloomiest paths of the surrounding grounds. He pauses before an Indian jessamine, and standing there with folded arms, he says in a low and earnest tone—

"On this very spot the confession of her love first escaped her virgin lips; the blush of modesty suffused her brow, and looking shyly down, her sweet voice murmured the sacred words, while I was too deeply moved, too wildly transported by my infinite happiness to speak, but stood trembling and silent by her side, as if the greatness of my good fortune terrified me. O thou who hast so often heard her sweet-toned voice—thou, the witness of those pure and rapturous hours! the spring has again crowned thee with young leaves, but at thy feet dwell no more either joy or hope!—the lamentation of a mourning heart alone rises among thy foliage! All is melancholy and silent; she whose presence breathed life into thy solitude is gone! We have lost the angel who, by a single word, could change this spot into a beautiful heaven, and spread around her joy, hope, and blessedness, as the sun diffuses light and life! Ah! it has left us, that soul of love! and nothing, nothing remains save memory!"

After a short silence, he struck into another path and wandered among the bushes, from time to time pausing before objects which were dear to him as witnesses of past occurrences, and spoke eloquently to him of her whom he mourned so deeply. He stood by the edge of the pond, and looked at the swarms of goldfishes as they sported in the water; and gazed with a loving eye at the pinks which adorned the borders of the broad paths, and which had been reared and tended by her with such motherly affection. And so he gave himself up to the past, and poured forth his sorrow to every object which she had known or loved, till at last, weary and desponding, he sank upon a chair under the old jessamine. He had sat there for a considerable time, indulging his **grief,** when the farmer's wife approached him with a book, and said cheerfully—

"Here is a book, sir, in which Miss Lenora used often to read. When at market yesterday, my husband recognised the man who bought it at the auction, and accompanied him to his house to get it. It must be a fine book; but had it not belonged to our young mistress, I would not have touched it for all the money in the world, for my husband says that it is called *Lucifer*."

While the farmer's wife was speaking, the gentleman had taken the book from her, and turned over its leaves with intense pleasure, without seeming to hear a word which the woman addressed to him. At last he raised his head, and said with a friendly smile—

"I thank you for your care and attention, Frau Jans. You cannot conceive how it delights me to get possession of anything which belonged to your mistress. Be assured that I shall not forget your willing service."

After saying this, he again examined the book, and seemed to peruse it with attention. The farmer's wife, however, still remained where she was, and at last said in a sorrowful tone—

"Permit me, sir, to ask whether you have yet heard any news of Miss Lenora?"

The gentleman shook his head, and replied—

"Alas! not the smallest. All our efforts have been hitherto fruitless."

"That is very unfortunate," said the woman sorrowfully. "God knows where she is now, and what she has to bear! She said to me when she was going away, that she intended to work for her father. Alas! one must have been accustomed to work from childhood, if one is to earn their bread by their own hands. Oh, when I think of it, it is heart-rending! To think that our poor young lady is perhaps at this moment serving others, and is forced to work like a slave for her daily bread. I, too, have served, sir, and know what it is to work from morning till night—and so beautiful, so refined, so amiable, and so kind-hearted! Oh, sir, it is too sad! I cannot help weeping when I think of it!"

She began to shed tears; and the gentleman, touched by the genuine and heartfelt sorrow which she displayed, looked at her in silence as she continued, with an effort at self-control, but with a choking voice—

"And now, when she might be so happy, and mistress again of Grinselhof, and all the rest of the possessions, in the midst of which she was born and brought up; now, when Herr von Vlierbeke might spend the rest of his old age in peace, and without any more troubles,—now they are perhaps wandering from place to place, poor, and neglected by everybody. Ah, sir, it is very sad indeed to know that a benefactor is unfortunate, and not to be able to do anything to help him, but pray to God, and hope for His compassion."

Without being aware of it, the simple woman had touched the most sensitive chords in the heart of her new master, and had moved him deeply. She now perceived that he shed tears, and wrung his hands with an expression of grief and despair; and with some anxiety and alarm, she added—

"Pardon me, sir, for having caused you sorrow; but my heart is so full of this, that it runs over, and I talk on scarcely knowing what I say. If I have done wrong, you are much too good to be angry with me for loving our young lady so much, and lamenting her fate. Has your honour any orders?"

She was about to go, but the gentleman raised his head, and said with suppressed but deep feeling—

"I be angry, Frau Jans, because you express to me your

love for Lenora? No; my heart rather blesses you for it. The tears which you have drawn from me, do me good—for I suffer much, and am very miserable. Life is a burden to me, and were the merciful God to call me away from this earth, I would die with joy. All hope of seeing her again on earth is gone; perhaps Lenora is waiting for me in heaven above."

" Oh, sir, do not say so," interrupted the woman anxiously; " that cannot be."

" You lament her, and sometimes shed tears for her sake, my good woman," he continued, without paying attention to her exclamation; " but you cannot understand the sorrow and pain which I feel,—how not a single minute passes without tearing my heart with some new agony. For eight long months to have prayed to God for the highest earthly favour He could confer—the being able to call Lenora my bride, to see her again, to overcome all obstacles, to make her happy! And then almost to lose my senses with joy and rapture—to hasten to my fatherland with lightning speed; and now, instead of the reward I hoped for, to find nothing but the most hopeless solitude—nay, what is more agonizing, to know that my beloved, my noble Lenora, is unhappy, and not have the power to alleviate her misery, and raise her out of her humiliation; to be compelled to spend the days of her sufferings in impotent despair, and not even to have the poor consolation that she still survives the miseries and hardships to which she has been exposed."

Profound silence followed this violent burst of grief. The farmer's wife stood with downcast eyes, and deeply affected. After a short interval, she said in a consolatory tone—

" Ah, sir, I understand your grief well. But who knows but some sudden and unexpected news may come, after all. God is good; He will listen to our prayers; and then joy for their return will make us quite forget all our sorrow."

"May your hopes be realized, my good woman! but it is now more than seven months since they left their home, and more than three since hundreds of men have received orders to search for them. Inquiries have been made in every city, and up to this moment not the smallest news, not the slightest trace, that they still live—that they are still in this world! My understanding tells me that I ought not yet wholly to despair; but my impatient, bleeding heart tortures itself with its own despair, and loudly proclaims that ' I have for ever lost them—for ever!'"

He rose and left the jessamine; but as he moved away, he suddenly raised his eyes with an expression of surprise, and pointing towards the public road, said—

"Listen! do you hear nothing?"

"The tramp of a horse's feet," replied the woman, without comprehending why the noise should have so powerful an effect on him.

"Poor fool!" sighed the youth, with a sad smile; "what has an over-driven horse to do with me, after all?"

"See, see, it comes this way," cried the farmer's wife, with increasing interest. "Heavens! it is a messenger from the city! There can be no doubt of it. O may he bring good news!"

The rider advanced to the gate at full gallop, but pulled the rein when he saw the gentleman and the farmer's wife coming to meet him; and, dismounting, drew a letter from his pocket, and gave it to the master of Grinselhof, with the words —"Herr Denecker, I come from the Herr Notary. He ordered me to ride at full speed, and, without stopping once by the way, to give you this letter." He then led his smoking horse to the stable.

With a trembling hand, Herr Denecker broke the seal, while the farmer's wife looked at him with a smiling and hopeful countenance.

When Herr Denecker read the first lines, he grew pale and trembled, and his agitation increased the further he read; but at last he exclaimed, almost mad with joy—

"God be praised! she is restored to me."

"Oh, sir, sir!" exclaimed Frau Jans, "have you good news?"

"Yes, yes, rejoice with me! Lenora lives! I know where she is, and I go to fetch her." And running to the house, he called his servants hurriedly, and said—

"Quick, the travelling carriage, the English horses, my portmanteau, my cloak. Make haste, fly!"

With his own hand, he then brought down several articles necessary for a journey, and placed them in the carriage, which had been already drawn out of the coach-house. The horses were yoked, and although they stamped their feet, and champed their bits with impatience, the lash was not spared. As if it had been swept on by the winds, the carriage dashed through the open gate, and the dust rose in thick clouds from the Antwerp road.

CHAPTER XL.

We must now transport ourselves to the French town of Nancy, in search of Herr von Vlierbeke and his daughter. Arrived there, we must pass through several streets of what is called the Old Town, and stop before a cobbler's humble little work-shop. Pass through the shop and ascend the stairs—still higher; now open a little door.

Here everything looks very poor, but extremely neat and clean. The curtains of that little bed are snow-white, the well-scoured stove shines with a brilliant polish, and the floor is strewed with sand in the Flemish fashion. Before the open window, stand daisies and violets in a wooden box, and blossom in the sun, and hard by hangs a cage with a gold-finch.

How still it is in this room—not even a sigh breaks the quiet and loneliness of the place; yet there sits, by the window, a young girl, who sews a piece of new linen with great assiduity, and is apparently quite absorbed in her work. The dress of the young worker is extremely plain, but so tasteful, clean, and neat, that an odour of freshness and life seems to envelop her.

"Poor Lenora! this, then, is thy fate! To conceal thy illustrious rank in the attics of a labourer's dwelling; to seek a refuge from mockery and contempt far from thy native land; to labour unceasingly, struggling with want and necessity, bowing under sorrow and shame, and, with a bleeding heart, scarcely bearing up under the incurable wounds of humiliation and despair !

" Certainly thy wretchedness has already given to thy countenance the sallow tinge of want ; adversity and trial have gnawed at thy heart, and robbed thy eyes of their once brilliant fire ; and thou art a dying flower, pining away in silent and uncomplaining suffering !—Heaven be praised, it is not so ! The hero blood which flows through thy veins has made thee strong against fate ! Thy graceful and lovely nature is more beautiful than ever ! If a residence in a narrow room has made the dark-brown hue disappear from thy face, it has only been to give it a tenderer, a mellower tone. As thy noble brow has grown more pale, the flush on thy lovely cheeks has become fresher. Still glances thy dark eye behind thy long eyelashes, full of fire and life ; still does that bright enchanting smile play round thy charming lips. It may be that thou still bearest in thy heart a rich treasure of courage and hope ; it may be that there still hovers before thy eyes a loved form. Is it out of the well of memory, then, that thou drawest strength to contend victoriously with misfortune ?"

See, some dream or fancy takes possession of her now ! she lets her hands fall, and pauses in her work. With her head inclined, she gazes intently on the ground ; her soul is elsewhere, and permits itself to be borne along unconsciously and unresistingly on the stream of self-oblivion.

She lays the linen on a chair, and slowly rises ; contemplates for a few moments her modest little flowerets on the window-sill, plucks a daisy, and dreamily tearing its leaves, gazes into the distance, where a noble chestnut exalts its leary crown above the surrounding houses. The sight of its well-known foliage works powerfully upon her soul ; a strange smile hovers round her lips, tears gush from her eyes, and, with visible excitement, she inhales, with long inspirations, the fresh air of the early spring, and seems to drink in the warm genial sunshine. The expression of her countenance changes; one would suppose that her fancy wanders among beloved but distant friends, and talks with them of happy and joyful things; unintelligible sounds escape her lips, followed by a sad and painful smile. Perchance she murmurs the name of some absent one. She now looks sympathizingly at the sprightly goldfinch, which flutters restlessly from side to side, and tries vainly to force its prison-grating with its little beak. She gazes at the bird with dreamy forgetfulness a while, and then says with a gentle voice—

"Wherefore would you leave us, dear one?—you, the dear companion of our misfortunes? Be contented. Father is well again, and now we shall live cheerfully and happily all together. Why flutter so restlessly in your wiry prison? But oh, it is a hard thing to be caught and confined in a narrow space, when one has been born in the free fields, or in the wild forest or untamed heath, where life and joy and freedom reign, and where alone, under God's blue sky, they can be enjoyed! Alas, poor bird! I am a child of nature like you; I also have been torn from my native fields—I also long for the solitude of my childish years, and for the great and calm old trees which overshadowed my cradle. Does there mingle itself with your sadness, too, the form of one whom you loved? Do you, too, lament something more than freedom? Why do I ask you? Is not this the season of love again? Love is for you, as for me, the most beautiful tale of life. I bought you in better times; you have been for long my sole companion and my pastime."

With these words she took the cage in her hand, and continued—"But I understand your little sorrows now. I will no longer be to you what inexorable destiny is to me. There,

fly—be free, and may God protect thee! Go and enjoy what
is most of all essential to every living thing—freedom and
love! O how you hop for joy, how gallantly you spread your
wings! Farewell, farewell, happy little one!"

Lenora looked for some time after the bird, as it flew heavenwards, dashing through air and light more swiftly than an
arrow; then returning with a smile of satisfaction to her chair,
she industriously resumed her work. About a quarter of an
hour after, she paused to listen to a sound on the stairs—

"Ah, there comes father!" she said; and rising, she went
to the door.

Herr von Vlierbeke entered the little room with a roll of
paper in his hand, and slowly approaching a chair, he sat
down, exhausted and panting. He had grown very thin and
wan, his eyes were hollow, his cheeks pallid, and his whole
face showed marks of suffering. One could easily perceive
that he had been the victim of a severe illness, and that mental
energy, as well as bodily strength, had been sapped.

His dress indicated great poverty, though kept painfully
clean, and evidently with great labour; it was everywhere
threadbare, here and there patched, and all too wide for his
shrunk and meagre body. Adversity and sickness had apparently quite crushed his once manly soul; he seemed dispirited
and heart-broken.

Lenora looked at him for a moment with deep concern, and
then said—"Alas! father, do you feel ill again?"

"O no, Lenora; but I am so unfortunate!"

She embraced him tenderly, and took his hand in an affectionate and consoling way.

"Father, father, eight days ago you lay in bed very ill.
We prayed God to restore you to health, as the greatest boon
He could confer on us. God heard our prayers; you are well
again; and yet you are cast down by the first little reverse

you meet with. Oh, what matters it? What prevents us being happy? Come, let us, as we have done hitherto, raise ourselves proudly to meet whatever additional misfortune may befal us. Let us be strong, and boldly look our poverty in the face. Courage is riches. Come, father, forget your sorrows; look at me—am I melancholy? Do I let despairing thoughts get the better of me? Yes, I wept, lamented, and suffered, when my father was ill; but now that you are well —now, come what will, your Lenora will continually thank God for His goodness."

The father looked sadly into the eyes of his high-spirited daughter, and sighed—

"Poor Lenora! you have power to make even me take courage and make an effort to console myself; may Heaven reward you for so much love! I know the source from which you draw this strength; and yet—you angel sent by God Himself to support me—your words and smiles work powerfully upon me, as if a part of your soul passed into mine. I returned to our little home here with a failing heart, a troubled mind, and quite powerless with despair, and your look alone has been sufficient to pour consolation into my breast."

"Come, father," interrupted the maiden; "you are always lavishing your tenderness on me. Let me know how it went with you, and I will afterwards tell you something which will give you pleasure."

"Ah, my child, I reported myself at Herr Roncevaux's Educational Institute, to recommence my English lessons; but I found that an Englishman had been engaged during my illness, and thus our chief means of livelihood is taken from us."

"And the German hour, with Miss Pauline?"

"Miss Pauline has gone to Strasburg, and does not return. Ah, Lenora, everything lost at once. Had I not good cause to be dispirited? Even you seem overcome by this unlucky news. It seems to me that you look pale?"

In fact Lenora had cast down her eyes, and seemed painfully affected by this intelligence. Her father's question brought her back to herself; and with an effort to appear cheerful, she replied—

"I was thinking, father, how these repulses must have pained you, and I felt the pain over again for you; but, notwithstanding, I have reason to be happy. Yes, father, for I at least have good news."

"So!—that surprises me."

Lenora pointed with her finger to the chair, and continued—

"Do you see that linen there? I have got an order for twelve fine shirts, and when they are finished, the order is to be repeated. I am to be well paid; and I know something better yet, though it is only a hope."

Lenora had uttered these words so quickly and cheerfully, that her father, borne along by her vivacity, was betrayed into a smile of satisfaction.

"Well," he asked, "what is this other thing which makes you so happy?"

Reproaching herself for having lost time, she sat down again to her needle, and resumed her sewing, visibly delighted at having succeeded in chasing away her father's melancholy, and, half jestingly, she replied—

"Ah, you cannot guess it: have you any notion, father, who has given me this work to do?—The rich lady in the large house at the corner. She sent for me this morning, and I went to her during your absence. You are astonished, I see, father, are you not?"

"Yes. You mean Madame Royan. for whom you received some beautiful collars to embroider? How did she come to know you?"

"I don't know; but probably the woman who sent me that troublesome work, informed the lady who had done it. She must have spoken, too, of your illness, and our poverty; for the lady knew more than you could have supposed."

"Heavens! she does not know . . . ."

"No, she does not know what our name was in our father-land."

"Go on, then, Lenora; you excite my curiosity. I see you wish to tease me."

"Well then, father, since I see that you are all right again, I will be more brief. Madame de Royan received me very kindly, and after praising my beautiful embroidery, she inquired into our former fortunes, and consoled and cheered me. Only hear what she said to me, after having ordered her maid to give me this linen to make shirts of : 'Go, my child, work on courageously, and be virtuous, and I will protect you. I require a great deal of work done for myself, and can give you two months' occupation; but this is not all : I will recommend you to my numerous acquaintances, and take care that you are always provided with sufficient work, to enable you to find a comfortable livelihood for yourself and your delicate father.' With tears in my eyes I took her hand and kissed it; for her beautiful and noble benevolence, which did not give me alms, but work, touched me deeply. When she saw in my eyes the gratitude which I felt, she said with still greater kindness, while she patted me affectionately on the shoulder—'Keep up your spirits, Lenora; a time will come when you will have to take in pupils to help you; and so, advancing from less to greater, be a mistress yourself some day.' Yes, dear father, she said so. I have her words by heart."

And so saying, she sprang up, and embraced him in the highest spirits.

" What do you say to this, father?" she continued. " Is it not good news? Who knows—pupils, apprentices, a shop, a *magusin*, a servant-girl! You keep the books, and select the wares—I stand in the shop and sell, or give directions to my workwomen. Oh! it is charming to think of—to be happy, and at the same time to be conscious that we owe it all to the work of our own hands; and then, father, then would your wishes be quite fulfilled, and you would spend your old age in comfort and peace."

Herr von Vlierbeke smiled cheerfully, and one could see clearly from the happy expression which revealed itself in his wan and wasted features, that the words of his daughter had allured him into entire self-forgetfulness for a moment. He soon perceived it himself, however, and shook his head pleasantly, saying—

" Lenora, Lenora, sweet Lenora! You charm me away from reality so easily; I hang on your lips like a child, and have perfect faith in all your hopeful promises of future happiness. However it may turn out with our future, we have indeed good cause to thank God for the present at least. But now to come to more serious matters : the shoemaker has again spoken to me about the rent, and begged me to pay him. We still owe him twenty francs—is it not so?"

" Yes, we owe twenty francs for rent, and twelve francs to tradesmen—that is all. So soon as these shirts are ready, we shall give the shoemaker my earnings, and he will be quite satisfied. They will give us a little longer credit in the shops ; and I have got two and a half francs here for my last work. So you see, father, we are rich yet. Within four weeks, all our debts will be paid. You are well again, and your strength will soon return. Summer has begun, everything smiles on us, and we shall be so very happy yet!"

Herr von Vlierbeke seemed quite consoled, and renovated

courage beamed in his dark eyes, and his spirits were considerably raised. He went to the table, and said, as he unrolled the paper—

"Lenora, I have a little work too. Professor Delsaux has given me some music to copy for his pupils: it will, in a few days, bring me in four francs. Be quiet now for a little, my child; my mind is distracted at present, and I should certainly make blunders, and spoil the paper."

"I may sing, though, may I not, father?"

"O yes, that gives me great pleasure, and never disturbs me."

The father now began to write, while Lenora, with a clear but low voice, sang beautifully a great many of her songs, and in this way gave free expression to the feelings of her heart. Meanwhile she sewed on industriously, looking up from time to time at her father, to observe whether any sad thoughts arose in his mind, which required to be dissipated.

A considerable time after this, Lenora heard the clock in the parish church strike; and putting aside her work, she took a basket from behind the stove, and hanging it over her arm, was about to leave the room, when her father, observing her intention, said with surprise—

"Already, Lenora?"

"It is half-past eleven, father."

Without making any further remark, Herr von Vlierbeke again applied himself to his music, and proceeded with his copying. The young girl ran quickly down stairs, and soon returned with the basket full of potatoes, and something else wrapped in a piece of paper, which however she concealed under her apron as she re-entered the room. Pouring water into a pot, she began to peel the potatoes, singing the while. She did not take long to finish this work; then lighting a fire, she washed the potatoes, and put them in the pot to be boiled. Behind this she placed another pot, considerably smaller, in which there was some butter and a good deal of vinegar.

Up to this moment, the father had not once looked up from his work. The preparation of the midday meal was no unusual sight, and it was seldom indeed that it varied. On this occasion, however, the potatoes were scarcely ready, when a very savoury smell diffused itself through the room. Herr von Vlierbeke looked at his daughter with surprise, and said—"Meat on a Wednesday! Lenora, child, we must be frugal; you know that well."

"Ah, father," replied Lenora, laughing, "never mind, the doctor ordered it."

"You would fain deceive me, I see."

"No, no; the doctor said you must have meat at least three times a week, if we could afford to purchase it at all. It will do you good, father, and restore your strength."

"But, Lenora, our debts?"

"Well, well, father, let me look after all that. Every one will be satisfied, I can assure you. Do not torment your mind about it any longer. I will answer for everything. Be so good as put aside your papers now, as I wish to lay the cloth."

The father shook his head, and did what Lenora had desired him. She then spread a snow-white linen cloth over the table, and set down the potatoes and a couple of plates. Everything was poor and humble, but so white and clean, that the table as it now appeared, would have pleased the eye of the wealthiest and most fastidious.

Father and daughter sat down to their meal, and bent their heads, as they thanked God for the food He had given them. While they were still engaged in this quiet thanksgiving, voices were suddenly heard on the stairs. Lenora was alarmed, and trembled violently. With strained attention and visible agitation, she listened to sounds which were heard indistinctly proceeding from below. The father, surprised to observe the unaccountable excitement depicted in his daughter's face, looked at her inquiringly, as if he would say, "What is the matter? what is it?" Lenora gave him a hasty sign to be silent. The sounds were again audible, and now at last Lenora recognised the voice. As if struck by a thunderbolt, she sprang up with a cry of pain, and running to the door, shut it, and held it firmly with her hands.

"Lenora, for Heaven's sake, what are you afraid of?" cried the alarmed and anxious father.

"Gustav! Gustav!" she exclaimed; "he is there—he comes! Oh, away with everything from the table; he of all others must not be a witness of our poverty."

The countenance of Herr von Vlierbeke grew dark when he heard this. He raised his head proudly, and his eye was vigorous and brilliant once more. Silently approaching his daughter, he removed her from the door. Lenora fled to the most distant corner of the room, and hid her face in her hands The door flew open—a youth hastened exulting into the room, and ran with open arms to the young girl. He wildly uttered her name, and, in his blind joy, would have fallen upon her neck, but the outstretched arm and stern look of the father held him back. He remained standing; and, looking round in silence, contemplated with a shudder the meagre dinner and the humble clothing of the old man and his daughter. What he had seen apparently affected him deeply, for he covered his eyes with his hands, and pressing them violently, said—

"O Lenora, beloved! look on me, that I may know whether your heart has preserved the sweet memory of our love!"

The maiden cast on him an earnest look—a look in which her pure loving soul was all revealed.

"Oh, what happiness!" exclaimed Gustav with ardour;
"still, as ever, my sweet, dear Lenora!   God be praised! no
power on earth can now rob me of my bride!   O Lenora,
come into my arms; do not refuse the bridal kiss!"

He opened his arms as he said this, and would have run
forward to press her to his beating heart.   Trembling with
anxiety and joy, Lenora stood with downcast eyes, though
longing to receive the fond embrace which was to be the
sign of their everlasting union; but ere the youth could obey
the impulse of his passion, Herr von Vlierbeke stood beside
him, and taking his hand firmly to restrain him, he said with
deep emotion, but with a severe tone—

"Herr Denecker, moderate your joy.   We too rejoice to
see you again; but it is not permitted either to you or to us
to forget what we are.   Respect our poverty."

"How! what do you say?   Who are you?   Are you not
my friend and my father?   Lenora is my bride.   Heavens!
what means that accusing look?   I lose my senses—I know
not what I do."

Then seizing Lenora's hand, and drawing her towards her
father, he said hastily—

"Listen!   My uncle died in Italy; he left me sole heir.
He commanded me on his deathbed to marry Lenora.   I have
moved heaven and earth to find you; have mourned and suffered during the absence of my beloved.   At last I have
found you, and come to get the reward of my suffering—to
lay my wealth, my heart, my life, at your feet; and to im-
plore you to grant me the happiness of leading Lenora to the
altar.   Father, O my father! do not refuse me this highest
favour!   Come, Grinselhof awaits your coming, I have
bought it for you—everything is there again.   The portraits
of your ancestors adorn its walls once more; and all that
was dear to you is re-purchased.   Come, I will surround

your age with honour—heap happiness upon your nead—love and adore your Lenora!"

The expression on the nobleman's face was still the same, but his eyes were moist.

"Oh!" exclaimed Gustav with enthusiasm, "no power on earth can tear me from my Lenora again. No, not even her father: God has given her to me!"

He knelt at Herr von Vlierbeke's feet, and raising his hands imploringly, said—

"Pardon me.—No, it is impossible; you will not inflict on me a deathblow! Father, father, for God's sake, grant me your blessing! Your coldness kills me."

Herr von Vlierbeke seemed at this moment to have forgotten the young man, as he raised his eyes to heaven, seemingly in earnest prayer. His voice became audible as he prayed, and tears of emotion gushed from his eyes, as he exclaimed—

"Margaretha! Margaretha! rejoice in the bosom of thy God! My vow is fulfilled—thy child will yet be happy on earth!"

Gustav and Lenora were now looking at him, trembling with expectation. He raised the young man, and, kissing him affectionately, said—

"Gustav, my dear son, may Heaven bless your love! Make my child happy—she is your bride!"

"Gustav, Gustav is mine!" exclaimed Lenora, and hastening into the arms of her beloved and her father, they were all united for a moment in a mutual and ardent embrace.

The first love-kiss—the sacred bridal kiss—was exchanged on the father's breast; while the old man moistened the heads of his happy children with his tears, and his hands rested upon them in blessing.

And now, dear reader, I must confess to you, that I have, for important reasons, concealed the true locality and name of Herr von Vlierbeke's house; consequently none of you can guess where Gustav and his youthful bride now dwell.

So far as I myself am concerned, I may inform you that I have often had the pleasure of talking with Herr Denecker and his amiable wife, and have frequently walked about the grounds of Grinselhof with their two lovely children and the aged grandfather.

The charming spectacle of domestic happiness—of perfect peace and love—which I have seen there, has imprinted itself deeply on my memory. The old grandfather sitting on a bench in the garden, and attempting thus early to explain to his two little grandchildren the workings of some of the powers of nature which are active around us: the little Adelina clambering upon his lap to stroke his cheeks, and the restless Isidor galloping on his knees with wild delight; while Herr Denecker and his wife stand beside them, and press each other's hands as they contemplate with feelings of intense happiness and gratitude the grandfather's delight, and the cheerful playfulness of their children.

I do not mean to tell you who it was that related this tale to me. It is sufficient to say that I knew every person who plays a part in it; and that I have sat more than once at table with Father Jans and his wife and their maid Kate, who are all great talkers, and are always very willing to speak of their benefactors.